PRAISE FOR *STRANGERS IN THE NIGHT*

"From New York to California, from Vegas and all through-out Europe, Webb captures Hollywood's golden age with all its glitz and glamour. Have a box of tissues ready and be prepared to be wiped out in the best possible way. A true marvel of a novel. I fell as hard for this book as Frank fell for Ava."

—Renée Rosen, author of *The Social Graces*

"Heather Webb writes illuminatingly about a love story that could easily have lit up the silver screen, but played out backstage. . . . Readers will find themselves wishing that the director didn't have to call 'Cut!,' that 'The End' didn't exist, and that they could stay immersed in this sumptuous story forever."

—Natasha Lester, *New York Times*
bestselling author of *The Paris Seamstress*

"Ava Gardner and Frank Sinatra's wildly rocky relationship in *Strangers in the Night* exposes the cinematic glitz of Holly-wood's golden age alongside Tinseltown's darker underbelly. Readers craving a story that's glamorous and deliciously dishy won't be able to turn these pages fast enough!"

—Stephanie Marie Thornton, *USA Today*
bestselling author of *A Most Clever Girl*

"Heather Webb gets under the skin of two of the brightest stars showbiz ever produced, and takes us inside their tempestuous, compulsive, alcohol-fueled love story. Crackling with sexual tension and full of insight about the pressures of megastardom, this is a spicy and addictive page-turner."

—Gill Paul, *USA Today* bestselling author of *The Manhattan Girls*

"Heather Webb has set a new standard in historical fiction by writing a story that was so engaging that I forgot I was reading a book and not actually embodying the characters. As a lifelong fan of the famous crooner, my own music listening will forever be quite impacted by Webb's captivating book."

—Camille Di Maio, bestselling author of *The Memory of Us*

"*Strangers in the Night* is a gorgeously written, impeccably researched historical novel that delves into both the glamour and darkness of old Hollywood, as it details the passionate and tumultuous epic love story of Ava Gardner and Frank Sinatra. By turns sexy and heartbreaking, beautiful and volatile, I loved this fascinating peek behind the curtain of a real Hollywood love affair."

—Jillian Cantor, *USA Today* bestselling author of *Beautiful Little Fools*

STRANGERS IN THE NIGHT

ALSO BY HEATHER WEBB

The Next Ship Home

The Phantom's Apprentice

Rodin's Lover

Becoming Josephine

Three Words for Goodbye (with Hazel Gaynor)

Meet Me in Monaco (with Hazel Gaynor)

Last Christmas in Paris (with Hazel Gaynor)

Ribbons of Scarlet

Fall of Poppies (anthology)

STRANGERS IN THE NIGHT

A Novel of Frank Sinatra and Ava Gardner

HEATHER WEBB

WILLIAM MORROW
An Imprint of HarperCollinsPublishers

P.S.™ is a trademark of HarperCollins Publishers.

FIRST EDITION

Designed by Diahann Sturge

Spotlight smoke © Matusciac Alexandru / Shutterstock
Curtain image © Es sarawuth / Shutterstock

Library of Congress Cataloging-in-Publication Data has been applied for.

ISBN 978-0-06-300418-4 (paperback)
ISBN 978-0-06-329711-1 (library edition)

23 24 25 26 27 LBC 5 4 3 2 1

821 4044

FOR THE DI VITTORIOS,
WITH LOVE

They were somethin'.

—TINA SINATRA, DAUGHTER OF FRANK SINATRA

He would never get her out of his system, nor
would she ever truly get him out of hers.

—JAMES KAPLAN, BIOGRAPHER

PROLOGUE

FRANK

Every important moment of my life could be measured in notes and captured by a song. That was never truer than the first night I saw her across the room, belonging to someone else.

As the brass finished and the lights went up, I stepped away from the mic. Cheers and whistles peppered the audience in the smoke-hazed room of the Hollywood Palladium. I mopped my brow and drank deeply from a water glass, parched after the set.

"Alright, boys, see you in twenty," Tommy said, bandleader and boss. He laid his trombone on his chair.

The orchestra wiped down their instruments, put them carefully in their cases before seeing about a refreshment or two. I ordered a drink from a cute waitress who batted her eyes at me and asked for my autograph. I obliged. I was never one to turn away a fan, never would be.

Whiskey in hand, I skirted the room, saying hello to those I knew and to anyone important, but really wasn't I the most important person here? They'd all come to hear me sing, after all. I'd taken Tommy Dorsey's Band to new heights and no one could deny it, not even Tommy, who still acted as if I should be kissing his ring in gratitude for the chance to tour with them. But it was my name the bobby-soxers screamed while waiting in a line that wrapped the building of every club or concert hall—not his.

I spotted Mickey Rooney across the room, Hollywood royalty and MGM's number one star, and headed toward him. One of these days I hoped to be taken seriously as an actor, too.

"Hiya, Mickey," I said, extending my hand. "Good to see you."

"If it isn't Frank Sinatra." Mickey shook my hand firmly. "That was some set. Dorsey's band is a favorite of mine. You were pretty alright, too."

I laughed good-naturedly. I liked this guy. "Good to hear man, thanks."

And then I saw her, perched beside him in a white dress: dark hair, almond-shaped eyes, cleft in her chin. She wasn't just beautiful—I'd seen plenty of women that fit that description— she was a goddess sculpted of the finest marble. The kind of woman that knocked the air from your lungs.

She also wore a ring on the wrong finger.

I cleared my throat. "Say, you've got yourself a real beauty of a wife." I gestured at her. "If I'd seen her first, I would have married her myself."

Mickey laughed, put his hand on her back. "Frank, meet Ava Gardner. She's one of Mayer's love goddesses."

Louis B. Mayer was the head of MGM and an all-around prick, but we put up with him to land a role in his pictures. It didn't surprise me that he'd snapped up this hot little number.

"I'll bet she is," I said, noticing the graceful neck and the ivory swell of her bosom. As she took me in, a sharpness framed her expression. I guessed too many people underestimated her intelligence—I wouldn't underestimate her in anything. She was a femme fatale of the highest order. There was no denying that, even at first glance. "Hello, Ava." I gave her my most irresistible smile.

Her eyes flashed with some imperceptible emotion. "Hello, Mr. Sinatra." She turned then, giving me her back, and signaled to a waiter to bring her a drink.

I stiffened at the slight but tried again. "It's going to be a good night, I can tell."

This time she reached for Mickey's hand. "It already has been."

My smile froze on my face. She hated me for some reason, couldn't care less who I was, and it was clear I should scram. "Fine, fine," I said, waving my hand as if to get on with things. "That's what we like to hear. Well, folks, I hope you enjoy the show."

I shook off the odd exchange and stopped to make plans with Lana about where to meet when the show was over. After, I continued through the room, shaking hands with members of the audience before making my way back to the stage. It was a packed house, an energetic crowd, their voices rumbling, their glasses clinking in celebration, and more than a few cigars glowing in the murky light of the club.

When the band moved into place and the familiar strains of the piano floated through the room, a hush draped the audience. All eyes fixed on me, and a familiar rush of satisfaction rolled through me.

On cue, I began to sing.

The music washed over me, filled me up until I brimmed with it, the emotion of the lyrics carrying me as if I'd written them myself. As my gaze drifted over the crowd, I found myself looking for that face: the one that had stopped me in my tracks, the one that had dismissed me almost instantly and left a lingering sting.

I locked onto a pair of vivid green eyes—Ava's eyes—to find them already intent on mine. A flame flickered to life inside me. She sure was something. I sang as if the song was written for her, and it was, at least for tonight.

If I'd known what she would come to mean to me, maybe I would have done things differently. Maybe I would have tried to change. How often would I grasp at time in a desperate attempt to hold it close, to rewind the clock to the moments I'd spent with her only to find they had slipped through my fingers like water, leaving me nothing but memories? Happy days and terrible ones, and the chasm left by her absence. I had regrets—plenty of them—but loving her wasn't one of them. Loving her was one of the things I'd done right, even if I hadn't done it well.

As the lyrics poured forth like molten lava and every part of me ignited, at last, I detected a smile on her lips.

We might have been strangers that night, but her smile told me all I needed to know. It was only a beginning.

Part 1

"I GET A KICK OUT OF YOU"

1946-1949

CHAPTER 1

AVA

Hollywood was everything and nothing I'd expected.

I'd expected billboards plastered with movie posters in vivid colors and grand theater marquees flashing with lights brighter than anything I'd seen in my forgettable hometown. I'd expected convertibles spiffed to a shine, racing down Sunset Boulevard beneath the towering palm trees and California blue sky. The most beautiful people in America walked those streets, frequented coffee shops, and graced the jazz clubs and martini bars in their elegant best. Everyone wanted to be a star in Hollywood: actors or writers or directors, singers and dancers, too. All of this, I had expected.

What I hadn't expected shook me to the very core, upending everything I thought was right in the world. Everything that was right about me, Ava Lavinia Gardner. I'd never forget the first few years I'd spent in Hollywood, feeling like a fish flapping around on a riverbank gasping for air, and frankly, that morning five years later, as I waited for my appointment in the illustrious offices of MGM studios, things still didn't look so different from the first.

A young woman with a curled blond bob glanced at a clip-board. "Miss Gardner!" she called.

I stood, clutching the little purse my sister Bappie had insisted I carry to look like a proper lady, and followed the woman into the office where my next lesson would take place. The odor of stale cigarette smoke permeated the walls and the carpet, and sunrays blasted through the window, heating the room to boil-ing. The waiting room itself was nondescript with the exception of a large potted palm in the corner by the window and a wall lined with promotional posters of old pictures—*The Thin Man, Gone with the Wind, Dancing Lady*—posters I'd seen a dozen times but still reminded me of the first time I'd fallen in love with movies.

"Wait here," the secretary said, gesturing to a chair. "Your coach will be with you shortly. Lilly is running a little late to-day. Oh, and we've added an hour of diction to your afternoon schedule," the blond secretary said, giving me an apologetic smile.

I suppressed a groan. I'd already spent several hours a day the last five years working on etiquette and, of course, acting classes with the famed Lilly Burns. Not that it mattered. Even I knew I couldn't act my way out of a paper bag. If I'd been able to, MGM wouldn't keep giving me photo shoots and parts so small I might as well have been a prop in the scene.

As much as I loved pictures as a girl, I'd never thought about acting. My secret dream was to be the lead singer of a band, probably because I'd had a crush on just about every hand-some crooner on the radio. My voice was competent, throaty in an appealing sort of way, but I knew I didn't have enough talent to make it a career. Besides, my knees locked and my throat went dry every time I had to do any kind of performance in front of others. Instead of silly dreams, Mama and Bappie had ensured I work toward learning secretarial skills and typing—until that fateful day the right man in the right suit saw my photograph hanging in a shop window.

Now, I was counted among the beautiful ones; the love goddesses, they called us. Except I carried myself all wrong and I spoke like the poor hick from Grabtown, North Carolina, that I was, or so I'd been told repeatedly during the years I'd lived in this city of fake smiles and golden dreams. I learned that all of my years of running barefoot after my brother and his friends through the tobacco fields of my hometown—something I'd always thought made me strong like them—didn't make me strong. It had made me naive to the ways of the world. Now when I looked in the mirror, I no longer saw the girl I'd known all my life. I saw every flaw and heard my coach's admonishments in my ears, felt the sting of the studio's constant rejections. I thought I'd come to Hollywood to be a star. As it turned out, I came to Los Angeles to be shown each and every one of my inadequacies.

This was what I hadn't expected about Hollywood. If I had, I would have better armed myself for the constant beratement, the stripping of everything I was but face and figure. Maybe I wouldn't have come at all.

"No, Ava," Lilly said, after thirty minutes of pure torture. "Try it again. Walk slowly, as if you're prowling. You're a tigress. You've done this before, you just aren't focusing properly today." She watched herself closely in the many mirrors that lined her office walls, as she so often did. The woman sure liked to look at herself.

I stalked across the room, trying not to show my irritation—of course I'd done this before, and nailed a few small parts doing it damned well, thank you very much—but I did as instructed, exaggerating my movements.

"Yes!" Lilly cried, clapping her hands like a nun in a schoolyard. "This time, watch your expression. Yes, that's it. Chin up and eyes on the prize. He is the most delicious thing you've ever seen and you're starving."

When the morning lessons wrapped, I felt a bit lighter and headed to the cafeteria for lunch. As I crossed the studio lot, I passed a street built to look like New York City with skyscrapers and brownstones, a backdrop mimicking the Texas wilds and the Alamo, and a street of small-town America complete with a newspaper stand and a candy cane pole outside a make-believe barbershop. I smiled to myself. I might be fed up with all of the lessons, but I hadn't outgrown the wonder and magic of a movie studio lot, not yet.

The cafeteria was crowded with famous faces, cameramen, producers, and other crew, and the smell of roasted chicken wafted from somewhere behind the cafeteria counter, covering the inevitable scent of far too much expensive cologne and perfume.

I spotted Lana Turner waving me over to a table and headed in her direction.

"How are things, Miss Ava?" Lana asked in the sultry tone I'd also learned to imitate.

"She was hard on me today," I said, unfolding my napkin.

Lana squeezed my hand. "She's hard on everyone."

I'd liked Lana the moment we met. She didn't put on airs even with her stunning fair beauty, wealth, and enviable fame.

I was grateful for her easy friendship in a world where I wasn't sure I belonged.

I devoured a salad with cold chicken and a hard roll with butter. As I reached for a second piece of bread, Lana gave me a look that said *Are you sure you want to eat that?*

I let the roll drop into the basket. I'd always had a hearty appetite and given that salads were about the only thing my coaches encouraged me to eat, my stomach grumbled all day until I went home, where I'd eat proper food with my maid and friend, Reenie. Steaks and fried chicken and buttered cornbread by the truckloads.

"Would you look at her outfit," Lana said, flicking her lustrous blond waves over her shoulder.

A young woman strolled past in a body suit and tiny sequined shorts, ostensibly for some role, but her bust was straining against the flimsy fabric. It looked as if she'd purposefully chosen not to wear a bra.

"She's probably on her way to give Louis a lap dance," I whispered.

Louis B. Mayer owned MGM and more or less owned every actor and actress employed by him. He expected his property to be preened and polished and churned through the studio factory. And like it or not, we all compared ourselves to each other, making the jealousy rampant. In fact, I was beginning to wonder if there was any loyalty at all in this town. I did my best to put it all aside. I wasn't the jealous type.

Lana laughed, poking me in the ribs with her elbow. "You're such an innocent thing and yet, you open that dirty mouth of yours and I can't stop laughing."

"I'm not so innocent these days," I replied. I'd come a long

way from the poverty and the stringent, pious upbringing Mama
had tried to instill in me. My, how she'd failed, I thought as I lit
a cigarette. Not only had I given up on God after Daddy died,
I'd been twice divorced and now knew how to wield my charms
to disarm men. It was all in a day's work.

"I suppose that's true." Lana winked and brushed invisible crumbs from her A-line skirt. She pulled out a compact to
brighten her lips with fire-engine-red lipstick and then touched
her hair gingerly, making sure all the pins tucked into her curls
were still in place.

"You're stunning," I said, checking my own reflection. Alert
green eyes, high cheekbones, pink lips, and a seductive smile—
ruined by spinach wedged between my two bottom teeth—
looked back at me. I worked the lettuce free with my fingernail
and closed my compact with a snap.

Another young woman joined us at the table then, Joanie
someone-or-other, and launched into a diatribe about a new
actress doing so-called favors for one of the bosses in exchange
for a role. Not an uncommon occurrence, I'd discovered, but
it was a nasty business. Someone told someone who told me
that little twelve-year-old Shirley Temple got an eyeful of a
producer's penis and that Judy Garland, star of *The Wizard
of Oz*, had her breasts groped by Mayer whenever he felt like
it, the poor girl. I'd been groped myself by an exec who had
lured me to a projection room. He didn't like it much when I
shoved him and raced down the hallway, ratting him out to the
publicity chief. I'd been carefully consoled and then promptly
told to keep my mouth shut. Marrying Mickey Rooney so soon
after I'd arrived in Hollywood a few years ago had probably
rescued me from being passed around the boardroom. Too bad

Mickey had turned out to be a bed-hopper, too—and that had been the end of that.

My second husband, Artie Shaw, split after a year of marriage because he thought no one was as smart or talented as he was. The result was the same: I was left heartbroken and wiser to the ways of the world and the merry-go-round of Hollywood love affairs.

"I've got to run," Lana said. "If I'm late again, they'll have my hide."

"I'd better get to it, too," I said, not interested in continuing the conversation with Joanie. She was dull as dirt.

"Are you going to the ball game tonight?" Lana asked, standing. "Everyone will be there. The money we raise goes to charity."

"Frank's team is playing?" I asked carefully. Lana and Frank Sinatra had dated off and on for a couple of years and she'd been devastated by the split. I didn't see how she could be, really. She'd known he was married, after all.

I'd crossed paths with Frank a few times, and though he had a nice voice, he was no Bing Crosby. Besides, I'd taken an instant disliking to him a few years ago when he'd tossed off some comment about marrying me. As if he stood a chance. I didn't understand why women swooned over him. He wore his conceit like a cheap suit, and really, he wasn't all that handsome.

"Yup," she said. "Come on, you should join us."

I shook my head. "Not tonight. I have plans with my sister. We're going to get some ice cream and stay in, listen to records."

"You're never going to meet anyone new if you keep that up, but suit yourself." She blew me a kiss and sashayed away.

Lana knew that I yearned not only for MGM to stop treating

me like a pretty little girl with a head full of air, but for a man who saw me as more than a notch on his belt. I'd been dating since my divorce from Artie, but no one of real interest. Unless you could count Robert Duffy, my on-and-off boyfriend of two years, and I didn't. I was looking for something I hadn't found. Something I was afraid might be mythical: the kind of love that made you feel as if it was your reason for living.

At the time, I didn't know I'd already met him—the man who would turn my life inside out and stay with me until my final breath.

But Lana was right. I could use a night out. Maybe I'd join the Swooners softball team that night after all.

★ ★ ★

As it turned out, it was a fine night for softball. The league was a success and had managed to pull in actors from MGM and Warner Bros. studios. The rivalry was all in good fun with a bucketload of taunting and teasing and dirty talk. Just my kind of thing. It didn't take Lana very long to convince me to join the bat girls and I was given a uniform.

"I can light a tennis ball on fire, but I never liked softball much," I admitted.

"Not to worry," Lana said. "You won't have to play. We're bat girls. And you look positively adorable in that jersey."

We were called the Swooners, a name Frank had obviously found funny, and it had stuck.

I tied my hair back and put on a ballcap that matched my softball uniform. It was a balmy summer night; the air was thick with impending rain. Though unusual for that time of year, the weather didn't put a damper on the buoyant mood.

Everyone was laughing and having a grand old time harassing each other.

Soon the field lights clicked on and illuminated the darkening sky. While a few boys swept the bases and raked the dirt to prepare for the start, Frank headed our way.

Lana scurried from the dugout and out of sight. She was trying to avoid him, the poor girl. That wasn't easy to do in this town. As far as I could tell, Frank Sinatra was just about everywhere.

"Look who's joined us," he said, punching his left hand into his mitt. A puff of dust lifted from the glove. "I wasn't sure if you'd show."

I smiled. "As long as you don't put me in the outfield, I'll be fine."

"I don't know. We may need you out there." He teased. "Hey, that jersey suits you."

"I'm not one of your swooning fans, but it'll do."

He laughed, clearly delighted. Sometimes men needed a good ribbing, and the best way was to insult their ego. They lapped it up. My brothers had taught me that.

"Let me show you what you'll be doing." He pointed out where they kept the bats in the dugout and explained that the most important thing was to cheer for the team.

"Aye, aye, captain," I said, with a mock salute.

He chuckled but his eyes were serious, intent on mine—and about the most piercing blue I'd ever seen. I wondered how I'd missed that before. I supposed I'd never really looked at him squarely.

"We're all going for drinks after, if you want to join," he said, scratching a line in the dirt with his cleats.

"Mind if I bring someone?" I asked, thinking of Duff. "I wouldn't want you to flirt with me."

"Now why would I do that?" He grinned. "Sure, that's fine. Well, I'd better get to it." He tipped the brim of his baseball cap and jogged over to the team, now huddled in a pack. It sounded like they were trying to decide on the batting order.

A short time later, the game began.

Lana and I caroused with the players in the dugout, collected bats left behind after a hit, and made jokes about a man's athletic ability translating to his performance in bed. I mean, really, who could resist the parallel?

When it was Frank's turn at bat, he took a few practice swings. The first pitch was a ball but on the second pitch, a satisfying crack of the bat split the air. The ball arced over the bases and into the outfield before it dropped into the grass not far from the fence. We cheered as he raced around first base and then second, and slid into third just before the third baseman caught the ball launched at him from the outfield.

"Lucky hit, Sinatra!" someone shouted from the Warner Bros.' bench.

Frank gave them the bird, eliciting laughter, and then looked toward home plate.

I glanced at Lana, who quickly looked away, pretending she wasn't watching his every move. I slipped my arm around her shoulders. "He's a heartbreaker, isn't he?"

"He certainly broke mine, but I'm over him, I really am. I'm trying to shake the lingering awkwardness between us, that's all. It's just as well that we're through. He'd never leave his wife."

I nodded. She was right, if the gossip was to be believed. Those Italian men who took lovers never left their wives. And since I'd moved to Hollywood, I'd learned most of the gossip turned out to be true.

Derek, the next teammate at bat, hit the ball down the first base line.

Frank made a run for it.

The other team scooped up the ball and the next instant, Derek was called out—but Frank slid into home plate.

"Safe!" the umpire shouted, throwing his arms wide.

Cheers erupted from the stands. Lana and I jumped up and down, screeching as Mickey dashed out from the dugout and jumped on Frank's back. Frank laughed, hoisted Mickey onto his shoulders, and staggered to the dugout. More laughter and catcalls peppered the stands. I was glad Mickey and I had remained friends. This town was too small—the studio even smaller—to make enemies. I'd even started to talk to Artie again. As it turned out, he was a hell of a lot nicer as a friend than as a husband.

When the game ended, Clayton's Bar was already closed so we high-fived and disbanded. I headed home, where Reenie set us up with a couple of bone-dry gin martinis and some music. Reenie had not only become a permanent fixture as my maid and assistant in the house, she'd become a true friend. When it would get on into the evenings, we'd have a drink or some dinner, or head out to a hot jazz club, ignoring the rules not allowing so-called coloreds to enter. No one would ask a young movie star to leave, especially not one who had been married to jazz king Artie Shaw, and I made it clear I would only be a patron if they allowed Reenie to enter, too.

I filled her in on the softball game and we talked for some time. At well past midnight, we finally decided to call it a night.

As I slipped under the covers, happy to surrender to sleep, a commotion outside drifted through the windowpane. I ignored it, assuming it was the group of college boys who lived in the Sunset Towers apartments behind the house. Sometimes they made a racket late at night.

A soft knock came at the bedroom door. "Miss G, do you hear that?" Reenie's voice was low but urgent. "Someone is shouting your name outside."

"What the devil?"

I threw back the covers and walked to the window, pushing aside the drapes. I craned my neck to see the full scale of the multistory building. Each apartment unit had a balcony and there, several floors above me under the moonlight, stood an extremely sauced Frank Sinatra.

"Hey, Ava Gardner!" he shouted. "Why don't you come have a drink with us tonight?" Several friends joined him. They jabbed each other in the ribs, laughing and shouting.

"They're going to knock someone over the banister, the fools," I said as Reenie looked over my shoulder.

"Ava Gardner!" Frank shouted again. "Come out and play!"

I reddened. That man was a real ass to wake up the neighborhood at this hour, and to drag me into it, drunk or not.

"Ava!" he called again.

His friends cupped their mouths with their hands and joined in a chorus of "Ava! Come out and play!"

"Will you pipe down!" a male voice came from the unit below them. "It's two o'clock in the morning!"

The men laughed as Frank cussed out the onlooker, and then tipped his head back and shouted again with gusto. "Ava Gardner! Come outside!"

"I said shut up, or I'm calling the cops!" the neighbor yelled back.

"Hey, jerk, why don't you go chew on some nails!" Frank replied.

His friends stumbled inside, pulling Frank along behind them.

"What was that all about?" Reenie asked, her large brown eyes reflecting the lamplight from the street that was streaming through the window.

"Men behaving like boys is all," I said, heading back to my bedroom. But as I turned off the light and pulled the blankets up to my chin, I couldn't wipe the smile off my face, even while I didn't understand my own amusement. Frank was something. He was a horse's ass, but he was something. Maybe I'd run into him again, sometime soon.

Maybe I was looking forward to it.

CHAPTER 2

FRANK

Hollywood was everything I wanted it to be and more. Sunshine and film sets and good-looking women; parties and late nights, and more talent in a few hundred square miles than in all the world combined. I liked being among it all, living the high life. I was glad to leave behind the lousy sods I'd grown up with, who knew how often I'd been beaten up by the kids on the block, taken a whack on the head from Pop, or worse, a slap from Ma followed by a stream of swear words that would make any sailor proud. I was glad to leave behind those who'd witnessed me begging for gigs at picnics and church halls and the bars in downtrodden Hoboken. I'd wanted to say goodbye to those who knew how often I was left on my own as a kid or pawned off on a neighbor. Who knew the kind of person all that loneliness had made me.

Hungry.

Hungry for success and for the kind of connection with someone I didn't yet understand. Hungry enough to fight my way in, or out, or over. Hungry enough to get back up and try again. To become the greatest singer the world had ever known. And none of it came easy. I think that made me love it all the more, made me proud and, some would say, it made me conceited. But I'd earned my success, and I wasn't the least bit sorry for it, or for moving to Hollywood, where I could live in a dreamland. Where I could be somebody.

Two years after my first musical with MGM and two years after my first slew of hits without Dorsey's band, I packed up my life in Hoboken for good and moved the wife and kids to California. I was in the big leagues, and I needed a lifestyle to prove it. When Mary Astor's waterfront house became available on Toluca Lake, I took that as a sign of good fortune and bought it. I believed in luck, probably more than I should. It turned out the neighborhood wasn't the friendliest to entertainers, or Jews, or Black people, but I learned that too late. It bothered me—I was no bigot and I couldn't stand anyone who was, so we wouldn't stick around for long—but in the beginning, for now, we were home.

I glanced at the house my wife Nancy had named Warm Valley and thought, for the tenth time, that I was glad we were here, in sunny California. I kissed our daughter, little Nancy, on the head and followed it with an identical kiss for my wife. She wasn't too keen to leave Jersey at first, but I coaxed her with a thousand sunny days, a big house with a lawn, and anything else she could want. She liked the idea of spending less time apart, and I liked the idea of having my daughter and Frank Jr. nearby. Though I'd never felt much passion for my wife, I loved her deep down more than just about anyone but my kids. She knew me, saw me for who and what I was, warts and all, and she believed in me. I never once doubted her affection or her support. What was more, she made our house a home.

And for now, she kept looking the other way while I dallied with women as I tried to find that something that always seemed just out of reach. That certain something I longed for to satiate my hunger.

"Grab the paddles, Nance." I motioned to my six-year-old and two other giggly little girls, the daughters of a friend. We were hosting a Fourth of July party, and friends and neighbors had begun to trickle in.

Nancy scooped up the paddles and nearly tipped over as she stood, their length making them cumbersome in her little arms. Still, she didn't complain or ask for help. That was my good girl.

"Get the other end of the paddles, girls," I said.

The lawn sloped to the water, where a brand-new dock that I'd rebuilt jutted onto the lake. Fifty feet from the shore, I'd installed a floating raft for swimming.

Nancy's friends took their job very seriously and helped her all the way to the water. I pulled the canoe from the shed and dragged it to the dock, stepping inside it and helping each of them climb in before pushing off onto the placid waters.

"Daddy, tell us a story," Nancy said, showing off how cool her papa was to her friends.

I made something up about a mermaid and they clapped and wiggled and the next thing I knew, we'd rowed far out into the lake and then back again. I wasn't the most present of fathers, always coming and going for the job, and I felt guilty about it regularly enough, but that didn't change how I felt about the kids. During our times together, I focused on them exclusively, and with all the affection in the world. I hoped that somehow made up for my failings. As idyllic as our home was, being there—and staying there—was difficult for me, impossible even, no matter how much I loved the family. Restlessness was rooted in my soul like a stubborn weed.

By the time I helped the girls out of the boat, the rest of the guests had arrived. I strode up to the house, ready for a cold drink.

"Do we have enough ice?" I asked, wiping my sweaty forehead with a towel. "We're going to need buckets of it in this heat."

Nancy flitted around the kitchen.

"We can always send someone out for more," she said, tying a clean apron around her waist. She'd insisted on doing all of the cooking and attacked a towering pile of sausages like she was on some kind of military mission.

It was a sweltering day, perfect for backyard lounging, canoeing, and swimming. We had a crowd as usual, milling on the lawn and through the house. I basked in the noise and activity; it distracted me from the ever-present buzz in my limbs.

I stepped outside to make sure the lawn chairs were set up and the yard toys had been put out for the kids: Hula-Hoops, a football, Frisbees, and a bucket of bubbles. Children raced through the yard like a flight of swallows, chasing each other from an activity in the yard to the water and back again. The sky was a deep blue I'd only ever seen in Southern California, and the sun bore down on our pale legs and arms. Within the hour, the women lounged on the patio in sunhats and swimsuits, glasses of lemonade and champagne on the tables between them. The men had already made quick work of a bottle of Jack Daniel's, sausages, and cold salads. I always kept my boys watered and well-fed.

"Everyone have enough?" I asked, opening one eye to peer at my pals stretched out next to me in the grass.

"More than enough. I'm stuffed," George Evans said.

Jimmy Van Heusen, songwriter and all-around pal, patted his stomach. "I'd say I'm good for at least an hour."

We all laughed.

"Frank, I need to talk to you later," George said, his tone heavy with meaning.

I glanced at him briefly to read his face, but his expression was inscrutable. He'd given me an earful the night before as a publicist and booking agent does from time to time, but his suggestions had recently turned to warnings. Not being able to serve in the war in France had damaged my reputation, and though I'd tried to enlist and been dismissed for a punctured eardrum, the doctor's note didn't seem to matter to the press. They chewed me up and spit me out. Now that the war was over, I'd hoped things would turn around. But I couldn't turn things around, George had said, if I continued to travel with politicians, speaking out on their behalf. People wanted me to entertain them, not preach to them.

I didn't know why I couldn't use my fame to help someone I believed in, that was all. And if I wanted to speak out against racism or try to help the Little Guy breaking his back working long hours for nothing, I'd do it. It was the right thing to do, the press be damned.

"I'd say it's high time we went for a swim, fellas," I said, not wanting to ruminate on my thoughts.

Danny, a new neighbor, and Jimmy got to their feet, and George followed me to the water's edge.

I raised my hands over my head in a mock stretch but with

a swift movement, I gave George a hearty shove. He yelped as he hit the water.

"Didn't see that coming, did you?" I called, laughing as he attempted to splash me. The cascades of water fell short by at least a mile. An athlete, he was not.

I dove in after him. I'd barely surfaced when two large hands dunked me under again. I rose to the surface again sputtering and laughing.

"Serves you right, you cad," George said, water dripping from his nose, his eyes bright with amusement.

I pushed the hair out of my eyes and looked back at the shore, where Danny and Jimmy were still perched like a couple of too-cool cats.

"Come on in, the water's fine," I shouted. They gave me the bird. I took aim and splashed them.

"Bombs away!" Jimmy called as he launched himself at the water, pulling his arms and legs together to form a cannon ball. He smacked the water hard, splashing everyone nearby.

The women near the water's edge screeched and moved their chairs back. George and I rewarded Jimmy with a face full of water as soon as his head poked above the surface. A splashing match broke out between us, and the next thing we knew, we all ended up on the shore, waterlogged, and poured another round.

We drank and told inappropriate jokes and basked in the ease of the day.

"Hey, Frankie," Jimmy said, slipping his hands behind his head as he lay down on a towel in the grass. "Which broad is it this week?"

"Any broad I want." I punched him in the ribs lightly.

Jimmy doubled over as if he'd been hurt, and we all laughed. "After the other night, I thought you might be carrying a torch for Ava Gardner."

We'd seen Ava at the softball game, and I'd nearly tripped over myself to say hello. She was as beautiful as ever, and single at last. I'd wanted to abandon the game and take her somewhere private. Too bad she'd been distant and polite, like I was her uncle or something. And then the fellas and I had acted like a couple of schoolboys on my balcony later that night, screaming her name. I could have sworn I saw the curtains moving in the back window of her house, but she never did step outside—and I never stopped thinking about the curve of her lips and the deep green of her eyes. Not that night, or since.

There was something about her, beyond her obvious physical attributes, and I wanted to be the one to find out what that something was. If she'd only give me a chance.

"She's a tough nut to crack," I said. "But if anyone can, I can."

We bantered back and forth a bit about my hubris and my five-foot eight-inch frame, all in good fun, but I couldn't help feeling for the first time in my life that maybe they were on to something. Maybe I just wasn't good enough for her and wouldn't catch her eye now, or ever. Maybe a crooner from Hoboken wasn't glamorous enough for her. She'd been married first to America's sweetheart after all, followed by Artie Shaw. Women went crazy for Shaw and his clarinet. I didn't get it.

"Did you hear they're courting Ava for *One Touch of Venus*?" Jimmy asked. "They couldn't have picked a better broad to play a Roman goddess."

"The musical?" I asked.

"They're talking about a picture."

"I'd watch her in anything." Danny whistled.

I laughed and slugged Danny on the arm. "I laid eyes on her first."

"I'm pretty sure Mickey Rooney and Artie Shaw laid her first," Jimmy said.

We broke into laughter again, but I couldn't help but feel a twinge of jealousy and for no goddamn good reason. Jimmy and Danny, and George for that matter, were as welcome to the sublime Ava Gardner as any other single man. I, however, wasn't available at all, at least not in any real sense. I may have had a lot of freedom and a lot of women, but Nancy still wore my ring.

George gave us the eye. "This isn't the place, gentlemen." He nodded subtly to the group of women behind us.

George was of the same mind as the Boys, my Italian friends, if I could call them that. They warned me off public displays with other women, told me I should keep my dalliances brief, the wife at home happy, and all would be well. I could do what I wanted discreetly, they'd said, but I couldn't walk out on my wife and kids—that wasn't up for debate. Problem was, Nancy was no fool and we'd argued about the stories in the paper plenty, and the diamond bracelet she'd found that had wound up on another woman's wrist. Mostly, Nancy looked at me with sad eyes when I rolled in late or decided to stay in the apartment I'd rented in town. I didn't know how to change things without ruining all we had and all we were—and I didn't know if I could live with that.

"I saw you in the paper again," Danny said after a gulp of whiskey. "Something about an Un-American Activities Committee. They after you?"

"Nah," I said. "They know I'm not a communist. They just want to point fingers because they're a bunch of racist pricks. I don't see how promoting the Little Guy makes me a communist."

"You're not a politician," George warned. "They eat their own. You think you're doing them a favor—and you are—by drawing a lot of the heat away from them. But you're the one who will go down, Frank. You need to cool it."

He was worried, and given the way the record company had been treating me lately, I should be worried, too. I'd had a real nice lineup of hits, but things seemed to be slowing down a little. It would pass. I knew we'd be right back on top with the next record.

"At least you weren't in the paper this week for threatening a reporter," Jimmy said, swilling his beer and swatting at a fly buzzing around his head. "They sure like to crucify you."

"One of these days Frank will learn to stop harassing the reporters and then he won't be crucified anymore," George growled. He poured tanning oil into his right hand and rubbed it over his arms and hairy barrel of a chest.

"And one of these days they'll learn to leave me the hell alone before I take a bat to their knees," I shot back.

George gave me another long look, brows drawn.

I winked at him and he rolled his eyes. I'd been in and out of the press for months and the stories were usually bad. Reporters stalked me, invaded my private life, started fights between Nancy and me, and gave Mayer over at MGM reasons to scowl. But I wasn't going to give them the satisfaction of being silent. I'd give them my fist instead, and soon enough, they'd find some other jerk to come after.

As the sky faded to dark, everyone got drunker than ever. We were dehydrated from hours of sunning and swimming and drinking enough whiskey and beer to fill a swimming pool. George ordered a taxi, but before he stumbled around the front of the house, he took me aside. The light through the window-pane reflected off his glasses.

"We need to talk. My office, tomorrow," he said.

"Sure, sure," I said, wanting to get him off my back. It was definitely time for him to go home. He was ruining my buzz.

He gripped my arm as I turned to go. "I know you're flying high right now and you think no one can touch you because you're a star, but that's not the case, Frank. The crash is even harder for someone like you."

What crash? He needed another beer.

"Don't be such a nag. I've got Nancy for that." I shook his hand off and sent him on his way, trying to put the conversation from my mind.

Some neighbors left, and a handful of others were arriving, but just as things were starting to get a little dull, I had an idea.

"Help me with these, would you?" I called to Jimmy. He put out his cigarette and together we dragged a large box of fireworks from the shed onto a raft.

"For heaven's sakes, what are you doing?" Nancy had her hands on her hips and her dark curly hair was wild from the day's activities. She was tipsy as well from the spiked punch. She looked happy and beautiful, and if the house hadn't been full of people, I'd have swept her off her feet and taken her to bed.

"Don't worry about it," I said, my tongue thick from all the whiskey. "We're just having a little fun."

I pushed off from the shore and paddled out into the lake.

The raft wobbled over the undulating water beneath me. I steadied myself and carefully stood, flipped open my lighter, and held it to the wick of one of the firecrackers. The flame licked at my fingers as I held the lighter steady, waiting for it to catch. It took several tries but at last, the wick caught and as it did, the flame burned my finger. I swore and dropped the lighter.

The lit firecracker landed on the pile of others. In an instant, the packages caught fire.

"Frank! Jump, you fool!" Jimmy shouted.

I dove off the raft, swimming away furiously, swallowing too much water. The whine and prattle of fireworks filled the air, and the small lick of flames grew to a soaring blaze.

"Well, damn! There goes the raft," I slurred.

"Splash it with water!" Jimmy yelled, stumbling sideways.

He hit the water with an enormous splash and swam out beside me. A couple of neighbors joined in and the four of us got to work, splashing the raft. When the last of the flames went out, we looked at each other, panting and out of breath.

"That was about the dumbest thing I've ever done," I said.

We all burst into laughter.

Yet, in spite of the laughter and the sun-drenched day and the hours we spent partying into the night, George's warning echoed in my mind. He'd always been a little stern, but this time, he wasn't bluffing. He was genuinely worried. I could see it in the set of his jaw, the way he'd smoked too much. The press was on my back, and I knew he was right. I should heed his warning.

Like it or not, I'd better watch my step.

CHAPTER 3

FRANK

Even though good sense told me to, I didn't listen to George's warnings, and as it turned out, I paid for it. Enemies to the causes I'd promoted and believed in smeared my name all over town right along with the politicians'. My record sales dipped and that did it—I stopped accepting invitations to speak for my politician friends, at least for the time being. I didn't, however, stop hitting the clubs and one night, I was stupid enough to get sloshed and land a right hook in a journalist's smug face. I hated being followed around by photogs; they didn't respect a man's privacy and they took a special kind of satisfaction in smearing me in the papers. I took a special satisfaction in introducing them to my fist.

In my Sunset Towers apartment, the phone rang, and a ripple of dread rolled over me. I knew it was George on the other end of that line and I didn't want to hear the latest. I let it ring until it stopped, only for another call to begin. This time, I picked up.

"Hiya, George," I said as I tapped the bottom of a fresh pack of cigarettes, knocked a smoke free, and lit it with a match.

He didn't bother to greet me.

"I've got some bad news. Old Gold cigarettes is dropping you."

"What? Why?" I looked down at the packet in my hands. My radio sponsor was one of my biggest fans, or so I'd thought.

"You're bad for business," George replied gruffly. "And imagine my surprise when I picked up the papers today." He started to read the headlines aloud. "'Frankie Makes Mischief in Hollywood. Sinatra's Left Hook Strikes Again.' Are you really beating up journalists? Jesus Christ, Frank. You don't have the luxury to act like this right now. Did you notice you didn't make the list of *Down Beat*'s top singers of the year either? You're losing touch with your audience. I've been warning you, but you don't seem to give a shit, and now it's catching up with you."

Pulling on the end of my cigarette, I dragged smoke into my lungs and pushed it out in a steady stream. "That reporter was asking for it. He's been dragging my name through the mud for months." Lee Mortimer—I hated the guy—he'd deserved every last punch I gave him, even if I did have to appear in court and pay nine thousand dollars in fines.

"I think we need to put you on the road, get you out of town," George said. "Get ready for a club tour. Let's see if we can at least put you on the charts again."

As I hung up, I swore under my breath. I paced out onto the balcony. The sky simmered with the last embers of a spectacular sunset. Why were things snowballing all of a sudden? I couldn't believe my radio sponsor had given me the boot. What the hell? That was what I paid George for—to manage things—though admittedly, he'd warned me plenty.

I sucked on the end of my cigarette and dropped it to the ground, crushing it with the heel of my shoe. Inside, I paced, anxiety crackling inside me. Perhaps things would be better on the tour. George seemed to think so.

Unable to stay inside another minute, I took the elevator and strode down Sunset Boulevard, trying to outrun the thoughts in my head. Things would turn around. George would think of something, I told myself. He always did.

After an hour, the roaring in my ears calmed. I headed back to the apartment, my hands in my pockets, wishing I had some plans that night, something to keep me from sinking. When I was this worked up, and the hours wrung themselves out, my thoughts turned dark and I had trouble staying out of my own way. It had always been that way.

When I rounded the bend and Sunset Towers came into view, I saw a woman just ahead on the sidewalk, her silhouette unmistakable even in the dark. Slender waist and full hips, a bandana tied over dark curls—it was Ava Gardner. A stroke of luck I hadn't expected.

"Ava!" I called and jogged to catch up to her. She turned at the sound of her name. "I thought that was you."

She gave me her megawatt smile. "Hey there, Frank Sinatra."

Something in my chest lurched at the sound of my name on her lips.

"That smile of yours is your superpower," I said.

"And yours is flattery," she countered. "You hand out praise like candy."

I laughed, shaking my head. "I only hand out praise when I mean it."

"Is that so." Her eyes gleamed and her ivory skin looked

luminescent in the pale glow of the streetlamp. It took all my strength not to brush my thumb across the soft roundness of her cheekbone.

I cleared my throat. "What are you doing out here at this hour?"

"Sometimes I like to walk at night," she said. "Helps me quiet my head a little."

"A woman shouldn't be out alone in the dark."

"Why? Because there might be strange men shouting your name off their balcony in the middle of the night?"

I tipped my head back and laughed heartily. "You heard us, then."

"I think everyone heard you clear to Malibu."

I chuckled again. She was always wittier than I expected. "We'd had a few drinks."

"You don't say." Her tone was sarcastic, but her full lips stretched into another pretty smile.

My stomach rumbled loudly, and this time, we both laughed. "I haven't eaten supper yet, have you? I'm not much of a cook, but I can make a mean steak, and there's probably something else in my fridge."

She hesitated a moment and then asked, "Have you got any gin?"

I felt myself grin. "I always have plenty of booze."

"Well, alright then, show me the way. I'm starved."

As we walked the short distance to my apartment, I could feel her beside me, hear her soft breathing, and I had to force myself to be cool, confident. Inside, I removed my sweater and rolled up my sleeves before rummaging through the refrigerator. The housekeeper had left steak and potatoes, and a medley of carrots and peas that I could cook up in a snap.

"This place is immaculate." Ava looked around the kitchen at the chrome polished to a shine and the counter that had become a makeshift bar with a cocktail shaker and rows of liquor bottles. She moved to the living room and glanced around at the plush couch and ran her finger over the coffee tabletop. "Not a speck of dust anywhere. You must have a maid."

"I do, and when she's busy, I clean it myself. I can't stand disorder. It makes it hard for me to think."

"I have a live-in maid myself. Reenie Jordan. Well, she's become something of a friend, too, truth be told."

"Is it a good idea to be friends with someone you've hired?" I asked.

"I'm not sure most of what I do is a good idea, Frank, but I do it anyway."

I chuckled. "Is that so? Well, that makes two of us."

I made us each a gin martini, extra dry as the lady requested, and got to work on the food. I couldn't help but look up from my chopping, to make certain she was really there. I watched her move, saw the liveliness dance across her features as she studied my place. She inspected the shelves that were decorated with a few odds and ends that I'd picked up at the gallery downtown: a desert landscape, a Waterford crystal decanter and glasses, and a series of marble statuettes. For the most part, the apartment had basic furnishings since it wasn't my full-time residence.

When she reached the record player, she crouched to look at the stack of records in the cabinet beneath it. "You have so

many records. Are you a collector?" she asked, running her fingertips across the stack.

"Of course," I said. "I'm in the music business. Besides, if you
host parties, you need music. Have you heard "Jungle Nights
in Harlem" by Duke Ellington?" When she shook her head, I
wiped my hands on the kitchen towel, crossed the room, and
pulled the record out of its sleeve. I blew on it to clear off any
dust and laid it on the turntable. "You've got to hear this."

Duke opened the song on the piano, followed by a trumpet,
a *tap-tapping* for rhythm, and lush saxophones cushioned the
whole melody.

She kicked off her shoes and sat on the floor, her back leaning against the sofa, her left foot moving to the beat. "This is
great."

"Isn't it?" I said, plating our food. "Let's eat."

After we ate, I made us another round of drinks and put on
one record after another. Soon we'd listened to big band and
swing, jazz, and eventually some of the classical greats: Wag-
ner, Strauss, Beethoven.

"Can you imagine composing something like that?" I asked
over the crashing of drums and cymbals.

"It sounds like someone is marching." She was stretched
out on the floor, her eyes closed, listening to the strains of a
magnificent orchestra. And all I could do was watch her: her
arched brow, the adorable apples of her cheeks, the way her
lips twitched into a smile. She'd made me laugh, too, more
times than I could count. She surprised me in the best of ways.
I didn't know what to make of it.

We talked about books and our favorite authors. She told

me all about the way Artie Shaw demanded she read his chosen list of books, and how he'd paid for chess lessons for her—until she beat him. The way he'd insisted she learn to behave like an upper-class socialite when she was a down-to-earth kind of woman. She'd even taken a few college classes to try to keep up with his expectations—and to ward off the constant barrage of insults. He sounded like a real prick.

"Don't get me wrong," she said. "I have nothing against self-improvement. In fact, I'm grateful to Artie for that. I learned so much from him. But in the end, I still didn't fit his imaginary view of who I should be." Her southern drawl emerged more and more as the night wore on and the drinks kept coming. "I'm nothing but a poor southern girl from rural North Carolina. I ran around barefoot, chasing my big brothers and their friends, or teasing my older sisters. I haven't been a lady a single day of my life."

"You're the best kind of lady, if you ask me," I said, my voice going soft. "A real looker, but you've got a curious mind, too. I'd say that's about the most important quality in life."

She smiled at that, and I held up my glass in a toast. We drank and a comfortable silence fell between us a moment before she began again.

"I do like to read, and to explore new places," she said.

"Me, too," I replied. "I read everything I can get my hands on."

"Tell me about your childhood," she said, her voice soft.

"I'm from Hoboken, New Jersey. Ran around with a pack of hooligans, beating up on each other in the city streets. Some of us stole things and cheated at cards. It was crowded and dirty, but I can't complain. My parents owned a bar, and Ma was in politics. Still is, really. Pop was a prizefighter turned fireman, so we had enough money to move to a real house a few blocks away from the worst of it. Wear decent clothes."

"You're an only child?" she asked.

I nodded. What I didn't say aloud was how often I'd yearned to be more like the other Italian families on the block. Large and loud and a whole lot of fun. "What about you?" I asked.

"I'm the youngest of seven. I was completely feral until I turned about fifteen."

"That explains a few things," I said, winking.

"Like what?" she demanded, a look of mock outrage on her face.

"The youngest is forgotten as often as they are put on a pedestal, at least from what I've seen."

"Well, that's true," she admitted. "Everyone treated me like a princess or completely ignored me—nothing in between. Were you always just Frank or is it short for something?"

"It's short for Francis."

"Francis." She smiled. "I like that."

I told her a few stories about my childhood friends, and she did the same, and the next thing we knew, it was late but neither of us paid heed to the time. At a lull in the conversation, she got up and looked through my records again.

"I love this song." She pulled out Bing Crosby's "Don't Fence Me In." "His voice is smooth and rich as cream."

I suppressed instant jealousy. I'd always looked up to Crosby and wanted to be just like him until I'd moved to Hollywood and had to compete with him for top spots on *Down Beat*'s best-seller lists.

"I've always wanted to be a part of a band, since I was a

girl," she said, a wistful look in her eyes. "I dreamed of being onstage one day. A silly fantasy, really. I'm not a great singer."

"That's not true. I saw you sing in *The Killers*. You have a fine voice. Sultry, I'd say."

"You think so?" She seemed genuinely pleased.

"As far as I can tell, everything about you is fine."

"There's that flattery again." She smiled, exposing a dimple in her cheek, and tossed her dark wavy hair—and I was completely smitten. She wasn't just beautiful; it was how she wore her beauty. She was intelligent and sharp-tongued and had a generous laugh. There was an edge to her charm. Something undefinable, intangible. I wanted to discover what that something was—I wanted to know everything about her.

"Here's a secret. Something about me that isn't so fine," she said. "I have the worst stage fright! I'm also shy in large groups. The martinis help with that," she said, sliding the Bing Crosby back into the stack and choosing a Billie Holiday record instead.

"That will get better as you make more movies," I said.

Billie's voluptuous voice filled the room and the energy between us shifted. I wanted her nearer. To take her in my arms, put my face in her hair. I'd wanted her the first moment I saw her, but it had been nothing like the need I had now to connect with her on every level. I held her gaze until she looked away.

"You're a night owl, like me," I said. "It's late and you haven't yawned once."

"I am." She turned on her stomach and propped herself up on her elbows.

"Me, too. I like to go all night. That's when all the fun happens." I winked and she rolled her eyes.

"I can't believe that works on women."

I laughed. "Did it work on you?"

"How about you get me another drink," she replied, dodging the question.

I raised a brow. She could hold her liquor as well as any of my pals, but I didn't mention it. Instead, I poured us another round and set the glasses on the coffee table.

"The floor must be pretty hard by now. Why don't you get more comfortable?" I sat on the couch and patted the cushion next to me.

She met my gaze and this time, the femme fatale that I'd watched on-screen emerged. Seductive, sexy, challenging. I felt a stirring below the belt.

"It is, come to think of it," she said, rising from the floor and settling onto the couch next to me.

I inched closer. She didn't come any nearer but neither did she turn away, and I took my chance, closing the slender distance between us. When her warm breath fanned across my cheek, I cupped her face in my hands.

"You're more beautiful than you have a right to be, you know that?" I said. "All I can think about is what your lips might feel like."

She glanced at my mouth and then met my eyes again. "So why don't you give them a try?"

I smiled and leaned in, brushing my lips over hers. I was gentle at first, but when her arms slipped around my neck, pulling me closer, an urgency built between us. I ran my hands down her arms and over her back, my body coming alive at the feel of her skin beneath my hands. I wanted to devour this woman from head to toe.

We kissed and caressed each other until our soft moans mingled.

Suddenly, she pulled away. "Well." She was breathless, her eyes dark. "Now that we know what that's like, I'd better be on my way." She scooted farther away from me, and I groaned at the distance between us.

"Now?" I asked, sitting up straight. "Come on, doll, stay a little longer. You didn't finish your drink."

"You're married," she said simply. "And I'm not interested in courting that disaster, no matter how much I like talking to you. Or kissing you." She slipped on her saddle shoes without her socks and grabbed her purse by the door. "Thanks for dinner."

And with that, she was gone.

As I stared at the back of the door, my body still pulsing with the need she'd elicited, I knew this woman wasn't anything like the others, and for the first time, that scared the hell out of me.

CHAPTER 4

AVA

I thought of that night with Frank for weeks: the heady sensation of his eyes on me, drinking me in, the weight of his hands on my back as an undeniable energy sparked between us. But it was our conversations that I couldn't stop thinking about. How easy they had been. I'd felt seen in a way that I hadn't before, and it was intoxicating—which was precisely why I'd avoided him ever since. There was no sense in wrapping myself around a man who had a wife and family. It would mean I was good for one thing, and I wasn't in any mood to have my affections toyed with, least of all by a man constantly on the road who also happened to be married.

Still, Frank Sinatra plagued my thoughts.

When an invitation came to get out of town, I accepted instantly and packed my sister up along with me. A few weeks in Palm Springs at a friend's place while I was between films seemed like just the thing. I needed the break. I'd been on the go for quite some time after *One Touch of Venus* released—another film owned by a studio other than my own. I frowned just thinking about it, frustrated by the way MGM continued to ignore me. The film had been a success and suddenly, there were plenty of other roles for me. My paycheck had quadrupled, and my name was not only all over town, but all over the country. I was ecstatic by the change in my circumstances and my success. And yet, MGM still refused to give me a decent role. I didn't understand it. Would they always overlook me, see me as nothing but a hick without star power? Whether I liked to admit it or not, the consistent rejection from the studio who had discovered me stung.

"Do you want a drink?" I balanced my sunglasses on the bridge of my nose and looked at my sister, who lounged in a chair next to me by the pool. "Champagne sounds just right, doesn't it?"

Even in the fall Palm Springs was hot until the sun burned itself out for the night. It was a beautiful town nestled at the base of a ridge of mountains that rimmed the valley. They were stark, lumbering giants of dusty brown and gray framed by vivid blue skies during the day and deep purple peaks swaddled by a blanket of stars at night. Grottos of lush palms and desert flowers adorned the properties of the rich and famous, fed by the local hot springs. A visual feast and the perfect escape to be sure. I adored it.

"We may as well keep the party going all day," Bappie agreed, and pushed her own sunglasses up the slope of her long, strong nose.

My sister was striking, though not precisely beautiful, and I loved her features for their character. She didn't live by them the way I had to with my own, and I envied that about her at times. I'd never tell her such a thing because I could already hear her reply: "Don't mock me, Ava." She'd tell me to be grateful for my beauty, and I was, but I was coming to learn that though my beauty was a gift, at times it was also a burden, the weight of which I felt as I avoided the lecherous men in the halls of MGM, or when it was suggested I eat more of this and less of that or told, "For heaven's sakes, don't get pregnant or you're through" by my manager, or by Mayer himself. I'd come to be defined by my beauty, and that was alright for now, but I couldn't help but notice the way most actresses "aged out" of the business and disappeared from Hollywood completely. As if age made one invisible. It was all the more reason to fully establish myself at MGM and beyond.

"I'll get it." I waved to an attendant who sat at a luxurious outdoor tiki bar decorated with cacti and fuchsia flowers on the opposite side of the patio.

He arrived pronto, took our order, and returned with a couple of coupe glasses and a bucket of ice. He popped the cork and poured the golden liquid.

"Isn't the pop of a cork the happiest sound in the world?" I said.

"It sure is," Bappie replied.

I took a hearty drink from my glass. I was looking forward to the next couple of weeks of sleeping through the morning and lounging poolside in the afternoon, attending an occasional party in the evening. It was a prime place to escape the rat race of Hollywood, and many people I knew had houses nearby.

"Did you keep that jewelry from Howard?" Bappie asked.

Howard Hughes—eccentric Texas millionaire, friend, and man on a mission to get in my pants. He'd even hired his own team of spies to watch my house and my comings and goings, to keep me safe, he'd said, but I knew it was because the man

STRANGERS IN THE NIGHT   45

liked to own things—and people. Somehow, I managed to forgive his awkwardness and his eccentricities, at least most of the time, and see past the wrinkled suit and body odor. We'd had a lot of great times together, talking like old hens, dancing, dining, complaining about Hollywood. The shopping trips to Mexico via his private jet with my sister along didn't hurt either. In the end, he amused me and he was loyal, and that was worth a lot in this life.

"Of course not," I said crossly, sorting through the chopped vegetables we'd ordered for a snack. "Sometimes, I swear he thinks I'm a concubine. I'm not going to sleep with him just because he gave me a bunch of diamonds."

"He's the richest man on earth, Ava. Even if you divorced him, you'd probably walk away with enough money to never have to work again."

"Would you listen to yourself? Why don't you go after him?" I drained my glass and reached for the bottle to pour another. "I'm not for sale."

Bappie swatted my arm half-heartedly, leaving a slick of tanning oil across my skin. "You know perfectly well he's in love with you and I'm the last person in the world he wants to date. I'm not a beautiful, mysterious movie star."

I launched a celery stalk at her, and it ricocheted off her sunglasses. I laughed heartily, reaching for another.

"Oh no you don't." Bappie shook her head vehemently. "We'll get a good scolding from the staff."

"We will not. He's barely pubescent." I motioned at the very young man who'd delivered the champagne bottle. "You think he's going to take on a pair of grown women?"

"You're probably right," she said, grabbing a handful of

chopped carrots and launching them at me one by one in a tiny bombardment.

We laughed hysterically and wound up knocking the champagne bottle over. The thick glass clanged as it hit the patio tile. The young man at the bar rushed over, his mouth falling open as he took in the scattered vegetables and overturned bottle that, thankfully, hadn't shattered.

"I'll just get a mop and broom," he said.

"You do that," I said, winking. "And we'd love another bottle."

"Um, yes, Miss Gardner. Right away."

"Thank you. And why don't you grab a drink and join us!" I called after him.

As he hurried away, we broke into a fit of giggles. My oldest sister was one of my favorite people in the world. I couldn't imagine living in California without her. I loved my other sisters, too, of course, but I'd never been particularly close to them. They didn't understand me. They'd married and gone on with their lives in the rural world where we'd grown up. I could never return to that life, much as I cherished my childhood memories.

My thoughts turned to Frank—again. How it must have been to grow up in a house without brothers and sisters. It was almost impossible for me to imagine. I'd lived in a tiny, crowded house, and later, in a boardinghouse for schoolchildren, where Mama worked as a cook. Home meant an ever-present hum of activity and the smell of boiled greens thick in the air, always too much washing, and bickering followed by peals of laughter nearly every hour of the day. It was no wonder I'd been wild as the youngest, an afterthought in many ways. I learned quickly to stay out from underfoot. Frank must have been incredibly lonely.

"What do you think about Frank Sinatra?" I asked suddenly.

"His music, you mean, or the pictures he's been in?" Bappie asked.

I shrugged. "Both?"

"I like his voice. His movies, not much, but then again, he hasn't played in anything of note. Why do you ask?"

"No reason. I see him around here and there," I said, cagey. When she cast me a side-eyed glance, I changed the subject. "What are you wearing tonight?"

"To the party?"

"Mm-hmm." I rolled lazily onto my side.

"The brown dress."

I wrinkled my nose. "What about the navy with the sash at the waist? Brown isn't much good for anyone."

"Maybe," she said, finishing her glass of champagne. She was living in her own place now. She'd become pretty autonomous, so I guessed the last thing she wanted was to take advice from her little sister. "What about you?"

"My halter sundress. The lemon yellow one."

"Oh, you're adorable in that one."

I blew her a kiss. "I might meet someone special there, who knows."

I'd given up Duff once and for all and had been on a few dates since, but still nothing serious to speak of. The single life suited me, except for in the heart of the night when the world dreamed and shadows invaded my thoughts. At night, all was quiet but me, and that was when I came alive. My senses heightened and my mind whirred, obsessing over every mistake I'd ever made. On the worst nights, I'd think about Mama and her cancer and how I wished I'd been able to spare her the pain of it all, or I'd think of Daddy and how taciturn he was. I could count the few times I'd heard him laugh or offer a kind word. He lived almost entirely inside himself, his thoughts locked away in a deep well that was unreachable. I pictured him, solitary among the leafy fields of tobacco he'd worked so hard to grow until we'd lost it all—and he'd lost his will to live right along with it. I wondered how he'd feel about having his daughter's face splashed all over the magazines and billboards, my divorces, and now, a spark of something with a married man. He'd order me home for a good paddlin', even if I was making all that money, and tell me not to put on such airs.

I flushed at the thought and reached for my drink, reminding myself that Daddy was no longer here.

A few hours later, Bappie and I were dressed and coiffed and ready for a little fun. If there was something I'd learned since my time in Hollywood, it was to accept invitations to parties and to make friends and play nice. The more the directors and producers liked you, the more often they considered you for roles. I liked parties so that suited me fine, but my natural shyness also made them difficult until I'd had a few drinks.

Producer Darryl Zanuck's home was beautiful with its airy rooms, potted greenery throughout the house, and wide veranda. I enjoyed a cocktail and then two, and once the liquor had loosened my tongue, I chatted with various colleagues and strangers. Most of the crowd I'd never met before. Bappie made a friend quickly and appeared to be having a grand ol' time. She'd decided on the navy dress after all and looked as pretty as a peach.

By my third drink, I felt properly lubricated and sidled up next to Darryl. "Aren't you going to play some music?" I asked the host. "I want to dance."

"After dinner," he said, eyeing my empty martini glass. He reached for it and called to the bartender. "Gerome, get this woman a fresh drink."

Within seconds, I had another drink in hand and edged around the crowded room. When I came to the patio door, I pushed it open, suddenly eager for a little fresh air. There was a brilliant pool lined with colorful Mexican tiles, decorative palms stationed around its outer edges, and a small lawn that appeared to roll all the way to the base of the mountains. Soft clouds dipped in plum and gold framed a spectacular sunset, and the heat of the day had begun to fade. I stared up at the sky, drinking in the sight for a moment before fishing in my handbag for a cigarette.

"Well, if it isn't Ava Gardner."

My stomach flipped at the sound of that familiar voice, the soft baritone I'd heard a lot recently coming from my record player. A voice, I had to admit, that was growing on me a great deal.

"Well, hello there, Francis," I said, not bothering to hide my smile.

CHAPTER 5

FRANK

*S*he called me *Francis.*

I hadn't given her permission to use the name that only my ma used from time to time, but I got the feeling Ava Gardner didn't need permission from me, or from anyone.

She stood at the edge of the porch, her silhouette as perfect as that of Venus de Milo: the curve of her hips, her narrow waist, and the dark hair that dusted the tops of her shoulders in a soft curl. She held a cigarette between two long, fine fingers, smoke curling and twisting overhead until it blended with the wisps of clouds in the sky. If it didn't make me sound like a broad, I might admit that my breath caught every time I laid eyes on her. But I wasn't a broad and I sure as hell didn't want to scare her away by being a fool for her. This woman would require finesse.

I leaned against a pillar beside her on the patio.

"How have you been?" she asked, flicking the ash from her cigarette.

"Thinking about you is how I've been."

She cocked a slim dark brow at me. "Is that so?"

"I saw your film. *One Touch of Venus*. Made me more jealous of Robert Walker than I could stand."

She laughed. "Whatever for?"

"He got to kiss you," I said.

"It's just a movie, Francis."

"And you're a goddess."

She laughed heartily this time. "Better not put me on a pedestal. I like to run around barefoot and get dirty."

"I bet you do." I grinned.

She slapped my arm playfully.

"That's some sky," I said, pointing at the edges of the mountain peaks gilded in gold. "Makes you want to drink champagne and count the stars as they come out."

"You're a romantic, aren't you," she said, blowing a stream of smoke through a pair of red lips.

"Aren't we all?"

Her eyes darkened from happy green to emerald. "Not all of us. Romance doesn't serve me well."

I angled my body toward her. "You can't let two lousy husbands ruin things for you."

Her eyes roved over my face and dragged down my frame. Studying, assessing, deciding. Was I worth her time? I wanted to remind her of the fun we'd had that night a few months ago. I wanted to know if she'd thought about me as often as I'd thought about her.

"Think supper's ready?" she drawled, her southern accent appearing. "I haven't had anything but rabbit food all day."

"They were setting up when I stepped outside for a smoke."

We went inside to find people taking a seat around one of the two large tables set for dinner. The scent of fresh bread and butter and some savory dish wafted through the room. Darryl had pulled out all the stops with candelabras and silver service trays, and porcelain dishes made to look like Mexican tiles.

"Well, aren't these pretty," Ava said, admiring the dishes with elaborate floral designs in cherry red, royal blue, orange, and white. "Sit by me?" she asked.

Something warm pooled in my chest, and I smiled, pulling out a sleek chair for her first and then myself.

As the hired staff served tenderloin with a mustard cream sauce, greens and garlic potatoes, and piping hot rolls, Darryl raised his glass. "I'd like to propose a toast."

I reached for my wineglass.

"Thank you all for coming," Darryl said. "To friends!"

"To friends!"

Ava clinked her glass against mine, her gaze on me steadfast.

Meeting her eyes made the blood in my veins hum. I drank and tried to play the suave fellow as the food was dished out, but I wanted nothing but to listen to more of her stories, hear her thoughts. Get her alone, even if only on the patio again.

"What are you working on now?" I reached for a roll.

"I'm between pictures at the moment," she answered, "but it looks like I'll be shooting again in a few months."

"Things are going great for you," I said. "I've seen your face on just about every magazine and billboard in town."

She pursed her lips. "Yes, well, it hasn't been easy convincing Mayer that I'm worth a damn, but things have been good elsewhere. Tell me about your music," she said, slicing her meat into bite-size pieces. "Are you recording anything new?"

My music. It was a sore subject lately. I'd watched my latest hits slide right off the charts. Worse, the movies I'd booked had mostly been panned, both because my parts were lousy and because those who didn't like my politics didn't care if my performance was right-on. They just wanted to sock it to me.

"I'm between records." I didn't want to look like I was a has-been, not to her. We talked about my manager and a few prospects I was hoping would come through.

I felt a twinge of worry in my stomach as George's warning came to mind and I changed the subject, asking her what she'd been reading. Over fine food and wine, we debated the brilliance of various authors from Fitzgerald to Agatha Christie.

After dinner, Darryl's staff pushed back the chairs and tables to make way for dancing. When someone turned up the music, the guests flowed onto the makeshift dance floor.

"Come on!" Ava grabbed my hand.

"I'm not much for dancing," I protested.

"Do I need to find another partner?"

"You'd better not," I growled, and we both laughed.

We moved along to the music in a Lindy Hop, her yellow dress twisting around her legs. She danced without even a hint of self-consciousness. She was beautiful, all charm and bright light, and as I looked down at her, her eyes sparking with mischief, I knew I was a goner. Ava Gardner might very well be my undoing.

"Let's get out of here," I said suddenly. "Go for a ride."

She hesitated a beat and then smiled. "Alright."

Relief rushed through me—she wanted to come away with me. It was my goddamn lucky day.

"I'll meet you in the drive."

I said a hasty goodbye to the host and made a beeline for the door. I'd never been more eager to leave a party in my entire life.

CHAPTER 6

AVA

I threaded through the crowd of dancers, looking for my sister, my stomach aflutter. What was I doing, leaving with Francis? But I didn't want to think about it too much. I wanted only to feel and do and be, at least for tonight.

I found Bappie slouched against a sofa cushion, deep in conversation with a man in a bright blue suit.

"I'm going for a drive with Frank," I said in her ear. "He's going to drop me off later. You take the car." I tossed her the keys.

Bappie's brow arched in surprise, but a smile touched her bright pink lips. "Don't do anything I wouldn't do."

"I'll do everything you'd do and more." I winked, and we both laughed.

I headed to the bar and rummaged around behind the counter until I found a mostly full bottle of whiskey. Tucking it under my arm, I met Francis in the drive. He revved the engine of his Cadillac convertible as soon as I appeared. I laughed in glee as I slid into the front seat.

"Where to, hot rod?" I asked, removing the lid on the whiskey and taking a swig straight from the bottle. It burned going down, but I hardly noticed. Francis was looking at me like a wolf eyeing a hen. He took in my face and then his eyes wandered lower. It was delicious and I was too drunk to pretend I didn't want to be in his arms again, the way we had been that night at his apartment.

"On an adventure," he said, tearing his gaze away and backing out of the drive.

It was dark as pitch except for the stars winking overhead like distant fireflies and the occasional pocket of light glowing from some house on the horizon. I could just make out the faintest silhouette of the looming mountains in the distance.

As we picked up speed, the wind caught my hair and blew it into a wild funnel. Laughing, I stuck out my right arm and let it ripple over the wind currents. I felt as free as a bird.

"You're goddamn sexy, did you know that?" he shouted over the noise of the wind.

"Faster!" I shouted, taking another slug of whiskey and passing the bottle to him.

He swallowed a large gulp and stepped on the gas. We rocketed down the road into the desert flatlands, kicking up dust behind us into the quiet night. I whooped and threw my hands overhead. He laughed as he swerved around a bend in the road. I tipped sideways at the unexpected movement. As I fell into him, he slipped his free arm around me to steady me and left it there. I didn't fight it, the nearness of him, and the night air whipping around us. It was all far more intoxicating than anything I'd drunk that night.

I turned in the seat to face Francis and study his silhouette: the long nose and full lips, his protruding brow bone. His wiry frame and enormous ego had faded, or maybe they didn't matter as much as I'd once thought, and all that was left was someone I had things in common with, who liked to live a little dangerously, and who knew what he wanted. Someone who oozed more charisma and energy than anyone I'd ever known. He was vibrant, vivacious—and utterly, perfectly wrong for me.

"You're not so bad, Francis," I said, smiling in the dark.

"Gee, thanks. That's a hell of a compliment."

I laughed heartily as he rolled his eyes.

When we passed the welcome sign for the town of Indio, he laid on the horn.

I shouted, "We're here everybody!"

He honked again, but as we rolled into the small town shrouded in darkness, the car slowed.

Frank grinned and reached for the whiskey, his hand brushing my thigh where I held it firmly between my legs.

"You pervert," I said, swatting at his hand.

"Honey, if I was going to be a pervert, I'd be a lot more aggressive than that."

"Oh yeah? I'd like to see that."

"Is that so?" He glanced at me and saw the wicked smile on my face.

"I don't believe you really live up to all of the talk, Mr. Sinatra," I goaded him.

"That does it." He jerked the car left.

I careened sideways and threw my right hand against the door to steady myself. "Francis!" I laughed at the screeching tires.

As we ran over the curb of a street corner, he slammed on the brakes and we jolted forward. He put the car in park and drank another big swig of whiskey.

"What have you heard?" he said, his eyes electric blue in the dashboard lights.

"That you're a Casanova," I teased. "But that's not what I see."

"Is that so. What do you see, Miss Gardner?"

"I see a man who's got it bad."

"It's worse than bad. It's a fever and I may not recover." He inched closer, putting his hand on my knee and sending a shiver of anticipation over my skin.

"I think you'd better show me just how right I am," I said. The words slipped out, and before I knew what I was doing, I leaned toward him.

He slid one hand around the back of my neck, caressing the soft skin with his thumb. Tilting my head back, he looked into my eyes as if searching for something.

"Ava," he said hoarsely.

"Shh," I whispered. "Just kiss me."

He pressed his lips against mine, slipping one hand around my waist, and crushed me against him. His other hand slid down my neck, over my bared shoulders. I tingled at his touch, felt a need building inside me as we kissed passionately, desperately.

I sat back suddenly, gasping for air.

"Your skin." He groaned, bringing his face to my neck and inhaling.

Something inside me released at that guttural sound, and a deep ache began to throb. I wanted him—God did I ever—but he wasn't mine to have, and I needed to remember that.

No married men, Ava. No married men!

I kept chanting the phrase in my head. They were trouble

and what was more, I didn't like thinking about their wives being brokenhearted. It was an ugly business. I didn't care how typical it was in Hollywood. But as I sat across from this man who had more passion than anyone I'd ever known, the air as electric as in a summer storm, I knew I'd surrender. Francis would be trouble, and trouble with him seemed like just the right kind.

Silencing the voice in my head, I wrapped my arms around him. He pulled me to him again, our lips finding the other's. This time, it was a slower, more tender kiss. His hands wandered over my bodice to my waist to rest on the curves of my hips. All my thoughts, all the warnings flashing through my mind, turned to whispers until I was filled to the brim with only him, his scent, his need.

We remained locked in an embrace for some time, until at last, I pulled away.

"Want to go somewhere?" he said, his voice hoarse.

"We are somewhere." I rested against the seat to catch my breath, to gather my thoughts. "Want a drink?" I reached for the bottle of whiskey.

He swigged and passed it back to me.

"Yes. Let's go somewhere," I said, wiping my mouth.

"You've got it, princess." He backed off the curb, put the car in drive, and mashed the gas pedal. "You wanted to go fast, baby!" he shouted over the engine and the wind. "Let's go fast!"

I whooped as the tires squealed once again and we tore down the main road that bisected the tiny town of Indio.

He reached across me and unlatched the glove box. Inside, sat a gleaming handgun. "This is what we do in the Wild West!"

He aimed the gun overhead and fired.

I screamed—and burst into laughter at my surprise. My heart racing at his antics, I reached for the gun. "Let me try!" I shot into the night wildly, not bothering to take aim.

A nearby hardware store window cracked and shattered, the glass tinkling as it hit the ground.

"Oh my God!" I said, covering my mouth.

The car swerved as he took the gun. "You've got to aim, baby. Like this." He pointed the barrel of the pistol at a streetlamp and fired. The light popped and went out, shrouding the street in darkness.

I shrieked. "You hit it!"

He handed me the gun. "We'd better beat it before anyone sees us." His foot was heavy on the gas, and we fled into the night.

I turned in my seat to face the back of the car as the little town receded and the night unspooled behind us. With a rebel yell, I fired one last time. Laughing and exhilarated, I turned around in my seat and tucked the gun into the glove box.

"That was damned fun!" I shouted.

In that moment, the sound of sirens split the air.

"Son of a gun!" Francis said, slowing the car.

I glanced over my shoulder into the desert night. A police car raced after us. I looked at Francis with wide eyes as a sobering thought edged its way into my foggy, whiskey-soaked mind.

We were in serious trouble. *I* was in serious trouble. Far more trouble than one silly police car, hot on our tail.

I was falling—and falling fast—for Frank Sinatra.

CHAPTER 7

FRANK

It's alright, baby. Let me handle this," I said, seeing the panic on Ava's face. She clearly hadn't had any run-ins with the law, and I'd had plenty. You didn't grow up on the streets of Jersey and New York without having it out from time to time.

Two cops approached the car, the taller cop stopping just outside my door. He beamed a flashlight at me.

"Well, what do we have—" He stopped and his mouth fell open in shock. He recovered quickly. "Mr. Sinatra, Miss Gardner! My wife and I saw you at the Palladium a couple of years back, Mr. Sinatra. It was the best show I've ever seen. And Miss Gardner, we saw *One Touch of Venus*, twice."

"Did you hear that, Ava?" I said. "He and his wife have good taste. You're a good man." I offered him my hand to shake on it.

Ava flashed one of her perfect, charming smiles. "Thank you, officer."

"Out for a little joy ride, I see," the other cop said, giving his colleague a stern look meant to be a rebuke. It was clear he had no interest in celebrities or in cutting us a break. "I think you'd better come into the station with us."

The more cordial cop nodded. "I'm afraid so, you two. You can't go around shooting up stores and drinking while you're driving. It's dangerous."

"And illegal." The other cop rolled his eyes. "Everyone out of the car. You're under arrest."

"Whoa, whoa, whoa. I think we can come to some kind of agreement, can't we?" I said, more than a little worried our pictures would show up in the police blotter.

"I said, out of the car!" the second cop demanded.

"No need to get a stick up your ass," I said, slurring my words. I opened my door, stood, and swayed a little.

"Francis, don't piss him off, sugar. It won't do us any good." Ava's voice was as sweet as southern honey.

The nice cop looked at his colleague, who roughly moved Ava to the side to cuff her. And that did it. I pushed the guy back.

"Mr. Sinatra," the nice cop said. "Let's keep this civil. You, too." He glared at the jerk cop.

I decided I'd better let the man do his job. I wasn't keen on the idea of staying in jail. We were steered into the back of the squad car, this time without complaint.

I glanced at Ava. Her expression had shifted and something in her eyes had changed. She looked frightened, a bit like a chastised little girl, and my heart melted.

"It'll be alright," I said, trying to soothe her. "I'll make a call."

We rode the rest of the way to the station in silence. Inside, they locked us in a holding cell. When Ava leaned against the wall, fatigue settled over her features and suddenly the fun of the night vanished. I needed to get her home, or she'd remember nothing about the passion between us—only the hassle and embarrassment of being arrested with that Frank Sinatra character.

"Listen, fellas, I think we can settle this without making a big fuss," I said through the bars. "I'll make it worth your while. Besides, don't I get a phone call?"

The policemen exchanged looks.

"What did you have in mind, Mr. Sinatra?" the nice cop asked.

I gripped the iron bars separating me from them. "I'd be happy to pay for the light and the shop window in town. And leave something extra for you boys for your trouble."

The jerk cop nodded. "Make the call."

Ava brightened and touched my arm.

I winked and then stepped back while they unlocked the bars. I called George, but it was two o'clock in the morning and he wouldn't pick up, so I called his assistant, Jack Keller. After I gave Jack a short explanation of the situation—that I'd creased a cop a little and made a scratch on an abandoned building and a streetlamp—he asked me to put the officer on the phone.

After a few minutes, the cop gave me the receiver.

"We've decided on a number," Jack said. "I'll charter a plane and bring the money with me. They're going to meet me at the landing strip. Most importantly, they agreed to keep this between us and out of the press."

I sighed in relief. I hoped so, or George would have a heart attack. He was already on my case constantly about the morality clause in my MGM contract.

A few hours later, it was all over, and Ava and I were dropped off at my Cadillac. Once inside the car, Ava laid her head on my shoulder.

"You sleep, princess," I said. "I'll drive."

She yawned and curled up in my lap like a cat and promptly fell asleep. When we arrived in Palm Springs, it was already midmorning. As I pulled into the drive of the house where she was staying, she sat up and stretched.

"We're here," she said.

"Yes," I said tiredly, and rubbed my thumb softly over her cheekbone.

She smiled at my touch. We got out of the car, and I walked her to the door. As she reached for the knob, she paused to kiss me on the cheek.

"That was a memorable night, Francis."

And she was one memorable woman.

"I'll say." I grinned and turned to go, but as I slid into the driver seat, I noticed her there, still on the porch, watching me. Her expression was part amused, part bewildered, as if she couldn't believe what the night had brought. And maybe, I hoped, what had happened between us.

A wave of tenderness washed over me then and I knew she was right. I had it bad—worse than bad.

I was in love.

Part 2

"COME FLY WITH ME"

1949–1951

CHAPTER 8

AVA

I liked to think the men—and the mistakes—I've made in my life have taught me something about myself, but I wasn't sure where Francis Sinatra fit into that equation. I'd thought of little else since the night we'd tied one on, kissed in an abandoned parking lot as desperate for each other as teenagers, and shot up a general store before we'd landed in jail. Without a doubt, Francis was not like other men. He was raucous and edgy, but because of the night we'd had dinner and drinks in his apartment, I knew there was another side to him. The side to him that was tender and passionate, loved music and books and art, and making the world a better place for everyone he loved and everyone he believed in. He was intent on reminding me of that fact. He'd sent flowers and small gifts every week since Palm Springs, but I'd avoided him, my mind in a state of turmoil. He was married, and I'd made the mistake of going down that path before.

And yet, Francis wasn't someone I could avoid, it seemed. He was always thrown into my path, or, somehow, he found me.

One night, after dancing and drinks with Bappie and a consistent nagging thought that I was missing something, or, rather, missing someone, the phone rang.

"Ava?" Francis's voice spread through me like warm brandy and curled around the hollow in my chest.

"Well, hello there, Francis," I said, glad he couldn't see the smile that betrayed me. I carried the phone as far as the cord could reach, plopped down on the sofa, and sank into a soft cushion. "It's late. Didn't your mama teach you any manners?"

"Did I wake you?" I could hear the grin in his voice.

"Of course not. I'm just home from the Mocambo. My feet will probably be sore tomorrow, but it was worth it."

"I've been thinking about you," he said. "About that night."

I paused, uncertain whether I wanted to admit the truth— that I was intrigued by him, infatuated, and damn it all, maybe more. I decided against it.

"Did you have a reason for calling?" I said at last. "It's almost dawn, and my pillow is calling to me."

"You need your beauty sleep."

"Something like that."

"Meet me for dinner tomorrow night. I'll pick you up at eight. We'll go to Gianni's." It wasn't a question.

I smiled. He always seemed to know what he wanted, and I had to admit, that was attractive. I never did like a man who hemmed and hawed. Come to think of it, I didn't much like women who didn't know their minds either.

"I have a red dress."

"And you'll be a knockout in it. Sleep well. I'll see you tomorrow."

"Good night, Francis." I laid the receiver in its cradle and looked across the living room at the blurry reflection in the windowpane. What was I doing? I hadn't even liked this man when I'd met him. Now I couldn't get his expression before we'd parted that night out of my mind. The mix of adoration and lust. It was intoxicating. *He* was intoxicating.

The next night I wore that red dress. It was crepe with a skirt that swayed prettily around my calves as I walked. I left my hair loose and though the studio insisted I always wear heavy makeup to play the part they'd groomed me to play—and to be prepared for photographers who might be on the prowl—I'd decided Louis B. Mayer couldn't dictate my life off set. I left my skin clean and brushed on nothing but a little mascara and lip gloss. It was chillier than I expected, too, so I slipped on a coat before I joined Francis in his Cadillac.

He glanced over at me appreciatively, his full lips turned up into a smile. "It's amazing. You're even more beautiful without that mask on your face. I've never liked a lot of makeup."

"That makes two of us."

I took in his perfect gray suit and tie, and the quiet seriousness I'd seen in him only one other time. This seemed to be the real Francis, not the boisterous and bawdy Sinatra of the newspapers and the spotlight.

He drove us to Gianni's, an Italian restaurant tucked away in a quaint neighborhood a good distance from the hubbub of Sunset or Hollywood Boulevard. As he held open the door for me, the aroma of garlic and homemade marinara filled the air and I inhaled deeply. I'd eaten hours ago, after a good, long swim, and suddenly I was ravenous. We settled at a table in the far corner away from the other guests and I glanced around to take in my surroundings. The décor was simple: lamps turned low, white table linens, a vase on each table with a single red carnation, and a string quartet playing classical music in the center of the room. It was charming and unassuming and perfect. I was beginning to understand that we were alike in this way, Francis and me. We had a lust for beautiful things, but we were simple at heart.

A waiter quickly tended to our requests. Red wine to start along with salads and fresh bread with olive oil. I copied Francis, who poured the oil from the miniature carafe onto his bread plate, forming a puddle of lime-green liquid and dipping his bread into it.

"Delicious," I said, sopping up the oil with my bread.

"I don't like food that looks like it should be in a gallery instead of on your plate," he replied.

"Me either," I agreed, smiling.

He watched me for a moment, his expression sober. "Ava Gardner, you're the most beautiful woman I've ever laid eyes on."

"And you've laid a few."

He barked out a laugh, unexpectedly. "You have a blade for a tongue, don't you?"

"I'm good for a sharp retort or two."

"I'll say." He smiled and picked up his water glass.

I adjusted my napkin, ready to initiate the conversation I didn't want to have but knew it was time. I wanted him to put everything on the table. I had the distinct feeling we were headed somewhere all of a sudden, and I needed to know the truth.

"Tell me about your family, Francis. It's the elephant in the room and we may as well discuss it. Here we are, on a dinner date, and you're perfectly married with children. Why don't you tell me why we're here."

He set down his glass and in an earnest tone began to tell me about his family. He told me how he'd met Nancy Barbato, a girl from Jersey who quickly became his sweetheart. How everyone had expected their marriage, including him.

"She fit the mold of a pretty Italian American whose family knew ours. Whose values were the same as all the others' on the block," he said. "Don't get me wrong. She's a good girl. Loyal and dependable, generous. There will always be a part of me that loves her, but the Hollywood life doesn't suit her. She's great at making friends, but she's not into the glamour and the parties and all the mess that goes with it. She's a family gal. In fact, her entire family has moved to the West Coast to be near us."

I watched his face as he talked more about Nancy and his friendship with her. I saw very clearly how he didn't want to hurt her, loved her even. There was no real animosity between them or serious reasons they should part ways, but it seemed like he'd outgrown their marriage the way a person outgrows a pair of shoes that crowds the toes and rubs the heel raw.

"It's the kids, too," he went on. "I love those rascals. I've imagined telling them their parents are getting a divorce and . . ." He stopped, drank a sizable swallow of red wine. When he met my eyes again, sadness shone in their ice-blue depths. "It ain't easy. But it's time to get on with my life, and Nancy needs to get on with hers. Besides, now I have feelings for someone else, and it feels impossible to stay."

My resolve to keep him at arm's length melted in the candlelight. He loved his children and was a family man at heart, even if something inside him yearned for more, whatever that more was. There was a hunger in his eyes I wanted to understand, and God help me, I wanted to help him satiate it. I reached for his hand.

He twined his fingers with mine and turned my hand over, placing a light kiss on the softest part of my palm. "Tell me more about you," he said. "I want to know everything. Do you want kids one day?"

"Doesn't every woman?"

And yet, even as I said it, the idea terrified me. I wasn't certain I was like every other woman. As much as I enjoyed a child's angelic face and playful innocence, having two failed marriages and a job that demanded I look sexy at all times had quashed much of that desire. Where would I be, had I been pregnant when I'd discovered Mickey was cheating on me? Or if I'd been saddled with children while Artie belittled me and finally tossed me out of his house?

I would never forget when Daddy passed away and left Mama with all of us to feed, with no money and scarcely a home. She'd worked herself to the bone. I wasn't in her position, but Hollywood never guaranteed an easy life or guaranteed anything at all. Hell, I'd learned that already.

"At least I think I want kids," I amended. "The timing hasn't been right." I speared the last tomato on my salad plate with my fork. "I'd like to travel more. See the world. I've always wanted to go to Europe."

He tipped his glass toward me before taking a drink. "Drink champagne in Paris."

"See a bull fight in Spain," I said.

"Walk the Great Wall of China."

"Barefoot," I said, giggling. The wine was going to my head. Or, perhaps, it was him. This. *Us.*

The waiter arrived then, and we sat back in our chairs as he placed a steaming plate of veal saltimbocca in front of Francis, and for me, linguine with a spicy marinara, basil, and fennel sausage. We ate silently for several minutes, enjoying the food, looking up only to stare at each other, sharing a smile between us.

"This is delicious," I said, taking a bite of the fresh pasta. It was the perfect texture, not that I was any sort of expert on cuisine, but I did like to eat more than just about anything.

We drained a second bottle of wine as I told him about my mama and daddy, about how I'd felt defeated so often by MGM and all of the lessons they'd inflicted on me. How hard I'd worked to make them see I was worthy of a real role. I'd been loaned out several months before, again to RKO studios, owned by my old friend, Howard Hughes, to act in a picture called *My Forbidden Past.* If the only way to be taken seriously and to earn real money was by working at other studios, I'd do it, and I'd not sign another contract with MGM when the time came, if the time came. They very well might still cut me loose. The thought didn't pain me—it made me as mad as a snake. I wanted them to realize my worth the way others had, but they didn't care when they had bigger actresses on their roster. I was just a small cog in a large machine that wanted quick, booming sales. Anything less was unacceptable.

Through it all, Francis listened intently.

"I know what it's like to feel like you're nothing," he said soberly. "I've been called a guinea and a dago more times in my life than I can count. I had to work like a dog to get where I am, and still I take a beating in the papers."

He told me how hard he'd worked on his diction and speech to sound intelligent like his friends who had gone to college, or like the politicians he knew. We were alike in that way, too. Always trying to make up for our upbringing, for the polish we lacked. We both wanted to improve what was less than in the eyes of others.

"Honey, if you ain't working like a dog, then you ain't working," I said.

"You're starting to sound like you're from North Carolina again." He brushed his lips over the sensitive skin on the back of my hand. "It suits you. All of that sass."

My skin tingled where his lips had been. Like it or not, this man had an effect on me, and I didn't want to fight it—couldn't fight it if I wanted to. And I didn't want to.

"Francis," I said softly.

His brow arched in a questioning glance.

"Come back to my place. For a nightcap."

He smiled like a little boy given an ice cream. "Better make it two."

I'd recently moved to a wooded neighborhood outside the city, so we both knew what I meant—there would be no return trip tonight—and within minutes, we were paying the bill and in the car, headed to the outskirts of town to my little pink house in Nichols Canyon. As I relaxed into my seat, Francis's scent of Yardley lavender soap floated around me and I felt absurdly happy, alive in a way I'd never been before.

"Why did you pick a place in Nichols Canyon?" he asked.

"The price was right. Besides, I don't like Los Angeles much. Oh, it's beautiful, sure, and exciting sometimes, but there's competition in the air all the time. Who's going to be the next big thing and who's the best at this and that. Who is the most beautiful. It dominates every conversation, and it's suffocating. And you know what else? None of it's real. Hollywood is the land of make believe, for better and for worse."

His brow knitted into a frown. "I feel the pressure, too, but most of the time I enjoy the hell out of the race to the top." He went silent then, lost in some thought.

I knew he'd had trouble with the newspapers over the last year—it was impossible to miss the headlines of his fights with journalists, the downturn in record sales, his suspected affiliation with mobsters—and I wondered if that was where his mind had gone.

"Well, you can't plop a country girl down in the middle of a concrete mecca no matter how beautiful it is. I missed hearing the crickets and the frogs at night."

"Maybe one day I'll take you to my new house in Palm Springs. You'd like it there."

"Maybe," I said with a sly smile. He was already thinking ahead, and I followed him there in my mind.

As we neared the house and pulled into the drive, I noticed a car with dark windows parked across the street. Howard had his men tailing me again. I frowned, annoyed that every movement I made was reported to a man who I'd never, ever consider more than a friend. Now he was testing those bonds as well. I'd give Howard a piece of my mind later, and for tonight, I'd be sure to give his men an earful from the bedroom. See how old Howard liked that.

Francis skipped around to my side of the car to open the door. I led him into the living room, poured us each a glass of whiskey, and sat next to him on the sofa.

"Thank you for dinner. It was perfect," I said, my voice soft.

"You're perfect," he said, cradling his glass in his hands.

I stared at him, struck by how quiet, how serious and intense he could be, and found I liked this side of him. I leaned close and traced his angular jaw with my fingertip.

He reached for my glass and set both of our drinks on the coffee table.

"At the restaurant, when I said I had feelings for someone else—"

I pressed my fingers gently to his lips, silencing him, and whispered, "Yes, baby, I know." I moved closer, wrapped my arms around him.

"And how do you feel?" He ran his hand down my back, his face only inches from mine.

"I feel like kissing you for a very long time."

His eyes darkened, and he closed the gap between us until his lips met mine. Our kisses deepened and grew feverish, our cheeks flushed. Something inside me ignited, and I found myself grabbing at him, eager to touch him, to feel him pressed against the length of me. I wanted him to ravage me, leave nothing on my bones—but was I ready for all that this entailed after the deed was done?

I pulled away from him an instant, hesitantly, and his eyes were wild, his breath ragged. I'd never seen a man look more beautiful than in that moment, and I knew the answer to that final question.

"Come with me," I said, standing.

We treaded barefoot on the cool wood floorboards to the bedroom. I'd scarcely stepped over the threshold when he pulled me into his arms again. He kissed a trail of fire down my neck, over my collarbone. With eager hands, he felt for the hem of my dress and pulled the soft red sheath over my head. He groaned as he took in my silky lingerie. He caressed the slippery fabric, his mouth finding mine again. As we pressed against each other, his hands wandered, his touch at once searching and tender. When he dragged his thumb across my nipple, I gasped.

"You like that?" he whispered in my ear.

I groaned in response, my hands reaching for the buttons on his shirt, freeing him of it, and tossing it to the floor. He slipped his fingers beneath one strap of my camisole and tugged it down my shoulder, then did the same with the other strap. His mouth moved lower, his fingertips caressing the swell of my breasts. I groaned at his soft touch. As he pushed the nest of lace out of his way, his lips closed around my nipple. I arched into him, my urgency growing. His hand cupped my other breast, squeezing and massaging the soft mound of flesh until I couldn't stand it.

I pulled the camisole over my head. He smiled like a wolf, and in one fluid motion, he lifted me and carried me to the bed. In seconds I was completely bare, desperate for him. He caressed every inch of my skin, bringing my cells to life, kissing me as he moved. When he stroked the velvet place between my legs, murmuring tenderly, I squirmed and rocked against him.

"Francis," I breathed his name.

"Angel," he said, his voice strangled with emotion.

I relieved him of the rest of his clothes and he was upon me, his lean body against mine.

And as we lost ourselves in the rhythm of our bodies, and

our feverish lovemaking turned from heat and fire and lust, to tender, our eyes locked. We fell into each other's depths, losing ourselves, and I knew this was real. This was what I'd been looking for, all this time.

This was love, baby, and come what may, we would be forever lovers.

CHAPTER 9

FRANK

I was lost, end of story. I was completely and thoroughly lost.

I thought of Ava constantly, sent her flowers and gifts, took her to restaurants and private locales on the beach or in the countryside. We talked and laughed and could hardly be together without falling into bed, losing hours and days and any sense of the world outside of us. I had never been so in love—never had a woman possess me so utterly. And yet, I had to do it all quietly, clandestinely, and out of view of the reporters. George was insistent I tread carefully as always, but this time he believed that I'd already burned through my second chances from the powers that be at MGM and the press, who loved nothing more than to prey on me. I used to think the press followed me because I was talented, that they wanted a piece of me. Now I knew better. It was about selling papers, even if it meant selling me down the river.

I riffled through the stack of bills Nancy had left for me in my study. Halfway through the pile, there was a notice from the IRS. My stomach clenched and I sat, knowing whatever was inside that envelope couldn't be good. I'd been audited recently and the way I saw it, the IRS had already put a target on my back. They were looking to trip me up. I tore open the envelope, my pulse racing, and scanned the contents of the letter.

I squeezed my eyes closed and collapsed against the back of the chair. They'd found a large discrepancy in my taxes. I owed nearly a hundred thousand dollars. Plenty of entertainers sheltered funds or used deductibles to pay less in taxes, but they had to come after me. I was the one who was busted. I rubbed my face with my hands. I'd overspent on the new house I'd recently bought in Palm Springs for sure, but I wasn't about to sell it. I liked nice things and I liked taking care of my people, giving them lavish gifts and making them feel special. Seeing their obvious delight had always been worth it to me, and what was money for anyway if you couldn't spend it the way you wanted? But a hundred thousand bucks . . .

I tucked the letter in my jacket pocket and pushed back from my chair. Nancy didn't need to know about this, at least not for now. Stomach in knots, I dressed in a clean suit for the day. I had a luncheon to get to and I couldn't be late. Mayer was hosting a silver anniversary celebration for MGM and he wanted photographs to memorialize it. *Life* magazine was going to write a piece. Like I gave a shit, especially today.

When I arrived, I searched the crowd for Ava. I needed to see her face, even if I had to keep my distance to maintain the charade of us not being an item to appease the studio and their ridiculous morality clause. She would calm me a little, give me something to think about besides the screwing the IRS was giving me. She appeared then and sauntered through the room, ignoring me completely. As I found her place in the lineup, I felt a desperation I'd never felt before. I wanted her to be mine. I didn't know how long I could keep this up.

I followed orders to pose with the others on a dais filled with rows of chairs. After the photographs, Mayer made a toast and we filed in line at the buffet table. Mayer, to my chagrin, stepped in line behind me.

"Frank, I need to see you in my office after lunch," he said.

I glanced at my boss, a pudgy little dump of a man who had total power over my career, and my stomach tightened for the second time that day. I didn't need more bad news and by his tone, whatever he wanted to discuss didn't sound good.

"Sure thing, boss."

He filled his plate with stuffed squab, scooped up a bowl of matzo ball soup, and found a seat next to an actress I'd never seen before. She smiled up at him in a way that made me think they'd shared more than a lunch date. The two-faced prick. He insisted his stars sign morality clauses while he hired women and doled them out to his male staff like two-bit hookers. Not that I was opposed to prostitutes; they were doing a job they were hired to do. But this was something else entirely: making women believe they were actresses and then bribing them to exchange jobs for tricks.

I filled my plate with some chicken dish or other and sat with a few of the fellas. I pushed the food around on my plate and watched the iconic lion's head made of chocolate ice cream melt until it was unrecognizable. I didn't feel like eating after hearing Mayer's stern tone. Instead, I downed another flute of champagne.

When the time came and the crowd dispersed, I walked to the offices.

"Have a seat, Frank," Louis ordered, motioning me inside and closing the door behind us.

"What's up, Mayer?" I sat on the edge of a chair.

He held out a newspaper toward me. "Do you want to tell me what this is about?"

I didn't need to read the paper. I knew he was referring to the interview I'd done with a correspondent about motion pictures. I should have said what they all wanted to hear: that working in movies was grand with so much talent around me every day, and that the opportunities from my employer were satisfying, inspirational even. Only it wasn't, and I was a bad liar. MGM had started to slide. Profits were down and we all knew it. People wanted to stay home with their televisions. Instead, I ran my big mouth as usual, saying what I thought rather than pandering to MGM. I didn't think the newspaper would actually print all of that garbage. I thought they'd write up a nice sunny piece like we'd all expected.

I was wrong.

"Look, I was joking around," I said. "Of course I don't believe that movies are junk and the people acting in them are lousy. Those creeps have it in for me. I'll sue them for slander. They'll never know what hit them."

Mayer's face looked like a red balloon about to burst. "You run up tabs at clubs and fancy restaurants, charge limos to the studio. Get into scrapes with the media. To say nothing of your visit to the White House and all of those political events, dividing your audience. You've got conservatives against you. And your last few performances were lousy! You're a sinking ship, Frank, and I've just about lost my patience with you."

I stood as the heat ran up my neck. "No one said I had to be a Republican to be in the movies. And I was speaking about civil rights at those rallies. It's the right thing to do, whether you, or anyone else, likes it or not."

"Sit down!" he thundered. "We're not here to debate our political views."

"Damn it, I'll sue them!" I said. "Those blasted papers are trying to ruin me."

"You're ruining yourself," he shot back. "I brought you in here today to see if you were big enough to offer an apology for your reckless behavior. To see if you would agree to tamp down on the spending and make me some sort of promise to get your ass back on track." He paused, waiting for my response.

"I'll see what I can do," I said at last, my tail between my legs. I couldn't afford to get fired from MGM, especially with the tax audit and my last few songs going sour.

"The next time I see you, Frank, you'd better have it together. I'm warning you, this is the last break I'll give you. Now get the hell out of my office!"

I tore out of the building with my head on fire, stalked across the parking lot, and jumped in my car, squealing the tires as I raced away. It wasn't until a fifth of Jack Daniel's and a few hours later of blustering to friends about it that the weight of the day's events really hit me. I was a hundred thousand dollars in debt to the IRS, and my prospects of paying for it were drying up quickly. My boss was on the verge of firing me. And the most dreaded thought of all: Ava wouldn't want anything to do with a loser whose prospects were going down the toilet. She'd want a man on top of his game—she deserved that and more.

I had to get myself in gear fast, just as Mayer had said, or I could kiss my career, and the woman I was in love with, goodbye.

CHAPTER 10

AVA

Spring was magical in Los Angeles. The winter rains washed the city clean and fed the endless array of palms in forest, lime, and bright Kelly green. Flowers sprouted in pinks and orange, and the days glimmered with warm, buttery sunlight. I peeked through the curtain to glance at the sky overhead. It was a perfect day for travel. I showered and packed a small bag with a couple of days' things. When a limousine pulled up outside, I all but raced down the front walk. I was looking forward to a weekend away with Francis. I'd been so busy with my shooting schedule that we'd hardly found time to meet up the last few weeks. He'd also seemed troubled, but I didn't press. Instinctively, I knew he'd want to work things out on his own. Still, I'd thought about him constantly, craved his touch, the sound of his laugh, the emotion that simmered in his eyes.

"Hello, beautiful," he said as I ducked inside the limousine. "Are you ready for a little adventure?"

"Where are we going?"

"It's a surprise."

I pressed up against him and we held hands until the limousine pulled to a stop at a landing strip. A small private plane sat on the runway.

I covered my mouth with my hand. "We're flying?"

"What better way to travel?" Francis said, winking.

I squealed in glee, unable to hide my excitement. He loved to surprise me with gifts, and this was certainly a gift. As we walked toward the plane, I noticed there was no pilot or anyone else inside it.

"Where's the pilot?" I asked.

It was then that he dropped the second secret for the day.

"I'm the pilot." He smiled triumphantly.

"This isn't a Cadillac, baby," I said, dubious. The man thought he could do anything, and I admired that, but this was a little much. "Are you sure you can fly that thing? Howard knew what he was doing and crashed his plane right into a lake. Killed some people and nearly killed himself." I'd been stupid enough to fly with Howard that day, too, while he was testing his amphibious plane, but thankfully I'd been dropped off at a hotel in Las Vegas before he continued back to the lake to practice his landings. That was when catastrophe had struck.

A cloud passed over Francis's face. He didn't like it when I mentioned Howard, but like it or not, he was a part of my life, though admittedly far less often these days and that wasn't a bad thing. I didn't miss his antics one bit.

"I'm not surprised that lunatic crashed a plane," Francis muttered under his breath. "But I've had plenty of practice, Angel. Don't worry about it."

I *was* worried about it, but I put on a brave face and tried to enjoy myself. We climbed inside the cockpit and buckled in, and Francis fiddled with knobs and switches until the engine roared to life. Soon, we lifted into the air.

As we soared over the landscape with a long strip of dark water on our left and on our right, a sprawling city changing to pastures and fields, I couldn't help but think of the other locations we'd been to—restaurants and hotels on the outskirts of town, or beaches outside the city limits. It suddenly struck me that all were remote or secluded. He was hiding me away, and it wasn't just from the reporters. He was hiding me from Nancy.

My mood dipped as the plane swooped toward the landing strip a few hundred yards from a copse of trees. Beyond the strip, a large pond shimmered like gold-tipped glass in the sun.

To my relief, we landed carefully and safely.

"What did you think?" Francis asked as he helped me gallantly out of the cockpit.

"It was better than I expected," I said. "We didn't crash."

He laughed and put his hand on my back, guiding me to the place we'd be spending the night. While we walked, I took in our beautiful surroundings and tried to bolster my mood. There was no sense in ruining things now. Besides, hadn't I known this would become messy? That it was a terrible idea to let him in? Now I had to pay the consequences. But not today. Today I wouldn't bring up the sticky conversation that awaited us. I wanted to enjoy the beauty and luxury of our surroundings.

We stayed in a remote historic farmhouse, quaint with its front porch and cheery yellow facade. An antiquated barn sat on the edge of the property but had been renovated and converted to living quarters for the staff. Inside the main house, the faded scent of Pine-Sol mingled with sugar and vanilla, and I fell in love with the place instantly. A basket threaded with gingham ribbon and filled with cookies sat on the night table in our bedroom, reminding me of southern hospitality. In all, it was a charming little love nest.

We christened the freshly laundered bed almost immediately and followed that with a long bike ride along the twisting lane beneath the gums and rosewood trees. Francis looked adorable in a peach sweater, his fedora tipped sideways as he rode, and I wanted to scoop him up and pull him to me all over again. And I did, on a blanket of grass near the edge of the pond. We were so far away from town, we shed our clothing, giggling like children who didn't want to be caught living in sin, as Mama would say.

I'd promised myself I would never be here again, falling for someone who couldn't commit to me in any real way, but as the sunlight fell on his hair and danced across the smooth skin of his back, I couldn't stop what had already begun. I knew I'd want more from this man than he could ever give me. And yet, here I was, offering everything I had to him, willingly. As we fell into each other the world disappeared. We were one, losing ourselves in our passion. Lips and soft hands, sighs of pleasure, and the mingling of something I hadn't known existed until now. I knew Francis hadn't known it before either. Not this. He hadn't said as much, but I saw it in the way he looked at me. The intensity between us couldn't be contained by expectations or rules, nor could it be put into words.

I lay back on the blanket, naked as a jaybird. He sat above me, tracing my collarbone with the tip of his finger, down the path between my breasts to my belly button. When he cupped my cheek in his hand, he bent closer, until his face was inches from mine, and I felt I could see right to the bottom of his soul.

"I'm in love with you," he whispered.

My heart fluttered with joy, and I felt my eyes fill. "I love you, too, Francis."

We held each other until a breeze wafted across our bare skin, making us shiver.

He leaned in for another deep kiss and after, we dressed and mounted our bikes. Riding along the lane felt like flying; we threw our arms wide as if we could gather up the lush carpets of grass and happy trees and carry all of it with us.

Love. We were in love.

When we returned to the farmhouse, we showered and dressed for dinner. It had been a glorious day and yet, try as I might to stop dwelling, I was bothered by still being hidden away from the world. He might love me, but we hadn't talked about what was next for him at home, or if there was anything next at all, and I felt myself go quiet as we were shown to our table.

Over barbequed chicken and creamy au gratin potatoes, the words spilled out on their own.

"This is all really lovely, Francis. The gifts and getaways, the dinners, but I can't help but feel as if you're hiding me away like some fling you're likely to forget one day in the not-so-distant future. Are you going to stay with Nancy, or are we really something?"

He put down his fork. "You're impossible to forget, baby. I'm in love with you. I told you that."

"But that doesn't exactly answer the question, does it."

His jaw twitched and I could see my questions were getting to him.

"This isn't the kind of love that comes and goes," he said.

"And yet, you still aren't answering me." I could hear my

buried southern twang rising to the surface and I knew I was both starting to get upset and a little drunk.

He shifted slightly in his chair. "It's over with Nancy, you know that. I just need to tell her."

"And when exactly will that be?"

"I don't know," he admitted. "It's complicated with the kids."

"Hell, if you wait long enough, after we've rolled around in the sheets for a few more months, you won't have to say anything to her at all, and we'll be through."

He grimaced and I knew I'd struck a nerve. He was holding back the anger that was beginning to brew, but I wanted him to know I meant business. I wasn't going to wait around for a man who was perfectly happy taking what he wanted from me—and happy to keep his wife at home.

The waiter filled our wineglasses for the third time and slid the stopper into the decanter. When he'd gone, Francis said, "I'll tell her this week."

I exhaled, relieved, and let him take my hand in his.

"I mean it," he said, the lines on his forehead deepening as he frowned. "I'll tell her, and we can get on with things."

I picked up my glass with my free hand and held it up. "So how about a toast. To getting on with things."

He picked up his own and tapped it against mine, the crystal making a dull clink. "To being in love."

As I looked into his face, all of his bright adoration for me as real as the ground beneath my feet, I quelled the pernicious voice in my head. He would keep his promise, and everything would work out just fine.

★ ★ ★

As the week passed, I waited for the news that Francis had told Nancy he wanted out. When a week turned into two and then four, I decided to let it all go—for now. It was a delicate situation, after all, and I could be patient when it was called for.

In the meantime, I was captivated, charmed, in awe of him. His charisma was like a drug, his intensity delicious. No one lived life as fully as that man, and I let myself be swept into his cyclone. Perhaps the most intoxicating thing of all was the way he saw me, the way he understood me. We'd both strived for success in an impossible business. We were both mocked for our humble beginnings. We both had a hole in our hearts where a parent's love should have been enough but never was, leaving us uncertain and raw in the secret part of ourselves. Those months when Artie had forced me to sit on a psychologist's couch had taught me that much, and I saw the same in Francis.

One afternoon, I pulled on a pair of trousers and a collared shirt, tied my hair up with a ribbon, and went out for a little shopping. I hadn't bought a new dress in ages and everything looked stale in my closet. I went to the farmer's market on Third and Fairfax, picked up some fruit for the bowl on the kitchen counter, and, afterward, drove to my favorite stores in Beverly Hills. I still had a little time before I was supposed to meet Howard for a late lunch.

I threaded in and out of the shops, posing twice for cameramen, and at last found a cute little number in white with red piping, and a black cocktail dress that cupped my breasts attractively and tapered to my knee. As I walked to my car in the parking lot, I spotted a torch of blond hair and instantly recognized the shapely beauty of my friend.

"Lana!" I called, waving.

She smiled brightly and walked toward me, swinging a cluster of shopping bags at her side. "Aren't you a sight for sore eyes," she said, kissing my cheek. "How have you been?"

"Things are the same at the studio, even after *One Touch of Venus* was such a hit. Mayer is still lending me out. I'm frustrated, but enough about me. You've been away!"

"Yes, I've been keeping busy on set." She smiled, her dimples coming into view, and patted my hand. "Don't you worry, your time is coming. They *must* see your success with other studios. You were born to be a star, darling, and they'll wake up soon and understand that."

I sighed heavily. "We'll see."

"So tell me, is it true?" Lana took off her sunglasses and her clear blue eyes met mine. "I hear you're seeing Frank."

I shifted uncomfortably, remembering how in love Lana had been with him for a time. But I was no liar and part of me knew they'd never been a good match, not like Francis and me.

"It's true," I said. "I know he's married, but they're on the outs."

"Are they separated?" she asked, her eyes round with surprise. "I haven't seen anything in the papers."

"Not yet but soon."

She took my hands in hers, her perfectly manicured nails digging into my palm. "Oh, you haven't fallen for him, have you?"

"We're in love, baby," I stated simply.

"Oh, Ava." She shook her head, her cascade of curls swaying around her face. "He'll never leave her, and Nancy will never let him go."

I looked down to hide the crush of doubt I felt. "I don't know," I said at last. "I guess we'll have to wait and see."

"Well, I hope you're right, darling. You deserve only the best. You take care." She kissed my cheek. "Call me sometime for lunch? I've missed you!"

"Of course. Good luck with your picture." I waved as she walked away in search of her car.

Though I was unsurprised by my friend's warning, it had turned my stomach upside down and later, as I sat across from Howard in a flashy place on Rodeo Drive, Lana's words still rang in my ears.

"You seem far away today." Howard plucked the wine bottle from the bucket on the table and filled my glass again. "What happened?"

We were civil to each other these days, after I'd socked him in the face, good and hard, for breaking into my house one night. He'd ended up in the emergency room. Now he was allegedly trying to curb his ridiculous behavior around me—his spies had recently stopped sitting outside my house—and I appreciated that. Demanded it, actually. I didn't want to end our friendship over his rotten side, but I'd made it clear that I would.

"Oh, it's nothing," I said. "I ran into a friend earlier today. She's been on my mind." I forced a smile and took a sip of crisp white wine, something French and obviously expensive, as was Howard's way.

He prattled on about some new airplane he was interested in buying. We dined on filet mignon and oysters, and I soon forgot about my conversation with Lana. Instead, my thoughts turned again to Francis and the promise he had made me.

As if Howard had read my mind, he changed the subject. "I hate to spoil the afternoon, but I have to tell you, you're playing a dangerous game with that man. He's friends with criminals."

"What are you talking about?" I said, growing annoyed.

"I've been keeping an eye on him. On Frank."

"Howard, you have no goddamn right!" I spat. "I thought we'd decided that you would butt out of my business."

"It's a bunch of those Italian guys," he continued as if I hadn't just admonished him. "They fly in from New York, meet him in clandestine places. The Mafia. They're up to something. I'm warning you, Ava, you're not safe."

"I'm not going to tell the man I love who he can and can't be friends with. Besides, Frank would never put me in jeopardy."

Howard's face twisted into a scowl. It was almost comical, with his thick dark brow and the hard angles of his face. He looked like a kid pouting on the playground when someone took his ball. "You're in love with him" was all he managed to reply.

"I am. Exquisitely so." I sipped from my glass again, relishing the last of the cold wine. There was no beating around the bush with Howard. Subtlety wasn't his specialty, so I had to give it to him straight. He needed to cool it. We were friends, nothing more, and it seemed as if he needed another reminder.

"How can you love that . . . that fop?" he spouted in frustration.

I stiffened and set down my drink. "If you call him a name again, I'll walk right out of here and you won't ever hear from me ever again. Do you understand me?"

"I'm sorry," he said, flustered. "I didn't mean that . . . I . . . Ava, he's dangerous. And he has girlfriends and hookers all over town."

"Kind of like you?" I replied tartly. I knew I had him there.

As for Francis, there were plenty of rumors about him that weren't true, and I was certain these were among them. He loved me like he was a man on death row. There wasn't room for anyone else.

Howard sat back in his chair in defeat. "I don't want to see you get hurt."

"That makes two of us, but it's already too late. I'm in deep. Luckily I'm a hell of a swimmer."

And yet, Howard's warning left me as unsettled as ever. He wouldn't lie about what Francis was up to, would he? Howard was desperate to get me in bed, so anything was possible, but Lana's warning came to mind again, too, and suddenly I wanted to go home. I could use a stiff drink with Reenie. She always talked through things with me until the dread coursing through me drained away.

CHAPTER 11

FRANK

Ava didn't want to see me after her date with that jerk Howard Hughes. She'd been open about meeting him, but when she didn't answer the phone later that night, it set me on edge and I found myself pacing. Every time I'd crossed paths with Hughes, he was disheveled and smelled bad. The man clearly didn't believe in Laundromats or bathing. I couldn't stand a wrinkled suit, much less a cheap one that didn't fit properly. I didn't understand it. He was one of the wealthiest men in the world but couldn't wear something decent? It solidified my suspicions: the man was completely off his rocker. And I didn't want him anywhere near Ava. They were friends, she assured me, nothing else. I wanted to believe her—she said she loved me—but I was no good at trust.

When it was good and dark and the moon was high in the sky, I drove by her house, relieved to see Howard's limo wasn't there, though she appeared to be. I felt like a heel and sped the hour and thirty minutes back to Palm Springs. At home, I sat in the backyard so I wouldn't wake the kids or Nancy, who were spending the next few days with me here. Leaning back in my chair, my legs outstretched, I stared into the night. Thousands of pinpricks of light studded the sky but there was no moon. I contemplated my place in the world as I gazed overhead and felt smaller yet. Somehow, the vastness comforted me. I was a tiny piece of infinity, part of the cycle of life, and nothing I did mattered all that much, good or bad. It helped keep what was important in perspective. That was one reason I'd bought the house in Palm Springs: to think, to gain perspective away from the noise of Los Angeles. I thought of Ava, how she would talk about this with me at length, for hours. Her curiosity, her active mind, was one of the things I loved about her. Nancy and I had never shared that link.

I pulled out a pack of cigarettes and lit one. How would I tell Nancy it was over? I couldn't see my way out of this, how to leave. I loved my kids—and I loved her, too, even if she wasn't the one who lit my fire. I worried constantly about how the kids would be impacted by the divorce, but perhaps it wouldn't impact them much at all. I was gone often enough already that it might not make a huge dent in their routines, and yet, I missed the little tykes even now as they slept in their beds.

Watery blue-gray light framed the edges of the mountains and seeped into the dark sky. It would be morning soon—and I was exhausted. I smashed the end of my cigarette in the ashtray and treaded softly through the house to the bathroom. I opened the cabinet to a neat row of pill bottles and reached for the third in the lineup. My anxiety got the better of me most nights, and I needed something to help me sleep and something else to help me wake up. I swallowed the red pill, changed into pajamas, and slipped into bed.

I'd been knocked out cold for hours when Nancy woke me for a phone call.

"It's George," she said. "It sounds important."

Bleary-eyed, I stumbled from bed. "Tell him I'll be right there."

She handed me a cup of coffee and I took it gratefully, slugging back half of it in a few gulps. It burned going down, but I needed something to shake off the drug-induced sleep. The drawback to the pills was the slow mornings. It took hours for my brain to fire properly again.

"Hello," I croaked into the receiver.

"It's about time," George said. "I thought you were dead."

"It's the sleeping pills. They knock me out."

"You've been offered a guest spot on CBS in New York," he said. "It sounds to me like he's courting you to do a running gig at the Copacabana."

I groaned. "I'm not interested in the club circuit anymore, you know that."

"Look, Frank, we're running out of options. We haven't had many offers lately. You know as well as I do that we're getting canceled left and right. This may be a way to stay afloat."

"Now's just not a good time to be away from home," I said, gulping down more coffee.

"Leave her behind, Frank."

"Who?"

"You know damn well who I'm referring to. She's not good for you or your career."

With Nancy ten paces away, I wasn't about to go into this now.

"Look, go ahead and get the contract," I said, avoiding the topic entirely. "I'll leave at the end of the week."

"Fine. I'm headed out there tomorrow for some meetings. I'll meet you there."

"Alright."

"And Frank?"

"Yeah."

"You need to be on your best behavior."

"Got it, George. You've told me that a thousand times."

"And you keep ignoring me and now look at the mess we're in. Behave, Sinatra."

I hung up the phone with every intention of inviting Ava to go with me. In New York, there would be fewer photographers hounding us and we'd be able to enjoy our time together in the open, at least more so than in Los Angeles. I whistled to myself as I shaved and showered and planned the way I'd ask her to come with me.

My girl liked to be courted, and I'd give it to her, better than anyone else. Courting was my specialty.

It didn't take any convincing for Ava to agree to go with me to New York. She hadn't been back in a while, and now that she was a star on the rise with cash in her wallet, she could hardly wait to go out on the town. We stayed in Manie Sack's place on Central Park South, the Hampshire House suite. He was a real pal from years before, a good boss, and an advocate for me through and through. He'd had my back from the beginning at Columbia Records, even though he was a top dog as a television and music executive and didn't have time to look after me.

He made time. I was looking forward to seeing him. He said he had something to tell me in person, big news. I'd been peppy ever since—I suspected it would be a new record deal and tour. Maybe my career wasn't in the toilet after all.

December in the city was as I remembered: one minute, mild enough to need only a lightweight jacket and the next, all blustery winds laced with snow.

"What do you think of my coat?" Ava said, twirling to show off her full-length mink coat.

"You look like a movie star." I refused to ask her where the gift had come from—I had my suspicions it was from creepy Howard Hughes, and I didn't want to have to come to blows with him about it.

"To Fifth Avenue?" I asked her, holding the door open.

"Where else is there?" she said with a smile.

We enjoyed a shopping spree and afterward sent the pile of bags from Chanel, Bloomingdale's, and half a dozen other stores ahead of us to the apartment. We weren't ready to head back and instead decided on a walk.

"This is the best time of year in the city," I said as we passed illuminated windows of Christmas displays. Toys and garland, beautiful dresses and suits. Santa Claus and Christmas trees and life-size gingerbread men. "But I don't miss the cold."

"It's so festive, I love it," she said, tucking her hands around my forearm and wiggling close.

Signs advertised their Christmas specials, and dance clubs posted about the kind of parties that only the wealthy could afford. The crisp city air smelled of pavement, electric cold, and the savory aroma of meat and fried potatoes drifting from food stalls and restaurants—it smelled like home. I found myself relaxing with my girl beside me, the scrutiny awaiting me in Los Angeles feeling far away.

After a late lunch, we strolled through Central Park, hand in hand, talking about how different Los Angeles was from New York, especially this time of year. The trees bore naked branches rather than leafy palm fronds, ducks skimmed across the cold, green waters of the lake near Belvedere Castle that perched on a swell of rock, and pedestrians huddled together in their wool hats, coats, and scarves, moving quickly against the brisk wind.

We spent the next day in bed and that evening dressed for the opening of a new show on Broadway, *Gentlemen Prefer Blondes*. The press would be at the opening, and so far, we hadn't had to deal with a single parasite with a camera. I downed a couple of shots of whiskey to calm the nerves.

"We should go. Get there early," I said.

Ava leaned toward the mirror to put on a slick of lipstick. "You think so?"

"We don't want to fight the crowds."

"And you also want to stay out of the papers," she said, her dark brow arched.

"Without a doubt." I reached for a scarf and my fedora, and then helped her into her fur coat. I was relieved she wasn't angry. Regardless of where I stood with Nancy, now wasn't the time to show up in the papers together.

As we arrived at the playhouse, only a handful of reporters were gathered outside the doors along with the line of people waiting to get in, but I knew their ranks would soon grow.

"This way," I said, my voice low as I grabbed Ava's hand. We slipped inside, miraculously without being seen.

I breathed a sigh of relief.

"That was lucky," she said.

"You're good luck," I said, squeezing her hand.

"Can I help you, sir—oh! Mr. Sinatra, Miss Gardner," the usher stammered as he realized who we were. He bowed slightly, eliciting a laugh from Ava.

"Look, Francis, I'm giving Queen Elizabeth a run for her money," she said.

The usher was hardly more than a boy and he blushed all the way to his hairline. "Oh, I'm sorry. I—"

"Don't you worry one bit. I like being bowed to," Ava said, winking, and eliciting another blush from the usher.

"Right this way, sir, miss," he said.

"How about some champagne first?" Ava said.

"I'd be happy to bring you some, Miss Gardner," the usher said.

"That would be mighty fine, thank you." She smiled and the kid nearly tripped over himself as he showed us down the aisle. I didn't blame him. She had that effect on just about every red-blooded male who crossed her path.

We sat in the best seats in the house, enjoyed our champagne, and the show. The production was grand, but as the song "Diamonds Are a Girl's Best Friend" began, I felt the sensation I'd come to know well—there were eyes on me, on us. Someone was trying to work out whether we were who they thought we were.

Annoyed, I glanced to my left to find not one but several people looking our way. They waved and one woman looked as if she would leap over the seats and make her way toward us.

We'd been discovered.

I diverted my gaze back to the stage, not wanting to encourage them. We'd have to make a run for it before the end of the show.

I leaned to Ava's ear, catching a whiff of her luxurious gardenia perfume. "We've been spotted. We should duck out just before the end."

She whispered back, "Who cares? Let them stare at us."

I frowned. Didn't she know how bad this would be for me to have a woman on my arm who wasn't my wife? Until I'd talked with Nancy about everything, I needed to keep things quiet. "It'll be a madhouse around here if we don't go," I insisted.

She frowned, her expression shifting from one of pleasure to irritation. She returned her attention to the stage, clearly disgruntled we would be cutting the show short, but I didn't care. I couldn't risk another bad scene in the press. George would have my hide and so would MGM.

When the closing number began, I tugged Ava's hand. We jostled over the other patrons until we reached the end of the row and darted up the aisle to the exit. Eyes followed us as we rushed away, but no one came after us.

As we stepped into the street, I breathed a sigh of relief, but Ava glared at me.

"We missed the closing scene!"

"I'll make it up to you. Come on," I said, noticing a few men lounging next to a car parked across the street.

She pulled from my grasp. "I don't like being your dirty little secret, Frank."

"You aren't my dirty little secret. I'm proud of having you on my arm, but I can't risk any more damage to my reputation right now."

"And now I'm bad for your reputation?" She crossed her arms.

"I thought we talked about this."

"I thought we had, too, and nothing has changed," she said pointedly.

And then it happened. The pop and flash of bulbs—so many they lit up the night sky like fireworks on the Fourth of July.

My stomach dropped. Son of a—

"Miss Gardner!" a reporter called. "Are you Sinatra's date?"

"Are you two an item?" someone else shouted.

"What happened to Lana, Frank?"

I waved over a taxi, and it screeched to a halt in front of us.

"Get in!" I said, shoving Ava into the car before shouting a stream of profanity at the jerks who were ruining our night. Just as I slammed the door closed, a last question floated toward us.

"Where's Nancy? Left her at home with the kids again?"

I cursed again, furious we'd been seen. I could already see the circus playing out in the media. George would be furious.

"What's the big deal?" Ava demanded. "We're celebrities. People want our picture. It's not as if they caught us with our pants down, for Christ's sake." When I didn't answer, she continued. "You're worried Nancy will see it, aren't you?" Her tone was cold but her green eyes flashed hot. "You haven't told her yet."

"In case you haven't noticed, there's been gossip in the rags about us for weeks," I said. "It's George, not Nancy. He's been warning me for months to keep my private life private. He's going to give me hell. MGM is looking for reasons to fire me."

Her face softened. "Oh, Francis. I'm sorry." Her anger appeared to dissolve and she leaned over and kissed me.

The driver watched us in the rearview mirror.

"What are you looking at?" I growled.

By the time we'd arrived back at Manie's I'd cooled off. I grabbed a bottle of whiskey from the liquor stash and steered Ava into the bedroom.

As we made love, I forgot about the scene with the photographers, Nancy, George, and every other confounded distraction that seemed intent on tearing us apart.

For now.

The following day we stayed in at the hotel, lounging and listening to records, hoping the press would die down—and hoping George wouldn't see the story. At least I hadn't punched anyone, and they had no proof of anything untoward between Ava and me. We could have been colleagues in town at the same time for all they knew. Sure, it wasn't likely, but it didn't matter what was likely. It mattered what they could nail us with, a little something I'd learned from the Boys back in Hoboken. This, I could tell Nancy: they liked to paint stories in the media that weren't true. She didn't question me as long as I had my story straight—and as long as I came home to her.

That evening, Ava and I dressed for dinner with Manie and his latest girlfriend at his place. I was glad for it, eager for good news. At dinner, Ava was subdued but gracious. I watched her pour on the charm of an accessible, earthy woman from the south coupled with her movie star persona who knew the power of her beauty. She wanted Manie to approve of her, but I knew it was a done deal. He took one look at Ava in a green dress, and he was putty in her hands.

I winked at her as we dug into oysters and crab-stuffed

mushrooms, and martinis made with the finest Russian vodka. The conversation lulled as we finished our meal, and the maids cleared the plates. When they began serving cake and coffee, and a carafe of cognac, I broached the topic Manie had yet to bring up.

"Well, I'd say I've been patient," I said with a grin. "Out with your news, Manie. I'll pour us another round for a toast."

He set down his fork and wiped his mouth with his napkin. He looked at me squarely and I noticed, for the first time, that his dark eyes were somber, his lips drawn.

"The news isn't good, Frank."

I set my martini glass on the table, disappointment crushing my precariously good mood. So it wasn't a new record deal and there'd be no new tour. I tried to keep my voice even. "What is it, man?"

Ava pushed away her dessert plate and reached for her martini, downing it in one quick gulp. She slipped her hand over my knee under the table.

"I'm being replaced," Manie said. "Mitch Miller is stepping in."

"Son of a bitch!" I swore loudly. Miller and I had exchanged a few choice words in the past. The songs he'd sent my way were garbage and embarrassing so I'd passed on them—noisily—but they'd gone on to become big hits, for someone else. I'd eaten crow to George, but I'd never told Mitch that I'd made a mistake, another in my growing list. Now it was too late. I was sure the guy hated my guts.

"Why didn't you tell me sooner?" I asked.

Manie's brow knitted into a frown. "I knew you'd take it hard, but there's nothing I can do about it."

That meant I didn't have a choice—I'd have to stay on in New York at the Copacabana for a while and work the night club circuit like a desperate has-been until Mitch deemed me worthy of another chance.

"You're a talented man," Manie said. "I'm sure Columbia Records will take good care of you. Just keep your head down for a while. Do some of the grunt work and you'll come out on top again."

Hadn't I done enough grunt work to last a lifetime? I'd peddled my voice at every seedy little tavern in Hoboken, worked myself to the bone practicing and learning about beats and rhythm and melody, making friends, kissing up to the people who could help me get somewhere. I'd done everything but sell my soul to find a band who saw my potential and took me on the road. Now that I'd finally risen in the ranks, started to become a household name, the whole thing turned rotten. I was free-falling straight to the bottom. I didn't deserve it.

I pushed back my chair and stood. "I need a walk."

"I'll join you," Ava said. "Just let me change out of these heels."

"Meet me later?" I asked Manie.

He nodded, a conciliatory look on his features. "You'll survive this, Frank. I know you will. You're a fighter and a real talent, too."

For the first time in my life, I wasn't sure about any of it.

CHAPTER 12

AVA

I stayed on in New York to support Francis. He was miserable over Manie's forced resignation and more bad news soon followed: his talent agency dropped him the moment Mitch Miller took over at Columbia. They'd claimed his temperamental nature was a liability and that he was difficult to work with—something I was coming to see wasn't far from the truth, at least in his work. He demanded perfection in others and above all else, he demanded he get his way. It didn't help his case that his record sales had fallen off drastically. He'd drunk himself into a stupor the past week, and I'd done my best to hold his head up.

"Come with me tonight, please," Francis implored me, wanting me to join him for his performance at the club. "You're leaving tomorrow."

I couldn't say no to him and dressed in a navy cardigan and A-line skirt, and brushed my curls into a smooth, wavy bob. I liked watching him perform anyway. At the Copacabana, the dim lighting and cigarette haze cast the room in a filmy glow. Men rattled the ice in their glasses, and women poised on the edge of their seats, ready for dancing. The place reeked of cologne and sweat and the promise of a good time. Bar girls floated from table to table, and at last, I made eye contact and signaled one over.

"I'll have a Manhattan," I said.

"Sure thing, miss," the young woman said with a bright pink smile before flitting off to the bar.

I looked around at the crowd as I was wont to do. I liked studying people and imagining what might be going through their minds. Two tables over, a couple inclined their heads toward each other like they were sharing a secret. They were falling in love, judging by their starry-eyed expressions. To my left, a group of women laughed and toasted, enjoying their freedom out of the house and, perhaps, taking a break from their children. I turned to see who was behind me and low and behold, George Evans, Francis's manager, sat near the tacky mural of painted palms on the back wall. He looked right through me, but I didn't care. I knew he didn't like me much and I didn't like him much either. He bossed Francis around as if he were a child. And Francis didn't need scolding—he suffered enough of it from the papers.

Behind George a few hulking creatures clustered together in their dark suits. When one of them stared a hole through me, I turned and gave him my back. I didn't like that look or the attitude he oozed. They had to be the gangsters that followed Francis around when they wanted something from him. I'd heard plenty of rumors about them at the studio and from Lana in the past, but I'd never seen them in the flesh. Everyone wanted a piece of Francis, it seemed, and he was struggling to keep everyone happy. Soon enough he'd learn he couldn't—

and that he'd need to make some tough choices starting with cutting the Boys loose so he could be his own man. This wasn't something I could say to him, at least not now. Francis made up his own mind about things.

Onstage, the band got into position and a chorus line of women all dolled up in flashy satin skirts, big hair, and Betty Boop heels flooded the stage alongside them. The crowd whistled and clapped as brass blasted through the room in a euphoric melody. Francis stepped out from behind the curtain to another round of applause.

"Good evening, folks," he said into the microphone. "Are we ready for some music?"

I smiled broadly as his voice poured through the room and over the audience, enchanting us all. I never tired of it, and though things were difficult for him at the moment, I had faith in those golden vocal cords and the brilliant way he put on a show. No one had the charisma that my baby did.

As song followed song, I enjoyed a great show, but I couldn't shake the unsettled feeling that I was being watched. I looked over my shoulder several times at the gangsters, and then at George. They always had their eyes on me. I ordered a few more drinks, anxious for the comfort of a good buzz. I didn't like that Francis was running around with the Mob. He didn't need any more trouble, God knew.

When the show ended, Francis made his way toward me, a grin on his face. He glowed with the energy he gleaned from the audience, and it was infectious.

I beamed right back at him. "You were incredible."

"It was you, baby. You're my good luck charm," he said, reaching for my hand. "Are you hungry? We could pick up lasagna from Patsy's. They always save me a nice plate." He hadn't eaten much since the news of Manie's resignation, and between the cigarettes, all the booze and little food, he looked haggard.

"Sure, baby," I said, glad he was hungry for a change. Patsy's was one of his favorite restaurants in the city, and their traditional Italian fare was about the only thing that might tempt him to eat.

The sound of a man clearing his throat drew our attention.

George wedged himself between Francis and me, nearly stomping on my foot in the process. "Good show, Frank. Are you up for a drink? We need to talk."

"Excuse me," I said, an edge to my voice. "You almost stepped on my toes."

George glanced at me and said not so much as a pardon me and returned his attention to Francis. "Let's go somewhere private."

I flushed. Crossing my arms, I waited for Francis to say something on my behalf or to at least properly introduce me. My fury mounted as the two walked away without the man acknowledging my presence—and without Francis saying a word. I watched them in disbelief. My fatigue, the vodka, and the disappointment with Francis melded into one big ball of hurt and I stood, steaming mad and prepared to say something to that effect, when they returned.

"This is Ava," he said to George. "We're on our way to Patsy's, if you care to join us."

The fat little man grunted and leaned into Francis's ear to say something I couldn't hear. And that did it. I'd had enough of the ingrate, and the both of them, being so rude.

"George can be your date. I'm out of here," I snapped, grabbing my purse.

I shrugged on my coat and headed to the door, ignoring Francis's shocked expression and his pleas to wait just a minute. I was sick of waiting just a minute, of being humiliated by the men in my life. First Mickey taking advantage of my naivete and then Artie with his imperious attitude, Mayer and his sexist lot, and now this manager, who had no business getting in the middle of my relationship with Francis, acted as if I were some sort of hooker not worth even a polite hello! Well, screw him and screw Frank for not standing up for me.

When I reached the door, George's voice drifted my way. "Let her go, Frank. She's just another bimbo. You'll get tired of her soon enough anyway."

I nearly turned around to slug the slob, but I couldn't bring myself to so much as look in Francis's direction. How could he listen to someone say those things about me? Not to mention just watch me go?

My vodka-fueled fury leading me on, I pushed through the door with a little too much force, hopped into a taxi, and promised myself I wouldn't let Francis into bed that night.

Tomorrow, I was flying home, and suddenly I couldn't wait to go.

★ ★ ★

An hour later, after I'd already locked the bedroom door and climbed into bed, Francis banged on the door.

"Ava, let me in," he said quietly, trying to avoid waking Manie.

I ignored him, pretending I was asleep.

The bang came louder. "Ava, open the door!"

"Sleep on the couch!" I shouted back and turned over, yanking the sheets and blanket up to my chin.

"I'll break the door down! Don't think I won't!" His voice rose in volume to match mine.

"Why don't you sleep with George! He'll keep you warm, I'm sure!"

He jiggled the doorknob, trying to twist it open, and pounded on the door. "So help me, Ava . . . open this door! You're going to wake up Manie!"

"You're the one banging down the door!" I shouted back.

I pictured Manie in bed trying to sleep and thought of the hospitality he'd shown us, and I felt a wave of guilt. Given the way Francis was carrying on, we'd probably wake him. The least we could do was fight quietly. I reached for the lock and yanked the door open swiftly, taking Francis by surprise. He raced into the room, leaning forward as if he were about to slam his shoulder against the door when I'd caught him midact. His momentum catapulted him across the room, and he stumbled over his feet, landing on the edge of the bed.

I threw my head back and laughed at the surprise on his face. "You should see your face right now."

He glared at me for an instant, but as he got to his feet he started laughing, too. He charged at me then, and we both landed on the bed in a heap of limbs and laughter.

I slipped into his arms and we made love savagely, taking my breath away. It was just what I needed.

After, he propped himself up on his elbows and gazed down at me, brushing a lock of hair out of my eyes with his fingertip. "I can't believe you just walked away from me like I meant nothing."

"You deserved it," I replied stubbornly. "You treated me like

I was nothing! And so did that jerk. If one of my friends had treated you that way, you'd have had some choice words."

"You're right," he said simply. "I'm sorry. But George didn't mean anything by it."

"He did, Francis, and you know it. I heard what he said about me. He thinks I'm another one of your bimbos." The vodka martinis had begun to wear off and with them, my anger. Now all I felt was a hole opening inside me as I imagined Francis tossing me aside, chasing the next best thing in Hollywood. I closed my eyes tightly against the image. As I did, I felt the soft graze of his lips over my eyelids.

"My love," he said.

I opened my eyes to see his searing bright blue eyes.

"You could never be just another girl. I'm mad about you, can't you see?"

"How am I supposed to believe you?" I forced a pretty pout, though I'd already forgiven him.

"You'll marry me, that's how. Marry me, Ava Lavinia Gardner. Make me your old man, for life. And the happiest asshole on earth."

I laughed joyously and wrapped my arms around his neck. His lips found mine and we lost time, passion rising between us again. When we came up for air, his expression was serious.

"I mean it, Angel. I want you to be my wife."

"I suppose that means you'll have to divorce the other one first."

He nodded solemnly. "I suppose it does. I'll move out after Christmas. Let the kids enjoy a last holiday with all of us together."

I kissed him again, this time softly. "I love you, Francis Albert Sinatra. The answer is yes. Yes, I'll marry you."

CHAPTER 13

FRANK

I felt lighter—thrilled the woman I loved agreed to be mine—and also heavier at the prospect of what lay ahead. Time was up. I'd have to come clean to Nancy. The holidays arrived in a hurry, and I left the snow-clogged sewers of New York for the sun-drenched hills of Los Angeles. I used to breathe deeper when I set foot in the city I'd come to know almost as well as my hometown, but not lately. Not while I was hunted by the media that seemed to enjoy watching my demise. Hell, they'd been a big part of it. The only thing that made me happy was Ava, and even then, she'd needled me about George for weeks. I knew I had to do something about my manager. He'd become a real thorn in my side, and if he was going to continue to treat Ava poorly, I couldn't keep him around.

At the house, Nancy and the kids had decorated for Christmas making everything look cheerful and bright. Garland wrapped the staircase banister, a wreath adorned the front door, and red ribbons and lights laced the branches of the Christmas tree. I wished I felt as cheerful. Ava would spend Christmas with her sister, and I'd have to wait out the holiday, watching my children be gleeful while joining Nancy and her family for the many celebrations until the feast of the seven fishes in January, all the while, knowing this scene, our lives together, would very soon come to an end.

In the end, I couldn't do it—I couldn't lie through it all. Instead, after a day or two, I decided to get it over with, to tell Nancy the truth.

I found her on the floor in Frankie's room playing blocks with him. As soon as she'd built a tower several blocks high, he'd knock it over with his fist and fall into hysterical giggles. The exuberant, childlike sound tugged at my heart and a pang rippled through me. I didn't want to do this, but I had to—I also didn't want to stay. I stood in the doorway, emotion clogging my throat, unable to find the right words.

"Blocks, Daddy," Frankie said. "Play with us."

I started to protest and promptly changed my mind. The kid wanted to spend some time with his dad. I'd known what that felt like at one point in my life when I'd really needed my pop, needed a man I could look up to, but that time had come and gone and I'd eventually realized he didn't have much to share with anyone. I plopped down on the floor next to my son, giving him the biggest smile I could muster, and played several rounds with him before I stood and brushed the wrinkles from my pants.

"Your mama and I need to talk, okay? You're a big boy now. Can you play by yourself for a few minutes?"

He nodded solemnly, liking very much the responsibility of being a big boy.

Nancy shot me a look. "What is it?"

I led her through the house to the back porch. A winter wind kicked up, blowing dust and withered palm fronds across the yard.

"It's cold, Frank. Why can't we talk inside?"

I'd prepared a speech, including a list of all the happy things about our time together, how much the memories meant to me, that I would always be there for her and the children. But as I looked into the gentle face I'd known nearly all my life, the carefully crafted words evaporated.

"I want a divorce, Nancy," I blurted. Heat crept under my collar, and I tugged at it, wishing I were anywhere but here.

Her face fell for an instant, but her calm demeanor quickly slid into place and I was struck by how much she'd changed. The circles beneath her eyes had deepened after three children; her clothing was more expensive but also more conservative. The pretty youth I'd met years before had shifted and morphed into someone new. She would never be unattractive, but she was the opposite to Ava's vigor and untouchable beauty in every way.

"Is this because of that Ava Gardner I saw in the paper?" she snapped.

"Come on, Nance, you and I are friends, but we aren't lovers," I dodged her question. "We made a good run of it."

"We just had another baby!" she shrieked. "How can you say we aren't lovers?"

I looked past her at the lawn and the terracotta roofs of the neighboring houses. What did she want me to say? That I loved Ava more? There were no words to describe the way I felt about that woman. When I wasn't panicked about the way my career was coming apart at the seams, she consumed every waking thought. Nancy had become something of a burden; she used to ground me but now she held me back. Hardest of all, she wanted something from me that I couldn't give her.

"I'll make sure you and the kids are properly looked after," I said. "I won't leave you in the lurch, you know that. I just can't do this anymore. We're leading separate lives."

"And whose fault is that?" She sniffed and swiped at her eyes, trying desperately to hold back her tears. "You can never keep your pants on! I knew that was your weakness the day I met you, but I thought you might leave it all behind once we had a family. Chasing women, desperately trying to prove your manhood. It's pathetic." She heaved, sucking in several ragged breaths. "We have it all! How could you possibly want more?"

I wanted to console her, an age-old habit I suddenly realized I'd have to leave behind, so I didn't. Instead, I watched her struggle to hold herself together as the pain sliced through me like a hot knife. "I'm sorry, sweetheart. I never meant to hurt you, you know that. You deserve better."

She wiped her eyes furiously. "How dare you ruin our Christmas!" She spun around to go inside but paused at the door. "I'm not giving you a divorce! You can tell that *puttana* she can go to hell!"

I stared after her, open-mouthed, as she slammed the door in my face.

I tried talking some sense into Nancy, but she wouldn't hear of it. She wouldn't give me a divorce, no matter what I said to her, so I decided to make a drastic move to send a message that I was done, even if she wasn't. I hired a moving van and packed up my suits and my office furniture at our house and installed myself permanently at the Palm Springs residence. Nancy watched in shock as I directed the moving van down the driveway.

I'd made my point: I wanted a divorce, and I wasn't coming back, at least not for her. The kids, I'd miss sorely.

"Where are you going, Poppa?" Little Nancy asked, throwing her arms around me.

I kissed her button nose and peered into a pair of brown eyes that had come from the Barbato side of the family. I searched for the right thing to say and finally settled on the truth. "I'm moving into my own house, squirt. But I love you and your brother and sister. I'll visit you all the time, and you can do sleepovers with me anytime you want. Doesn't that sound like fun?"

She nodded, her eyes wide, but I could see the sadness in their depths. "But I want you to live here with us."

"Sometimes things don't work out between grown-ups. I care about your mom a lot, but we don't make a very good husband and wife anymore, so we want to make sure you're happy instead. Do you understand?"

She pondered my words for a moment and said, "Like how Julie Milton used to be my friend until she was mean to me, and now I don't like her anymore?"

"A little like that, yes."

"But why were you mean to Mommy?"

I kissed her forehead. "I wasn't mean to Mommy. Things have just changed. One day you'll understand. But listen to me. I will always be your dad, you hear me? I'll never leave you."

She nodded and tucked her head into the crook of my neck. The sweet smell of shampoo and strawberry jam wafted around me and the knot of pain I'd been carrying in the pit of my stomach unraveled. I hoped I hadn't let the kids down too much. I kissed her head and kissed Frankie and little Tina, too. When I'd finished, Nancy took the baby from my arms and walked inside the house without a word.

I drove to Palm Springs gripping the steering wheel to keep my eyes from filling. I wanted to go—needed to—but that didn't make it any less painful, or the guilt any less of a burden. I didn't want to be that guy who left. And yet, here I was, hating myself as the pain rolled over me in waves.

Later that night, George called.

"You should know, I've left Nancy," I said.

"Christ, Frank. You really don't care about your career, do you? You need to take Nancy back or you'll never repair your image, and you'll be out of work entirely."

I'd heard it all before, but his tone was different this time and I knew we'd reached a crossroads. I couldn't take any more gloom and doom, least of all that night.

"I think we're done here, George," I said. "I'll be hiring a new manager."

"Jesus, Frank, right now? You need me now more than ever! Who the hell is going to agree to represent you in this state?"

"I don't need another mother, and that's what you've become. Scolding me and telling me who I can and can't see. We're done. You're fired. And now I've got to go. I had a lousy day and I have a plane to catch tomorrow morning." I slammed down the phone. The only thing I'd do for now was try to keep my relationship with Ava as quiet as possible—and the divorce. I didn't want the studio to know my business, or for anyone else to either.

I dialed Ava, desperate to hear her voice. Though I felt heavy and unsettled, I knew the news would make her happy and that, one day, it would make me happy, too.

CHAPTER 14

AVA

When Francis called to tell me he'd finally left, I was at once relieved and sad for him. I could hear the pain in his voice, bless his heart. I knew he must be wrestling over leaving those children. They were precious, even if they weren't mine, and I knew it must be eating him alive to feel like he was walking out on them. I'd tried to reassure him that I'd never come between him and them. They needed their daddy. After we spoke that first night, I'd given him some time and space to figure things out.

As it turned out, I didn't need to avoid him. He was avoiding me, and I worried he was having second thoughts.

To take my mind off things, I spent a few days with Bappie in Los Angeles, swimming at the beach, practicing my lines for another role, waiting to hear from Francis. I might be crazy about him, but I also wasn't about to stop living my life while he was in a mess of a relationship with Nancy either. I'd like to say I felt some sort of guilt about our affair, but I didn't—I wasn't even close to the first woman he'd chased while married, and if that wasn't a sign the marriage was broken, I didn't know what was. Nancy needed to face the facts. The man she'd married was scarcely a husband to her and he wasn't in love with her that way anymore.

One morning, I rose early and headed to the studio. On set, they paraded me around in a polka-dotted bathing suit and sunglasses to pose for promotional shots.

"Turn your head to the right," the photographer said. "Yes, perfect. Now show us those dazzling emerald eyes."

I pretended to seduce the camera, giving it my best smoldering look. He took several more shots and then told me to take a break, to my relief. I could use a drink. I headed back to my dressing room, pulled on a silk robe, and fished around the drawer of my vanity for the emergency bottle of vodka I'd come to store there. My performances were smoother, and I was able to go deeper into character, when I'd had a few shots of vodka or bourbon. It loosened me up, calmed the nerves. I set my shot glass on the tabletop and filled it to the brim. I threw it back, the burn in my nasal cavity and throat always a little shocking. I poured one more before sliding the bottle back into the drawer. Now I could finish the preproduction tedium after lunch without wanting to kill someone.

A light knock came at the door. I closed the gaping lapel of my robe and tied the sash around my waist. Smoothed my hair. It was always a guess as to who was on the other side of that door.

As I threw it open, David Hanna, my publicist, waited there with a grin the likes of which I hadn't seen in a long, long time.

"Well, David, what is it?" I said. "You've got a shit-eatin' grin on your face."

"I have good news," he said.

David could be tough when he wanted to be but mostly he took good care of me. We were friends of a sort, though we knew we shouldn't mix business with pleasure. No one followed those kinds of rules in Hollywood, or they'd never have an ally or friend.

"If it's good news, then come on in and have a drink with me."

"It's eleven o'clock, Ava."

"Like that ever stopped anybody before. Here," I said, pouring him a finger of vodka and then pouring myself another shot. "What is it?"

"They've got a picture for you."

"Who has?" I asked.

"MGM," he said with a smile. "It's a big role, lead billing. It's called *Pandora and the Flying Dutchman*. The director is Albert Lewin, and they've already got me looking into how to pitch it to the news media."

I gasped, lunged for him, and hugged him tightly. At last! Maybe MGM didn't have their heads up their asses anymore after all. I'd been preparing to cut ties with the studio as soon as my contract expired, but perhaps they finally saw me as more than a pinup girl, or someone to lend out. My heart soared. I was proud, thinking of how far I'd come and how long it had taken me to get here. How I'd persisted.

"When does filming start?" I asked.

"Mid-March."

"Soon!" I said, thinking immediately of Francis. Maybe he could visit me on set.

"That's not the best part," he said with a sly smile.

"Well"—I hit his arm playfully—"Out with it, you devil."

He laughed. "You'll be filming in London and also a small town in Spain called Tossa de Mar."

I squealed, covering my mouth with my hands and undoubtedly smudging my set makeup. "I've always wanted to go to Europe!"

"I know." He held up his glass, clinked it against mine, and we both swallowed the booze in one gulp. David sputtered at the bite of the alcohol.

"He's finally giving me a chance, that grouchy old Louis," I said. "I can hardly believe it."

He smiled. "You've more than earned it."

"I never thought I'd see the day!" I said eagerly. A starring role for MGM—in Europe! I opened the vodka bottle again and poured David another healthy glass.

"Take it easy, Ava. I still have almost a full day's work." He laughed but when he saw me grinning ear to ear, he held up his glass again without complaint. "To the next step!"

"To London and Spain!" I could hardly wait to tell Francis. He'd be so happy for me.

Or so I thought.

When I called him late that night after his show in New York, he sounded more sullen than usual, and lately, that was saying something. He felt guilty about the kids so he was truly wrestling with his decision to leave Nancy. I hated that he had to give up more time with them, but we both knew staying wasn't what he wanted either. I guessed he felt guilty about Nancy, too, but I didn't ask the question because I didn't want to know the answer.

"You're going to Europe?" he said, his voice pained.

"Not until March, baby. We can spend some time together before I go. I'll fly to New York first."

"Who's the costar?" he growled. "I don't like the idea of some loser with his paws all over my girl."

"James Mason. And don't be silly. You're the only man in the whole world for me, Europe and beyond," I said.

"Maybe I can get away from this pathetic show and visit you there. We're not selling out, baby. No one wants to see me play anymore, not even in New York."

"Oh, Francis—"

"My talent agency fired me."

My mouth fell open. He really was on a downward trajectory and falling fast.

"My God, I'm so sorry," I said, wishing I were there to console him. In the short time I'd come to know him, I'd learned how deeply he felt everything. His raw honesty and profound feelings were what made him so magnetic. It was also his cross to bear, especially when things weren't going his way.

"What am I going to do?" he groaned.

"We'll think of something. What does mean old George say?"

"He doesn't say anything. I fired him."

My mouth dropped open for the second time. Francis fired George! I hated the guy, but still, I couldn't believe Francis had let him go.

"Well, good," I said at last. "You can do better. You don't need to pretend like you're someone you aren't just to appease the media. You have more talent than just about anyone in this town."

"When can I see you?" he asked, his tone pleading. "I miss you."

"Soon . . . I don't know. I need to talk to David, see what my schedule is, and I also need to talk to Reenie. Hopefully she doesn't mind watching the house."

"Will you take Bappie with you?"

"Of course, if she wants to come, and I'm sure she will." I knew my sister wouldn't want to miss the chance to see Europe for anything.

"I'd feel better with her there," he said. "She looks after you."

I laughed. "I don't need my big sister to look after me, Francis."

"I know, I know. Listen, the fellas here want to get some drinks. Call me tomorrow."

As I laid the receiver in the cradle, I realized he hadn't said congratulations. He was happy for me—I knew he was—he was just having a bad day. A really very bad day. Yet I couldn't quiet the nagging voice in the back of my head that said he was burdened by my success as his career faltered, that he was embarrassed to be shown up by a woman. He hadn't said as much, but I was coming to understand what it meant to love a man who was traditional at heart, even if he loved my strength and my independence.

But it really had been a very difficult day for him—and week and month—and for now, I'd let him off the hook.

★ ★ ★

I thought Francis had received all the bad news possible, but days later while he was en route to Houston, he got another difficult phone call. George had died of a heart attack. I'd disliked the man, but I didn't wish him ill, and I knew Francis would be devastated. I secretly booked a flight to join him at the Shamrock Hotel, where he was playing at a special event and joining the mayor for supper after the show. I suspected Francis was in no mood to perform and would be very happy to see me.

When I slipped into the concert hall, the audience tittered, and some people whispered and pointed. I'd never get used to such a thing, being recognized so far from home. I supposed this was what it was like to become a star. You were recognized no matter where you were. I smiled and found a table near the stage that quickly and conveniently opened up for me.

As the curtains parted and the show began, Francis spotted me immediately, and it was as if a lantern had switched on in the room. He radiated happy surprise from the stage. I warmed from the inside out, loving him so completely it made my heart ache. He needed me and appreciated my support, and I knew I'd made the right decision in coming.

I ordered a martini, the alcohol working its magic as it warmed my blood, and soon I was jiving along to the music in my seat. The band was wonderful, even if the audience was paltry compared to the crowds Frank had played to in the past. He'd win those crowds back, and I'd help make sure of it. I couldn't stand to see a man as prideful and as talented as him—and a man I loved—lose everything. On top of it all, he was also losing his family, for me. I downed the last of my martini as I thought of how worried he was about his kids. I needed to be patient with him. He'd made a show of commitment in the right direction by moving out of the family home. We'd get to what was next.

After the performance, he kissed me hard in the taxi.

"You're the best." He pulled me to him and held onto me as if I were a lifeline.

"I'm sorry about George, baby. I know you didn't end on the best of terms, but that's just business. He knows you cared about him as a man."

"A heart attack, can you believe it?" he said. "He wasn't even sixty years old."

I shook my head solemnly and stroked his cheek. The car swept us through the city to Vincent Sorrento's Italian restaurant, recommended by the mayor, Oscar Holcombe. Oscar was a huge fan of Francis. I was glad; Francis could use a little fawning over him to lighten the mood.

When we entered the restaurant, we were quickly shown to a quiet corner with lamps that glowed and an array of comfortable chairs stationed around a table backed against the wall. We had a view of the entire place.

"It's always better in the back," Francis said, leaning to my ear. "There aren't any surprises that way."

"There wouldn't be any surprises if you'd stop making friends with gangsters," I replied.

He grinned as we took our seats.

We introduced ourselves to the mayor and after we ordered drinks and appetizers, the chef emerged from the kitchen to greet us in a white coat that was smeared with something that looked like marinara.

"Mr. Sinatra," Vincent said, smiling broadly. Holding out his hand and shaking Francis's vigorously, he seemed like a genuine fellow. "I'm honored you're eating in my restaurant."

"Happy to be here, Vinnie," Francis said, raising his wine in a toast.

Francis was saying all the right things, and doing all the right things, but I knew better. I didn't miss the edge in his voice. He needed some relaxation and time in private to mourn. I slipped my hand under the table and felt for his, squeezing it briefly to remind him that I was here, beside him.

We chatted politely with the mayor and all seemed to be going well until we finished the first course.

Out of nowhere, a man approached the table and a light flashed, blinding us, followed by two others.

"What the hell?" Francis complained loudly. His show of polite eagerness instantly took a dive.

"Mr. Sinatra, it's great to meet you, sir," the photographer said. "Mr. Sorrento gave me permission to take your picture for the *Houston Post*."

"No one asked me," Francis snapped. "Who is this clown?" he turned to the mayor. "I can't even have a decent meal with an esteemed guest without being interrupted."

Taken aback by the outburst, I laid my hand on Frank's arm. "Francis, I don't see the harm in letting him take one—"

The bulb flashed again, and Francis sprang to his feet. "Get out of here!" He shoved the photographer away from the table. "I'm not allowing any pictures tonight!"

The photographer stumbled backward, knocking into another patron, whose wineglass tipped and shattered and red liquid oozed around shiny speckles of glass across the floor.

"I'm so sorry, Mr. Sinatra," he stammered.

But Francis wasn't alright. He'd snapped. He pushed the photographer again, yelling obscenities.

"Francis!" I said, reaching for his arm. "That's enough! You're overreacting."

Mr. Sorrento arrived then, his face ashen. "I'm terribly sorry, Mr. Sinatra. I thought you wouldn't mind. I'll ask them to leave immediately—"

"You should be sorry!" Francis shot back. "Everyone wants to make a quick buck off my hide, and they don't even have the common decency to ask me first!"

The mayor's face had gone white and then red. He was clearly embarrassed by Francis's absurd reaction. I wanted to hide.

"Frank!" I hissed. "That's enough! You're upset. We should go." I wanted to be understanding, but I couldn't believe he'd made such a scene in front of an entire restaurant and especially in front of the mayor. He was making us both look ridiculous.

"I didn't realize it would upset you, sir," the chef interceded. "I gave the paper permission to take a promotional photograph. I thought it would please you. I'm truly sorry, sir. I'm sorry, Mr. Mayor."

Oscar held up his hand. "No need to be sorry, Vince, it isn't your fault—"

"We're sorry for the mess," I cut in. "Frank hasn't been himself. He's just lost a good friend who passed away."

The spell of rage that had seized Frank lifted at the mention of George's passing, and he gruffly turned back to the dinner party. He slid into his seat again and downed the rest of his wine in one gulp. "I should show them my fists," he said when he'd finished. "You'd think by now those bastards would leave me alone."

The rest of our party stared at him, open-mouthed.

Mortified, I sank into my chair, flushed, knowing this couldn't be good publicity for either of us. Things might be tough for him right now, but it didn't give him the right to act like a child in front of everyone.

Later, I apologized profusely to the mayor, who kindly brushed off the incident, but I knew better. He was as appalled by Francis's behavior as the rest of us. With every step closer to the door on our way out, I grew angrier and angrier with him. He was grieving and down on his luck, I chanted in my head, trying to keep my anger at bay.

Yet as we drove away, it took all my self-control not to give him a piece of my mind.

CHAPTER 15

FRANK

'd really done it this time.

I'd upset the wrong person and the story exploded. I made the front page in Houston and Los Angeles and so did Ava. The photographer managed to get a shot of the two of us at the table before the kerfuffle. My little altercation with the press made the papers as well, and that was only the beginning. After the initial story broke, a tidal wave of bad headlines from every journalist who'd ever hated me hit newsstands across America. There was no hiding my relationship with Ava now. It was all there in black and white: her hand on my arm, the surprised look on both of our faces as the flash went off, the ill-timed confrontation. This time there was no hiding my indiscretions from MGM.

I flew back to New York with the sinking feeling that I might be fired from the Copacabana. Thankfully, management needed me more than they could afford to let me go so I stayed on, but my crowds dwindled to an embarrassingly paltry less than half-full and for the first time, it really sank in: George was right. My fans wanted to see me as a family man: a clean-cut, perfect American hero who was a lovesick fool writing songs about his wife. I didn't understand why they couldn't love a regular guy who struggled, who was down on his luck sometimes and made bad choices but who still fought like hell to make a name for himself. Wasn't that the American dream? To strive every day for something greater, even while we came up short? And what about all of the charity events and speeches I'd given, my fight for civil rights and the self-made man scraping together a living—the Everyman—who built America on his back? The media seemed to forget everything good I'd ever done after a lousy run-in with a lousy reporter who didn't have the decency to ask if I wanted my dinner interrupted.

I reached for the phone, anxious to talk to Ava before the show that night. She'd been supportive as the hits kept coming, but I knew this had been hard on her, too.

"How are things at the studio, baby?" I said, lighting a cigarette to give my hands something to do.

"Busy," she said. "We've been doing a lot of promotional photo shoots. The costume director is insane. He's made us try on about a thousand different outfits. Oh! And there's going to be a bullfight scene in the film! Isn't it the most romantic thing you've ever heard? I can't wait to see one!"

That was precisely what I was worried about. My girl, the most beautiful creature in the whole damn world, was about to be on set in Spain and now there would be some hot-blooded bullfighter in it, too? A wave of nausea swept over me.

"You don't really need that role, do you?" I asked. "Please, Angel. Stay here with me in New York. I'll take you to Europe just as soon as this gig is finished. We can fly to London and Spain and France, or wherever you want to go."

"Are you out of your mind?" she said, the shock in her voice plain. "I've already negotiated the contract. And you know I can't turn down a starring role from MGM right now. It's what I've been waiting for."

She was understating things. She'd been on dozens of magazine and newspaper covers, been the source of gossip for nearly four years now. She already was a real star—and I was a sad, pathetic Joe, down on his luck. I had to find my way out of this before she realized I didn't deserve her. The thought made me desperate. I loved her more than I knew what to do with, more than what made sense.

"Consider it, please," I said. "My life has gone to hell and you're the only good thing I've got."

"I'm packing my bags, baby," she replied firmly. "I'm flying to New York in a few days to stay with you the last two weeks before I go."

I let loose a relieved breath. Maybe I could convince her to stay once we were together. There was no reason she couldn't choose a picture closer to home.

But days later, I couldn't change her mind—and another bomb landed right in our laps.

"That was David," Ava said, pushing the phone away from her forcefully and lighting a cigarette. She walked around the mahogany coffee table and a potted ficus tree to pace in the open space of the hotel suite. She inhaled and blew out an agitated cloud of smoke. "That damned Houston trip is causing a real stir. Apparently there are letters about us flooding the mailbox at MGM from all over the country and they aren't good."

"What did David say?" I asked, going straight to the cocktail cart and pouring us each a glass of whiskey. I handed one to her and she threw it back instantly. I refilled her glass and did the same for me.

"They're calling me a slut who ruins marriages. They say I'm a vixen on the prowl and you're my latest victim. Nancy, of course, is painted as the saint." She filled her glass a third time. She was pale and upset, but as I reached out to gather her in my arms to reassure her it was all worth it to be together, she stepped out of my reach. "Not now, Frank."

Frank. She only called me that when she was angry.

"This will blow over," I said. "Trust me. The media is like a dog with a bone but eventually they get tired of it after they've chewed on it for a while. They'll move on to something new in a flash."

"David said it's getting worse. They're trying to ruin your career and very well may ruin mine! Jesus Christ, I'm the next Ingrid Bergman!"

Ingrid had made the fatal mistake of falling in love with a married man, too, and having his baby. She'd ignored the gossip and gotten hitched anyway. The gossip never really had blown over—it had blown up—and they'd destroyed her in the press. Now she had her man, but her career was in the toilet—couldn't book a picture to save her life. Puritan America didn't seem to believe in shades of gray; they either lived their lives in a black lane or a white one. What a load of bull.

"It's harder for women," she said, stubbing out her cigarette. "We don't get second and third chances. They'll exchange one pretty face for the next, and after a certain age, most of us can't get work at all." Her eyes were a stormy forest green.

I hadn't thought of it that way before, but she was right. I was already hated in the press, but she wasn't, and it was likely she'd pay for it far longer than I would, and in a more vicious way.

"I'm finally starting to really get somewhere, too," she lamented a bit too forcefully, sloshing whiskey over the rim of her glass and onto the floor.

I rubbed her shoulders. "I know, but look. You're a love goddess to them so of course they're going to assume that's who you are in real life. When we get married, they'll shut their big fat traps and leave us alone."

She slammed down her whiskey glass. "I need some air."

"I'll go with you." I reached for my coat.

"Oh no you don't," she snapped. "I don't want another photo of us floating around out there right now. I'm going alone." She pulled on her hat and gloves, slung her coat around her shoulders, and slammed the door behind her.

I wondered if this would break us—if she would give up on me. I'd never been so afraid of losing something, or someone. I wouldn't be able to sustain the pain, after everything else that had happened, should she never walk through that door again.

As the echo of that slammed door still reverberated in my ears, I reached for the Jack Daniel's one more time.

CHAPTER 16

AVA

I hadn't foreseen the pressure of being a mistress to one of the most notorious men in Hollywood. I'd had lovers and high-profile husbands, but none had attracted the ire that Francis did. In part, it was his fault. He behaved like a child having a tantrum with every press photographer or reporter who crossed his path. He couldn't seem to keep his insults to himself. Though I tried to explain that the press could either destroy him or make him into the star he wanted to be, he refused to play nice. Under the strain, I found myself counting the days until I could leave for Europe. I needed a break from the circus—and from him. I needed to focus on my career. I finally felt like I was getting somewhere.

I tossed a tabloid that David had mailed to me on the floor. "'Hurricane Ava,'" I seethed. "I'm the temptress they watch and dream about one day, and in real life, they turn on me. I don't understand it. Everyone in the free world knows you cheated on Nancy before you were with me!"

"I know, baby. It isn't fair." He dropped the latest letter he'd received that morning on the sofa cushion beside him. Willie

Moretti had added his chiding to the pile with the kind of quiet menace I'd expected a mobster like him to dole out. He wrote that he was surprised to read what was in the papers about Frank's darling wife. When Frank hesitantly read it to me, I lost my mind.

"Why doesn't Moretti mind his own damn business!" I demanded. "I hate the way you let those gangsters boss you around."

"I don't let them boss me around."

"Like hell you don't." Blinded by anger, I picked up my shoes and flung them across the room.

"You show them, baby," Francis said, dodging the shoes.

If I wasn't so fed up, I would have laughed.

"They think they're so damned clever. Screw them!" I shouted.

I'd never been the target of negative press in a direct hit. Sure, there'd been news splashed across the papers about my former husbands and occasional boyfriends, but it wasn't this . . . this dogpile of insults that made me want to wring someone's neck. I felt sick to my stomach.

I wasn't the only one who was a wreck. Francis was all over the place with his pills and booze, and I thought I might be witnessing the true unraveling of the man I loved. I'd read that Hollywood could do this to a person, but I'd never witnessed it firsthand.

At last, my final day in New York came and I was exhausted, ready to escape to Europe. That morning had brought one of the worst letters of all: *Dear Bitch, I hope your plane crashes* . . . It had sparked tears. First I called Reenie, who'd listened and consoled me the way she was so good at doing, and then I called David.

"That's awful," he said, his voice mournful, and I wanted to hug him for being kind. "It all seems a little unfair, doesn't it?"

"You can say that again," I said, sniffling.

"If you didn't have a film abroad, MGM was going to ask you to go into hiding until the storm passes."

"I'm getting on a plane tomorrow."

"Just lay low in Spain. Do your work, enjoy the sights, and stay out of trouble," David said.

"Of course I will."

Little did I know, the promise I'd made wouldn't hold water for long.

Bappie arrived in New York, ready to go with me to London the next day, and I filled her in on everything only to get a terse shake of the head.

"I don't like what you're up to with Frank," she said. "It's not right, Ava."

"He's left Nancy! And he asked for a divorce. They aren't officially separated, but they may as well be."

"But they aren't yet," Bappie added quietly.

I glared at her. "We're in love! He's asked me to marry him."

"He did? Oh, Ava." She slipped her arms around me in that big sister way, and I laid my head on her shoulder.

"This will all stop, as soon as we get married," I sniffed. "We're just being kept apart is all, and it's stressful."

"It'll be alright," Bappie said, brushing my hair off my forehead. "Ride out the storm. In the meantime, let's make a list of the sights we'd like to see in London and maybe in Spain, too. It'll be a good distraction."

I blew out a breath, more grateful than ever that my sister was here, and that she would go with me, at least for part of the time I was in Europe. I was moving up the MGM ladder at last and I wanted to enjoy it. To bask in my success a little. I also wanted to give the role my all and I couldn't do that if I was mired in anger at the world and worry about Francis. Couldn't he understand that?

"That sounds perfect," I said. "I'll just get us a pen and some coffee."

Bappie smiled, her dark eyes approving. "That's my girl."

Later that night, I dressed for Francis's concert, opting for something pretty but subdued in a dark skirt and blouse with a cardigan, and black flats to match. I didn't want to attract attention to myself, not tonight. All I wanted was to show him my support and then the next day get on that airplane to London, where I could breathe again.

I ordered a martini followed by another, trying to stifle my anxiety. By the time I was drunk, my anxiety had shifted to irritation. The crowd was particularly ornery that night, chattering during the show, being rude to Francis. Some walked out early. A few booed a song they didn't care for. I had to admit, his performance wasn't like any I'd seen in the past. His songs were flat, his usual swagger absent; he was exhausted and cheerless, burned by the very fans who had once loved him. He didn't know what to do with himself. I didn't know what to do with him—or us—either.

When the show ended at last and he did his usual walk through the dwindling crowd to shake hands or sign autographs, I went to the bar for a last round. It was going to be a long night of listening to his litany of complaints. He'd begged me all day not to go to London. I'd tried to make him see how important it was to my career, but he didn't seem to care that it was something I needed, not just something I wanted to do. That didn't sit well with me, but I didn't want to pick a fight.

We decided on dinner at a steak house several blocks away in a quieter part of town. The restaurant was still bustling, however, and the owner welcomed us inside with a smile. I ordered chicken and roasted vegetables, but hardly touched my plate. Instead, I made my way steadily through another dry martini.

I watched the happy patrons around us finish their meals, eating and talking and heading back into the night. It was a relief to not be bothered here, to be able to have dinner without anyone eager to snap our photograph or beg for autographs.

"Not hungry?" he asked.

"No, are you?" I glanced at his plate. He'd hardly touched his pork chops.

"I don't want you to go," he said.

"We've been over this," I said, my tone a warning. I didn't want to rehash this for the hundredth time, especially here.

"I don't want you to forget what we have."

"How could I ever forget you, especially after the last two weeks?" I snapped. I loved the man intensely, but I couldn't keep this up for much longer. The pleading, the despair, especially now, after what we'd been through. I was a patient woman, but my patience was now wafer-thin.

"I saw the letter from this morning," he said.

"Yeah, let's not talk about it."

"Good idea."

I took a few bites and excused myself to the ladies' room. As I took my seat again, a beautiful blonde waved Francis over to her table. He nodded back politely but didn't get up.

Good boy, I thought, as I reached for my napkin.

The woman wouldn't be put off and crossed the room.

"Why, if it isn't Frankie Sinatra." She eyed me up and down. "And are you Hedy Lamarr?"

"Who's asking?" I said, slugging back some of my martini so I didn't slug her.

"I'm Cherrilee Williams," she said, putting one perfectly manicured hand on her hip. She looked like she was trying to imitate Marilyn Monroe with her bleached out hair and heavy makeup. What she didn't know was Marilyn wore that makeup only when she had to and not on the regular, same as me, and she was stunningly gorgeous without it. Furthermore, Marilyn was smart as a whip—not just beautiful—but no one outside of Hollywood knew that either.

"Well, hello, Cherrilee," Francis said with one of his charming smiles.

She leaned over him, dipping her breasts forward so he could see down her dress. "Can I have your autograph?"

I rolled my eyes. Why did he have to encourage her? My annoyance escalated and I found it harder and harder to keep my mouth shut.

"Sure thing, but I don't have a pen," he said in an almost purr. I'd know that voice anywhere; it was his bedroom voice and—I'd thought—something he reserved for me.

She moved closer to his ear, said something, and then giggled prettily. Her breasts nearly brushed his face when she stood erect again.

"As you can see, I'm having dinner, Cherrilee," Francis replied.

Cherrilee faked a pout and smiled again before sauntering away.

Francis glanced at me then, his smile fading quickly. "What? I can't help it if they come on to me. What am I supposed to do, tell her to leave?"

"For starters, yes," I said, now fuming. "We're trying to have a private dinner." I pushed my plate in front of me, my appetite now completely gone.

"Come on, Ava, can't we forget it? I've been looking forward to dinner with you all night."

"Then why did you have to flirt with little miss desperate, right in front of me? She looked like a strung-out version of Marilyn Monroe."

He barked a laugh at my insult. "I'd hardly call that flirting."

Heat swept up my neck and spilled over my cheeks. "She shoved her knockers in your face, practically giving you a lap dance, and you sat there, smiling through it all!"

If there was one thing Francis couldn't ignore, it was a beautiful woman. I knew this about him no matter how many times he told me he loved me, and it gnawed at my trust in him. There were also rumors he hired prostitutes regularly and the rumors made me crazy, even if I didn't necessarily believe them. It all drove me to do stupid things to make him jealous. I thought about the time I'd sat on a friend's lap at the studio on purpose, just as Francis arrived. He became incensed, and I felt like a cad for making him angry, all because I'd heard a rumor that he kept a list of the women he'd slept with in his dressing room.

The words to that morning's letter flashed again through my mind. *Dear Bitch* . . . Well, yes, I could be one, and it was time Dear Bitch showed her face again. After all we'd been through the last two weeks, I was fed up.

I threw my napkin across my half-eaten dinner. "All of a sudden I can't wait to leave." I knew it would hurt his feelings, and that was precisely why I'd said it.

"Fine. Leave. See if I care!" He pulled his money clip out of his jacket pocket and threw a wad of cash on the table.

"Why don't you follow Cherrilee home. I'm sure you'd make her day."

"Come on," he growled, gripping my elbow to steer me across the restaurant and through the doorway. "You know you're the only woman I want."

"Then why did you look down her dress? I can't so much as glance in the direction of another man without you giving me an earful about it."

He gritted his teeth. "She threw herself at me. What was I supposed to do? I told her no, only to get a lousy talking to."

"Lousy?" My voice raised an octave and the next words came out as a shout. "I'll tell you what's lousy! Lousy is drowning in hateful letters! Lousy is watching the man I love come unhinged every time a reporter is nearby. Lousy is watching women throw themselves at you and I can't do anything about it!"

A few patrons turned to watch us, but I didn't care.

"Calm down, Angel," he said holding out his hand as if to keep me quiet. "Let's get out of here. We can talk about this—"

"I don't want to talk to you! I want to leave." I jerked away from his grasp and started for the door.

"Ava!"

Somewhere inside me, I knew I was being irrational but the stress of the last weeks, coupled with too much vodka, set loose all the frustration that had been building inside me. I dashed outside and into the street, flagged a taxi down, and jumped in, slamming the door closed just as Francis stepped outside the restaurant.

"Go!" I ordered the driver, and we screeched away from the curb. I turned to look out the back window.

Frank stood there, holding his napkin, fury etched on his face.

Served him right.

Once back at the suite, I couldn't stand the thought of seeing Frank so soon—of him crowding me. I paced, trying to decide where to go when I spied my address book by the phone. I flipped it open, scanning the list of names. Artie—he was in town. I'd forgotten my ex-husband was living in New York these days with his new girlfriend. In spite of our split, we'd somehow managed to remain friends of a sort, and we talked from time to time. It was a gift of mine, to befriend old lovers and boyfriends, and I knew Artie would be up late.

I picked up the telephone and dialed his number.

"How about a nightcap?" I cooed. "I'd like to meet that new girl of yours. Besides, I can't sleep."

He invited me over and not long after, a taxi dropped me at his apartment. I hadn't bothered to close the address book. If Francis really wanted to find me, he could—and it would serve him right to find me at Artie's. I knew, underneath it all, Francis was jealous of him. He hated that I'd been Artie's wife once upon a time, and that the man I'd been with before him was an incredibly talented musician. Francis couldn't dispute Artie's skills, much as he wanted to.

"Come on in, Ava," Artie said. He wore silk pajamas and slippers. "This is Ruth."

A beautiful woman with mussed brown hair tied the sash of her robe into place before saying, "How do you do, Ava? Why, you're more beautiful in person than you are on-screen. I didn't think that was possible."

I liked her immediately. "How kind of you to say so," I said, accepting a bourbon from Artie and following them both into the living room to a set of overstuffed pin-striped chairs.

"So tell me," he said, "what brings you to the city?"

As we talked, I felt my anger cool and I was glad I'd stopped by, even if I knew I'd interrupted their evening. They didn't show any signs of irritation at my late arrival. Artie had always been the quintessential host when he wanted to be, and a good friend. Just as long as you weren't his wife.

Our peaceful conversation didn't last. Soon, someone pounded on the door.

"What the devil?" Artie's face tensed and he stood to answer it.

I knew who was on the other side of that door and braced myself for a fight.

"Frank?" Artie said. "Come on in. Take your coat off, have a drink."

A large man in an immaculate dark suit pushed in behind Frank. I rolled my eyes. Frank had brought one of his goons, though he'd call him his manager and bodyguard. He denied Hank Sanicola was a part of the Mafia, but Hank shadowed us regularly while in the city. Any fool could see that, and I knew he'd been put up in the hotel a few floors down from us, probably by Willie Moretti.

"What's going on here?" Frank demanded, his voice loud.

"I wanted to get away from you!" I snapped.

"Let's go. Now," Frank said, pointing at the ground as if I was to scurry to his side. The very hubris of it made me laugh. He fumed at my amusement, and by the shade his skin was turning, I thought he might burst.

"I'm not going anywhere with you," I said. "I'm enjoying myself with Artie and this lovely woman. Ruth, meet Frank."

"Hello—"

"Ava," Frank interrupted her, "get your coat. We're going, or I'll drag you out myself and it won't be pleasant."

"You should watch your tone, Sinatra," Ruth cut in. "This isn't your house, and she's welcome here."

I smiled, daring him to continue. I wondered whether Frank would make more of a scene than he had already. I was just drunk enough to test him to find out.

"You mind your own business, lady," Frank snapped.

Hank Sanicola flexed, stepping closer to Frank.

"You'd better watch yourself, or I'll make good use of my pistol," Artie said, his voice quietly menacing.

A shiver ran over my skin. I knew that tone—Artie had reached his limit. He wouldn't hesitate to use his gun, should he need to. God knew he'd been trained how to use it while serving in the war.

Frank paled and went silent. Hank Sanicola balled his hands into fists as if poised for a brawl.

"I think it's time you were on your way, too, Ava," Artie said, motioning to the door. "Our visit has taken an unpleasant turn."

I stood, tossing my hair to hide my embarrassment. I don't know what I was thinking, egging Frank on to follow me here. It couldn't have gone well no matter what.

Frank stepped backward into the hall. "Alright, we're going."

"Good night, Artie. Thanks, Ruth," I said, walking out after Frank. I pushed past him to the elevator and tried pushing the button to close the door before he could enter.

"Where do you think you're going?" he asked, pushing open the door.

"Back to the apartment to lock you out!"

"Come on." He stepped inside and Hank followed. "Let's forget all of this. You're leaving tomorrow."

"Don't touch me," I fumed.

Hank crossed his arms over his chest and looked from me to Frank and then trained his eyes on the ceiling, not saying a word, probably wishing he were anywhere but here.

When we'd made it back to the hotel, I staggered inside, pushing into the bedroom I was sharing with Bappie. I was glad Frank was across the hall for the night. At this point, I didn't want to talk to him and I didn't care about anything but drinking a giant glass of water and resting my bone-dry eyes.

From the bedroom, I heard some rustling around in a cabinet and then the apartment went blissfully silent. I climbed into bed and was about to drift off to sleep when the telephone beside the bed rang. Who the hell could that be?

"Hello?" I said, irritated to be roused from sleep.

"It's all over." Frank's voice drifted through the receiver. "So long, baby, it's been fun, but it's over."

"What are you talking about—"

The sound of a gunshot boomed over the line.

I screamed, dropped the phone, and dashed into his room, heart racing. No. No, it couldn't be true. Francis wouldn't take his own life! This was all a mistake. I loved him. I couldn't lose him.

I kicked open his door. "Francis! Baby—"

My words stuck in my throat. He lay in the bed on his side, his back to me.

Panic stole my breath and I raced to the bed, touched his shoulder, terrified of what I'd find. I may have been angry with him, but goddamn it, I loved him. I loved him more than just about anything on this earth. I couldn't imagine a world without him in it.

Bappie raced in behind me, her hair mussed from sleep. "What's happened?"

Francis rolled over then and peered up at me, mirth in his blue eyes. There was a gaping hole in the mattress and a pile of stuffing and feathers that had blown apart from the gunshot.

"Got you," he said.

"You scared me, you jerk!" I screeched. Too relieved to be angry, I pulled him into my arms, kissed his face, stroked his hair. "That wasn't funny! I was afraid you'd offed yourself. What would I do then?"

He wrapped his arms around me for a moment, whispering, "I love you."

"You're crazy, do you know that?" Bappie shook her head as she treaded back to the bedroom.

"I always did like a good prank," he said, a wicked gleam in his eye.

"That's not what I'd call a prank, you asshole," I said, stomach still churning with adrenaline and too much vodka. "What would I have done without you, Francis?"

We kissed hotly until our argument and exhaustion and the terrifying prank were forgotten. I wanted him beside me, over me, inside me. I grabbed at him greedily as his hands reached for my nightgown. He slipped it off quickly and pinned me beneath him. I yielded to him and we were lost in each other—hot breath and caresses, the musky scent of his skin.

What was it about him—about the way we were together—that drew me to him even when I wanted to sock his lights out? I didn't know, but here we were, loving each other again as if the world would end.

A loud knock on the front door split the air.

"Ignore that," Francis said, kissing me again.

"Do you think someone heard the gunshot?" I asked.

The knock grew more insistent.

He rolled off the bed and pulled on his trousers. "I'll handle this."

I dressed hastily and followed him to the living room while he opened the door. He pinned an innocent expression to his face. "Yeah?"

Hank's large body filled the doorway.

"Jesus, Frank, was that your gun I heard?" Hank had pulled on a pair of trousers but still wore a green nightshirt with pearlescent buttons.

"You could hear it three floors down?" Francis asked with a laugh.

"Half of Manhattan heard it," Hank said. "What did you shoot up? I hope it wasn't your girl."

"My mattress."

"We'd better get rid of it." Hank pushed inside the suite. "Oh, hiya, Ava. I'm glad it wasn't you."

"Too bad it wasn't you," I quipped.

We both laughed. I always did like a good laugh at a tense moment.

"Look, I passed a couple of staff and some old lady in the hallway," Hank said. "They heard it, too, and it sounds like they know what direction it came from. Police will be here shortly."

"Damn!" Francis said. "I can't afford to be arrested again."

I watched them heave the mattress out of the apartment and down the hall to the elevator. Minutes later, they returned with Hank's pristine mattress. Sweat beaded Francis's forehead, but in a strange way, he looked like he was enjoying himself, like a little boy trying to get away with murder. I remembered then why I loved him, the mischievous prankster side to him as much as anything—even if I could have slapped him for that stunt earlier.

"Better hide my gun, too," Francis said, handing it to Hank, who left in a hurry.

Moments later, an ominous knock came at the door.

"Open up! Police," a gruff voice called from the hallway.

Francis opened the door to two policemen, who looked none too happy to be there.

"Mr. Sinatra, someone reported a gunshot," one of them said. "Everyone alright in here?"

"A gunshot?" Francis asked, gaping in mock innocence. "Who the hell would fire a gun in a hotel, of all places? I didn't hear a thing, officer. I've just returned from a late-night dinner."

I smothered a smile. Sometimes it paid to be an actor.

After the policemen were satisfied with their search and went on their way, we dissolved into laughter—and into each other's arms until the sun rose.

CHAPTER 17

AVA

Sometimes Francis was as crazy as a bedbug, but I forgave him for his stunt. The night had ended well, but still, I was never more relieved than when Bappie and I boarded the plane to London. For now, I was leaving the mess Francis and I had made behind me, and I could divert my energy to new things, to the new picture.

I dozed off as soon as we were aloft and the next thing I knew, we'd landed and checked into Claridge's, the hotel where Bappie and I and the rest of the crew would be staying for a few nights for preproduction chores. After a deep sleep, I took my sister out into the city to see a few of the sites: the Tower of London, Buckingham Palace and St. James's Park, Westminster Abbey. Big Ben's clock tower was just as I'd always pictured it: regal and tall, overlooking the bustling silver waters of the Thames like a sentinel. I delighted in the double-decker buses and telephone booths that painted bright spots of crimson against a mostly gray landscape of stone and moody sky.

Though London was a bustling city, it had a different energy to those I'd known in America. It felt prim, somehow restrained by centuries of hard-learned lessons. It was wiser, too, and full of secret nooks and gardens. Though the perfectly pruned rose bushes and flowerbeds were stripped bare, I could imagine them bursting with blooms. Many of the neighborhoods were sleepier than I'd expected, tucked away from the hubbub of Piccadilly and the main attractions. Each day, I bounded out of bed ready to explore. I loved everything about the city and made a pledge to return one day for a much longer stay.

After the film crew was fitted for their costumes and we'd wrapped up the preproduction items—including a failed attempt at getting the silly guards at Buckingham Palace in their fur hats and red coats to smile—it was nearly time to move on to Spain.

"We have a couple of days before shooting begins," I said. "What do you think about a quick trip to Paris?"

Bappie smiled and clinked her glass against mine. "*Vive la France!* That's what I think."

For our final evening in London, Bappie and I decided to dine on a proper English meal. When the waiter served us the steak and potatoes with mushy peas that we'd ordered, I stared at my plate. The portion was minuscule.

"Bappie, have you ever seen a portion so small?"

The waiter reddened. "I'm sorry, Miss Gardner. We're still under strict war rations."

"Really?" I sat back in my chair. "But the war has been over for five years now. I know they say things move slowly in the old world, but that's downright glacial, wouldn't you say?"

"You don't have such rations in America, I take it," he answered politely if a little stiff.

"I live in California, honey," I said. "The land of plenty and the land of variety. You can eat as much as you want and get just about any food you can imagine."

"Ah, the American appetite," he said. "I've heard it's rather large."

I paused at his unexpected rudeness for an instant, then burst into laughter. "That's probably true, so you're going to have to bring me another order, Jeeves." I knew full well his name wasn't Jeeves, but he'd acted like a valet from some stuffy English picture and I couldn't help myself.

"Ava!" Bappie hissed, smothering a laugh. "You're terrible."

Jeeves got the point and moved away quickly, clearly put off by my reply.

I found myself wishing Francis were here. He'd have had a good laugh with me, probably joke around with the guy. Struck by my thoughts, I realized that was the first time I'd missed Francis the last few days. Everything had been such a trial for him lately, and then there were the letters and the threats from the studio. Away from it all, I realized just how much things had been wearing me down.

By the time Bappie and I had finished in glorious Paris and boarded our flight to Barcelona, I'd once again packed away the hateful letters and the stress back home. I was ready to take on legendary España and play the best dang nightclub singer I could. I knew this was it—I could feel it to my very core—things would be forever changed in my career. I was about to discover a real, honest-to-God star inside of me.

I was also about to risk losing the love of my life.

CHAPTER 18

FRANK

After Ava left for Europe, I drifted around New York like a loser whose girl had dumped him. I worried she'd fall out of love with me, or worse, fall in love with someone else. I was a man down on his luck and I couldn't afford to take care of her the way I wanted to. What was attractive about that? Nothing, that was what. She'd paid for many of our recent meals and excursions—she'd even paid for some of the gifts I'd given her. It was humiliating, but I'd promised to pay her back, just as soon as I was back on my feet. I hated myself for every stupid move and every wrong turn, and yet, I didn't know how to be anyone else but the person I was. A fighter, a big mouth, and a heart on two legs.

The telephone rang, rousing me from restless sleep. I knew it was going to be "one of those days" when I heard my lawyer's voice on the line.

"Nancy wants a big cut, yearly, for the rest of her life," he said.

"How much?" I asked.

"$150,000 per year for life, and that's just for the separation. Right now she still refuses to file for divorce."

I swore into the phone. "I don't care about the money. I'd take care of her and the kids anyway, but Jesus, she wants all of that now when she won't even file for divorce?"

"According to her lawyer, she wants to put aside a nest egg for the two of you. She says when no one wants you anymore and you're finished fooling around, you'll be back and she'll be prepared for the both of you."

I barked out a tense laugh. "That's insane! *She's* insane. I'm not going back. We're through."

My lawyer cleared his throat. "She believes Ava is nothing special."

I swore again. "We're crazy about each other. We're going to get married when this is over."

"You sure about that, Frank?" He paused a moment. "Have you read the papers today?"

"Should I?" I demanded, hopping around my room while I pulled on a pair of trousers.

"Ava is up to something in Spain," he said. "She's been photographed with some bullfighter. There are pictures of her everywhere, receiving flowers from him in a stadium, getting in a car together. You'd better take a look."

My blood ran cold. No, it couldn't be. I didn't believe it. We loved each other—she was the love of my life. She wouldn't betray me. And yet, my raging doubt resurfaced and I felt like I was going to be sick.

"I've got to go." My voice was strangled.

I raced to the market and bought a copy of every last newspaper and tabloid I could get my hands on with her face on it. I tore through the articles in a rush, gleaning every detail I could. Panic crashed over me as tabloid after tabloid showed her, gorgeous as ever, smiling and on the arm of a bullfighter. I closed my eyes, the pain tearing through me. I knew it. I knew if I let her out of my sight that she'd forget me. She was too beautiful, too independent and successful, and I wasn't good enough for her.

My head reeling and my heart in my throat, I headed home and dialed for a long-distance line to Tossa de Mar. I had to hear her reassurance that this wasn't what it looked like. MGM was famous for publicity stunts. Maybe this wasn't any different?

I waited . . . and waited as the line crackled and cut out a dozen times. At last, two hours later, the call went through.

When her voice came over the line, I didn't even greet her. "Who the hell is this Mario Cabré! I'm going to kill that motherf—"

"Calm down, Francis. He's my costar, that's all."

"I've seen you all over the papers. The flowers in the stadium. The two of you in a car. Did you sleep with him? I'll kill him!"

"I said it's nothing!" she shouted over the static. "Al is having me ride around with him to drum up publicity and MGM is encouraging it to distract the media from my mess with you. It appears to be working, or I wouldn't have gotten this ridiculous phone call from you. Francis, this bullfighter is about the most pompous ass you've ever met. I'm not interested. I'm in love with you, God help me."

An unexpected laugh burst from my lips. Jesus, I loved this woman to the moon and back. She owned me.

The static grew as loud as an ocean wave over the line.

"Francis! Are you there?" she shouted into the phone. "I love you!"

"I love you, too, doll. And if that man so much as lays a finger on you, I'll have his ass."

"I have to go! The crew is meeting for dinner. Call me tomorrow!"

I hung up, my fear assuaged a little but not completely. I wanted to be there, to spend some time meeting this clown in tights so I could show him a thing or two about respecting another man's woman, but I couldn't walk out on my contract at the Copacabana. It was one of the few paying gigs I still had going.

I paced the living room, fearing that Ava wasn't telling me the entire truth and was placating me. If only we could get married and truly be together, I'd never have to worry again. We'd be bound to each other, bound by hearts and souls and a vow.

A vow I was breaking with Nancy so why would it be different with Ava, my doubt whispered. And I thought I'd go mad.

The telephone rang, and I pounced on it like a cat on its prey.

"Mr. Sinatra," a soft voice came over the receiver. "I'm calling on behalf of Mr. Mayer at MGM Studios. He'd like to meet with you at your earliest convenience."

"It's not convenient," I shot back. "I'm in New York on a job."

"He needs to see you, sir. I can book a ticket for you tomorrow."

I knew what this visit would be about—Mayer wasn't pleased by the negative publicity surrounding Ava and me, and I guessed he'd give me another lecture, the old windbag. It would have to be a quick trip. I had three shows at the Copacabana on Friday night.

"Fine," I said, "but it'll have to be a quick meeting and then I'm back on a plane."

By midafternoon the next day, I landed in Los Angeles a ball of nerves. If Mayer wanted to give me a work-over, why didn't he just call? It would be a hell of a lot easier and faster. Besides, then I wouldn't have to look at his smug face. I drove to the studio in Culver City, trying to talk myself down. This time, I'd apologize if he wanted me to. It was probably time.

Inside the security gate, I parked and headed to Mayer's office. His secretary sent me in and I noticed she didn't offer me coffee this time. Swallowing my apprehension, I put on a brave face and chose a chair next to his desk.

Mayer left me waiting for nearly an hour.

Every minute that ticked by, I shifted in my chair, picked at stray threads on the armchair, looked back at the clock, my anxiety rising. Just as I'd made up my mind to leave, he limped into the office and eased himself into the chair behind his desk. He looked like he hadn't healed from his recent equestrian accident.

"Hey there, how are things?" I asked. "I see you're having trouble getting around."

"I could be better," he said, his tone curt.

So he was still hurt and in a mood. Terrific. Not wasting time, I got right to the point. "You wanted to see me."

"Don't you have something to say to me?" Mayer barked, spittle collecting in the corners of his mouth. I would have offered him a tissue but now wasn't the time. He'd think I was being a smartass, and maybe I was. I'd been guilty of that a few thousand times in my life.

"I don't know what you mean, boss," I said.

He tossed a tabloid on the desk and pointed to the article. "Read it."

I skimmed an article headlined "Sinatra Takes Aim at Mayer, Studio."

"They'll write just about anything, won't they?" I said. "They're so desperate for a real story, they have to go and print a silly joke I made and try to spin it into a drama."

"A joke," he said. "Is that what my life is to you?"

"Of course not," I said, frowning. The joke I'd made was about how Mayer had fallen off his girlfriend and not a horse, and that was why he was injured. A little crass, I supposed, but what man didn't make jokes like that among friends? The last thing I'd expected was for some weasel reporter to write about it.

"Look, Louis, it was in good fun. Don't you horse around with your pals about women?" I paused, realizing I'd used the wrong choice of words. Mayer clearly wasn't in the mood for puns.

His round face went beet red until the vein in his forehead pulsed. He looked like he was ready to blow.

"Look, that's not what I meant to say—"

"My wife," he interrupted through gritted teeth, "did not take your *joke* well. After hours of dealing with her tears and her rants, I had to sleep on the couch last night. While injured."

I bit back another snide comment about him taking up permanent residence on the couch. He'd always had a series of girlfriends and everyone in the business knew it. Instead, I forced a contrite look. "It's too bad about your wife, but—"

He held up his hand. "You can't even apologize, can you? That's the only reason I've brought you in here today. To see if you could put aside your ego for one goddamn minute and apologize for making your boss, and consequently the studio, look bad. But you can't, can you?" He stood over his desk and leaned forward on his knuckles. "And that, Frank, is how you get yourself fired. You can take your pompous ass right off my lot. And don't come back."

I fell back in my chair as if I'd been decked in the mouth. He wouldn't—he couldn't fire me.

"But my contract hasn't expired," I pleaded. "This is all a misunderstanding."

He gave me a menacing smile. "I understand perfectly. You cost the studio more than you're worth and you don't play nice with administration or the press. Your contract is null and void under the morality clause. Now get out!"

I stormed out of his office, swearing loudly in a show of bravado and insult, but the minute I slid into the front seat of my car, I felt as if I'd been beaten like a punching bag. This was it, then. I'd finally gone and done it with my big mouth. I'd reached the end of the line. No manager, no sponsor, no studio or record contract.

I was all washed up.

CHAPTER 19

FRANK

After Mayer fired me, I disappeared inside myself. I'd always been a performer, until now. Now I was nothing and no one. Now I couldn't tell what end was up. I couldn't make it through the day without my anxiety medication, or sleep without my prescription. I dissolved in a sea of Jack Daniel's and martinis, seeking the comfortable oblivion of alcohol. Yet even while wasted, I couldn't erase the worst of it all: the image of Ava cavorting all over Spain with some prick, again. She'd insisted it was for publicity, but I felt in my bones that it wasn't. It was almost impossible to get her on the phone with the poor connection, and when we did talk, it was brief and strained. As story after story hit the tabloids, I reached a new low.

I headed to the club, trying not to think about the outstanding bills on my kitchen counter, trying to talk myself into believing I'd sign with another studio one day. Most of all, I was trying not to think about Ava but was tortured by imagining another man's hands on her.

As soon as I walked in the door, I downed a couple of quick

drinks and talked myself into the three performances ahead that night. The sound of horns and woodwinds, and the piano, drifted from the main stage where the band was already warming up. I went backstage and when it was time, the lights dimmed, and the very lean audience meandered to their seats.

I plastered on a smile and attempted to summon up a little charm. As I held the microphone to my lips, I belted out the first lyrics. Oddly, my voice felt thin. I kept going, straining to shape the notes but they sagged and fell flat. After two songs, I drained a large glass of water. What was going on with me? I nodded to the band and when the next song began, the taste of blood filled my mouth.

I swallowed quickly, panic winding through me. I cast a glance at my pianist, Skitch Henderson. Concern was etched on his face, and then I knew I sounded as bad as I thought I did. I'd been putting off going to the doc for weeks, but this was the third time I'd had blood in my throat while singing. I closed my eyes for an instant and forced out the next song, all the while praying my voice would hang in there.

Tomorrow, I promised myself. I'd see the doctor tomorrow. I just needed to get through the shows tonight.

I finished the first show and the second, though they were rocky at best. I downed as much water as I could stand to lubricate my vocal cords before going on for the final show. It was two thirty in the morning, and the joint was now nearly empty. I blew out a relieved breath. For the first time ever, I was glad the audience was so scarce.

The show began and this time, we opened with the theme song from *South Pacific*. As the strings filled the room, I opened my mouth to sing "Some Enchanted Evening."

My voice faltered. No sound came out.

I looked at Skitch. His eyes widened and he gave the band the signal to backtrack a few chords, setting me up to begin again.

I focused on the back wall, trying to control my panic. That had been a fluke. I wasn't losing my voice—I couldn't be. These pitiful shows were the only thing I had left.

As the song wound up again, I opened my mouth a second time—not so much as a squeak came from my throat. My heart pounding in my ears, I gave the band the signal to stop. At the very least, I was through for the night.

I leaned to the mic and whispered, "Good night."

The audience looked bewildered as I shot across the stage, down the back stairs, and out to the exit. I couldn't believe it. My voice—gone. What if my vocal cords didn't heal? If I lost my voice for good, I didn't know what I'd do. Who I'd be. Frank Sinatra was a singer, first and foremost, and if I couldn't sing . . .

With shaking hands and a churning gut, I lit a cigarette and walked the dark streets to the hotel, my head bowed.

It took twice the medication to knock me out. When I finally woke up a groggy mess, I took myself directly to the doctor.

"You've hemorrhaged your vocal cords," the doc said as he shined a light down my throat. "You said you've been singing three shows a night, several days a week?"

I nodded, trying to speak as little as possible.

"And smoking and drinking, too?"

Another nod.

"Your vocal cords need time to heal. Take two weeks off, and no cigarettes or alcohol. This includes no talking except when absolutely necessary. This is very serious. If you don't take the time to rest, you may damage your voice permanently."

Those words struck a bolt of fear in me so strong, I nearly puked up my breakfast.

I'd give up my favorite vices for a short period of time if it meant saving my voice. I'd scale a damn mountain naked if he asked me to.

I tried to whisper a question and the doctor shook his head.

"No, Frank. If you need to communicate, write it down." He gave me a notepad and I took it, scribbling down my question. "Yes, I'll write you a doctor's note to release you from your shows," he said. "We'll start with two weeks off and see how we do. If they're healing well, we'll get you back onstage."

I perked up at the best news I'd had in a while. Sure, two weeks without work would mean a hit to my bank account, but it also meant I had a two-week break. And the first thing I'd do was book a flight to Spain to surprise Ava—and that lousy, scheming matador.

It was time to reclaim my woman.

CHAPTER 20

AVA

If London was slate gray with splashes of red and green, Spain was bright gold and ochre and brown. Tossa de Mar charmed me with its terracotta roofs and walled medieval city that had stood the test of time, and the grape vines that scrolled through the valleys and over the rocky earth beyond the town. The Mediterranean lapped against a glimmering sandy shore in vivid blue and aqua, so unlike the steely waters of the Pacific to which I'd grown accustomed. Something sultry drifted on the breeze here, and as the blazing sun dropped into the sea in the evenings and the sky twinkled with stars, the night came alive with the kind of energy I'd never experienced before, an ancient beauty full of story and song. It spoke to me in a way no other place had. The heat, the music, the simple emphasis on the day-to-day, and as Spain soaked into my skin, I felt as giddy as if I were in love.

I made friends on the set of *Pandora and the Flying Dutchman*; it wasn't difficult when you spent endless hours with the same people, day in and day out. We shared jokes, poked fun at our blunders on set, or shared a bottle of bourbon. We had more fun than anyone had a right to for something we called work, and for the first time, I truly enjoyed being an actress. I did my best with Al's demand for many, many retakes—something this director had become known for in the business. Most of all, I gave him what he wanted: a young woman who'd enchanted three men, all to their demise. Somehow that seemed fitting that I should star in such a role.

Maybe it was the combination of Spain's lurid, dark charm and my own natural lust for adventure that intoxicated me one night when Mario Cabré, the bullfighter both in the film and in real life, made his move. I was seduced by his regal features, and by the perfume of the night. I was also very, very far from a lonely—and desperate—Francis.

"Can I buy you a drink?" Mario asked, his eyes as dark as ebony, the scent of sandalwood and earth rolling off his skin. The soft glow of lamplight illuminated his crooked but beautiful smile. Conceited though he was, he was also handsome— and I was alone.

"A *vino tinto*," I replied, ordering the typical local beverage of readily available Spanish red wine.

"You're an enchanting woman," Mario said, leaning entirely too close to me.

"And you're pushy," I said, sipping my drink.

He laughed darkly. "I face life and death each day I step into that ring. You'd learn what you want very quickly, too, in that case."

I smiled slowly. "Honey, I always know what I want."

"And what is that?"

"Another drink," I said, but his smile reflected the wicked gleam I knew must be in my own eyes, too.

He motioned to the bartender.

Another round arrived instantly.

After several drinks, plenty of dancing, and a surprising proposition from the bartender that I declined, Mario and I danced all the way to bed. For me, it was all fun and exhilaration and freedom from the stifling press coverage at home. Ava the homewrecker, Ava the slut. I wasn't the one who was married and yet I was taking so much of the heat. It had been exhausting, crushing even, and now I finally felt like myself again. Wild, flying free, taking life by the horns any way I damn-well pleased.

It wasn't until the next morning when the booze had worn off and the sensation of Mario's lips and eager hands had dissipated that the guilt crashed over me. I didn't even like Mario. He was a pompous ass, and he wasn't worth losing the man I loved, no matter how hot the nights were here. Yet, the studio had other plans. They used our pairing in the picture as a way to drum up publicity and insisted we be seen all over town together. I obliged but prayed Francis wouldn't catch wind of what had really happened between me and the matador. It was all a big mistake.

During a day off from filming, Mario showed me around some of the small surrounding villages and the beautiful countryside; the cattle and markets, and a sky so wide it nearly swallowed the landscape. Afterward, we returned to my bungalow for some lunch.

As we pulled into the drive, the production assistant stood from the solitary chair on my porch. He held a clipboard and his features were arranged into an ugly pout.

"Where have you been?" he asked as I got out of the car. "We've been looking for you everywhere!"

"I wasn't aware I needed babysitting," I quipped, annoyed with the presumption I should be reachable at every moment. A day off was a day *off*.

"Frank Sinatra has been here for hours! He wanted to surprise you," he said. "We showed him around set and introduced him to the crew. He's been playing poker while waiting for you."

I felt the blood drain from my face. "You have to go, Mario. Now."

Mario glanced from me to the assistant and back again, anger turning his brown eyes almost black. He was jealous and I didn't give a damn. Mario was a flash in the pan. A little entertainment while I licked my wounds and tried to figure out what was next for Francis and me.

"Ava," he began.

"Not now, Mario," I said, shooing him off my porch like an unwanted rodent that had gotten lost. "You've got to go."

He stomped away dramatically, and I rolled my eyes as I ducked inside my cabin. I straightened it quickly, fluffed my hair, and raced back to set. There, I found Francis. He wasn't even playing poker, he was watching the others play.

At the sight of him, my heart somersaulted in my chest.

"Darling!" I exclaimed, inserting myself between him and the two men holding a full hand of cards. "What on earth are you doing here? What a wonderful surprise! Did you just get in?" I kissed him and then slid my arms around his neck, trying to hide my nervous energy. "You've gotten here just in time for my days off."

His sharp blue eyes captured mine—and he took my breath away. How had I forgotten their power in such a short time?

"Where the hell have you been, woman?" His voice came out a whisper. "I've been here for hours."

His vocal cords!

Alarmed, I asked, "Baby, what's wrong with your voice?"

He started to speak but thought better of it and scratched down a short explanation on a pad of paper.

"Oh my Lord! Well, the only good thing about this is your time off. I'm so glad you're here!"

"I missed you," he said. "Where have you been?"

I reached for his face and cradled it in my hands. "Shh, darling. Don't tax your voice. I've been out driving in the country. I had to get away from set for a while."

We stood and he picked me up off my feet, swinging me around. I squealed, gripping him tightly as a whiff of his familiar lavender cologne washed over me. When we'd stopped twirling, he kissed me hard, right in front of everyone.

Some looked away, others whistled.

"Are you hungry?" I asked, smiling. "Or do you need to sleep for a while? You must be exhausted. It's a long flight."

"Can we go somewhere alone?" he rasped.

"I know just the place," I said.

We loaded into the car—he insisted on driving—and as we pulled away, I studied him. His thinning hair, the bags under his eyes, his rail-thin frame.

"Francis, my love, you look like hell. You're thin as a ghost. What's happened?"

"Things haven't been going well." He filled me in on the performance when his voice cut out on him, and then he started in on the tabloid stories about me. Again. We talked about them every time we got on the phone, and he was quickly making me wish he'd stayed home. "I've been missing you," he rasped, "and seeing all of that trash about the bullfighter messed me up."

"You know he's nothing to me but a costar," I said, wishing like hell I hadn't slept with Mario. It wasn't even particularly satisfying. "You're the man I love. You know that. Let's talk about something else, baby. I can't believe you're here!" I squeezed his knee and snuggled up next to him, kissing softly along his jawline.

He groaned. "I'm so glad to see you."

The car rumbled over the rocky, dusty roads in silence until the town disappeared behind us and we neared the ocean.

"What else is going on?" I purred in his ear and enjoyed watching him shudder.

He coughed, cleared his throat and said, "I got fired."

"What!" I sat up straight in my seat. "From the Copacabana? Why on earth didn't you tell me?"

"Not from the Copa, from MGM. Turns out Mayer has the humor of a wet mop. I don't know, baby. I'm afraid I won't be able to book anything else. You've seen what's happening to me in the papers. And with Columbia Records . . . I'm trying to pick myself up, but I'm getting nowhere. And then there's my voice."

Regret slashed through me. Regret that I wasn't there for him when he needed me, and regret that I'd wasted time with the matador, who meant absolutely nothing to me. Francis and I were a mess together, but I loved him something awful, and he needed me right now.

I stroked his hair. "Baby, you know I'll do anything I can to help you. Maybe I can call my manager, see if there's a part we can find for you? There are other studios."

He didn't reply. We both knew MGM was the largest and one of the most powerful studios, and if they fired someone, the other studios would hear about it. They might very well choose to snub a so-called troublesome actor, too.

We drove through the countryside for an hour, catching up on friends and gossip from New York and Hollywood, and I regaled him with tales from the set from the last few weeks. By the time we arrived at a little tavern on the beach, we were laughing again—and we were as together as ever. At the restaurant, we ordered a Spanish aperitif and the owner brought plate after plate of tapas: oily fish, grilled octopus, mushrooms *a la plancha*. By the time we opened our second bottle of wine, the difficulties of the last few weeks had faded and all that remained was the way this exasperating, darling man looked at me and the way my heart responded when he was near. I might not have been a romantic, but my love for him made me a believer. Perhaps when we married, the fears and doubts—and the circus in the media—wouldn't matter a lick and we could get on with being in love.

I knew he needed to hear me say it, to reassure him.

"I love you, baby."

His eyes softened and he leaned in to kiss me. After, he reached for the wine bottle on the table and refilled both of our glasses. "So who is this jerk I keep seeing in the papers?"

"Who? Mario?" I feigned an innocent expression.

"You two are everywhere. I know you've said it's a publicity stunt but—"

"Darlin'." I brought his hand to my lips and kissed it. "You know how the press is. We're making a movie together, and that's all I have to say about him. I'll never see him again after this and that's fine by me. He's a bit of a horse's ass, truth be told." I held up my glass. "Let's toast, to our love."

He hesitated a moment and raised his glass.

"Together again," I said with a smile.

"Together for always."

He seemed appeased—for now—and we enjoyed our first night together in my bungalow. First thing the next morning, we left for a romantic getaway in the country. We watched the landscape undulate with verdant meadows or olive groves and endless yellow flowers that bloomed in the sun, until we were hours from Tossa or anywhere I recognized. We stopped in a tiny town, if one could call it that, where there was nothing but a general store. Not even a gas pump could be found within miles of the place. Luckily, we'd thought to fill up before we'd left.

Francis brought up Mario again in the car, but I brushed away the conversation like a noisome fly. We didn't need to go over it again and again, especially since his visit would be short. We needed to focus on us. We pulled into the drive of a small house I'd rented that faced a vast field covered in scrub and dotted with trees. The land was wild and unsettled and the vastness of the sky bore down upon us. It reminded me a little of Palm Springs, though far more temperate, and we were both enchanted by the untamed beauty of the place.

I'd arranged for someone in the village to stock the refrigerator with the basics before we arrived, and to the Spanish, it appeared the basics meant olives, eggs, potatoes, a little cheese, and some beef. Two fresh loaves of crusty bread lay in paper sheaths on the countertop next to a long-necked bottle of olive oil and a half dozen bottles of red wine. They'd definitely gotten that right. We could go to the general store if we needed more later.

"I brought some fruit, too," I said, taking some oranges from my bag and setting them on the counter. "And whiskey."

Francis smiled. "My girl knows what I like."

He brought in the suitcases and left them in the hall. Then he reached for me.

I ran my hands over his shoulders and chest, and every cell in my body tingled. He didn't hesitate and swept me into his arms, carrying me to the bed. We made love tenderly, and lay together afterward, telling stories and planning for the future.

Francis reached for a pack of cigarettes, shook one loose, and put it in his mouth. He handed another to me and lit the ends for each of us with his gold lighter. After we finished a smoke, we migrated to the kitchen. I poured us each a glass of red wine and cut some cheese and a hunk of bread. We were enraptured with each other all over again and everything felt right. I was glad he was here.

"I've brought something for you," he said.

"A gift?" I smiled, sitting at the dining table, my white silk robe tied loosely at my waist.

He reached into his luggage and pulled out six bottles of Coca-Cola.

I laughed in surprise. "Francis! I can't believe you carried that for me all this way."

"You said you missed it, and I want my lady to have whatever she wants."

"Thank you, baby." I kissed him. "It'll be hard to ration it!"

"Well, I think my other gift will make up for the impermanence of that one." He pulled a velvet box from his bag and placed it in front of me on the table. I grinned, a ribbon of warmth winding through me at his expression of anticipation. He really was so adorable sometimes, so vulnerable and loveable.

I opened the box, eager to see what he'd bought—but it was empty. "What's this about? Is this another of your jokes?"

He laughed—a contagious, musical sound I'd missed so much I nearly ached with it. A happy Francis was the most delicious, charming man in the world.

"I wanted to give you something beautiful, but it got impounded by the Spanish authorities at the airport. Apparently you need permission for expensive imports." He rolled his eyes. "You'll have to pick it up when you fly out to London."

"Is it a necklace?"

"Yes."

I kissed him again. "I'm sure I'll love it."

"The next time I see you, I want to make love to you with the necklace on."

"And nothing else," I added wickedly.

He gave me a boyish smile.

We ate and after, we fell into another hour of bliss. I was his again, and thoughts of Mario Cabré were as distant as the horizon.

We belonged together, Francis and me, and no one could deny, we were magic.

CHAPTER 21

AVA

A few weeks later, I hated to say goodbye to glorious, steamy, intoxicating Spain, but I was also thrilled to be heading back to London for a while. We still needed to film the movie's interior shots before we headed home. The American dollar was strong in Europe so filming abroad made sense. There were also the tax breaks on the income earned while there—if we waited out the extra mandatory weeks to make them worthwhile. Staying on suited me fine. I had fallen in love with Europe and regretted having to return to the shark-infested waters of Hollywood, or to the United States at all. The only problem was my job and home were there. And so was Francis.

I found myself marveling at the culture shock I felt after months in a place with heavy religious trappings but also a wildness that infused the air. In general, the English were rarely direct and didn't prefer to be overly emotional about things unless in private—the opposite of my experience with the Spanish, and the opposite of me. And yet, no one had a better sense of humor than the English; the jokes were sometimes biting and other times raunchy enough to make your toes curl.

I adored it, and it didn't take long before I loved being in London as much as I had Spain.

Francis returned for a visit a month later, this time to perform a series of shows at the London Palladium. He brought a new friend with him.

"His name is Rags, after my friend Rags Ragland," he said, holding out an adorable puppy with large ears and a long body with caramel, black, and white fur. "He's yours, baby."

Rags jumped into my lap, yapped happily, and licked my face. I gathered him to me, scrubbed him around the ears and on his belly. "Hello, Rags," I cooed. "You're the cutest thing I've ever seen. Is he a corgi?"

"Yep," Frank said.

"I've always wanted a dog."

"I know, doll." He kissed my nose and turned on the shower as hot as it would go, then hung his midnight-blue suit on a hanger on the curtain rod to steam out any wrinkles from traveling.

When it was time to get dressed, I noticed him fumbling with his tie before huffing in frustration.

"Let me, baby," I said, putting Rags on the floor.

"I'm nervous," he said.

"I know, but it'll be great. You'll be great," I kissed him on the cheek.

He'd finally booked a show with CBS and would be making a tidy sum for the next two years. The fortnight at the Palladium before returning home would kick off his new gig. He was relieved to be able to pay down some of his debt, and to be able to meet Nancy's separation demands. More than anything the money could provide, though, the new show helped his wounded pride. Still, he wanted to nail his opening night, to prove to the press that his voice had recovered and that he was headed for the top again. I didn't blame him.

I played with Rags for a while after he left, and then dressed for the evening. I slipped on a green dress with black and white trim in a geometric pattern that accentuated my waist and set my hair in rollers. As I finished getting ready, I thought of my director's warnings. Mario Cabré hadn't taken my hints about ending things and now had plans to share—at the Spanish Institute in London—some love poetry he'd written about me that was sure to embarrass the hell out of him, or at the very least, embarrass me. I wasn't sure if he was off his rocker, or if he was just melodramatic—I'd cut him off weeks ago—but he'd turned out to be needy and insecure. Now I ignored Mario completely, even though we still had interior shots to do together for the picture. If I was portrayed as a black widow in the press, I might as well live up to the reputation. Besides, if I reacted at all, Francis would combust.

When I arrived at the Palladium, a renowned and beautiful theater in the West End on Argyll Street, I was shown to my seat amid the rows of velvet red chairs at the front and center where Francis could see me. He'd been good about resting his voice, at least from singing—Lord knew nothing could keep the man from talking—and he was ready to go. I couldn't wait to see him nail it.

The lights dimmed and the partition lifted. Stage lights burned bright along the edges of the platform and a spotlight found Francis in the center of the stage. The band began to play and with his characteristic swagger across the stage in his impeccable suit, my man began to sing. His opening notes sent shivers over my skin. He had a voice, no doubt about it, but it was his delivery that set him apart. He communed with the audience, his rhythm at times speechlike, and at others, melodious and so full of heartache that tears shined in the eyes of every person in the audience. He believed what he sang; he felt the lyrics to the bottom of his soul, and he shared a piece of it with all of us. How could anyone deny him in the face of so much beauty? Lord knew I couldn't, and I didn't want to. I smiled as he worked across the stage with his microphone, his voice carrying through a silent room riveted by his performance and by him. It appeared England hadn't given up on Francis the way much of America had.

When he found me in the crowd, he held my gaze and sang the next song as if I were the only person in the room. "It Had to Be You," one of the first songs I'd heard him sing in person, years ago. How could a voice convey so much emotion? I laughed quietly to myself, and I caught the nearly imperceptible smile at the edges of his mouth.

As the night progressed, he physically relaxed while one wonderful song after another poured from his lips. His stint in London would do him good, help him regain his confidence. When the final song began, he half-smiled and sang with all his heart. This time, though, he looked past me.

I frowned and glanced over my shoulder.

Several rows behind me sat Marilyn Maxwell, one of Frank's old flames—the woman he'd bought a diamond bracelet for that Nancy had found and assumed was for her. It had made the tabloids and I'd heard all about it through the grapevine at the studio once upon a time.

Marilyn gave me a sweet smile, and I felt my face flush. Perhaps he hadn't been singing to me all along but to her, and I'd

STRANGERS IN THE NIGHT 181

been mistaken. My stomach soured. As Francis wrapped the song, the audience applauded, and the house lights went up, I made my way to the bar, trying desperately to avoid Marilyn and to keep myself from crying. I'd thought we were back on track—that we really were meant to be together after all of the awful scrutiny, after Mario and the time apart. But maybe Francis had played me for a fool the whole time.

Shortly, he joined me at the bar.

"How did I look up there?" he said. "I felt great. It's been too long since I sang to a real audience."

"Great. I'm sure Marilyn Maxwell thought so, too," I said, my tone clipped.

His brow arched and he laughed. "Don't be ridiculous. She's a thing of the past."

"Then why did you make eyes at her?" I said, my anger flaring. The vodka had worked its way through my system and suddenly I was ready to go to battle. "I know other women want you, Francis. You don't need to rub my nose in it every chance you get!"

"What the hell are you talking about?" he said, suddenly looking tired. "You're ruining my night."

"And you ruined a perfectly good cocktail." I downed it, slammed the glass on the countertop, and headed to the door.

He didn't stop me—neither did he follow me. I staggered into the night, ignoring the steady drizzle from the sky. It suited my mood. As I slowly became soaked to the bone, I looked for a place to huddle until I decided what was next. I spotted a newsstand and ducked under the awning to wait for a taxi. My gaze wandered over the news rack and one magazine headline jumped out at me:

"Ava Gardner Seduces Frank Sinatra in London While Wife Cries at Home"

I let out a frustrated wail. I was tired of being the woman with the scarlet letter and tired of being second place in Francis's life. And yet, when I considered a life without him, I felt a little like dying. I loved him too much for my own good.

"Everything alright, miss?" the vendor asked while picking at his teeth with a toothpick.

"Not really."

"Here, this will help." He held out a chocolate bar. "My wife says chocolate makes everything better."

"Thank you kindly," I said, hearing the echo of my mama's admonitions about manners in my words. The last thing I wanted was a chocolate bar, but it didn't hurt to be nice.

"How about I get you a taxi?"

"That's exactly what I need."

The man darted out into the lightly falling rain, put two fingers in his mouth, and whistled loudly. A car zoomed toward him—just as Francis darted outside of the theater.

"Where the hell do you think you're going?" He ran toward me, his hair turning black with rainwater.

I dodged his hand as he reached for me. "Leave me alone, Francis."

"Jesus, Ava, what's your problem? Doesn't my word mean anything to you?"

Guilt needled me as I thought of Mario Cabré. I had no room to be angry, especially about his word, but I couldn't seem to help myself. Francis made me insanely jealous—something I'd never felt before in my life—and I became incensed and unfair and desperate to torture him the way I was tortured.

"You and your women is my problem," I shot back. "And all those stupid headlines! Everyone hates me now because of you! Lana was right. You're never going to leave that damned wife of yours, are you?"

"I did leave Nancy! What are you talking about!" he demanded, eyes flashing. Rainwater dripped from his nose.

"Don't give me that," I spat. "It's not as if moving out changes much. You already lived apart from her most of the time. You still haven't filed for divorce!"

"Stop this right now!" He yanked on my arm and I shoved back. He stumbled, soaking his shoes in a puddle.

I used the distraction to my advantage and jumped into a taxi that had just pulled up.

"Haul ass!" I said, slamming the door.

"Miss?" the driver looked confused.

"Giddy up! Go!"

We screeched away from the curb, but I couldn't help myself—I turned around to look out the back window. Francis stood in the now-pouring rain, watching after me.

I remembered all the other stories I'd read about Francis in the papers, everyone's warnings. He might be separated from Nancy, but would he ever really sign on the dotted line? I just didn't know. The only thing I knew was how much my heart ached pulling away as he stood in the rain, and how lonely my world was without the fiery, infuriating, brilliant Frank Sinatra in it. Still, I had to go, and to keep him at arm's length for a while—until he realized I meant business. No other women, no Nancy.

Either he was finished with his wife and filed divorce papers, or he was finished with me.

CHAPTER 22

FRANK

I didn't know what to do with that woman sometimes. Ava loved me better than any man deserved and then turned around and walked out on me when she felt like it. Her jealousy reassured me as much as it made me steaming mad, and yet, she was right to be jealous. I thought of the woman I'd hired last night while Ava stonewalled me, refusing to take my calls, and the girls I'd had while she was in Spain. Prostitutes fit the bill; they did their job and left. Sometimes a man just needed a professional without any hassles. It was Ava I loved without question, but when she was gone, I needed a reprieve. And now, more than ever, with the stress from her walking out on me and with Nancy ignoring my request for a divorce, I needed a way to relieve the pressure.

The only good news was we were both back in the U.S., even if Ava was on the opposite coast, filming a new picture while I stuck it out in New York.

The on-air light switched off.

I removed my headset and motioned to the band to signal that we were finished. Everyone began to wipe down their instruments and pack up. Smoke clouded the soundstage—and my head. The bourbon didn't help much either, but it had been another canned radio show at CBS Studios and if I didn't drink something before the show, I could scarcely make it through the humiliation. I'd thought the show might be my saving grace, but it hadn't been. My records still weren't selling and my ratings were poor. The pit in my stomach told me what I already knew: soon, this show would be canceled like the others. I was at rock bottom, which meant one thing: I'd need to reach out to the Boys in Hoboken, see if they could get me a gig or two at the clubs in the city to pay the bills. I didn't like being in their debt, but it was better than having the IRS haul me to jail.

I put on a hasty smile for the producer, who didn't bother to so much as grimace back, and I knew I was definitely screwed. My head down, hands in my pockets, I walked to my dressing room, not knowing what was next or if there *was* anything next.

On my way, Bobby, a new pal I'd met who worked in the studio, gave me a wave. "Hiya, Frank. Hey, you might want to look at this." He gave me a folded newspaper.

"Nah, man, I try not to look at them," I said.

"You might want to today." Bobby's bright eyes were serious even if his striped tie was crooked and his suit was wrinkled to hell. The guy needed to meet an iron. "It's the third one I've seen like it," he continued.

My stomach dipped. Though not in any detail, Bobby knew about my troubles with Ava. I'd confided in him a little over drinks one night. And I wasn't ready to see her splashed all over the papers with some other man—again.

Reluctantly, I took the paper and skimmed the article. "They're comparing us to Romeo and Juliet?" I said with a smirk. "Things didn't end well for those kids, did they? I think I'd prefer them to call us something else."

Bobby chuckled. "No one has ever been more of a Romeo than you are, Sinatra."

"That's not good news for me."

We both chuckled.

"Anyway, you're missing the point," Bobby said. "This means people are starting to side with you and Ava. This whole Saint Nancy business is through. They see her as someone trapping you in a marriage that isn't right. She fell in love with the wrong man and is keeping you from your true love and such. This is good, right?"

"Maybe?" I was skeptical of anything the media wrote so I didn't see how this would help.

"Seems to me that the public is starting to think you aren't the cad they thought you were. And Ava is just a woman in love who can't be with her man. That's got to be a good thing."

I grimaced. "Maybe, but it's too late to save my reputation. MGM already dumped me, and I'm not sure I'll be here much longer either."

"There will be others, man. Hang in there." He cupped my shoulder with his hand in a show of solidarity. "You're too good to fall off the map."

I gave him a wan smile. "Thanks, Bobby. I appreciate that. Have a good night. I'm heading out."

The truth was, it was hard to feel optimistic about anything. I felt lower than low and I didn't see any way up.

I lit a cigarette and walked several city blocks, weariness seeping into my bones. The last time we'd spoken, she'd said she was sick of Nancy being between us, tired of being pulled into a negative spotlight. But maybe Bobby was right. Maybe things were turning around on that front, at least. Maybe. I couldn't tell Ava if she wouldn't answer my calls.

I stamped out my cigarette and jammed my hands in my pockets. The night was alive; neon lights buzzed like a thousand bees, taxi drivers honked their irritation as they weaved through traffic, and the subway trains rumbled beneath my feet. Sometimes I still couldn't believe things had gone so fantastically bad so quickly. The show ratings were an embarrassment, and every new poor review or canceled film was a dagger in the gut. I was like a dog that kept getting kicked and no one gave a damn if I had broken bones or a bleeding head. I hated feeling sorry for myself—it was weak and I couldn't stand feeling weak—but after so many endings, so many disappointments and wrong turns, I couldn't see a way out.

I stepped over a slightly ajar sewer cap that spewed a rush of steam into the air before I rounded the corner. The Paramount Theatre came into view, concertgoers gathering out front and spooling down the block in a long line. They were boisterous, excited about the night's show. I glanced up at the marquee. The headliner was Eddie Fisher? I stopped in my tracks, bewildered. I had more talent in my pinky finger than that hack had in his whole body. They'd once loved me at the Paramount. Now they wouldn't return my calls—but they made Eddie Fisher a headliner? Made me want to kick something.

I walked past the crowd, hoping I might be recognized— and I was recognized alright.

I caught a man's eye and his smile faded. He cupped his

mouth with his hands and booed at me. It caught on like a match to an old newspaper. Jeering followed the booing and I picked up my pace, anxious to get the hell out of there.

"That's right! Get lost, Frankie! This isn't your show!"

"Your music is rotten!"

"Where's your whore tonight, Sinatra?"

All I'd accomplished before didn't matter, it seemed. My music, my pictures. I was utterly forgettable, a passing fancy, and everyone had moved on to the next best thing. Everyone but me.

My head ached as a black fog rolled over me. I walked on, not seeing, not hearing, only feeling. I gasped in air as my pulse thumped in my ears. I could hardly breathe beneath the crushing weight of my bleak reality: not knowing where to go next, of who to be.

"Mr. Sinatra" a voice called to me in what felt like hours later.

I turned in the direction of the voice. A doorman in navy livery with brass buttons and pristine white gloves stared back at me.

"Aren't you going to come inside?" he asked.

I looked at him, confused a moment, and then realized I'd passed Manie's apartment, where I was staying, several times already.

"Oh, yeah. Thanks, man."

"Lost in your thoughts?" he asked.

"You could say that," I replied. "Or just lost."

In the apartment, I poured a large glass of Jack Daniel's and sat on the sofa in the dark for a long time, refilling my glass twice, three times. I imagined Ava sitting next to me, her gardenia perfume, the sound of her laugh when she was up to something. Ava wrapped in a bedsheet, her hair wild around her beautiful face, eyes bright.

I picked up the phone and dialed her number again. It rang five times, ten, fifteen. I hung up and called again. Nothing but her silence—that had been her way since our argument in London. Silence. Avoidance.

As I drained another glass, I staggered through the hallway and flipped on the light. Catching sight of my reflection in a mirror as I passed, I paused to study the gaunt person in the glass. I barely recognized myself. My cheekbones protruded from my face, and deep purple smudged beneath two lifeless eyes. I didn't know where to go from here.

Maybe there wasn't anywhere to go?

I headed to the kitchen, flipping on the light as I slugged another gulp and I choked on the burn in my throat. I'd had too much too fast but what did I care? I had nothing holding me back, nothing to live for. I stood over the stovetop a long minute, the image of the spiral eyes blurring until I felt dizzy. I couldn't take it anymore. The pain was unbearable.

I turned on the gas, kneeled, and pulled the oven door open, sticking my head inside. As the smell of gas filled the oven, I inhaled—and coughed. It could all be over in a matter of minutes. I'd never face another humiliation, never suffer another night feeling like I was so alone that I echoed with the emptiness. I closed my eyes and inhaled again. My head grew foggy after another minute and I lay my face down on the edge of the oven rack, ignoring the cold metal digging into the flesh of my cheek. Spots formed behind my eyes.

From behind me came the sound of a door. The flicker of light.

"Frank! Jesus, man, what are you doing? Holy shit!" Manie's voice.

Everything was hazy, my vision blurred.

I was vaguely aware of being pulled to the floor, half carried, half dragged to the bed, and everything else shifted around me like a ride on a merry-go-round.

When I woke minutes later, Manie stood over me.

"You just scared the hell out of me," Manie said. "You've got to get it together, Frank. It's time to see a psychiatrist."

Despite the fog in my brain, I nodded. "Okay," I rasped. "I'll do it."

Maybe that was what I needed, someone to talk to who could help me see my way out of the dark. Maybe. Maybe there was nothing anyone could do. I didn't know but for now, I'd give it a shot.

CHAPTER 23

AVA

Manie told me about Francis. Worried sick, I called Francis several times a day, even from set. That night in London, our argument about Marilyn, and then my pride that followed . . . it had been a stupid fight. I didn't know why I let Francis's old flames get the better of me. The man clearly loved me, and when I could see past my jealousy and the vodka, I knew that truth to the depths of my soul. Still, Nancy's stubborn refusal to let him go and the nastiness in the papers had worn me down. For now, the fact that he was still in New York was for the best. It gave the rumors more time to cool.

To keep myself distracted, I spent a lot of time out on the town, meeting with friends. One night after a house party, several of us headed to a club to go dancing. Lena Horne was among the group and she was a riot, smart as a tack and a real talent at singing and acting, too. We had a grand old time together, stirring up trouble. She liked a party as much as I did, as it turned out.

I clinked my glass against hers. We were sweaty after an

hour of swirling around the dance floor and decided to take a break for a fresh drink.

Lena sipped from her cold martini glass. Her hair was brushed into a dark wavy bob framing her face, her lips blazed red, and her pretty little dimples made her seem innocent and sweet. "My manager said they won't play my films in the south, or my roles have to be reedited with a white woman in my place," she said. "Some towns and theaters even boycott Black performers."

Lena was a gorgeous Black woman with fair skin, from a well-off and well-educated family, and yet, she was treated like a pariah in certain circles. Just like with my Reenie, it made me furious to see the way she was treated.

"That's appalling," I said. "Have you thought of hiring a new manager? Maybe someone else will have better luck beating down doors on your behalf."

She shook her head. "For now, we're taking things as they come. I'd rather sing, but the NAACP has been pressuring me to stay in Hollywood to promote their agenda. I'm all for equality on screen, of course, and everywhere else for that matter, but I also have to look out for myself, too, you know? I just signed a club tour contract. It might complicate things for my next movie role, but I figured I'll cross that bridge when I get there."

"You've got a wonderful voice," I said, laying my hand on hers. "In *Words and Music*, you were stunning. I could listen to you sing all day, baby."

She smiled brightly. "You're too kind, little sister."

I smiled at her nickname for me. "You know I speak only the truth."

"I know, I know." She winked and took another sip from her glass. "I leave next week, after we hear back about *Show Boat*."

I hesitated an instant. "You know they're putting me up for that role, too?"

The role in *Show Boat* was a tragic singer of mixed race who could pass for a white woman. She was driven to drink because her marriage to a white man was illegal and caused all kinds of complications. It made a lot more sense to cast Lena for the role, both because of who she was and her singing skills, but I also knew there was nothing sensical or fair about Hollywood. I'd like to land the role, it was true, but I wasn't one to begrudge anyone their success or what they deserved. Never had been, never would be, especially for a friend.

Lena nodded. "I did know, yes, and if they pass me over, it may as well go to you. At least I know you'll do a fine job."

"No one has your voice, baby," I said. "I couldn't possibly compete."

"I'd desperately like to land that role. It was made for me, wasn't it? If I don't get it, I'd rather be out on the road than in Hollywood," she said. "I'm not a big fan of this town."

"Well that makes two of us," I said.

We set down our drinks as the next song began and she grabbed my hand and led me to the dance floor. We giggled like schoolgirls but swished our skirts like vixens, dancing until the lights went up and the club closed down.

In the end, MGM offered me the part, and Lena was as gracious as ever, wishing me luck and promising me a night out when she was next in town. I hoped she truly hadn't felt slighted. We were neighbors and friends, and I'd learned that in Hollywood, real friends were hard to come by. Meanwhile, the fact that I was chosen over someone with superior singing skills made me self-conscious. I was no chanteuse, after all, so I reached out to Phil Moore, an old friend and a rehearsal pianist. He didn't hesitate to help me out, the lamb.

One evening after rehearsals at the studio, I headed to his apartment for a lesson.

"Come on in, Ava," he said with a smile.

"Thanks for doing this, Phil," I said. "I don't want to make a fool of myself."

"Anytime." He ushered me into the small studio space in his apartment. His piano was nearly as big as the room itself. The only other furniture was a small bench and a pair of identical, hideous lamps with clunky brass feet that looked like the claws of a gnarled old man.

"Do you have the music with you?" he asked.

"I do." I handed him a folder with the sheets of music.

He ran through several practice takes and when it was time to begin, the familiar stage fright reared its ugly head again. I tried to muster my courage but every time I should begin, my heart stuck in my throat and my words faltered.

"I don't think I can sing in front of you, Phil," I said after the fifth attempt.

He laughed in disbelief. "Isn't that why you're here?"

"Can we turn off the lights?"

"I suppose I know the music well enough, sure."

Under the cover of darkness, I practiced my range and sang my heart out with Phil, then also later at home in the shower, and finally, with the rest of the team on the demo recordings. I may not have had the range of a professional, but my whiskey tenor had a style all its own. I was proud of it after so much hard work.

On my way to set one day, I parked and walked to the back lot. Behind the studio building was a lake that had been dug long ago for another picture and now, with its trees and muddy banks, truly looked like a real one. It would serve as the Mississippi River for our production, a stretch if you asked me, but anyone watching the picture probably wouldn't notice, especially since the life-size model of the boat was what held the eye. The boat was the largest set prop in Hollywood production history, and as I peered up at the enormous structure, the paddlewheel at its back, and its two towering smokestacks, I could believe it.

We did a few takes of different scenes and after hours of shooting, an argument broke out between the producer and the director. He waved us off, so we took a break.

"Back to my place, for a little fun?" I asked my costars, offering my dressing room as the usual party location.

Everyone mumbled noncommittally and I left, secretly glad for the snatch of alone time. I knew this picture was going to be something special—I could feel it—so I'd been throwing myself into my performance day after day, and I was plum tired. I needed a little peace and quiet—but apparently that wasn't to be.

As I opened the door to my dressing room, a telephone call was put through to my line.

"This is Ava," I said, leaning back in my chair. I attempted to smother a yawn.

"Hi, Angel." Francis's New Jersey accent filled my ear. "Why haven't you been returning my calls? I'm dying over here."

"I hope you don't mean that literally," I said a bit too sharply.

He laughed, and I appreciated that. The man had a dark sense of humor. "How's the shoot?"

"I'm working hard, but it's coming along."

"I miss you. When are you coming to see me?"

Between my exhaustion from a long week's work and the thrashing I'd taken in the media, I wasn't in any hurry to book a flight east, even if I loved him. Even if I missed him terribly, and I did.

"I'll see you when you file for divorce," I said. "I'm nobody's mistress, Francis. I can't go on like this. *We* can't go on like this. Things will never get better if we can't really be together."

"What do you expect me to do? Hold Nancy at gunpoint to make her file and sign the papers?"

"For starters," I snapped, losing my patience. "Figure it out, Francis. I'm sick of being painted as a whore in the papers."

"I guess you haven't seen the latest? Now we're Romeo and Juliet. The whore is Nancy."

"You're kidding," I said, opening the drawer in my dressing table, brushing aside a scrap of royal blue silk and a few pieces of costume jewelry encrusted with paste jewels to find the bottle of vodka.

"Juliet is the east and I am the sun," he said jokingly.

I softened, laughed at his attempt at poetry. "My romantic is at it again, but I need to go, baby. I need to focus on my part. It's awkward to act in scenes where we've already recorded the songs. I feel like an idiot lip-syncing."

"You'll nail it, Angel. You always do," he said. "Call me tonight?"

I supposed it was time to thaw a bit. I'd frozen Francis out for a couple of weeks now, and the truth was, I wished I had him in my bed at night and his shoulder to lean on while I was working my tail off to please the director.

"I will."

"I was hoping you'd say that."

I threw back a shot of vodka and walked back to set. Joe Brown and Kathryn Grayson, the other leads, were already there, but most of the rest of the cast hadn't returned yet, so I bummed a cigarette off a cameraman.

A moment later, the director sidled up next to me. "Ava, I'd like you to meet someone. This is Annette Warren."

"Well, hello there, Annette." I gave her a big smile. "I'd offer you a smoke, but I borrowed one myself."

She smiled, hesitated an instant, and held out her hand to shake mine. "Hi, Miss Gardner. Gosh, I'm your biggest fan. I've seen all of your pictures."

"Why, thank you." I gave her a genuine smile. She was pretty if a little unsure of herself, with her shy smile and hunched shoulders, and a dress that was too plain for her face.

"Annette will be the stand-in for your singing parts," George said. "So you don't have to worry about anything, Ava. I know how nervous you've been about them."

I dropped the woman's hand as if it were on fire. "What do you mean she's my stand-in? I've trained for weeks. I thought the recording went well."

He cleared his throat and looked down at his clipboard. "The team decided the best thing for the picture would be for Annette to sing your part." He shifted from one foot to the other. The lout was too weak to even meet my eye and give it to me straight. "She's experienced," he said, "and she has a perfect soprano. Her voice coupled with your face will only make the picture more of a success."

I felt my cheeks flame with fury. "Is this some kind of joke? These other clowns"—I waved my hands at the cast that had started to trickle back to set—"Are no better than me. Do they have doubles, too?"

He frowned. "Come on, Ava. Don't be like that. Listen—"

But I was no longer listening. I stormed off the stage, grabbed my purse from my dressing room, downed another shot of vodka, and headed straight for my car. A professional soprano, my ass. I had worked for weeks! For this? If they'd wanted someone else's voice, why the hell had they chosen me in the first place? My character was a woman born on the levee, a sad drunk living a simple life. My sultry voice matched the part!

I turned over the ignition, revved the engine, and squealed out of the parking lot.

As I torpedoed down the boulevard, I pictured the director listening to my recordings and deciding they were subpar, and I flushed with embarrassment. I hated being incompetent more than just about anything and worked hard to prove myself, and yet, MGM seemed to continually remind me that I wasn't good enough. I wanted to scream.

I drove to the beach in Pacific Palisades, parallel parked haphazardly, and took off my shoes, throwing them in the back seat. As I walked on the sand, I listened to the waves crashing and felt the cold, clear surf as it swirled over my feet. I looked ahead at the mountains where they tapered to the ocean. I didn't understand it. I was given starring roles by practically every other studio in Hollywood and now that I was finally starring in bigger roles for MGM—and making them plenty of money—they still treated me like nobody special. Like I was second-rate. As I walked across the beach, my anger eventually turned to pity. I liked acting. I really did, but I didn't like the business, and I disliked it enough to dream about giving up acting entirely. If I had any other skills, any other way to make money, perhaps I would.

I watched the sun streak the sky in a riot of orange and searing pink that any painter would be jealous of and suddenly realized how alone I felt. The one person who understood me better than anything—who understood the hard knocks and the way the business gnawed away at your soul better than anyone—was very far away.

I wanted Francis. I *needed* Francis.

I didn't go back to set for three days. I ignored the telephone calls, the telegrams, the insistence I return. I tortured myself with thoughts of what they'd said about my voice and my performance, and I grew angrier and more despondent by the day. I didn't want to finish the film and was seriously considering quitting, even if I was penalized with a fine from the studio.

I called Francis and talked to him about it at length to keep me from doing something stupid.

"At least they'll include your recording on the soundtrack," Francis said. "You'll get your royalties. And people will still hear you sing."

He was right and I was sulking, I knew. What was done was done, and at least I'd be paid for my role, even if MGM still treated me as an inferior. Besides, I didn't want to pay the fine I'd have to face if I quit.

"You need to go back in there." Francis's voice was somehow firm and gentle at the same time. In this moment I was so glad to have him in my corner. "Finish it up, baby. Don't walk out on this now. I know you'll regret it."

He was right, I would. And so, I did finish the picture.

No sooner had it been edited and was ready for screening, my trepidation returned, and I doubted myself all over again. What if the movie was panned? There had been so much negative press lately. Betsy Nobody from Iowa might give the movie a terrible review just because she saw me as a homewrecker. The studio might want to cut their losses rather than take another chance on me. I worried myself sick over how the film would be received and finally decided the only thing that would make me feel better was seeing the man I loved.

I flew to New York to be with Francis. He took good care of me. We had dinners out, lazed in bed, and passed the time until weeks later, at last, the time came for the early reviews of *Show Boat*.

To my relief, praise flooded in from nearly everyone who had attended the screenings.

"Ava Gardner stole the show."

"Ava Gardner was so wonderful."

"Miss Gardner excels anything she has done in the past."

"Best scenes, Ava singing."

I grinned widely when I read that one. "Did you see that? The best scenes are of me singing. Poo on the director!"

"I told you it would work out, didn't I?" Francis kissed me. "You're a talented woman. They'd be blind not to see it."

"Want to see another way I'm talented?" I asked, giving him my best heavy-lidded vixen look.

He pulled me to him, and I sat atop his lap, kissing him deeply. The next thing we knew, our clothes littered the floor. Afterward, I curled into him, laying my head on his chest. He smelled of musk and lavender and the salty scent of sweat.

"Francis?"

"Hmm," he said, twirling a lock of my hair around his finger.

"Why won't you introduce me to your parents?"

I felt his body stiffen beneath me. "We aren't getting along right now."

"What happened between you?" I looked up at him, our faces only inches apart.

His eyes had hardened. "I borrowed some money from Dolly, my ma. I've been in a bad way here and there, and right now, I don't want to fight about it. I'll pay her back as soon as I'm flush again. Working this idiotic show on CBS will get me there soon enough. I should be able to pay her in a month or so."

"If we're going to get married, I have to meet your parents," I pressed. "And we're both here in the city right now. Besides, maybe she'll help us convince Nancy to move on."

"No. I'm not going. *We're* not going. No way," he said, sliding out from under me, pulling on his trousers, and hastily buckling them. He stalked into the other room and returned with two snifters of whiskey.

I sat up and reached for the glass, taking a sip. He threw his back in one gulp.

"It's not just the money," he said. "Ma never knows when to let something lie. We'll be quarreling before I've taken off my hat, and I'd likely get a good slap or two to the skull."

His mama had hit him? I'd heard about plenty of less-than-happy fathers knocking their kids around from time to time, but rarely a mother. I peered at him over the rim of my glass.

"Surely your mama has changed," I said.

He shook his head. "You think an Italian mother has changed?" He barked out an angry laugh. "You don't know Dolly Sinatra."

"No, I don't," I replied tightly. "But I'd like to."

Maybe Francis was wrong about her—or maybe not. In general I didn't believe we changed as people. That had been my experience my whole life. We were who we were and the sooner we accepted that, the faster we could get on with our lives and stop worrying about what everyone else thought. And yet I was a complete hypocrite, given how on edge I'd been waiting for the *Show Boat* reviews.

"Are you embarrassed by me?" I asked.

"Of course not!" he said crossly, drawing his brow into a deep frown. He walked into the other room, signaling the end to the conversation, or so he thought.

I pulled his shirt over my head and followed him. He was in the midst of pouring another whiskey, this time two fingers deep.

"I want to meet her, and your daddy," I insisted, crossing my arms over my chest. "You're not going to talk me out of it, baby."

"I don't have to talk you in or out of anything." He left his glass on the countertop. "Now, let's not ruin a perfectly good night arguing about my parents. I'll introduce you to them another time."

I was never one to back down just because anyone said I should. When Francis hopped into the shower, I called the operator and had them put me through to the Sinatra residence in Hoboken.

"Hi, Dolly, this is Ava. Ava Gardner. Francis and I are here in town and would love to pay you a visit. Are you free this week?"

I listened to Dolly's excited exclamations and agreed to dinner for the four of us the next night. Satisfied, I hung up the phone just as Francis walked out of the bathroom with a towel around his waist. Water droplets still clung to the pale skin on his chest and his hair stuck out in wet clumps, emphasizing his rapidly receding hairline.

"We have dinner with your parents tomorrow night." I drained the rest of my whiskey. "Dolly was very sweet. I don't know what the big deal is, Francis. She's thrilled to see you and can't wait to meet me. I think I'll wear my black and white dress. The one with the big collar?"

His face had gone red, his eyes round. "You what?" he demanded. "You called after I told you not to? Damn it, Ava, do you ever listen to me?"

I got up from the bed and sauntered over to him, my hips swaying, and tugged at his towel. It slipped from his waist to the floor. "If you want to marry me, Francis Sinatra, you'll have to introduce me to your parents. Now you can."

He shook his head and opened his mouth to launch into another of his tirades—until I slipped my hands over his bare skin. He gasped and almost instantly, he was ready for me again.

"You'd better make it up to me," he said, tugging me against him again.

I glanced down and smiled slyly. "Honey, I plan to."

The next evening, we took the ferry across the Hudson River

and a taxi to the Sinatras' house on Park Avenue, Hoboken, a town house in the classic New York City style. The house had multiple stories and a set of steps ascended from the street to an oaken door with glass panes, exactly as I'd envisioned it. Francis had spent most of his childhood in a different home in the heart of Little Italy on Monroe Street, so I asked him to take me there before heading back into the city. I was curious if the neighborhood still looked as rough as he'd always said.

When Dolly opened the door, a personality as large as Francis's greeted me.

"Hello, come in, come in!" She smiled a grand, wide thing, her blue eyes sparking with delight. "Frank, where the hell have you been? I've been trying to get you home for months. Come here, let me look at you." She grasped him by both arms, looked him up and down. "It's a good thing I've made lasagna. You need some meat on your bones. You're skinny as a train rail."

"Hi, Ma." He kissed her cheek then took my coat and hung up his hat on a rack in the hall.

"And you must be Ava," she said. "You're a knockout, doll. I see what all the fuss is about."

I laughed and gave her a hug as if we'd known each other for ages.

Inside, their home was cozy if a little cluttered with statuettes of the saints and the Madonna, floral accents that were less of an accent and more of a dominant feature, and a set of comfortable chairs and sofa that you never wanted to get out of.

While we ate antipasti and lasagna with fresh bread, Dolly regaled me with tales from Francis's childhood. How he'd run around with a pack of boys from the neighborhood and sing at night in the family's tavern. They'd named it Marty O'Brien's to keep the police away and to prevent them from looking into operations too closely like they did with the other Italian establishments on the block. Their tavern even remained open during Prohibition, one of the few allowed. Between the tavern, Marty's work as captain at the fire department, and Dolly's work as a midwife, they did better than most in their neighborhood.

I smiled at Francis's father all evening, trying to get him to relax, but he was a quiet man. He seemed withdrawn and stern, or perhaps he wasn't much for socializing. Either way, something about Francis clicked into place as I watched his daddy. In a way, he reminded me of my own daddy, long gone.

Dolly was his opposite in every way. I saw where Francis got his vivaciousness.

"You chained yourself to the railing at City Hall?" I asked in disbelief, astounded by Dolly's courage and determination. I pictured her on the steps in the pouring rain, shouting at the top of her lungs, and banging down doors until someone listened to her.

"Sure did," she said, her eyes twinkling. "I wasn't about to give up on the right to vote for women. We're as smart as men are. Probably smarter."

"I've definitely been outsmarted by women a time or two," Francis said, winking at me, and we all laughed.

Dolly talked about the abortion clinic she'd run for the poor, and her midwifery, delivering babies in the middle of the night in all sorts of homes in the area or in the hospital. She swore as heartily as any man and more. She was an absolute force of nature. I adored her.

"Ma is involved in politics," Francis said proudly. He'd

relaxed at last and was genuinely enjoying the visit. I was happy to see it. No one should be estranged from their mama, least of all the man I was in love with. "People have always listened to her," Francis went on. "Still do or they get a good wallop."

We laughed again, but I knew Francis retained a healthy fear of his mother. She was tough and bold but also friendly and seemed like the kind of person that would stick her neck out for a friend—very much like her son.

We put away four bottles of wine and some limoncello afterward, and eventually it was time to go.

I couldn't help but beam at Dolly as she took my hands in hers.

"It's been wonderful to meet you, Ava. I've been following you in the papers and the magazines. The minute I saw that you two were together, I knew my Frank was a goner." She smiled that infectious smile again.

"I suppose it was inevitable for me, too," I replied.

"Now, listen, don't pay attention to what they're saying about you," Dolly said. "Love is difficult and we have to fight for it sometimes. Nancy is a good girl, always has been, but I can see now she wasn't right for Frank, not in the long run. Still, she'll always be a part of the family."

"Of course she will," I agreed. And though I wanted to throttle Nancy for hanging on to Francis for dear life, I couldn't blame her. She was also Francis's children's mother. Even when the divorce came through—if it ever did—she'd still be a part of his life, which meant she'd be a part of mine, too, if only peripherally. "Thanks again for the wonderful meal," I said with a smile.

We said good night and Francis slung his arm around me. "That wasn't so bad."

I arched my brow at him. "It was terrific. I love your mama."

And what I didn't say was that I understood him better— and perhaps even loved him now a little bit more.

CHAPTER 24

AVA

Francis and I flew home to Los Angeles together when he had a break between his shows in New York. We were happy to spend some time in Palm Springs, soaking up the sun and sitting by the pool. But the peace between us didn't last. Nancy wouldn't budge on the divorce papers, though she'd told her lawyer she would sign them. Francis and I were both at our wits' end waiting for her and got at each other's throats. We were up and down, left and right, together and apart. I was fed up with the whole scene so I took a breather from the drama that inevitably played out between us: the arguing, the jealousy, the threats. I screened my calls for weeks until one night, I decided to answer. I was beginning to miss him too much, drama or no.

"Is it over?" I asked. "Has she filed the papers?"

"Listen to me, I've called her—"

"Are you getting divorced or not?" I demanded.

"I'm working on it—"

I cursed and slammed down the telephone. As I expected, Francis called right back and I let the telephone ring ten times, twenty times, thirty, until finally Reenie answered it to put us both out of our misery.

"Mr. Sinatra, Miss G doesn't want to talk to you."

I hovered nearby, waiting to hear what he had to say.

She covered the receiver with her hand. "He says he has a plan. He's going to Tahoe and wants you to go with him. He's going to force Nancy's hand."

He would live in Nevada until the six-week residency period passed and technically he could be divorced the following week. I'd done it myself when I'd divorced Artie.

I took the telephone and put it to my ear. "Francis," I said simply.

"I'm going to Tahoe, baby," he replied. I could hear the barely controlled desperation in his voice. "Come with me. Let's put this to bed once and for all."

I felt myself giving in, the longing to be with him returning with a vengeance. "I love you."

"I love you like a man in the desert in need of water, Angel."

"You always were a bit of a poet, weren't you," I said, laughing softly. "I guess that's what makes you irresistible."

"I'm glad you still see me that way."

"Of course I do, baby. I'm just tired of playing second fiddle to that kept woman of yours."

"I know," he said. "But that's done. I'm leaving tomorrow."

"Alright," I said. "I'll see you in Tahoe."

We met in Tahoe the next day.

It was far more beautiful than I'd remembered. The mild fall weather brought a sky painted in eggshell blue without a single whisp of clouds. Vast pine forests swept across the flat lowlands, hugged the slopes of the Sierra Nevada, and encircled the deepest lake imaginable in a thick green embrace. I'd heard rumors that bodies didn't decompose in Lake Tahoe because the water was too cold. Of course Francis and I had to know the truth, so we hunted down some books. He read me snippets out loud as we lay on the couch together, our limbs entangled. He regaled me with facts about the area, including the deplorable way the Chinese laborers who'd helped build the railroads were treated. Rumor had it many of their bodies probably drifted in the deeps somewhere. A ghastly business. I read to him, too, from Daphne du Maurier's books and Salinger, and a sprinkling of nonfiction about the Wild West of yore.

The first two weeks were blissful, filled with making love and taking long strolls or reading on the lake's sandy shores. In the evenings, we'd head to the club where Francis was singing. He was able to book a gig while we were in town, and that seemed to help his mood, alleviating some of the stress about his bills. He hated asking me to cover them—God knew his ego was threatened by the idea of a woman paying for things—because it made him feel like less of a man. I did my best to take care of things quietly and not mention it.

One night, we returned to the rental house after a midnight dinner following his show. He was lying on the bed, his ankles crossed, and rummaging through a stack of magazines. On top sat a copy of *Time* magazine that my publicist had sent to me. I was on the cover, but I hadn't mentioned it to Francis. He was proud of my success, but I knew it bothered him, too, that I was doing so well while he was struggling. That was a casualty of our industry: the constant comparisons and competition. It had a way of making you feel inferior nearly all the time—desperate for more success to ensure you really did have talent—and it ruined plenty of friendships along the way.

"Will you look at this! My baby on the cover of *Time* magazine!" He flipped through the glossy pages. "Why didn't you tell me about this?"

I watched his face as a ferocious wave of pride warred with his jealousy. "I don't know why they used that picture of me." I plucked the magazine from his hands. "There had to be others that were better. You've got to love the title, too. 'The Farmer's Daughter.'" I rolled my eyes. "I'm never going to live that down."

"What are you talking about? You look like a dream."

I smiled. "It is a dream to be on the cover, I suppose, and I shouldn't complain."

"That's the spirit. You know what I'd give to be on the cover?" He shook his head. "I'd give my right eye."

"Don't say things like that," I said, running a brush through my dark hair until it was silky. "You'll bring yourself bad luck."

"In case you haven't noticed, doll, I've had bad luck for months."

I pulled on a pink French negligee that had cost as much as a night's rent at our cottage, and smeared cream on my face and hands. "You won't for long. You'll be on the upswing soon, you'll see."

He brightened slightly. "I hope you're right."

I didn't mind bolstering him when he needed it, though it could be tiresome at times. He'd been through a lot, losing his fame, fortune, and contracts. His family. It had only made things worse to have his reputation eroded by all those straitlaced, dull-as-dirt nobodies who hated us for falling in love.

"Have I ever been wrong?" I asked.

"I can think of a few times," he replied, grinning.

I huffed in a playful way and smacked his thigh with the back of my hairbrush, making a loud thwap. He grabbed my hand and pulled me toward him, tossing the brush across the room. I squealed and landed beside him on the bed.

"Tell me something," he said. His hand ran gently over the curve of my shoulders. "Tell me you've never loved anyone the way you love me."

"I've never loved anyone like you," I said, meeting his vivid blue eyes.

"That isn't the same thing."

"I love you, Francis Albert Sinatra, and I've risked my reputation and my career for you. If that doesn't tell you how I feel about you then you're a moron."

He chuckled and then turned serious again. "Have you slept with anyone since we started seeing each other?" he asked, unable to keep the question to himself—even if I'd already answered it a thousand times.

"Why would you ask me that? You know I love only you."

"Do I know that?"

I frowned. "I should say so."

"Did you sleep with that Spanish cad? What's his name? Mario."

"You've asked me that a hundred times and my answer is still no." I plumped my pillow a little too hard and nestled down into it, not wanting to get into it after such a nice couple of weeks together. "It's two o'clock in the morning, Francis. I'm tired. Let's go to sleep."

He knew I wasn't being entirely honest with him. He could

sense it. Or maybe he'd fooled around, too, and that was what made him so suspicious? I bristled at the thought.

"Come on, baby, you can tell me," he said, cajoling me.

"I don't want to talk about Spain. That's over and he was my costar, nothing more."

He nibbled my ear. "Then what's the big deal, anyway?"

Exasperated, I turned over to face him squarely. Maybe if I told him the truth—or at least a small fraction of it—he'd let it go. It had been a mistake, after all, and Francis and I had been stressed so much at the time and living so far apart, with me in Europe and him in New York, that it felt like our relationship had been less . . . solid. Frankly, he was still married, too, so it wasn't as if he could say much.

I studied his face and decided it was now or never, that we could be honest with each other. We had been until now. Why keep a dirty little secret?

"I slept with him," I admitted. "Once, okay? And I regretted it the moment it happened. You and I were fighting. We were . . ." My words trailed off at his expression.

His eyes shone with an odd brightness and rage blistered his tone. "I knew it! That no-good . . ." He shouted a string of slurs and, unable to hold in his fury, jumped off the bed. "Am I not enough for you?"

"Calm down. Of course you're enough for me!" I said, sitting up, the sheet sliding down my body. "It was a mistake and things were difficult between us."

"I'm clearly not enough if you're getting boned by someone who prances around in tights and britches like a goddamn ballerina."

We argued for another hour, lobbing insults back and forth, wounding each other, and I'd had enough. I stormed to the bedroom and yanked my suitcase out of the closet, tossing clothes in it willy-nilly. Our fights were always the same, and my leaving was, too, but this time, the ending felt like a new shade of bad. We were reaching an inflection point.

I dragged my suitcase to the car, threw it in, and headed home to Los Angeles.

Hours later, I sighed in relief and exhaustion when I pulled into the drive at last. I'd barely staggered into the kitchen when the phone rang.

"Hello," I said, my voice raspy. A doctor introduced himself and I felt my pulse suddenly speed up. Something wasn't right. "Yes, go on. This is Ava Gardner."

"I'm calling about Mr. Sinatra," he said. "He's taken a large dose of sleeping pills. The maid found him on the floor and called the police."

I didn't hear the rest.

I dropped the phone and jumped back into the car. Sobbing, I backed the car out of the drive and dashed into the night, bleary-eyed, terrified of losing the man I loved once and for all. This was my fault. He'd threatened suicide before, but this time it seemed he might have succeeded. My hands shook as I covered the miles. He was a mess, a real disaster and there was nothing I could do about it.

Unless . . . maybe I could help him find a film role, something to help him back on his feet again. Perhaps then he'd stop this madness. I'd do anything—anything for him, to help him get better. I'd go to a psychologist, and he could go, too. My mind circled the possibilities feverishly with each mile. I'd call my publicist and my manager immediately tomorrow. Whatever it would take to help him get to a better place.

If only he would be alright. Please, God, let him be alright.

I pushed the gas pedal harder, driving faster than ever, desperate to get to him.

When I arrived hours later, I burst through the front door and raced to the bedroom. And there he was, propped up on pillows. A doctor stood beside the bed.

"Good timing," the doctor said. "I've given him a saline solution to clear his system, but his vitals are fine. It appears he's taken just enough to give us a scare, but he'll be in top shape by tomorrow. Mr. Sinatra, I suggest you seek some professional help."

"You came," Francis said, a groggy smile on his lips.

"Of course I came!" My hands shook with adrenaline and the fear I'd been fighting during the drive I'd just finished— twice. As the truth crashed over me and the realization settled in, my fear drained away and all that was left was fury. How dare he do this to me again!

"Do you know what you've done to me?" I fumed. "Jesus! I thought you were dead! Right now I wish you were!"

"Come on, Angel, don't say that." He grinned sheepishly at me.

"I just drove all night long, terrified I'd lost you forever, and you're sitting here with a grin on your face!"

He patted the bed next to him. "Come here. I'm sorry. I shouldn't have done it, but you left and I thought—"

"Don't you dare blame this on me!" I shouted, anger burning my throat.

"Angel, I—"

"Screw you!" I stormed off and headed to the door, ignoring his calls from the bedroom.

But as I reached for the handle, ready to head to my car yet again, I stopped. A sense of deep weariness emanated from my bones. I was far too tired to drive again—but I'd be damned if I was going to stay in the bedroom with him.

I poured myself a whiskey, cursing him one last time, and passed out on the sofa.

★ ★ ★

Francis and I made up after the latest fiasco, but I told him if he ever did that again, he'd better be dead because I'd never come back. I'd been feeling more wrung out than usual after that night, and queasy in a way that made me nervous. I took the precaution of leaving Tahoe to let Francis finish out his time there for the paperwork while I headed to Los Angeles to consult with a doctor. It was as I feared: I was pregnant. Having a kid out of wedlock with another woman's husband wouldn't do my career, or my relationship with Francis, any favors so I made a difficult decision. My doctor directed me to a discreet—and illegal—clinic and I had the deed done. I tried not to think about the implications, but afterward, I had a good, soaking cry. Even if having a baby wasn't what I wanted, my emotions swung from relieved to devastated and back again. I knew Mama would have plenty of things to say about my decision, and despite it, I wished she were here. A girl needed her mama, and so did a woman.

Meanwhile, my publicist put out a statement that I was recovering from exhaustion. I didn't tell Francis. I knew it would crush him—I'd never met a man so eager to have a big family—but frankly, he already had one and we were in no position to discuss it at the moment.

After I recovered, I returned Mayer's call to come into the studio. I dreaded it. I knew it probably had something to do with Francis. Everything had to do with Francis these days. I drove to the studio with the windows down and lit a cigarette to put my hands to work and my nerves to rest. On the lot, I parked, reached for my little black patent leather purse, and headed inside, trepidation rolling through me.

Mayer's secretary showed me in immediately.

"Hi there," I said as I slid into one of the guest chairs.

Mayer's gaze traveled over my body as it so often did. I knew the old codger would take me to bed in a second if I let him. The thought still made me ill.

"What's this meeting about, Louis?" I said, crossing my legs and leaning forward. "You've been hounding me for weeks to come in and I've been indisposed. Treated for exhaustion."

He grunted and threw his pen down on the desk in front of him. "I'm sure you *are* exhausted after what I've seen in the papers. Why did you have to get mixed up with Sinatra? He stinks. His reputation, his attitude. He's nothing but bad news. You've taken quite a fall from Mickey to Frank."

I gave him an icy glare. "I appreciate the fatherly advice, but really, I can choose who I date just fine, thank you."

He pressed his lips together, giving his already chubby cheeks an inflated look like a beaver's. "Apparently you can't. You shouldn't be running around with a married man, all over the country. You've left a trail of pissed-off journalists and offended fans in your wake." As he rubbed his face, I bit down on my tongue. Nothing I had to say would make his little lecture any better. "Look, Ava, you're one of our biggest stars these days, and I can't have you destroying your career, and the studio's reputation, in the process. You're practically flaunting the fact that you're breaking our morality clause."

So he admitted it, at last. I was a hot property at MGM. It had taken nearly a decade working for them, dozens of magazine covers, popular films with *other* studios, and resoundingly good reviews for *Show Boat* for him to admit it. It was a moment to be savored and celebrated. I'd arrived, hadn't I? At last, my own studio, the people who had given me my first chance, considered me a star. And yet, the feeling of victory I'd hoped for was nothing but a sharp instant and silent thrill, a hummingbird hovering over a red bloom before it buzzed away. I still hadn't been nominated for an Oscar—and I was still under Mayer's thumb. Worse, the ache for more hadn't been satiated, even if I didn't know what more meant or how to get it. I'd have to ponder that another day.

"I'm glad you agree, Louis," I said, allowing my southern drawl to surface. "I *am* one of your stars and that's why I decide who I will and won't be with, regardless of this ridiculous, outdated morality clause. If you want this mess to end with Francis and me, then help us instead of chastising us. Francis has done everything he can to get divorced and Nancy still won't budge on the paperwork."

His cheeks reddened and sweat was beginning to dampen his temples. I knew I'd gotten to him. He wanted this mess over with as badly as we did.

"What do you need from us?" he said.

"Pressure Nancy to sign the papers. Frank has done his time

in Nevada, waiting for his appeal to come through. She just needs to sign on the line."

"I'm not sure we can do that."

I smiled a feline smile. "I'm sure you'll think of something."

He sat back in his chair and ran a hand over his head. "If we get Nancy to sign, you'll need to get married as soon as possible."

"Of course," I said. "That's all we want. Once we're married, the press will settle down and we can get on with acting."

He sat back in his chair, eyeing me a moment. "You sure you want to marry him, Ava? He's trouble."

I grinned. Mayer didn't know I brought my own kind of trouble. "I'm sure," I said.

"Alright. I'll make some calls."

CHAPTER 25

AVA

Mayer made good on his promise.

When the call came that Nancy had finally signed and filed the papers, Francis and I didn't waste any time. We headed to New York to plan the ceremony where we'd have a handful of our friends and family join us. Always a beacon of hospitality, Manie Sacks opened his home at Hampton House. The first night in town, Francis took me to dinner at the famed Frankie and Johnnie's Steakhouse. We were joyful if tired after the flight and from the flurry of excitement that came from, at last, knowing we would be married. When we returned to the hotel, we were intent on heading straight upstairs to change clothes, make love, and read a good book in bed, but the concierge waved me over to his desk.

"There's a letter for you, Miss Gardner," he said, extending a sealed envelope.

I peered at his nametag and gave him a big smile. "Thank you, John."

He blushed like a Catholic school boy. Some men were like that; they didn't know how to react when I was near and it

baffled me still, even after the last ten years of seeing men follow me around like lost puppies. I was still only me, a simple
woman who liked to dance, swim, or play tennis when I could,
and act now and again. And I liked good gin and a good . . .
well. Francis knew very well what I liked.

I laughed softly at my thoughts as we headed upstairs.

"Who's it from?" Francis asked.

"I don't know," I said, tearing the envelope open as we
closed the door behind us. I pulled out a sheet of stationery
and quickly scanned its contents—and stopped.

Heat bloomed in my chest, filled my throat, and spread
through me until I thought I might burst into flames. It was a
letter from a hooker—a hooker who had slept with Francis repeatedly, and I knew it was true, instantly. She knew the things
he said in bed, the way he moved, his moles, his enormous . . .
member. The prostitute knew everything.

I rushed to the bathroom and splashed cold water on my
face. All this time, Francis had given me hell about Mario and
here he was, hiring women for sex? Didn't he get it enough?
The tears began, joining the dark rivulets of mascara and eye-
liner that ran down the smooth contours of my face.

He'd been fooling around behind my back after all. I sobbed
as I stalked across the suite to the kitchen and poured a large
vodka, downing it in two gulps.

"Whoa, Angel, take it easy," Frank said as he pulled on a
pair of slippers. "I thought we were going to share a nightcap?"

"I don't want to share anything with you," I heaved. I couldn't
do this. I couldn't go through with the wedding. I didn't give a
damn what we'd overcome to get here—and apparently neither
did he. I was going to be just like Nancy, the woman pushed

aside while he got on with his life. I tossed the letter onto the counter and made to leave, but Frank grabbed me, holding me tightly in his grip.

"Oh no you don't. Tell me what the hell is in that letter!"

"Let me go! The wedding is off!" Tears spilled from my eyes. I didn't understand it. Why did he need whores when he could have me anytime?

"You have some nerve giving me hell while you were off gallivanting with some bullfighter! Who's the real hooker?"

I slapped him—hard—across the jaw, leaving a searing red welt. He reeled backward from the unexpected blow, knocking into a table and falling on his rear end.

"What the—!" he shouted, pushing to his feet.

"You don't need a wife!" I seethed. "You need a woman you can call anytime, to answer your every whim, you egotistical bastard." I stalked to the window, shoved it open, and removed my six-carat emerald engagement ring. With a swift movement, I tossed it out of the fourteenth-story window.

Frank gasped. "What the hell is wrong with you?" He shouted to his friend who was holed up in the guest bedroom. "Tony!" Dark-haired, small-framed Tony Consiglioni was one of his lackeys who jumped every time Frank told him to, and within seconds, he appeared.

"What is it, man?" Tony glanced from Frank to me, at the letter, and the table that laid on its side. He'd obviously been trying to ignore the racket we were making, but now he had to witness it from a front-row seat.

"My bride just tossed her engagement ring out the window!" Frank shouted. "Can you find it?"

"Out of that window?" Tony asked, dumbstruck. "In Manhattan? Are you nuts?"

"Can you just go!" Frank looked as if his head was about to explode.

"Yeah, sure thing." Tony ran to his room to pull on his shoes, fished around in the kitchen drawers and cabinets to find a flashlight, and headed outside.

"You're so full of shit!" I shouted at Frank as the door closed behind Tony. "You've been harassing me about Mario, but all along you were with some whore!"

"That letter is a lie," he countered. "I bet it was Howard Hughes, paying off someone to break us up. That clown is obsessed with you. Come on, baby. Let's forget this." He reached for me, but I wrenched away, slammed the bedroom door in his face, and locked it.

The night went on like that for hours, our friends becoming involved, going back and forth between us, trying to convince us that it was just a horrible joke. At last, after much cajoling and a thousand apologies, I forgave him and we fell into bed, taking out our frustrations and fears on each other. I needed him like he needed me, despite our flaws and hurts and arguments, something that I didn't understand—that neither of us understood—but we did know one important thing: nothing could keep us apart. Not even some stupid little mistake like cheating on each other.

As the following day dawned, we learned the press was already waiting, and given Francis's proclivity for picking fights with journalists, we thought it best to avoid them altogether. We made the decision to get married in Philadelphia instead.

I slipped on my engagement ring again—Tony had recovered it in the street gutter, amazingly—and the wedding party packed up and drove to Philadelphia, only to find that the press had caught wind of our change in venue. As our plans for a private ceremony came apart at the seams, we drove back to New York while Manie made a few calls. At last we found an officiate, a police court judge named Joseph Sloane, who agreed to marry us at Manie's brother's home in the West Germantown neighborhood of Philadelphia. We'd return to Philly again and after the brief ceremony, we'd take a plane to Miami and on to Cuba for a short honeymoon before Francis had to be back onstage.

Our wedding took place on a miserable day in November. The wind howled as if it were being tortured by some unseen deity in the sky and cold rain sheeted from the clouds. Francis and I didn't care—we were eager to get on with the ceremony and put this chapter of our lives behind us. We were hopeful that everything would change for the better then, and we could focus on creating a home together.

Finally, we pulled into the drive of Lester Sack's—and reporters had, once again, found us. They swarmed the front walk, ignoring the driving rain.

I put my hand on Francis's arm to restrain him. "Baby, let it go. They're here and what's done is done. Let's just get married already."

"They ruin everything," he growled. "They're not going to ruin my wedding day, too." He kissed me quickly on the cheek and flung open the car door.

Light bulbs flashed and he stumbled, blinded by the light and distracted by the rain. He ran around the car to open the door for me. Instantly I was pelted with rain—and with questions.

"Ava, do you love him?"

"How does MGM feel about this match?"

Ignoring them, I held my purse over my head as we darted for the front door.

"Frank, didn't you just divorce Nancy? Is she at home with the kids?"

"Does she know you're getting married already?"

"I heard you were dropped by MGM."

That did it. Francis swiveled around, the vein in his neck bulging. "How did you parasites know we were here? Who wants me to punch him out?"

"Come on," I said, dragging him inside. "Who cares if they're here?"

He screamed and swore all the way to the front door. At least he didn't throw cherry bombs at them—that had become his new favorite parlor trick with the press.

Inside, Bappie, Francis's parents, and Manie's family had already begun to gather. At the last minute, Francis's bandleader, Axel Stordhal, agreed to stand in as best man, his wife as matron of honor. Bappie had already had the honors twice and this time wanted to be another member of our small but mighty audience.

I didn't waste time and headed upstairs, where I slipped into a gorgeous halter dress made of gauzy marquisette with stiffened brocade and a pink taffeta top. Howard Greer made the dreamiest designs and this one was no different; it fit like a second skin. The only problem with a second skin was I couldn't wear anything underneath it. For jewelry, I fastened on a double strand of pearls and diamond earrings. Finally, I touched up my lipstick and I was ready or not.

When the "Wedding March" began, I walked slowly from the bedroom down a set of stairs to the living room. I tried to ignore the fact that the piano was out of tune and so did our pianist, Dick Jones.

My heart fluttering, I smiled brightly as I looked at the faces of our nearest and dearest. Francis's eyes met mine and his face beamed like a spotlight on a dark stage. We were rich in people who loved us—we were rich in each other, and even after the events of the last few days and the last few months, his flaws and mine, I loved this man with all my heart. We were an outrageous yet perfect pair. Life was an adventure after all, wasn't it?

I glanced at the white carnation in the buttonhole of his dark suit. Dolly had probably put it there. Tears pricked my eyes at the sight, and I blinked rapidly to hold them back. I wished Mama could be here, too.

When I reached the fireplace posing as our altar, Francis took my hands in his and the judge began the ceremony. When it was time for the magic words, I swallowed the lump in my throat.

"Do you, Francis Albert Sinatra, take this woman to be your lawfully wedded wife . . ."

Francis grinned and his blue eyes sparkled. "I do."

I smiled back at him, wanting to take him in my arms.

"Do you, Ava Lavinia Gardner, take this man to be your lawfully wedding husband . . ."

"I do," I managed over a lump of emotion in my throat.

"By the power vested in me . . ." The judge finished and we sealed the deal with a fervent kiss.

The audience erupted into cheers and applause.

I laughed and looked at the guests, seeing I wasn't the only one who had tried not to cry. Every woman in the room was dabbing at her eyes and all were smiling. I went immediately to Dolly. She hugged me fiercely.

"Honey, I'm so glad this day has come," she said. "You love him, don't you?"

"Maybe too much," I said, laughing and wiping at the tears.

Francis kissed us both, looking happier than I'd seen him in weeks—maybe ever.

"She's the one, son," Dolly said, and he smiled.

"She is, Ma."

We cut a four-tier cake and drank champagne, and within a short couple of hours, the party was over and we were on the road to our honeymoon. At dawn, we arrived in Miami, exhausted but happy. At the Green Heron Hotel, I discovered I'd taken the wrong luggage and sent for it back in Pennsylvania. I ordered out for groceries and cooked Francis his favorite breakfast of fried eggs in olive oil; we ate companionably, fueled ourselves with coffee, and decided to go for a walk on the beach before our flight to Cuba later that day.

I shivered in the wind that whipped over the water and swept us along the sand.

"Here, Angel. Take my jacket." Francis slipped it over my shoulders, and I tucked my hand into his as we made our way down to the beach.

We sauntered along the water's edge, taking in the raw beauty of the ocean, churning and foaming and communing with the land that contained it. And for a few hours, we were quiet, relishing nature and our place within it, our toes in the sand, our hopes in the sky. We relished each other and all that lay ahead. Things would be better now—we were together, truly together, and nothing else mattered.

Perhaps marriage really was the cure to our madness after all.

Part 3

"ALL OR NOTHING AT ALL"

1951–1953

CHAPTER 26

FRANK

We were married at last, after more guilt and pain in the ass than I'd anticipated, but we'd made it. We enjoyed a week in Cuba, but no sooner had we returned from the honeymoon than my hot-headed woman was spitting nails and driving off into the desert, leaving me alone in Palm Springs. We'd argued about an old flame of hers and somehow the conversation returned to the hooker's letter. I did know the hooker, but Ava didn't need that information, especially when we were trying to get married and get on with things. It would have only added fuel to the fire. After looking into matters with a little help from the Boys, I discovered the stunt was Howard Hughes's doing. The man had more money than God and he liked to play at being him, too. He'd paid the hooker off to send the letter, to prevent Ava from marrying me. I was going to have to teach him a lesson or two, see how he liked meeting my fists.

I drove to Los Angeles after Ava like the back end of the car was on fire. By the time I arrived at the house we were renting in the city, she was passed out in bed. I wondered how much she'd had to drink. It worried me, how much booze my lady could put away. It seemed to be growing by the day.

I slid in beside her warm, languid body. Immediately, all was forgotten and I wanted nothing but to pull her into my arms.

"Hi, Angel."

"You came," she said, opening her eyes. She gave me a sleepy smile.

"Of course I did." I kissed her mouth softly.

"I'd yell at you some more, but I'm too tired and too happy to see you." She wrapped her arms around my neck.

My body responded as she pressed against me. She was all round breasts with pert nipples and soft skin that demanded to be touched. She ground against me, and I took her like we were running out of air and life. And this was how it was between us: hot or hotter—never cold, never dull. We couldn't seem to help ourselves. We'd argue and love each other and argue some more. It was exhausting—and sometimes I wondered why I'd given up my life with Nancy and the kids for the wild, untenable relationship I'd dived into headfirst—but I loved her in a way that didn't make sense, even now. Even after all we'd done to each other and all we'd been through.

When we'd both been satiated, she lay in my arms. I drew circles with my fingertip on her shoulder.

"Did you hear about *From Here to Eternity*?" I asked.

"The book?"

"The picture. Rights sold to Columbia for eighty-two thousand dollars! Harry Cohn gave it to Zinnemann to direct."

"Good grief," she said, resting her chin on her arm. "I guess Harry really wanted it."

"Well, it did win the National Book Award. I heard it sold a million copies or more."

"Mm-hmm," she said. "I'm not surprised. I loved that book."

"I did, too," I said, sitting up and propping a pillow against the headboard. "I'd give about anything to be cast, but they probably wouldn't give me a screen test, never mind a role."

"You don't know that, baby," she said, laying her hand on my knee.

I sighed heavily. I did know that—it would be the most sought-after picture with those numbers behind it already—but I was dead in Hollywood and they wouldn't even give me a chance. "I'm going to London," I said, changing the subject. "Will you come?"

"I can't," she said. "I have a meeting."

I frowned. "You don't even know when I'm going."

"When are you going?"

"Next week."

"That's exactly when I have a meeting," she replied.

"How many times have I joined you on set?"

"I'm meeting with David and a director, Francis. It's not like I can blow them off. They'd be furious, and it's unprofessional."

"Come on, wifey. A good woman stands by her man. Besides, it's for the Royal Command charity show. It's a good gig for me, good press for us. You'll get to meet the legendary Duke of Edinburgh." I tried to tempt her. "I hear he throws a mean cocktail party for the stars."

She slapped me playfully on the arm. "I stand by you plenty. But it does sound like a good time. I'll see if the director doesn't mind rescheduling."

I smiled and tugged on a damp strand of her hair. "Atta girl. Will you sing a number with me, too?"

She laughed. "And look like a fool next to you and your sexy voice? Not a chance."

"You've got a set of pipes. They're sultry and soft. Come on, you know you can sing."

Basking in my flattery, she smiled. "One song."

I grinned. "You've got it."

We made the flight over the pond, but the party wasn't as we'd hoped. Though the royal set and their guests wore their best suits or sparkled in sequined gowns and satin, and plenty of top shelf booze was on hand, it was a stiff, formal affair. Ava and I were expected to follow English protocol that we didn't know. We bumbled our way through the series of awkward bows and handshakes around the royals and tried to make the most of it.

"I need another drink," Ava whispered, her eyes on the duke. "If I have to have one more conversation about the weather in Los Angeles, I'm going to die of boredom."

"We've already had three and I get the feeling they're all keeping track," I replied. "Better keep it to a minimum. Besides, we're going on soon. We can party after, baby."

"There's no way I'm going to perform to that crowd," she said, finishing her drink. "They're tight as virgins."

I nearly spewed the whiskey in my mouth.

She laughed at my expression. "You know it's true."

"It'll be fine. Regardless, you'll be great."

She shook her head. "No way. I'm not singing. I'll look ridiculous and they'll all think I'm terrible."

"You promised," I said, feeling my face go hot. She was going to bail on me now, at the last minute?

We argued quietly until it was time to begin—and I soon learned that she meant what she'd said. She wasn't going to sing. I didn't sing well either, and I scolded the band during a number, which ticked everyone off, leaving me with only Jimmy as accompaniment on the piano. The crowd looked on in restrained but clearly surprised amusement and I wanted to get out of there the minute I could.

Tired and in a foul mood, we went back to the hotel, arguing the whole way.

Inside our suite, Ava kicked off her heels and removed her earrings, but as she reached for her travel bag she screeched.

"My necklace, it's gone!"

"The emerald necklace? Are you sure?" It was the same necklace that had been impounded in Spain. Bad luck seemed to follow it and I'd spent a fortune on that thing. Well, she had spent a fortune—I'd asked her for money to cover it, but I did pay her back. Another embarrassing admission I'd had to make as a grade A loser.

I yanked open the drawers one by one and sorted through the few things inside. After I'd opened them all, and dug through her suitcase, I swore loudly. Her face crumpled at the realization that it really was gone, and the anger that had stuck to my ribs all night began to fade.

I wrapped her in my arms. "We'll get it back, doll. I'll call the hotel manager and the police."

Tears brimmed in her eyes. "It was my favorite. It matched my engagement ring."

"I know," I said, and swore again. We'd arrest whoever that son of a gun was, or I'd beat him to a pulp once we found him. I dialed down to the front desk and we also filed a report, but in so many words he let me know we'd probably never see the necklace again. A perfectly terrible end to a terrible trip.

As I stared at her tear-stained face, an unsettled sensation lodged in the pit of my stomach. I didn't want to think of the necklace as a sign of bad luck to come and yet it was impossible not to.

★ ★ ★

After the lousy trip to London, Ava and I returned to New York, where we planned to live for the next several months to wait out my show commitments. The problem was she was in demand, so much so that she spent only a few days with me before she had to jet back to Hollywood or some other destination for a promotional shoot or screen tests for a new film. I couldn't stand it, watching her constantly go, leaving me behind to wallow in the pathetic life I was leading. It left me in a constant foul mood, and I'd pick a fight with her every chance I got. But no matter what I said or did, Ava did things her way. If I told her to stay in New York, she'd fly to California or Europe or Mexico and show up all over the papers in pictures with a man on her arm, her costar or some local celebrity. I'd fly into a rage, blow off a concert, and go to her, wherever she was, to tell her what I thought of the photographs. She would laugh them off, tell me how ridiculous and jealous I was being. She'd insist they were publicity stunts and a fun way to get under my skin. I was jealous enough to grind my reputation deeper and deeper into the mud. The jealousy would come over me like something violent and unrestrained. I was headed straight for the edge of a cliff, and it left me wondering if I'd have to drive myself off it before I'd make a change.

As it turned out, the change did come, but not by my own hand.

Universal canceled one of my few remaining deals, and CBS announced it was dropping my program. I suspected they might, though not for the reason I thought. They were peeved because of my refusal to rehearse. I wasn't about to rehearse some of the worst music I'd ever heard and if they thought I would waste my time, they were out of their damn minds. Barking like a dog, parading around like a fool in an advertisement—I was a musician!

I was still licking my wounds when the biggest blow of all came in the form of a bill. My booking agency dropped me and charged me forty thousand dollars in expenses. I lost it, trashed my hotel room, and then got savagely drunk. As the news of my dismissal reached the Hollywood gossip mill, the jokes followed: "Even Jesus couldn't resurrect Frank's career" and "He's a dead man walking."

I was on the verge of a breakdown. What was show business anyhow? A way to prostitute ourselves? Sell ourselves for a little applause or a few autographs? Somehow I had to put this business—my livelihood—into perspective, or I knew I wouldn't be able to carry on this way, sliding deeper, darker into an abyss.

One night, after a show at the Copacabana, one of my less-than-savory connections waved me over to a dark corner near the back wall. Some of the Boys were from the block where I grew up, and none were the kind of people I wanted to cross, so I was cordial enough, shook their hands, and thanked them for coming.

"Frankie, nice to see you," Johnny said, pulling out a chair for me. He had what you'd expect in a guy that delivered unwanted news: thick hands, the shoulders of a linebacker, and a nose that looked like it had been broken a few times. The two men with him had their eyes glued on a pair of women with big tits that stuck out too far and that could only mean one thing: they were hookers.

"How's things?" Johnny asked.

I waved the waitress over for a whiskey, straight up. "In the toilet, to be honest. I'm struggling."

"The Copacabana isn't enough for you." He swirled the ice cube in his glass to water the whiskey.

I shrugged. It wasn't a question. Of course it wasn't and we both knew it, but I wasn't going to get into it. "How's Frank?"

"Who wants to know?" Johnny said.

I was referring to Johnny's boss, Frank Costello, the head of the Luciano crime racket. Ever since Lucky Luciano was deported back to Sicily, Costello had taken his place. Much as I tried to steer clear of Costello, Joe Fischetti, and Willie Moretti, I'd known them most of my life and there was just no escaping them. Secretly, I admired them and their power, their invulnerability. No one messed with them unless they wanted to get hurt.

"Nobody wants to know," I said, trying to hold back my irritation. "I was just making conversation."

He eyed me for a minute, and I glared back. I wasn't afraid of this chump. He might have been Costello's muscle, but I knew too many of the Boys to be worried.

"So you're struggling," he said, changing the direction of the conversation. "We might be able to help with that."

I knew what that meant. Nothing was for free.

"I know just the man," Johnny went on. "George Wood."

"At William Morris?" I asked. William Morris had the biggest nightclub roster in the business. It was no secret the Mob backed some of the most famous performers in New York and Chicago, and they were looking to move into Las Vegas. They were building a new casino at that very moment called the Sands.

"The same." He threw back the rest of his drink.

"Can you get me a meeting?" I'd been through the ringer, sure, but I'd avoided explicitly asking for help from the Boys—on purpose. Now . . . well, maybe I'd been wrong. Maybe I had to take my breaks wherever I could get them, no matter who served them up. Besides, Italians looked out for their own and that was good enough for me. Loyalty among friends was something I prized over just about anything.

"Sure, but you can't botch it up, Frank. He still needs to like you to take you on."

"I'll fold his goddamn laundry if I have to."

Johnny clapped me on the back with a little too much force. "That's the spirit. I knew you had it in you."

The first glimpse of hope I'd felt in months flickered to life in my chest. I knew George Wood had a roster of difficult clients, or at least that was what I'd heard, but he'd gotten them work—lots of it—and made careers out of nothing.

And godammit, I wasn't nothing.

"I've got it in me, alright," I said, and lit a cigarette, thinking for the hundredth time that I was glad I was an Italian American and that I had friends, no matter what the papers, or anybody else, had to say about it.

CHAPTER 27

AVA

After my latest row with Francis, I was relieved to start a new picture. The time apart would do us some good. MGM, once again, lent me out to Twentieth Century Fox studios, this time for an adaptation of a Hemingway novel, *The Snows of Kilimanjaro.* Francis pressured me—and them—to shorten the shooting time so I could join him on his nightclub circuit. I humored my new husband, who continued to battle his demons and a raging sense of inferiority after a couple of hard years. I wanted to stand by him, encourage him to stick it out—and he leaned on me—but when he pushed back on my commitments, it really started to tick me off. He wasn't the only one with a career or with struggles.

"I need you here," he said over the phone.

"I'm trying," I said. "I really am. I can't ask them to change the entire shooting schedule for me."

"Why not?" he grunted. "You're one of their biggest stars. You need to start acting like it, baby. They need you."

Francis liked to strut around as if he were the center of the universe and he expected others to treat him that way, too, even after things got rough for him. I knew they didn't need me, but I liked the sound of that anyway. And maybe I should be a little more demanding—take charge of what I wanted a bit more. So I did. I pushed my publicist and the director to meet my demands. If they wanted me in their film, they'd have to do all my scenes in a twenty-four-hour period.

I booked a flight to New York, ready to head back east with Francis after the shooting on the lot, but Fox soon fell behind in the production schedule. I was exhausted, the director was exhausted—we were all working as fast and as hard as we could—but we still needed more time to finish. I put in the dreaded phone call to Francis, knowing he wasn't going to take it well, but he had to understand. It was my work, and there was nothing I could do about it.

"Baby, the schedule got away from us," I said. "The production crew has been pushing hard, but we're going to need another day or two."

"Which will turn into a week or two," he said, not bothering to cover the irritation in his voice. "Damn it! Just walk away. They didn't fulfill their end of the contract so now it's null and void. You aren't obligated to do anything else for them—"

"Are you out of your mind?" Anger bloomed inside me. We'd worked nonstop on the film—never mind the many phone calls and negotiations early on—and he still wanted me to walk away? Given how much he cared about his career, he had to know I felt the same way about mine—but he sure as hell didn't act like it, or maybe he didn't care. "I'm not going to walk off set and be in breach of contract!" I continued. "How could you ask that of me?"

He flew into a tantrum—and I slammed down the phone.

And that was only the beginning of Francis's absurd expectations.

I blew off a movie role entirely to join him at a rain-soaked, pitiful little concert under a leaky tent in Hawaii. It was another garbage film anyway and I couldn't believe MGM had reverted back to dumping the worst roles on me, but still, I'd had to break contract, for him.

When the call came that I'd been suspended and my royalties were being withheld—all for being there for my husband—I returned to the studio to do as they demanded. I had to work nonstop for several weeks to make up for the little incident, until finally one day, I had a break to relax. I was looking forward to a languorous day doing nothing but meeting Francis's daughter, Nancy. I'd heard so much about her, and I loved children, even if I wasn't going to have any of my own. Something I had yet to tell Francis. And he hadn't pushed the idea either, not yet.

While waiting for him to arrive, I asked Reenie if she wanted to join me on the patio.

"Sure," she said with a smile. "I don't have anywhere else I need to get to today."

I was always happy to see Reenie go on about her life, visiting with friends or family, pursuing the things she enjoyed outside of her work for me, and outside of our friendship. I didn't want to be the kind of employer who demanded their staff devote their entire lives to their employers. What kind of life would that be? Made my skin crawl to think of it.

"I miss my sister," Reenie said, batting a fly. We sat on the veranda sipping gin martinis beneath the shade of a palm tree at the house Francis and I were renting in the Pacific Palisades.

"When's the last time you saw her?" I asked.

"At least a year ago." She sat stretched out beside me on a lawn chair, her long brown legs crossed at the ankles, looking positively adorable in a gleaming white sundress.

"Why don't you visit?" I said. "I'll buy you a plane ticket. How about next week?"

"Really, Miss G?"

"Of course. Go spend a couple of weeks with your family and catch up." I adjusted my large black sunglasses. "I'll get on fine here. I'll miss you, but I'll survive."

We grinned at each other, and I reached for my pack of cigarettes.

"Reenie, what am I going to do about my contract?"

"Is it time to sign again?"

"Mm-hmm." The sun sprayed a fan-shaped pattern of light across my bare legs and feet. I laid my head back against the lawn chair and closed my eyes. "I'm getting tired of this business. MGM has broken my heart a hundred times."

"Shouldn't your talent manager negotiate something for you?" she asked. She'd learned nearly as much about show business as I had over the years, being my closest confidant and all.

"Yes, he said I have to agree to the next picture, even if it's a stinker since I got suspended. But I was also thinking about asking for a role for Francis. Would you do that?"

"Do what?" She stirred her martini with the tip of her finger and took a sip.

"Put your neck on the line for your husband." I'd already made a few attempts to help him, but nothing had panned out yet. No one wanted to touch Francis right now, but I couldn't tell him that, and now I wasn't sure how far I should go to jeopardize my own reputation. Like it or not, my husband was a liability.

She shook her head. "I don't know, but I'd do it for my family, or my friends," she added with a smile and reached for my hand.

I squeezed back. "You would, wouldn't you? I just want him to be happy. If I could help him get an audition for a really good role, he could jump-start his career again. Maybe then we'd stop fighting." It sounded like a good solution, but would we really stop all that arguing? I couldn't imagine it at this point. It seemed to be who we were together.

When barking came from inside the house, I peered over my shoulder to see Francis. A warmth spread through me when I saw his face, happiness sparking in my chest and I knew that was why we were still at it, still working on being married. He opened the back door and Rags dashed outside. My little corgi had grown long and thick with big ears that stood on end. He was cute as a button.

"Come here, Rags," I said. "Come sit with your mama."

He barked and put his paws on the edge of the chair, his tongue lolling happily from the side of his mouth.

Francis reached down to scrub him behind the ears and then called his daughter's name. "Nancy, come meet Ava."

I jumped to my feet. "Why, hello there." I smiled at the pretty girl in her dress and flats. "I'm Ava. It's nice to meet you." I held out a hand and took hers in mine. "Goodness, you have a nice firm handshake."

Nancy smiled shyly. "Hi," she said.

She stared at me as if awestruck, so I set about trying to make her feel at home.

"Nancy, this is Reenie," I said, gesturing to my right.

"Hi, Miss Reenie," Nancy replied.

"Hi, Miss Nancy," Reenie said, proffering a smile at the young lady. "Would you like some lemonade?"

"Yes, please."

Reenie set down her martini and headed to the kitchen, calling over her shoulder, "I'll bring some out to the patio."

"I have a gift for you," I said. "Should we go get it?"

Nancy's face brightened.

I winked at Francis, and he beamed at us both. I led Nancy back inside the house and produced a beautifully wrapped package. Her face lit up as she opened a tube of neon orange Tangee lipstick.

"It's a magic lipstick," I said. "Do you see how bright it is? But when you put it on, it changes to match your natural color, and if you're lucky, your mood."

"Thank you," Nancy said with a shy smile.

"Would you like me to help you put it on?"

She nodded, and I led her into the bathroom. In front of the mirror, with a steady hand, I slid the soft stick of makeup over her lips. "There. Isn't that gorgeous?"

She blushed hotly. "Thank you."

"Well, now. Let's go have that lemonade."

Francis had plunked down in a lawn chair and was thumbing through a copy of *From Here to Eternity*. "I really want to play Maggio," he said, laying the book on the table with a big sigh.

"You'd be great at it," I agreed, taking my seat again. "He's scrappy and a good friend, with an air of desperation about him."

He nodded. "If that doesn't describe me right now, I don't know what does."

"Are you going to audition?" Nancy asked after taking a big gulp of the sunny yellow beverage in her glass.

"I'd like to, sweetheart, but it's not that simple." He fished in his pocket and pulled out a roll of cherry Life Savers, his favorite sweets that he always had on hand, and gave them to Nancy. She accepted it happily, peeled one piece of candy off, and handed the roll back to him.

I made the final decision right then that I would try again—pressure someone to give Francis an audition. In fact, I suddenly knew who the right person was to ask.

"You leave that to me, baby," I said, winking at him. "I'm going to make this a whole lot simpler."

He smiled broadly for the first time in ages, and I felt my heart melt a little. I'd give Joan a call that afternoon.

★ ★ ★

A few days later, I met Joan and Harry Cohn for dinner. Harry was the owner of Columbia Pictures—and now owner of the film rights to *From Here to Eternity*. The restaurant was a divine five-star establishment with mosaic tiled floors in greens and purples and gold, potted palms and flowers, and a jazz trio. Naturally, the crowd was a who's who in Hollywood, and I was glad I'd dressed for the occasion in a black crepe cocktail dress with cap sleeves and hand-stitched vines that rolled across the bodice.

Joan's full red lips weren't the least bit smudged despite her two martinis and salad. I wished I had that kind of class, but I had never been the overly feminine type. When I could get away with it, I still looked like a tomboy in tatty trousers.

"The fish is delicious," Joan said. "You really should try it, Ava."

"Sure. You know I'm not shy," I said, swapping some of my lemon chicken piccata and fried potatoes dusted with salt and sprinkled with herbs for her salmon. We talked about the latest studio gossip at Columbia Pictures, but Cohn kept turning things back to my contracts. I could tell he was fishing, but I'd rather donate a kidney than work for Harry Cohn. Truthfully, I wasn't a fan of Harry's. His nickname was King Cohn, and he was known as the biggest tyrant in Hollywood. I'd heard he had listening devices on the various soundstages at his studio and cracked a horsewhip on his desk to get people's attention. Francis told me Cohn had connections with the Mob in Chicago, not that Francis had a right to say anything. Francis had struck up a friendship with Sam Giancana in Chicago recently. Made me sick to my stomach. I hated Mob scum.

"I have this picture that's perfect for you," Harry pressed. "*Joseph and His Brethren*, set in Egypt. I'll pay you what you deserve. You know that."

"As tempting as that sounds, Harry, I'm booked solid." What I didn't say out loud was the script sounded like a real dog.

He reached for his martini, the light of the table lamp transforming the rim into a ring of gleaming silver. "Promise me you'll think about it."

"Of course," I drawled. The waiter poured my third glass of

an outrageously expensive Burgundy wine. Cohn could afford it, and I was glad to have something nice to wash down a difficult conversation. "Thank you for the offer."

Joan met my eyes and reached for her glass. "Darling," she said, turning her attention to her husband. "Have there been any casting calls for *From Here to Eternity*?"

"Not yet, but we have several people in mind. Why?" He aggressively cut his lamb chop, making it wiggle across his plate as he sawed at it with his knife.

"Well, I was thinking you should give Ava's husband a chance at a part."

"Frankie Sinatra?" The furrowed lines on his forehead reached all the way to the bald crown of his head. "He isn't an actor. He's a singer."

"What do you mean he isn't an actor?" she protested gently before I could. "Of course he is."

"He's played himself in a handful of musicals is all."

"What about a smaller role, Harry?" I cut in. "Maggio, the lightweight Italian who's down on his luck. My son of a bitch husband is perfect for it."

He laughed abruptly. "Oh, Christ. He may be an Italian down on his luck, but he's no actor."

"Just give him a test," I said, touching Harry's forearm lightly. "You won't be disappointed. You've never seen a man so ready to eat crow and work hard. He's willing to work for free, even."

"Come on, Harry," Joan said, slipping her hand under the table onto his knee. "It's just an audition."

"I'll think about it," he said finally.

I gave him my most winning smile and said, "That will do, Harry. You're a peach."

Joan winked at me over her glass, and I knew we had him. It wasn't a guarantee, but it was something. I could hardly wait to tell Francis.

★ ★ ★

Francis was thrilled I'd spoken to Cohn, and he showered me with affection. There was no certainty he'd get the part, but his chances were suddenly much greater. He wasn't so thrilled, however, about my next film. I, on the other hand, was beside myself with excitement. MGM was pulling out all the stops for *Mogambo*, a picture set and filmed in Kenya. I was cast along with Grace Kelly and Clark Gable to play in a sort of love triangle in the dangerous wilds of the African bush, and no expense would be spared. I could hardly wait to go, to take a break from the never-ending bickering with Francis, and to escape his incessant melancholy. It was something of a problem, I supposed, to always look forward to an escape from my husband, but I wasn't ready to do something about it.

And yet, I wouldn't escape him entirely. He chose to come with me for a few weeks.

The night before we left Los Angeles, we went to Frascati's, one of our favorite Italian places, to celebrate what was coming next. We enjoyed our fettuccine primavera and spaghetti Bolognese, the pasta tender and the sauces satisfying—until Francis mentioned casually that Lana Turner was borrowing his house. I knew he still held affection for his ex-girlfriend. Lana had always been hard to ignore with her blond locks, buxom curves, and box office hits. She was sex on legs, and though I knew I was the dark version to her blond, and that their past relationship didn't compare to our love, I couldn't help myself. Jealousy rushed over me like a swollen creek after a summer storm. It didn't help that we'd been drinking—it never seemed to.

"Well, isn't that convenient," I said, stabbing at a slippery noodle. "You have a beautiful movie star waiting for you in your bed!"

"What's the problem?" he said. "She's fighting with her boyfriend and needs a break, so I told her she could stay there."

"Why can't she stay somewhere else? You're seeing her again, aren't you." I pushed away my plate.

"What are you talking about? Calm down," he said, giving me a look like I was insane. "I'm not with Lana. I'm married to you, remember?" Francis threw a wad of cash on the table. "I'm out of here."

"Where do you think you're going? Don't walk away from me!" I followed him outside and he slid into the car.

I swore at him and kicked the tire with my boot. He rolled down the window and as he roared out of the parking lot, he screamed obscenities about what he'd do to Lana when he got home.

"Enjoy her!" I shouted back before I realized a startled elderly couple, a valet, and a family had stopped to watch the spectacle. I didn't care—the alcohol had gone to my head and Frank made me incensed. I called my sister to pick me up and she showed several minutes later.

"Take me to Palm Springs," I said, my voice shaking with unshed tears.

She frowned, her brow arching into one thick dark line. "What's going on?"

"I think he's cheating on me. With Lana."

"Frank? Isn't Lana your friend?"

"Some friend," I scoffed, crossing my arms over my chest.

"Are you sure?" Bappie asked, putting the car in reverse. "The man worships you and yet you assume the worst."

"Whose side are you on?" I said, fumbling in my handbag for a cigarette. "I assume the worst because it's true! Don't you remember the hooker?"

Sighing, Bappie steered us onto the highway. By the time we arrived in Palm Springs, I still hadn't calmed down. The sight of Frank's car in the driveway propelled me up the walk. I banged my fist against the front door, noticing suddenly, for the first time, that the house was dark. And what was I doing? I didn't have to knock to enter. I reached for the knob when Ben Cole, my business manager, answered the door.

"What are you doing here?" I asked, pushing my way inside.

"I'm having a drink with Lana," he said, closing the door behind me. "Frank just showed up, too. Everything alright?"

I felt myself blush hotly. He hadn't been lying after all.

As we walked into the living room, Francis took one look at me and rolled his eyes. My anger sparked all over again.

"Hi, Lana," I said, blatantly ignoring him. "I just thought you should know what Frank has in mind for you tonight." I repeated the crude comments he'd made.

She looked taken aback, set down her drink, and grabbed her purse. "You two can fight this one out without me. For what's it worth, Ava, I may have loved this guy once upon a time, but I don't anymore. Besides, I'd never do that to you."

I knew she very well would do it to a friend because she had in the past, but before I could reply, Ben jumped to his feet.

"I'll join her. Good night, all." He scurried after her, the front door closing with a decided bang.

Frank's face went purple as a plum. "What the hell is wrong with you?"

"You're what's wrong with me!" I shouted back.

Storming into the kitchen, I reached for plates and dishes and anything else I could get my hands on and smashed them, one by one, on the floor. I'd lost my mind, and though some part of me knew this, I couldn't seem to stop.

The maid looked on in abject horror, as if she was trying to decide if she should get the broom and dustpan or call the cops.

"Get out!" Frank roared as he stomped into the kitchen. When I didn't obey him, he reached for the telephone. "Hi, yeah, officer, I've got an intruder."

I couldn't believe it. I couldn't believe he'd called the cops on me. We'd have the press on us in no time, but maybe he didn't care anymore. Maybe I shouldn't either.

And yet, this was our way—to love and fight and struggle desperately against our insecurities and our own brand of darkness. It was a mad, addicting cycle, but I was wrung out. Tired of jeopardizing my career for him, tired of the bickering over nothing, of the jealousy, and the way he expected me to follow him no matter what. I was tired of it all, and one day soon, I would have to decide if I wanted Frank in my life at all.

CHAPTER 28

FRANK

After the ridiculous fight when I'd called the cops on my wife, I followed Ava to Kenya. It was one of the worst decisions I'd ever made, and that was saying something.

Kenya was beautiful and otherworldly with its black mountains, a rich savannah of grassy plains, Acacia trees, and wildlife I'd only ever read about, but it was a lot more rugged than I'd expected. The crew and the talent lived in Tent City near a river where the bugs were unbearable and the beds were scarcely more than a straw mattress on the ground. I wasn't the kind of guy who liked to rough it in the wild. I wanted the comfort of my own bed, or silk sheets at the Ritz. Maybe that made me spoiled, but I didn't care. I liked nice things and after years of having them, I was in no mood to give them up.

I hated being idle on set, watching my wife be at the top of her career while I wallowed, waiting for news about the audition I so desperately wanted, wishing I weren't a nobody, and worst of all, wishing I'd done a million things differently. I took the shuttle to and from Nairobi for a little civilization on many days, but it wasn't enough of a distraction from my misery, and I picked fights with Ava constantly.

We'd been in Kenya a week when a commotion came from the kitchen tent.

"What the hell is that?" I demanded, sitting up in bed.

"Better go see. We're not in Kansas anymore, Toto," Ava quipped.

We pulled on our shoes and dipped outside to see what was happening. The crew gathered around a tall, lean man in a safari outfit standing aloft of the kitchen tent. He brought his finger to his lips, signaling us to be quiet, and then waved his arm to push the crowd back. He had a long scar on his calf muscle, and I wondered how he'd gotten it. Probably from wrestling with a cheetah, the dumbass, I thought wryly.

Ava leaned to my ear. "What's in there, do you think?"

"Something we don't want to meet face-to-face, I can tell you that," I answered.

The safari man pulled a rifle from his shoulder holster, cocked it, and ducked inside the opening of the tent.

A roar tore through the air.

"Jesus Christ, it's a lion!" I said, sweeping my arm across Ava and pushing us farther back.

Another roar rippled the air and goose bumps raced over my skin. I was glad I wasn't that guy. He was nuts.

A shot rang out. We jumped at the sound.

Two lions streaked out of the tent, raw steaks and chickens in their mouths. The crowd gasped and then broke into laughter as the animals galloped away with their prizes. We watched them until their furry golden haunches disappeared in the thick grass beyond Tent City.

"I guess we aren't the fresh meat around here after all," Ava said, earning more laughter from the crew.

I slung my arm over her shoulder and steered her back to our tent. Wild animals, insects, constant bickering . . . I didn't know how much longer I could stand to be here.

As it turned out, I didn't have to wait long. Days later, I received a message and had to travel to Nairobi to retrieve it. Impatient, I rode the sweltering, smelly community bus over the rough terrain that could hardly be called a road, shifting constantly in my seat, praying it would be the news I'd been hoping for these last weeks. When at last the countryside gave way to flattened streets and colorful markets and storefronts that could hardly be called a city, I pressed my face against the dirty glass of the bus. I couldn't stand the suspense—who had called, and when would the infernal bus stop?

As we finally pulled to a halt, I pushed to the front of the bus and raced across the square to Western Union, dust coating my Italian leather shoes.

"Hi, there's a message for Frank Sinatra?" I asked the attendant, straining to hold back my enthusiasm.

"Yes, sir." He handed me an envelope and I tore it open on the spot.

It was a message from George Wood, my new manager. I placed a call to the U.S. immediately.

"George?" I shouted into the receiver over the static. "Tell me some good news."

"You got the screen test for *From Here to Eternity*," he said.

I punched the air with my fist. "Yes! Get me out of here!"

He laughed. "Not enjoying Africa?"

"Hell no!" I replied. "It's beautiful and wild, but let me tell you something, George. There's no such thing as a cold drink and the place is swarming with flies."

He laughed again. "I get you. Listen, Frank, there are five actors auditioning for the part including Eli Wallach, the Broadway star. You're going to have to do the best work you've ever done. Are you ready for that?"

"I've never been more ready," I said, forcing a confidence I didn't feel. There were five others? How would I beat out Wallach? Everyone loved that guy. But I had a shot, and for now, that was good enough—I was going to use it well.

"I'm going to act my ass off, George."

"Atta boy. I'll book you on a flight to LA for tomorrow."

When the bus dropped me off in Tent City, I leapt off the shuttle and raced to our tent to find Ava lounging with a book.

"I got a screen test!" I shouted in greeting.

She sat up and dropped her book. "Oh, baby, that's wonderful! When do you go?"

"Tomorrow. I'm going to pack up my things tonight and head back to town on the first shuttle."

"Are you ready for it?" she asked, hugging me to her.

"Am I ready! I already know all the lines!" I smiled for the first time in I didn't know how long. I'd never been so ready for anything in my entire life. I'd show them I wasn't some two-bit has-been. I wasn't going to disappear from the spotlight without a fight.

I picked up the woman I loved, who'd helped me get this

chance and who, no matter what happened between us, I couldn't seem to live without, and twirled her around. It was one of the few moments of peace we'd had since we'd arrived.

She laughed and kissed me hard. "Knock 'em dead, baby."

"I will," I said enthusiastically. "I've got nothing left to lose."

CHAPTER 29

AVA

I hated to admit it, but I was relieved the minute Francis got on that plane. I hoped like hell he'd land the part. Auditioning would give him a sense of purpose, if only for a little while. If he didn't get it, we'd have some things to figure out. I couldn't go on living this way. We'd been in more screaming matches since we arrived in Africa than we had even at home, but that wasn't the only reason I was glad he was leaving. I was pregnant, again.

"Gracie, I'd be the worst mother in the world," I confided in Grace Kelly, who had become a good friend. Working on set closely and intensely, even for short stints, had a way of bringing couples together or sparking new friendships. I adored Gracie's determination and warmth and goodness—a goodness that was tempered with a little fire and bad behavior on occasion. She was my kind of woman.

"Don't say that," she replied, retying the bandana covering her golden hair. "You'd be a wonderful mother. Look how charming and friendly you are with everyone."

"Everyone but Francis, and he'd be the father," I said, sullenly. I unscrewed the cap to my water canteen and took a deep drink.

"You could always hire a nanny to help," she suggested. "Think of the baby's sweet smiles and little toes." She sighed. I knew she was longing for marriage and a family. She was a romantic, just like Francis. I, however, was not.

"And the diapers and the screaming in the middle of the night. The schooling while we're on the road. What would I do, drag the poor child with me on set? She'd grow up rotten."

The truth was, after the first abortion something soft and vulnerable had broken inside me; a childhood dream I'd been carrying was switched off like a porch light on a Carolina winter night. I was too frightened of being pregnant and even more terrified of being a mother. I'd never forget Mama's exhaustion and the pain she'd suffered because of her children, and later, her ovarian cancer. I wasn't like her. I couldn't devote my life to others who depended on me for everything. I could barely take care of myself. And somehow, I knew Francis would expect that of me; he'd want me to give up everything and raise our children. That wasn't me. If he didn't understand that by now, well . . . then we really were doomed.

I was grateful to my publicist, who discreetly leaked to the press that I was being treated for a tropical infection while I flew to London for the procedure. When I returned to set, there was hell to pay. John Ford, the director, was a real grouch. Constantly swearing and demanding retakes, insulting the cast when he felt like it, even if it wasn't warranted. I had to shoot several scenes quickly that they'd paused while I was away, and after an exhausting day, I bungled my lines in one of the cabin scenes with Clark.

"Well, that was a real disaster," John said. "This is why I wanted Maureen O'Hara for the part instead of you."

I stared at him a moment, stunned by his blatant insult, but ever the sharp-tongued straight shooter, I recovered quickly. "You've been nothing but hateful all day, and I don't deserve it," I fumed. "You can take the dirty handkerchief you're chewing on and shove it up your ass!"

Clark and the others stared open-mouthed for a minute and glanced at the equally stunned director. I stormed out of the cabin but hadn't gone far when I heard Clark's voice.

"You can count me out, if you don't knock it off, Ford," Clark said. "She's been working her tail off all day and I, for one, am sick of putting up with your foul mouth."

I smiled and headed to my tent for a little of that whiskey Francis had left behind.

A couple of weeks later I took the shuttle into Nairobi to put in a call to Harry Cohn. I pressured him into choosing Francis for the part, and then I called Francis. I may have been glad he'd left to give me some breathing room, but still, I was lonely. Clark and Grace had been shacking up together, their on-screen affections turning into a steamy affair. They'd teased Francis and me endlessly about my loud, squeaky mattress, but now it was them I could hear. I started talking with the crew, hanging around the cameramen and the producer, looking for company, especially in the evenings when the work was done.

On days off, there wasn't much to do, so one day I downed a quick breakfast and headed to set. I thought I'd ride out into the bush with the crew, see the sights. Clark and Grace were filming a scene in a jeep and would be followed by a camera truck. Frank "Bunny" Allen, the professional hunter hired to protect the camp from wild animals, would be riding along in the truck for safety's sake. I squeezed in next to Bunny, happy about my good luck. He'd be interesting to talk to if nothing else. He was tall and light-eyed with a dark brow and a slightly crooked smile. His British accent only added to his appeal, as did the way he slung a gun around like he wasn't afraid of anything. He'd been raised in Africa and moved like a leopard, and I could see he felt as much a part of the land as the wild animals he loved.

We bumped and swayed over the uneven roads, if one could call them roads, following closely behind Grace and Clark. Grace's hair had come loose from her bun in places and was fluttering in the wind, and though Clark handled the vehicle well despite the potholes, they had trouble delivering their lines.

I, meanwhile, enjoyed the ride and the landscape.

"Bunny," I said, laying my hand lightly on his forearm, "what kind of bird is that?"

He squinted in the sunlight. "A grey crowned crane."

"They're beautiful. Elegant."

He nodded. "There's a lot of beauty in Kenya, especially from where I'm sitting." He held my gaze and a sly smile crossed his face.

"Is that right?" I said, my tone turning flirtatious. I knew he was married but still had a reputation for being a ladies' man. I could see why women flocked to him. It was all of that raw male energy, the whiff of danger.

The next instant, thunder rumbled from behind a copse of squat trees and a tangle of brush. The ground trembled and the truck began to shake. I gripped the sides of the truck to steady myself and stared wide-eyed at the dust rising like a malevolent fog into the air.

Clark and Grace turned to look at us, fear carving up their faces.

"Ah, hell," Bunny said, cocking his gun.

Three rhinos dashed from behind the cover of the trees.

My heart leapt into my throat. Of all the animals in the Kenyan wilds, rhinos were the most dangerous. Bunny had briefed everyone on our first few days at camp with details about how to protect ourselves. His advice flashed through my mind: with a rhino, you were to stay very still so with their poor eyesight they mistook you for a tree, stay downwind to throw them off your scent, climb a tree or hide in a bush, or run in a zig-zag pattern if on foot.

We were breaking all the rules. The beasts charged straight at us.

"There's two more!" I screeched, pointing at the small herd.

Grace screamed as the powerful animals descended upon their truck.

The rhinos ducked their heads, bashing them against the metal, their horns scraping the sides of the truck until a terrible screeching sound mingled with our screams. I watched in horror as they used their enormous, muscular bodies to push the jeep to and fro as if it were a toy truck.

Clark wrapped Grace in his arms protectively. I could do nothing but stare, open-mouthed, my heart racing.

Bunny stood with his gun, aimed, and fired.

One rhino collapsed to the earth with a thud.

Bunny fired a second shot and another animal went down. The remaining rhinos took the hint, turned abruptly, and galloped away.

My hands shook and my mouth remained agape as I watched the crash of rhinos dash off, the earth trembling beneath us.

John and Bunny jumped from the truck and raced over to the others.

"Are you alright?" Bunny asked, reaching to cup Grace's shoulder.

She nodded, sending a cascade of tears down her cheeks. "I'm alright."

"That was the craziest damn thing I've ever seen," I said. "Thank God we've got Tarzan with us."

At that, everyone broke into laughter, cutting the tension. Bunny laughed, too. He held my gaze a moment longer than what was comfortable, but I didn't look away. I never was one to cower or play coy.

Later, I couldn't stop thinking about the incident with the rhinos. It had shaken me, but it had also exhilarated me—so had Bunny's intensity. He hadn't even flinched at the animals' approach. Suddenly I wanted to see more wild animals up close, especially if it meant seeing more of Bunny and his big gun.

"Are you sure you're up for this?" he asked the following afternoon. "You don't seem like the type who's into wildlife."

He had me pegged. He'd seen me swat at the incessant swarming flies, mosquitoes, and other insects intent on taking a bite out of me until I'd gotten irritated and zipped myself up inside my tent with much loud complaining.

"Whatever do you mean?" I batted my eyes innocently, eliciting a laugh. I'd followed his instructions to wear long pants and boots, but it was too hot to wear long sleeves.

"Here, rub the exposed skin on your arms and neck with this."

I took the tube of lemon eucalyptus oil and filled my palm with a glistening pool of it, liberally spreading it over my skin. I'd gotten used to the smell of the stuff, so I barely noticed its pungent woody scent.

As we rode away from camp, I found myself soaking in the scenery—miles of red clay and brush, patches of lush grasses and trees, a range of mountains pointing toward the heavens—but the most magnificent thing about Africa was the infinite sky. It was a vast desert of blue all day, and at sunset, the embers of a smoldering fire.

At last, Bunny pulled the truck off the dirt road to park.

"See there?" He pointed to a patch of tall, thick grasses. "There's a stream, and where there's water, there are usually elephants and plenty of other animals, too."

We left the truck, walking briskly until we reached the edge of the thicket.

"Now," he whispered. "We have to be very, very quiet. We don't want to be trampled so move slowly. Do your best not to make a sound. There's a herd just ahead."

I was ready to ask him what sort of herd when his finger pressed against my lips, and he mouthed the word, "Shh."

I smiled and his finger traced the curve of my lips.

My throat went dry at the look in his eyes. We shouldn't go down this path. We couldn't. I'd never forget Francis's hurt and fury when I'd told him about my bullfighter.

I looked away.

Bunny led us painfully slowly through the grass. At last, the grass parted to make way for a brown ribbon of water glistening in the sunlight. On the banks of the stream, a herd of cow elephants lazed, drinking and spraying water over their papery skin. They were beautiful, majestic, and unbelievably enormous.

Bunny looked back at me and winked. When I smiled, he grabbed my hand, pulling me into a crouch beside him. We hid from view in a spray of weeds, where we watched them in awe. They spoke to each other in soft rumbles and playful nudges, their ears flapping to keep the flies away. There was one so close, I could hear her snuffling, felt as if I could reach out and touch her. I leaned closer—and jumped suddenly at a splashing sound.

"It's alright," Bunny whispered, his lips brushing my ear. "She was just taking a crap."

I burst out laughing.

The sound split the air and I clamped my hand over my mouth—too late. The beautiful animals were spooked.

Bunny yanked me backward and we stumbled through the mud, splashing across the swamp, pausing only briefly to see the elephants stampeding, mercifully, in the opposite direction.

Relieved, he exhaled a deep breath and removed his hat to wipe the sweat ring from his forehead with his arm. "So much for staying quiet."

"You have to admit, that was funny."

"You're funny," he said. "The way you see wonder in everything. You're kind of adorable."

"Am I now?" I gave him one of my brightest smiles.

As his eyes locked on mine, I knew then that I'd even the score with Francis. His hookers for this one night. I'd put the hurt aside for an adventure, for one wild night in the bush. There wasn't much I valued more than making memories, and that night, I'd make another.

That night, I would find myself in Bunny Allen's bed.

CHAPTER 30

FRANK

flew to Los Angeles all nerves. I prepped for the screen test for hours and then went in for my appointment for *From Here to Eternity* as assured as I could be that I was ready. I gave my all like nothing I'd ever done before.

If the director didn't see I was right for the part, he was a moron—if he didn't see I was right for the part, I was done. Through, finished for good. I tried not to think about it, but who was I kidding? I obsessed over it. This film that I could feel in my bones would be a huge hit. This role could turn everything around for me if they would just give me the chance.

When I was finished, I couldn't sit still and paced the house for a week before I decided it was time to get out of town, spend some time with Ava. Besides, it was Christmas. I flew back to Kenya, hoping time on set with my wife would help calm my anxiety, but instead, we spent Christmas in shouting matches. She didn't care one bit that I was there and showed no interest in the extravagant gifts I'd brought.

To make matters worse, I discovered she'd had an abortion without telling me she was pregnant in the first place.

"How could you do that to me?" I said, slumping into my chair after an hour of cussing and throwing pots and pans and upending the vase of flowers I'd brought her. The vase had shattered on impact. I was shattered, too. When I didn't think that woman could hurt me anymore, she twisted the knife. "Don't you want kids?" I asked. "I thought we were going to start a family."

"And what exactly would I do with a baby on set, Francis?" she asked, her hands on her hips. "Or when you're at three gigs every night, dragging your sorry ass home at five o'clock in the morning? What then? I'm not doing this by myself. Besides, we can't spend a week together without going at each other's throats. What kind of life would the kid have? You only think about yourself, Frank."

She was right, I knew, but how could I trust a woman—the woman I was crazy enough to drive myself right off a cliff for—who went behind my back about something so important? The short answer was, I didn't and I couldn't.

I cut my trip short and took a job in Boston.

Ava and I patched things up long distance, but I was restless. There was no word on the screen test, and as week after excruciating week passed, I still didn't know if I'd landed the part of Maggio. I railed against the capriciousness of Hollywood and the gatekeepers who made the decisions. Who were they to say I couldn't act? Who were they to call the shots, anyway? They were just suits, men with money who wouldn't know a good film or good music if it bit them in the ass. It was all about sales to them and nothing more.

I consoled myself with Jack Daniel's and too many late nights at the bar after hours. Called up friends, Jimmy and Bogie—

Humphrey Bogart, who was becoming a real pal—but though I appreciated their friendship, I still couldn't see where to go from here, and the black dog found me again.

After a particularly grueling day, I was getting ready for a show when the phone rang. My stomach clenched at the sound of my talent manager's voice.

"You're the luckiest son of a bitch alive," George Wood said matter-of-factly into the phone. "Apparently your screen test was great. They were impressed with you, Frank. And that's not an easy feat these days."

My heart racing, I ignored the dig. "Well? Did I get it?"

"They chose Eli Wallach." He paused and my heart crashed to the ground like a fourteenth-story elevator. "But you're in luck, Sinatra. Wallach took another role on Broadway instead. The part is yours."

I screamed like a little girl. I'd gotten the part!

"You're not pulling one over on me, are you?" I said, my voice hoarse.

"Not my style. You know that."

I did. George wasn't one to mince words. It was one reason why he was so successful. He didn't take any crap and he didn't push any either.

I hollered again as the back of my eyes pricked with overwhelming emotion. This would change everything. I knew it would—I'd make sure of it.

"Now," he went on, "filming begins next month in Hawaii. And unfortunately for you, they took you at your word when you said you'd work for next to nothing, so you'll only make a lousy thousand dollars a week."

"I don't care about the money," I said breathlessly. I was

playing the long game, and I knew, given my current status in Hollywood, I'd have to take what I could get. I'd already had one death in this town, and it was hell trying to resurrect myself. I'd be on my best behavior from here on out. I couldn't wait to tell Ava.

"Good," George replied. "That's where you need to be right now. And listen, Frank, I have a lead on a record contract, but it's not a sure thing yet so don't go blabbing all over town about it. But I wanted you to know. Keep your head up. I think your luck is about to change."

I would have hugged the man and beat him on the back if he'd been in the room. Instead, in a serious tone, I said a paltry, "Thanks, George. I owe you, and I won't ever forget that. I mean it. I'm Italian. My word is everything."

"You pay me, remember? Besides, I'm looking forward to seeing this ship turn around."

I grinned. "Me, too, man. Me, too."

The film turned out to be everything I wanted it to be. The director was brilliant, the cast was top notch, and I enjoyed working my tail off day after day on set in Hawaii. I was focused and attentive, on my best behavior, at least during the day. In the evenings, I let loose with Montgomery Clift, my costar who played Prewitt in the picture, and James Jones, the author of the novel. A former soldier, Monty could party like the best of them and even better, liked to philosophize the way I did after a few beers. We'd grab Jones and head to the hotel bar or out to the tikis on the beach, shut down the bar and go back to our suite to talk about life and politics, art and women, and everything between. I missed Ava like hell, but we both needed time away from each other. Some part of me was relieved for the separation.

One night after filming, the fellas and I were half a dozen beers deep and happened onto the topic of civil rights.

"Look, Monty, people have called me names my whole life," I said. "Some people are nothing but a bunch of small-minded pricks who can't tolerate a person who doesn't look like them. I grew up in the city, you see? There were all kinds of people and we got along just fine. No one was better than the other. We worked hard, we lived hard, we made friends."

He nodded, puffed on his cigar, and swigged from his beer can. "I don't understand segregation. Can you imagine being told to drink at a different water fountain? What does that accomplish anyway, man?"

"What a crock of bullshit that is," I answered. "I've spoken out against inequality plenty, and I will again, no matter what my manager says. I was told to keep my mouth shut, because it hurt my career, but I can't stand it, man. The injustice." I'd won a Golden Globe and Academy Award for a short about racial and religious tolerance called *The House I Live In*. Equality was a principle I was passionate about and I'd be damned if I'd back down now or ever.

He wagged his head in sloppy agreement, and I knew he was as lit as a Christmas tree. Made me laugh.

"It's good to see you happy," Monty said, lighting a cigar and squinting at me. He was a pretty boy, and the women were lured in by his brooding looks and bright eyes. He was a hell of an actor, too. I'd never met anyone into method acting, but he'd taught me a lot in our short time working together.

"I'll be heading to London soon to see Ava," I said, puffing on my own cigar and blowing a plume of smoke overhead.

"I've never seen anyone so whipped by his old lady," Monty said, laughing at his own joke.

"You've never met Ava, have you?" I said. "She's a witch. Casts a spell on just about everyone she meets, male or female. Most beautiful damned woman you've ever seen."

"Those are the best kind," Monty said. "Love isn't enough. There has to be something else there."

I nodded, contemplating his words. "We fight like a couple of cocks in a ring. She won't hear of settling down or doing anything a woman is supposed to do. And yet, she owns me."

"Maybe that's why," he replied.

I contemplated his words. I thought being married and truly belonging to each other would end the arguing between us. I thought it would mean she'd want to make a home together and put her career second, after us. We'd start a family, be happy. I was beginning to see how foolish that assumption was. The very things I loved about Ava—her unpredictability, her independence, and the drive that brought her success—meant she would never agree to what my idea of being married meant or my traditional views of a woman's duties. She'd slug me at the mention of it.

I looked down at the drink in my hands and finished the last swallow.

Noticing my pained expression, Jones said, "She's really got you tied in knots, hasn't she?" He cracked open another beer. Cans littered the room and a cloud of not-quite dissipated cigar smoke hovered in the air. Combined with our sweat and Monty's unwashed socks, it smelled like a locker room.

"Hey, Jones, open that window, would you?" I asked.

Jones, who had been quietly drinking himself into a stupor as he listened to us, jumped up to open the window. The ocean air rushed through the suite, catching the tendrils of smoke and whisking them out to sea.

"We should clean up. This place is a dump." My words were slurred.

Monty bent to pick up one of the empty beer cans and launched it out the window at the dumpster below. It ricocheted off the lid with a clatter and fell to the ground. "Damn, I missed."

"You're a lousy shot," I said, and scooped up a few of my own. I launched them at the dumpster next. After we'd all missed a few, we realized the cans were too light to aim properly so we smashed them, flattening them into discs, and spun them like saucers.

"Bull's-eye!" I shouted, hitting the target.

Monty and Jones cheered.

After several minutes of chucking cans and anything else we got our hands on out the window, we heard a loud knocking at the suite's main door.

Monty grinned. "It's probably for you."

"Nah, I didn't hire any girls tonight," I said, stumbling to the door. With Ava so far away, I'd helped myself to prostitutes and a couple of cute girls I'd met at the bar. No big deal. It wasn't as if I ever wanted to see them again, so Ava didn't need to know about it. I loved that woman enough for ten men. Meaningless sex with someone else couldn't change that.

"Debbie?" I said, scratching my head. Our costar, Deborah Kerr, stood on the other side of the door.

"What the hell are you all doing?" she demanded. "It's three thirty in the morning!" Her eye makeup was smeared and her hair was disheveled, and if I didn't know any better, I'd say she'd been making mischief of her own. "I could hear you down the hall."

We laughed at that but abandoned our game. It was late and we had an early wake-up call in just a few hours.

"Come on, boys, it's time for bed," she said, ushering us out of the living room.

We obeyed like naughty children and once we were all in our rooms and in bed, Debbie said good night.

"See you soon," she said.

"Can I get a good-night kiss first?" I called out, eliciting laughter from the other two.

"Not on your life, Frank. Good night."

I chuckled, feeling happier than I had in ages. I might not have been on top of the world, but baby, I was back in the game.

CHAPTER 31

FRANK

I returned from Hawaii feeling like a new man. I'd given it my all and I knew, deep down, that I'd done a great job. I hoped things would start looking up from there. It was no secret that Ava was getting fed up with my constant low moods, and I didn't blame her. She needed a man who could take care of her; a real man who didn't have to beg, borrow, or steal just to stay afloat; and I hoped I could finally be that for her.

I had scarcely walked through the door at home in Palm Springs when the telephone rang.

"More good news, Frank," George, my talent manager, said. "The record deal with Capital Records got the green light."

A wave of sheer joy crashed over me. I wanted to kiss the man—I would've also kissed Johnny the Meathead who'd set me up with George in the first place, had he been around. George was as ballsy and no-nonsense as everyone said he was, and he got the job done.

"Good man!" I all but shouted into the telephone.

"There's just one thing, Frank," he cautioned.

"Anything," I said. "I'll do anything."

"You'll need to pay for the studio fees"—he paused—"And you'll also have a new arranger."

My mood dimmed slightly. "I'll pay the fees, but no new arranger. Axel is my man."

"He *was* your man," George corrected. "Look, this guy Nelson Riddle is brilliant. One of the best out there and he's going nowhere but up. You want to ride this train, believe me. He's worked with Bing Crosby, Nat King Cole, Mel Tormé. Besides, it's time to shake off the old image of Frankie the sweetheart crooner and bring on Frank Sinatra, a man reinvented."

He was right. I needed a brand-new everything. New look, new attorney, new accountant. There wouldn't be any more cute Frankie Sinatra bowties, suspenders, and screaming young girls. It would be Brooks Brothers suits and a fedora, a pinky ring, Cuban cigars, and a healthy dose of swagger after a few years of hard knocks. I'd have a complete redo. I wanted to come back swinging.

When recording day arrived, I walked into the Capital Records studio a ball of nerves. I hadn't recorded anything in six months, and most of what I'd been forced to sing the last two years was trash. Could I pull this off? Was I as good as I needed to be? I didn't like the idea of a new arranger, and the pressure to be prefect—to not make a single wrong move— had my guts twisted in knots. I made a silent deal with myself that I'd record a few songs with the new arranger to see how things went, and when they turned out to be garbage, I'd put in a call to George and insist we bring Axel back.

I checked in and was shown to the recording studio. I hung my hat and made my way around the room, shaking hands, offering a smile, pouring on the charm. I was more grateful than they knew, and I would act the part, show them they weren't wasting their time and money on me. The band, at least, looked to be top notch and I knew right then we were in business.

"Hi there, Frank," one of the executives said. "Meet Nelson Riddle. He'll be your arranger."

Nelson had a head of thick dark hair, a widow's peak, and pointy eyebrows, but his face was open and friendly, and in spite of myself, I liked the look of him, even if I didn't trust him to do a good job yet.

"Great to meet you, Frank," he said.

We shook hands and he gave me the sheet music. We talked about which notes I should emphasize and the tempo of the accompaniment, exchanged a few comments about the lyrics, and got to work.

I stepped up to the mic, earphones on, and after a few run-throughs, I was ready to give it a real go for recording. When Nelson signaled the band to start again, I closed my eyes to block out the people in the room and focus. When I finished, my eyes flicked open to see Nelson looking at me thoughtfully.

"Your voice has deepened since the last record I heard," he said. "It's a little brassier than I remember, too."

"Well, I'm not twenty anymore," I said, reaching for my water glass, suddenly nervous my voice wasn't quite what they expected—or wanted. Was I losing my touch?

"No, this is a good thing," he said reassuringly. "It lends itself better to the music. It means . . ." He paused, scratched at the light stubble on his face. "I'd like to start with the brass first thing on this one, and if you could open with some vibrato. While singing, think about the lyrics. You're mad about a girl so you're the happiest man in the world. You've got the world on a string. Let's see it."

"I don't have to stretch for that one." I smiled.

He didn't smile back but nodded. The guy had a real serious air about him, but if anyone could appreciate intensity in a fellow, I could.

I gave him what he was asking for; the lyrics flowed from my tongue and mingled with the renewed sense of hope that had buoyed me over the last month. Afterward we recorded a couple of ballads, too.

"This is perfect. Really, Frank," Nelson said. "Your delivery . . . it carries a wounded soulfulness to it. You're fantastic at bringing the emotion."

Well, alright. Looked like Riddle understood me. I'd give this man a chance, but if the recording sounded lousy, that was it. I would still call Axel no matter how much Riddle complimented me.

"Let's listen to the playback," I said, reaching for the pack of smokes in my jacket pocket.

"I've Got the World on a String" began to play and I glanced at Riddle, who was frowning in concentration. The next few songs played, sounding different from anything I'd done before. They had more of an emphasis on my own rhythm, the way I liked to enunciate every syllable. Nelson had conducted the band so the music could bend around my voice and elevate it in a different way from Axel's arrangements. It sounded fresh, upbeat. It was utterly damn brilliant.

He replayed "I've Got the World on a String" and as it ended, a genuine smile stretched my lips. This man knew what the hell he was doing. More than that, it took a lot to impress me, and I was astounded at the way he'd conducted the orchestra.

"That went a lot better than I thought," I said. "It was great!"

He returned my smile. "I think we've found ourselves a hit, Frank."

I was pretty sure we'd found ourselves a partnership.

I left the studio, whistling, my hands in my pockets to keep myself from skipping down the road. Maybe we did have some hits on our hands, maybe not, but one thing was for sure, I was relieved to be developing a more mature sound with a group of great musicians. *This music* I could work with. There would be no more songs with dogs barking in the background and all that other nonsense I'd been forced to sing for CBS. Between *From Here to Eternity* and my work with Riddle, for the first time in ages, I felt the inklings of honest-to-God happiness. I couldn't wait to tell Ava all about it. Since George booked me for an international tour, I'd be able to tell her in person, in England where she was filming *Knights of the Round Table.*

I still couldn't fill a theater in the United States, but I hoped I could abroad. My manager insisted it was a good move, especially with promotion for a new film about to begin. I needed the cash anyway.

But my buoyant mood plummeted fast and hard on opening night of the tour. In a theater that seated thousands, only four hundred showed. As I looked out at the paltry showing, I could barely make it through the night.

"Shake it off, baby," Ava said when we had gone back to the hotel that night. "It'll be better elsewhere. Maybe the press didn't hear about the show because there wasn't enough advertising. It was a fast booking."

"How am I supposed to shake it off?" I said, fuming after more embarrassments in Scandinavia and Milan. No one gave a damn who Frank Sinatra was there either. We were four drinks deep and it had been a spectacularly bad night. The crowd watched Ava, not me. They wanted her autograph, not mine. They went mad for her, taking photographs and chasing her on foot or by car. They cornered her at the clubs. I couldn't take it much longer, and I wished George hadn't booked the tour.

"It's like taking a beating publicly, over and over," I said. "It's humiliating. No one even knows me in Europe."

What I didn't say was how humiliating it was to be thought of as Mr. Ava Gardner and not the other way around.

"That's probably good," she quipped. "It'll keep your ego in check."

"What the hell does that mean?" I thundered.

"Ever since you finished recording with Nelson Riddle, you've gone on and on about how great you are," she said, her eyes glossy from too much gin. "You don't have to remind me of it every day, Frank. I married you, remember?"

So I'd been reduced to Frank again. My head exploded. "Look who's talking! You prance around like you're the queen of Hollywood, waiting for people to fall at your feet!"

"Aren't I, though?" she volleyed back at me. "Stop acting so jealous. We aren't competing. I'm on your side, remember?"

I swore at her, abused her with rough language that I didn't mean but couldn't seem to keep myself from saying. She had that way about her, the needling that set me off when I was already on edge. And she was no saint herself—something I'd always loved about her but was beginning to like less, all of a sudden.

We slept in separate rooms that night, and the following day, we trudged onward to Naples, miserable and desperate for this wreck of a tour to end. Ava refused to go with me to the show after another row that afternoon, but we eventually agreed to meet at a club in the city when the show wrapped.

The theater was smaller than the others I'd been to recently, but I was relieved to see a crowd lined up down the street. They packed the place; people stood in the aisles, voices boomed from the rafters, and excitement electrified the air. It was Italy, welcoming one of their own, and I wouldn't disappoint. I swelled with excitement. At last, I'd have a real crowd—and I'd give them a heck of a show.

I warmed up with the band and when it was time to go on, the curtain parted. We began the first song with flair. I was hot tonight—we all were, I could feel it. When the song concluded, the crowd cheered and I beamed. It had been too long since I'd felt this way, like my music mattered. Like I mattered.

The band shifted to a new melody, gearing up for the next song, but the crowd wouldn't stop. They cheered and chanted, and as they grew louder and more insistent, I finally caught wind of what they were chanting.

"We want Ava! We want Ava!"

I felt my face go hot.

They were cheering alright, but they weren't cheering for me and suddenly I felt like the biggest heel in the world. Once again, I was reduced to Mr. Ava Gardner. They didn't care about my show. They wanted her.

I stomped off the stage and blustered and shouted behind the curtain until I nearly gave myself a heart attack.

"I'm sorry, man," my trombonist said. "I heard they promised the crowd a stage appearance from Ava. They sold the tickets for a higher price and told people they'd see her."

I closed my eyes. They'd sold on her name, not mine? What the hell was the owner getting at, selling my wife? I'd felt humiliated throughout the whole tour, but this was worse—this was a betrayal. I wanted to light the stage on fire and crawl into bed. I wanted to cancel the tour. Go home and leave Ava to shoot her picture on her own, where she could tend to her adoring fans and leave me the hell alone.

Eventually, though, the owner persuaded me to go back out there. I finished the show, but I skipped the club after and left Ava to fend for herself. She wouldn't miss me. She'd be surrounded by her adoring fans and forget I existed anyway. And yet, we continued on the tour. I had an obligation to fulfill and I was in no position to turn down work. Besides, George would be pissed and I respected the man. He'd done me right. After that terrible night in Naples and plenty of arguments with Ava, we headed to Rome. I was prepping to go on that night when a call came through from my manager.

"George, I'm in hell," I said, lighting a cigarette. "No one wants to see me. They want to see my wife. Not that I blame them, but Jesus, this is a waste of time."

"I've seen some of the headlines," George said. "It's not looking good over there."

"Tell me you've got something better than this and I'll cancel the rest of the tour," I said, sucking furiously on my cigarette. "There's only a month left anyway. What will they care?

The press keeps taking cheap shots at me. The owners can't be making much when they can't fill a theater." I winced saying the words out loud.

"I've got something better for you. Cancel the tour."

I exhaled in relief and covered my eyes with my hand. Jesus, I needed to hear that. "What is it?"

"Zinnemann wants to start publicity for *From Here to Eternity*, pronto. He said the early reviews are smashing charts. People are eating it up, and your name has been thrown around a lot."

"God, man, that's fantastic!" I paced, unable to remain calm. "Get me out of here. I'm ready for the real deal."

"I'll put you on the earliest flight home."

"You've got it. Tomorrow." I was grinning from ear to ear, thrilled at the prospect of blowing out of here to avoid limping through another two dozen shows.

I hung up and gave Ava the news.

"Oh, you'll have to go?" she said, looking up from her magazine. "It sounds like it's important work, baby," she continued. "It's probably for the best."

I stared at her as she said it. Her hair was wrapped in a bandana, her nails were chipped, and she didn't wear a lick of makeup. She'd barely made eye contact and worse still, didn't give any indication that she gave a damn that we wouldn't see each other for weeks, if not months. And that's when I knew—something had changed between us.

I didn't bother picking a fight with her and that was, perhaps, the most disturbing thing of all. I didn't care to argue, I just wanted to go home. Home to a world that wanted me—at last—once again.

CHAPTER 32

AVA

'd never been so glad to see Francis go, and that was saying something. He was miserable and when he was miserable, everyone around him had to suffer, too. Thankfully things at home seemed to be changing for the better for him. A few weeks later, I flew back to the States to attend the premiere of *From Here to Eternity* in August, and to our relief, the film was a sensation. Everyone crowed about Francis's acting as well as that of the other stars, Donna Reed, Deborah Kerr, Burt Lancaster, and Montgomery Clift. I had to admit—and I told him as much—that it was truly one of the best films I'd ever seen, never mind one of the best films of the year, and we both had high hopes it would turn everything around for him. I was proud of him and proud of being his wife.

After a few weeks, I headed back to Europe to shoot another picture. Francis and I spoke on the telephone when we could, but I could feel the distance growing between us as the days turned to weeks. When the movie wrapped, I planned to stay in London the few extra weeks needed to avoid the wage tax. Though I'd be home in a matter of weeks, Francis wasn't having it.

"I'm back, baby, I'm back!" he shouted into the telephone from Palm Springs. He'd clearly drunk his weight in Jack Daniel's and it sounded as if he wasn't the only one celebrating. Voices and crashing noises sounded in the background. Frank's entourage of admirers who followed him everywhere had multiplied in the last few months, and he loved every minute of being the puppet master and the man about town.

"Everyone loves me!" he exclaimed and then laughed loudly at something someone said.

I was happy for him, but I'd received a dozen of these sorts of calls from him already, and I was getting tired of hearing him stroke his own ego every time we got on the phone.

"You're drunk!" I shouted back.

"Whoa, Angel, no need to shout," he said, his voice now sounding far away, as if he'd pulled the telephone away from his mouth. "When are you coming home? I miss you. My success isn't as much fun without you. Besides, women are throwing themselves at me again. Don't you want to come put a stop to it?"

"What do you need me for if you have all of them?" I said. But I wanted to punch him right in the gob, as my new English friends would say.

"Come on," he said. "You know you're my girl. Come home, won't you? Meet me in New York. I'm flying out tomorrow morning for a run at the Riviera club."

"You know I can't give up my tax break," I replied, irritable. "I'd lose over a hundred thousand dollars."

"That's a drop in the bucket for you lately. Please, I need you here. We need this time together," he pressed. "Are you really going to choose your career over our marriage again?"

"That isn't fair and you know it," I snapped.

"I know," he said, his voice growing softer. "Come home, and I'll treat you like a queen. I'll pick you up at the airport."

"Oh, alright," I replied, suddenly so tired of it all. Tired of the constant struggle to keep our relationship together, tired enough, in fact, that I did as he asked. I booked a flight and flew to New York—and lost every cent I was going to save by staying in Europe a few more weeks.

When I landed, Frank was nowhere to be found.

Exhausted and bitter, I flew into a rage. That bastard had begged me—acted as if he couldn't go on without me—and didn't have the common decency to make good on his promise to be waiting for me. I'd made a huge sacrifice and he didn't give a damn. I thought of returning to California the next day, without seeing him at all because screw him, but the truth was, I wanted to give him a piece of my mind.

When he called, I let the telephone ring until I finally took it off the hook. Hours later, after a long nap and a hot shower, I replaced the telephone on the receiver. It immediately rang.

"Hello," I said, ready to lay into Frank.

"Ava, it's Dolly." My mother-in-law. "Why don't you come over for dinner, honey? I heard you're in town."

"Your son lured me here, and he didn't even greet me. How did you put up with his insubordination, Dolly?"

She laughed. "I didn't. Just like you, honey. Come on over and I'll make you a nice meal. You can see the new house. We've moved over to Weehawken."

As it turned out, Frank had called his mother and pleaded with her to talk me down. I knew she was playing matchmaker and I could blow her off—and tell him to stick it—but I was too tired to resist, and I loved Dolly just that much.

As I expected, Frank was there when I arrived. His expression was contrite, but his blue eyes were as bright as ever. He wore a new suit and had a new air about him; things were changing for him. He seemed happier—and he certainly hadn't suffered without me.

After a nice visit with Dolly and Marty, a home-cooked meal and a couple of bottles of wine, Frank and I made up and I followed him to his show that night.

"I'm really sorry, Angel," he said, kissing my hand in the car on the ride to the club. "I'm glad you're here."

"You'd better be," I said, but I was smiling.

At the club, people lined the block, begging to be let in to the exclusive show. I smiled as I passed and several people recognized me, calling my name—but this time, they called his name, too. I was proud of Francis. He'd really found his way back after such a disastrous fall.

Inside moments later, the lights dimmed and the band began, and my infuriating, adorable husband stepped into the spotlight. He electrified the crowd with "I've Got the World on a String," and I basked in his happiness, his assuredness as he stalked across the stage, one arm outstretched. He was a hell of a performer no matter what had happened between us and no matter how insensitive or difficult he could be. I could forgive a lot when I listened to him sing.

When the band started a tender number, he met my eyes. They shined with raw emotion. Our love filled up the room and I couldn't resist him—didn't want to. This was precisely why we put up with each other.

As I blew him a kiss, he smiled at me from beneath the bright spotlight on the stage. I returned his smile and gave him the smallest flirty wave.

No matter what—no matter time, distance, or aggravation—he would forever be mine.

If Francis was easing back into the spotlight, my star was reaching a pinnacle. A whirlwind of films, publicity, and large crowds of fans.

We attended the premiere of *Mogambo* at Radio City Music Hall, and I was thrilled to hear the whispers of Oscar nominations in the air. I felt truly validated for the first time in my career in a way that MGM—or anyone for that matter—couldn't take away from me. I'd come so far, suffered a hundred small humiliations and larger ones, and I'd finally, truly carved out a place for myself amid the greats.

After the premiere, Francis and I decided to lie low until his show began at the Sands Hotel and Casino in Las Vegas. He would be performing, as requested by the Boys and Jack Entratter, the hotel owner, and he was jazzed by the opportunity. The night before Francis's premiere, we decided to enjoy a last quiet meal together in LA before the parade of shows began. I'd go with him for his debut performance and then fly home for a few weeks until filming began on my next picture.

The dinner started off well as it often did—until someone spotted us.

"Frank Sinatra, how the hell are you?" the man said. His face was open and friendly, and he wore a light blue sweater over a shirt and tie. I didn't have the faintest idea who he was.

"Charlie, good to see you, man!" Francis shook his hand. "This is my wife, Ava."

"Hello," I said and then nodded at the waiter who'd just arrived with our dinner.

Frank rattled off a list of polite questions and the men went back and forth for some time. I put on my showgirl smile, waiting for the man to realize he was interrupting us.

He didn't.

As the minutes ticked by and my food started to get cold, I dug into my plate, growing more annoyed with each bite. This man clearly had no manners. Couldn't he see we were trying to have a quiet dinner? Francis was being as rude as the man was!

I nudged Francis under the table.

He glanced at me quickly before returning his attention to his friend. My irritation flared. He made more fuss than a woman about us spending time together and yet he didn't seem to value it. Sometimes I'd swear that he was happier with his male friends than anything, and if he could give up women, he would.

When at last the man left, Francis had a congealed mass of cold food on his plate and I was hot with anger.

"I guess that cinches it. I can see how important I am to you." I didn't hide my sarcasm. "First I fly back to the States to be with you and you blow me off, and now one of the few moments we have alone together before we're going to be apart again for months, you ignore me when some guy I've never seen before is rude enough to talk through our entire dinner. And you let him!"

"What was I supposed to do? Tell him to get lost? He's a friend of mine!" Francis said, signaling to the waiter to bring him another plate.

"You could have told him we wanted some time together! Enjoy your food alone. I'm out of here." I grabbed my purse and made for the door.

It was a practiced, tired scene; an argument at a restaurant, one of us peeling away in a car going a hundred miles per hour. How many times had we replayed this routine? We couldn't seem to get things right no matter how hard we tried, and I couldn't take it anymore.

Frank followed me out, shouting at me as I went. "Where are you going? Don't you want to spend time together?"

"Nope," I said, walking to the car. I opened the trunk and dragged his suitcase out, dropping it on the ground. "And you can find your own ride."

"Fine!" he shouted.

He waved for a taxi and threw his things in the trunk and within minutes, sped off into the night. Without me. Without a word about our plan to fly together. Without a word about his grand premiere. *He didn't care if I went. Now that he was back on his feet, he didn't need me.*

As the realization struck, the tears began. Frank cared more about himself than our marriage. He wanted to mold me into something I wasn't. Expected me to hang on his every word and follow him around as his career soared at the expense of my own. And yet, I knew what he loved most about me was that I wouldn't put up with his garbage and that I was the exact opposite of everything he allegedly wanted in a woman.

He just couldn't quite stomach it. He couldn't quite get past his traditional views, much as he seemed to want to.

I roared down Sunset Boulevard, the tears coming faster until I was choking back sobs. I drove to Sydney's house, the chief hairstylist at MGM, a good friend from my early days at the studio. He'd know what to say, what to do, and honestly, I didn't know where else to go. Bappie was in North Carolina for a spell and Reenie had flown home again.

By the time I'd arrived at Sydney's, I was nearly hysterical.

Sydney immediately scooped me into his arms and led me to a seat on the front porch.

"What is it?" he asked. "Do you want to come in and have a drink?"

I shook my head. "I need air," I said through a shuddering breath. I paced on the lawn for hours, sobbing, filling Sydney in about the last several months. The arguments, the prostitutes and female fans, Frank's struggle to gain traction in his career and then his sudden change of fortune. His soaring ego and constant goading about other women to make me jealous. I even told Sydney about my own transgressions with Mario Cabré and Bunny Allen. Sydney didn't have much to say, but I needed a shoulder to lean on. Perhaps, above all, I needed to hear myself say it all aloud—to not only feel and see but to accept the torturous path we'd been down, and to figure out what to do next.

When I'd finally calmed down enough to drive, I'd made up my mind. I wasn't going to Vegas. Instead, I drove to Palm Springs.

The moment I walked through the door, the telephone rang. I knew it was him. If there was one thing that son of a bitch had, it was uncanny timing.

"Come on, baby, it was just a misunderstanding," he said when I answered. "Come to Vegas, please. Jack put me up in a really nice suite. You can order whatever you want and go to the spa."

"Not this time," I said, gripping the receiver until my knuckles turned white. Something was changing between us, or at least it was for me. Something irreparable.

"Come on, you're being ridiculous."

Was I? Was I expecting too much to have a dinner without a fight or without having to ask him to prioritize our time together? I hung up on him.

He called every night after, and I ignored him.

One day, when I finally cooled down and I was more certain in my path forward, I picked up the telephone.

"When are you coming to Vegas?" he asked. By his tone and the volume of his voice, I could tell he was bombed. "Come on, Angel, can't we just put this behind us and try again? We'll do it right this time. I can finally be the man you deserve."

There was a soft whisper on the other line followed by a chuckle from Francis. When the whisper came again, I froze.

It was a woman's voice.

Bile rushed up my throat. He didn't have the common decency to call me when there wasn't a whore in his bed?

"You have a woman with you, don't you? You asshole! I knew you were cheating on me!"

"If I'm going to constantly be accused of infidelity, I'm going to at least enjoy the benefits of being guilty," he replied.

I slammed down the phone.

I'd endured too much—we'd endured too much—and our wounds were too deep. There were too many arguments, too many slights and infidelities. Too much lost. We could barely be civil to each other. And then I knew what I had to do.

The next day, I met with my manager and with Mayer at MGM—and I didn't bother to call Frank first to warn him. MGM immediately issued an announcement that we'd separated.

I couldn't do it anymore. I couldn't stay. Frank and I were through.

Part 4

"MY WAY"

1953–1966

CHAPTER 33

FRANK

M r. Sinatra." My housekeeper's voice drifted through the receiver and my hope plummeted. "No, Miss Gardner is not here. She moved her things out, sir."

"She moved out?" I asked, incredulous.

Ava hadn't bothered to tell me. I pictured her in a fury, packing her things at the house in Palm Springs and tearing out of the parking lot. We'd been through it lately but this, moving out on me without a word about it? I swallowed hard. It was a line we'd never crossed. Sure, there had been plenty of volatile arguments, but we'd never been able to be apart from each other for long. Maybe I assumed too much—that our passion for each other would always be enough in the end. Maybe I was a damn fool.

"Yes, sir," the housekeeper replied. "She told me not to call you, sir."

I called all over town, called my friends, my manager, her sister trying to find her. No one would tell me where she was. I left desperate messages with everyone until finally, one afternoon, I roused from bed to the shrill ring of the telephone.

"Hello?" I rasped into the receiver.

The voice I'd longed to hear was edged with ice. "I'll be out of the country on set for a while, so you can stop harassing my sister and everyone else."

"I'm sorry about that night, Angel," I said, relieved to hear her voice, even if she was still pissed. "Come to Vegas before you leave. I miss you. I'll give you a tour and—"

"What do you need me for? There are plenty of showgirls to keep you company in Vegas."

"Why did you have to bring that up?" I said, raising my voice. And yet, it was true. I'd been lonely, in need, and she had shut me out entirely. What was I to do, sit idly by and not expend some stress? Deny myself a good time when things were finally going my way? And where was she in all of that? "Come on, baby. Please? Come see me."

"I have to go, Frank. I hope your show is swell."

The line went dead.

Swell? I held out the phone and looked at it like it was a foreign object. My wife had blown me off like I was just another Charlie on the street. A terrible heat swept over me, a feverish regret. No matter what we'd been through, I still couldn't imagine my life without that woman in it.

The following day, as I sat in the dark in my hotel room at the Sands, my mind a morass of worry and regret, my head in my hands, I received a call from George.

"I've got bad news for you, Frank," my manager said. "Or hell, maybe it's good news. Maybe it's time to cut ties so you can get on with it. Stay out of the tabloids."

"What's the news, George?" I asked, testy.

"Ava filed for a separation."

Another thing she hadn't bothered to tell me.

I dropped the phone, puked my guts out, and wailed on a bottle of bourbon that night, washing down a load of sleeping pills before I passed out on the hotel floor. I guessed we were through. She was done with me, for real this time.

And I couldn't see my way out of the pain.

Yet, the next day, I picked myself up and got ready for the show because that was what they were paying me for and that was what my fans wanted. Ava or no, I had a job to do and bills to pay. I was putting everything I had into the show that Jack Entratter hired me to perform. After where I'd been, I couldn't risk giving less than a thousand percent.

I settled into the routine in Vegas, marveling at how much it had grown since I'd last been in town when it was nothing but dust and blue skies and the distant mountains of the Mojave Desert. Now, everything seemed to be under construction. The Sands was spectacular, one of only seven resorts on Fremont Street and the most modern, too, with its geometric designs and neon lights. Inside, the casino boasted the Silver Queen Bar, decorated with panels depicting the Nevada desert, an elegant restaurant and sprawling gambling floor, a sunrise terrace adjacent to a large pool, and, finally, the room where I performed: the Copa Room. It was a dinner theater with tables and ruby red chairs tucked around a stage that was lit by spotlights on its outer edge. The stunning casino was a playground for not only the wealthy, but for those with a little extra pocket change to bet at the tables.

Jack made sure I received a king's welcome in a suite with nightly champagne on ice, and my name in bold lettering on the marquee. The Boys had set me up for real this time, and it was like an electric shock straight to the heart. I was no longer a man at the bottom of a well enrobed in darkness. I'd climbed out, stronger and smarter.

The journalists changed their tune about me, too, when the reviews for *From Here to Eternity* released and the new record dropped. Suddenly I was an outlaw hero who refused to die, and I leaned into it, sliding into my role onstage like a hand in a glove, this time with a learned confidence and a new sense of appreciation for being wanted. I drew on the energy of the growing crowds and the new enthusiasm for a man you couldn't keep down. I was no longer some loser with bad press. I was a man about town. Hell, I *was* the town. And God, it felt good to be back.

Night after night, I stood beneath the bright lights, looking out at the mass of growing fans, and tried to put Ava out of my mind. During many of my shows, the Copa Room showgirls backed me up, the crowd delighting in their energy. They were young, vibrant, beautiful. I charmed them and they charmed me with their sequined outfits and feathers and red lips, and the next thing I knew, they took turns keeping my bed warm. It eased the ache in my gut a little—a very little. I called Ava every night, desperate for her regardless of who lay in my bed, but no matter the time of day or night, no matter how many times the telephone rang, she didn't answer it, not once. I tried to get on with things—life was looking up in almost every way—but she was a specter hovering in the dark corners of my mind and shadowing every move I made.

A few weeks into the new show, I headed to New York to do some recording. Nelson Riddle and I had some smash hits on our hands, and I hoped this would help me shake the black dog that had descended again. It didn't. I could barely make it through the days.

One quiet night, I waited at Jimmy Van Heusen's apartment, where I was staying. He'd wanted to make a night of it, go out on the town, and he persuaded me to go with him. When I got the call that he'd been held up at the studio, I relaxed. He was having a bad recording session—we'd all had them.

As the hours ticked by, and the silence of the apartment deepened, I lost myself in my thoughts. All I could think about was how I'd ruined things with Ava—how I'd destroyed what most made me happy. What did my success matter all on my own? It was great, sure, absolutely, and it also meant nothing. No matter what I did, I missed her in a way that made me ache. I couldn't manage the suffocating emotions that came over me, at times like a dense fog that I couldn't see my way out of, and I started to wonder if something was truly wrong with me.

I stared at the ceiling and the crown molding along its edges where it met the wall. What the hell was I going to do? I paced, unable to be still, until my shoes and jacket grew heavy, uncomfortable and I realized that no matter what time Jimmy came home, I wasn't going out. I was in no state to do anything.

I pulled on a pair of pajamas, poured a tall whiskey, and downed it quickly before pouring another.

Sleep. I needed sleep. I reached for the little red pills I'd stashed in my suitcase and washed them down with another double pour. After, I lay down on the couch and tried to relax enough to fall into a dreamless sleep but my mind was winding up, not down.

I couldn't face another minute of it all—the disappointments of this life, the desperation of loving someone too much. Of feeling too much. A sixty-four-carat manic depressive, that's what I was, and as I glanced down at my withered frame, less than a hundred and twenty pounds, I realized I looked like I was on the verge of death. Why not finish it off? End my misery?

I stumbled to the kitchen and yanked open every drawer until I found them—the knives. I pulled out the largest, sharpest knife I could find. I stared at it, the ridge of the cool steel blade, felt the heft of it in my hand. I could end the pain here, make it all go away.

Blurry-eyed, my head spinning, I slid the clean blade across my wrists.

A scarlet slash bloomed on my arms and I dropped the knife.

Somewhere in the narrow tunnel of my lucid mind, I heard the knife clatter to the floor. I backed up against the cabinets, sliding down to the tile floor. Warm blood oozed from the perfect slit, staining my hands red in a matter of seconds and dripping to the floor in a flowery pattern. Vaguely, I wondered what Ava would say when she heard the news that I'd finally done it. I'd followed through on a threat that she'd stopped believing could be true. Could I blame her?

My head grew light and I closed my eyes. Death didn't feel painful after all; it was fuzzy, indistinct, and quiet. An inexorable pull toward the deepest silence of all. Wouldn't we all arrive there one day anyway? What was the point in fighting it?

A door slammed somewhere in the distance. A voice rippled through the quiet and found me, wherever I'd gone, hovering, aching.

Footsteps and a sharp intake of breath, and then, Jimmy's voice.

"Jesus Christ, Frank! What have you done?" Jimmy hauled me to my feet. "We're going to the hospital."

I didn't respond. I hardly made any sound at all. This was all too familiar, too painful and tragic and I had nothing to say.

Minutes later at the hospital, as the medical staff tended to my wound, I looked for her—waited for Ava to walk through that door and tell me that I was a fool but everything would be alright. We were meant to be together, weren't we? Or was I the ridiculous romantic she accused me of being? I didn't know if it mattered. All that mattered was that she didn't show.

As the doctor explained that I needed to be treated for nervous exhaustion, I attempted to let go, of her, of us.

"Mr. Sinatra, you need time off to rest so you may recover."

I knew it was more than bone-deep exhaustion. It was a bone-deep need to be accepted, to be loved. To be the big man in the room. It was also a bone-deep need for her, and like it or not, she was gone.

CHAPTER 34

AVA

Francis tried to off himself again—or rather, he'd done just enough to make a scene but not truly end his life. Again. Though I felt sympathy for his morbid obsession with suicide, and the dark spells that overtook him—I had them myself in the middle of the night when the world was quiet and I was left alone to examine my life—I couldn't stand his melodrama anymore. And yet, wasn't I the pot calling the kettle black? Maybe, but I didn't care. That man had broken my heart a hundred times in a thousand ways and I couldn't sustain the ups and downs anymore. Besides, I had a new picture to shoot.

I flew to Rome, worse for wear and heartbroken but relieved to be as far from LA as possible. I was assured *The Barefoot Contessa* would be sensational given the director Joseph Mankiewicz's eye for beauty, and that was good enough for me, for now. I only cared to get out of town. Hollywood never was my thing, and it was becoming harder to bear as the years passed.

When I landed in Rome, I made my way from the terminal to the pickup area at the Ciampino airport. I was greeted with the unmistakable roar of voices.

"Is that what I think it is?" I asked one of the two body-guards that I'd recently hired. They were both the size of a Mack Truck. With the paparazzi in Rome, I'd learned not to go out on my own.

"It is, ma'am," one of them said.

"Damn. That means the press will be here, too." I slipped on my sunglasses to hide my eyes that were puffy from crying.

The guards stood on either side of me, ushering me forward. As we stepped outside, bulbs flashed in a constant chain until we were blinded in the confusion.

"Miss Gardner! Welcome to Roma!"

"I love you, Ava!"

"Where's Frank?"

"Ava! Ava! Ava!" A mob chanted my name.

Breathless, I was packed quickly into a Cadillac. I received some fan attention in the U.S., but nothing like that of Italy.

The crowd parted slowly as the car nudged crazed fans out of the way. Several foolhardy men threw themselves across the windshield. You'd have thought I was the savior himself by the way they were acting. The thing reached a whole new level when a man pressed his bare chest against my window and shouted my name.

I screeched and leaned away from the window as if I could avoid them. "I can't believe there are so many of them."

"You're a favorite here in Italia, Miss Gardner," the driver said.

"Well I guess so, good Lord," I said, equally pleased and aghast. I was only human, after all.

I'd never seen anything like it. Perhaps my name was bigger than I'd ever realized. During the drive, I contemplated what it meant to be famous, the perks of owning nice things: being shown to the best table in a restaurant or the best seat in a theater, of having my way when I wanted, most of the time. There were so many admirers and gifts . . . but it also meant the press was always hounding me. And then there were the nasty letters and a lack of privacy everywhere I went, and the pressure to be perfect all the time. It was exhausting. I slumped in my seat, trying not to wish that Francis was here with me. At least with him, I wasn't facing it all alone.

As I arrived at my flower-filled suite at the hotel and was swept away to dine on champagne and the biggest bowl of fettuccine they could find, I relaxed a little. The Italians sure knew how to greet a girl. I was instantly in a better mood.

After a few days of rest and endless bouts of tears over Francis, I rented an old dark house on the noisy Corso d'Italia. I liked that it was close to the action—I also liked the essence of the past that was so evident in its ancient décor and crooked frame. In the evenings, I drank Italian wine and danced the nights away, meeting people, waiting for the heartache to subside. I had to take my mind off Francis and try to move on. I was good at that after three failed marriages, or so I thought. Francis proved to be different. He didn't fade the way the others had, so I threw myself into the nightlife and beauty of the city. Anything to distract me from the gaping hole inside me, and a truth I didn't want to face: I was a spectacular failure at love.

Thankfully, the preproduction for the film also kept me busy. The costume fittings were the most fun of all, as I tried on dresses made by the spectacular Sorelle Fontana. I swooned over the designer sisters' couture beadwork, the delicate stitching and fanciful detailing along a hem or neckline on luscious fabrics of silk, satin, and velvet. In the afternoons, I posed for

sculptor Assen Peikov, a passionate if irritable Bulgarian artist commissioned to sculpt a marble statue in my likeness for
the film. The artist had what I'd call an interesting mustache
that I couldn't help but stare at—truthfully, it made it hard
to take the man seriously. I soon learned he was demanding
and wanted me to remove more and more of my clothing, and
though I felt unsettled by the request and unnecessarily exposed, I went along with it. Who was I to get in the way of art?

One afternoon on set, pretty little Lauren Bacall—Betty to
those of us who knew her by her real name—arrived to spend
time with her husband and my costar, Humphrey Bogart. It
was a nice surprise, though seeing her reminded me of home in
not the best of ways.

"Why, Betty! It's great to see you," I said, giving her a hug.
"What do you have there?"

"I've brought you a gift," she said, her blue eyes sparkling.
She held out a pastry box from a shop I recognized in Los Angeles. "It's your favorite coconut cake, for your birthday. It's
from Frank, flown all this way. Isn't he the sweetest?"

"You traveled all this way carrying that thing?" I asked,
more stunned by her dedication to her husband's best friend
than I was by Francis's gesture.

She laughed. "I did. Here, it's all yours."

I took the pastry box, thanking her profusely, and as she
drifted away to get cleaned up after the long flight, I dumped
the box in the garbage. I didn't need to get fat and Francis's gift
didn't mean much. Besides, I couldn't help feeling a twinge of
suspicion. Betty was a little over-dedicated to my husband, and
I wondered if something had sprung up between them behind
Bogart's back—and mine. Not that I blamed her. Humphrey

Bogart was a toupee-wearing, complaining, grade A asshole. I would have cheated on him, too.

"I'm sure Frank will be happy to learn you didn't bother with his gift," Bogart's voice came from behind me.

"You saw that?" I said, putting my hands on my hips. "Not that it's any of your business, but we're separated."

"After chasing men in ballerina slippers and tights, I'm not surprised." He smirked and I wanted to punch him right in the mouth. I didn't see how anyone could find Bogart handsome. It took one conversation with him to turn me off him for good.

I gave him the bird without turning around and started toward my dressing room. I didn't care if Bogart was one of Francis's closest friends. He picked at me and pried and thought himself entirely too funny when really, he was a bully, seeking out the most sensitive part of a person so he could use it against them. He'd step into my dressing room and make relentless comments to get a rise out of me, and worse still, he'd interrupt me while I was trying to concentrate on my lines.

Filming wasn't a picnic either. Mankiewicz might be considered a genius, but he didn't grasp my method of acting. I liked to react to my fellow actors on set as if the words coming out of their mouths—and my own—were true, that we weren't acting or channeling some other personality at all but living inside the scene. The director would explode at me and force me into an awkward situation that felt unnatural, and we'd have to do another retake. I couldn't wait for filming to wrap.

I'd never been so relieved for the holidays to come. I called the airlines and booked a flight to Madrid for Christmas; it would be good to get away.

In Madrid, I visited my expat friends Betty and Ricardo Sicre. Though I enjoyed my time with them, as the holiday crept closer, I felt as lonely as ever, and I found myself off to the bull-fighting ring. The suave and handsome Luis Miguel Domin-guín, the most renowned bullfighter in Spain, appeared to be the perfect distraction.

The distraction didn't last.

One night, Francis called.

"I need to see you, Angel. It's Christmas." His voice was hoarse with emotion.

I hated myself for it, but my heart still thumped wildly at the sound of his voice. "All we do is fight," I protested weakly. "What'll we do when you come all this way and we can't stand to be in the same room?"

"All I want is to be in a room with you," he cajoled. "Especially a bedroom. I love you, Angel. No one can replace you."

I still loved the bastard, too. Things were definitely over between us, and yet, here we were, unable to hammer the final nail in the coffin. Maybe after this trip it would all be done and finished.

"No one can replace you either, baby," I said.

Within twenty-four hours, he joined me in Madrid. We were swept up in a reunion briefly—this time less than a full day—before he accused me of seeing someone else and as he seethed, I nearly admitted my liaison with Luis Miguel. Nearly. I knew better now than to admit anything, and we were separated after all. Instead, I launched a litany of suspicions of my own. I knew he was sleeping with every showgirl in Vegas.

The only thing to calm our fights was a terrible bout of the flu.

We recovered over the course of the week and when we were well again, we went to Rome to host a New Year's Eve party as a publicity stunt for the movie. To help create a sensation with the press, we invited a few other stars who were traveling or filming in the area. At least, that was the plan. The only sensation was our fighting—in public, at the event—and our parting afterward.

His visit was another disaster, and as he left Rome early to shoot a film with Marilyn Monroe, I waved goodbye in relief.

And once again, I went looking for solace. Once again, I put in a call to my bullfighter.

When it was time to return to set, I pushed myself through the final weeks of filming, putting up with Bogie when I had to but despising every minute around him and the clueless director. I couldn't deny it, I was at the top of my game, living the high life of the rich and famous, but I felt a little bit lost.

The only good news came from David in February.

"Darling, you've done it!" he said over a long-distance telephone call.

"Done what? Don't tease me, David. Out with it!"

"You were nominated for an Oscar!"

I screamed into the phone. "Go on, you're lying!" I said after catching my breath.

"Would I lie about something like this? Best Supporting Actress for *Mogambo*."

I smiled the biggest smile I had. After all this time, after twelve years of working my tail off and eating crow at MGM, I'd gone and done it. I'd gotten the nomination for the golden statuette.

"Who else is in my category?" I asked.

"Audrey Hepburn, Leslie Caron, Deborah Kerr, and Maggie McNamara."

"Ah, so I don't have a snowball's chance in hell, do I?" I said, some of the joy leaking out of the moment.

"The nomination is enough," he reassured me. "When your contract is finished at MGM, you'll be worth a fortune."

"I'm already worth a fortune," I said, smiling again, but he was right. The nomination had come at the perfect time.

"Yes, you are," he said, laughing. "Oh, and you might like to know that Frank was nominated, too."

I couldn't help it, my heart leapt into my throat, and I felt the kind of soaring joy you could only feel when a good thing happened to someone you loved. Someone you loved so deeply it hurt—hurt too much—especially when you weren't together.

I swallowed hard. "That's great news! I'm sure he's thrilled."

"If you want to go to the show, we can make arrangements with the director. I'm not sure how he'll feel about you leaving set, but that's too bad for him. This is huge news. He'll have to understand."

I was starting the preproduction for a new picture to shoot in Europe that very week. "You know . . . I don't think I need to fly all the way to Hollywood for one night, just to put on a fancy gown and lose the Oscar in front of everyone."

"Are you sure? This is once in a lifetime," he said, his tone colored with a hint of regret for having such a stubborn client. He'd probably wanted to go with me.

"I'm sure. Thanks, David. I'm thrilled, truly. I'm going to celebrate tonight."

I hung up the phone, bouncing between happiness and the loneliness I'd been trying so desperately to ward off. Finally, I called my sister to tell her the news. Promptly after, I got drunk, alone. Congratulations to me.

CHAPTER 35

FRANK

After Madrid, I returned home to Palm Springs rather than Los Angeles as planned. The film with Marilyn wasn't going to happen after all. It was just as well. I needed a week's rest anyway to think about things. I sat on the patio for hours, looked at the sky until I shivered with cold night air. On my way inside, I strolled past the statue of Ava in the garden, gleaming pearlescent in the dark. The sculptor who had made it for *The Barefoot Contessa* was happy to sell his work, and I was even happier to have it. My baby had inspired art. I missed her—I missed her so desperately, I wanted to crawl out of my skin. But she wasn't here, and she wouldn't even attend the Oscars with me.

I'd done it—received a Best Supporting Actor nomination for *From Here to Eternity*. I'd never been prouder of anything I'd ever done And the woman I'd most longed to share it with didn't give a damn. I consoled myself with too much whiskey and too many late nights, but it didn't take the edge off. Nothing could.

The night before the Oscars I spent the evening at Nancy's to celebrate. Despite all we'd been through, she was happy for me and welcomed me with open arms. She cooked an Italian feast with a few of my favorite things; I could count on her for meals that tasted like home. Over dinner, I looked around the table at my family: Nancy, already fourteen and no doubt turning the boys' heads; Frank Jr., starting to fill out; and little Tina, now big enough to sit at the table without a stack of books. They told me stories about school and about the neighbors' kids. Nancy updated me on all the family gossip and the word from back home, and for a few hours, I felt like I was home. I wished violently in that rare moment of peaceful contentment that I could have stayed—that my life with them was enough—but even as I wished it, I knew the feelings of being suffocated and restless would return. I knew it would never have anything to do with them. I was the one who was broken.

"Dad," my daughter Nancy said, jumping up from her seat to grab a wrapped box off the kitchen counter. "We have something for you."

"You have something for me?" I said, raising my brow. I tossed my napkin on the table. "Should I save it for later?"

"Open it!" Frankie Jr. said with a toothy grin.

I smiled and shook it slightly, watching their faces as they looked on eagerly. I opened the box slowly, teasing them, drawing out the suspense.

"Hurry up!" Frank Jr. said.

I chuckled. "Oh, alright." I opened the lid to find a shiny gold medallion. I plucked it from the case and turned it over in my hand. There was an inscription on its face:

Dad, All our love from here to eternity

I gazed at it a moment, overwhelmed by the love I felt for

them, and by the realization that tomorrow night, I'd be seated among the Hollywood elite once more, reaching toward one of my life's greatest goals. Even if Ava wouldn't be there with me, her absence couldn't diminish this honor.

"Nancy, you kids," I began, my voice wavering with the weight of emotion. "This is the best gift I've ever had. Now come over here and give your poppa a hug."

They gathered around and hugged me tightly, smiling and giggling.

"We're going to watch it on the television, Poppa," Tina said.

It was only the second Academy Awards to be televised. The first had been an enormous success, and Bob Hope had been the right man for the job as master of ceremonies. I hoped the second would be equally successful and, more importantly, that I wouldn't let my family down.

"Congratulations, Frank," my ex-wife said with tears in her eyes. She knew how much this meant to me, and I could see the pride in the soft contours of her face. "You've earned it. You were wonderful in that picture and if you don't win, the world doesn't make any sense at all."

I kissed her on the cheek, hugged her to me fiercely. If only Ava was as loyal.

"Thanks, sweetheart," I said.

As the evening drew to a close, I made plans to have the kids over the next weekend. I'd cook up my special pancake breakfast, take them shopping for goodies, go swimming. I was looking forward to spending some real time with them.

With a smile and a wave, I put on my hat, more grateful than ever that I had a family—even if I was often gone, even if I wasn't capable of staying put the way I should—and backed out of the drive turning toward home and the long, lonely night that awaited me there.

The following night, I arrived at the Academy Awards at the RKO Pantages Theatre in a pressed tuxedo, all smiles and nerves. I didn't know what to expect, but the fanfare of red carpet and stars, photographers and reporters, and fans jamming the thoroughfare was electric. I buzzed with the excitement and smiled at the photographers for the first time in ages. I would win, wouldn't I? I had to. I craved it, yearned for the validation winning would bring. I'd already proved something to the director and the studio head with the nomination, but this win was for me—and for them—those who'd ridiculed me or turned their backs on me when I was down. A man didn't forget that kind of betrayal.

The only thing slowing me down was Ava's absence. I'd felt it keenly all day; it was a knife in the ribs, the sort of pain that didn't ease up. As I made my way around the lobby filled with women in glittering gowns and men dressed like elegant penguins, I chitchatted with old friends with her in the back of my mind, shook hands and walked to my seat while thinking about her. Somehow, I couldn't believe she'd do this to me— abandon me when I'd worked so hard for this—and I couldn't believe she'd do this to herself. She'd received her own nomination, too, but instead of attending she'd chosen preproduction chores for a new movie shooting five thousand miles away. She could have come for a couple of days. She should have come.

As the production unfolded, I shifted impatiently in my seat. When they finally reached the nominations for Best Supporting

Actor, I held my breath. I tried to look nonchalant, but the truth was, my heart was racing, my palms were sweaty, and I was pretty sure I was about to lose my lunch.

"Ladies and gentlemen, our nominees are Frank Sinatra in *From Here to Eternity*, Eddie Albert in *Roman Holiday*, Brandon deWilde in *Shane*, Jack Palance in *Shane*, and Robert Strauss in *Stalag 17*."

This was it, the moment.

"And the Oscar goes to . . ."

I gripped my hands together and tapped my foot impatiently against the leg of my chair.

"Frank Sinatra, *From Here to Eternity*."

My stomach dipped wildly, and I leapt to my feet. The audience broke into thunderous applause as I jogged down the aisle in exuberance. I couldn't believe it! I'd shown those bastards! I'd shown everyone! Emotion rushed up my throat and as I took the stage, a huge smile stretched across my face like sunshine after a storm.

"Ladies and gentlemen, I'm deeply thrilled and very moved, and I really, really don't know what to say because this is a whole new kind of thing . . . ," I began.

I finished to more applause and a kind of exhilaration I'd never felt before. I was a winner, goddammit. I was a winner!

I shook hands and received lots of pounding on the back and drinks pushed into my hands. But as the evening wore on, my exhilaration faded.

I stopped by one of the parties after the program, only to find I couldn't seem to rally my rapidly deflating mood. Everyone had a plus one, a spouse or girlfriend, or, in some cases, a relative on their arm. In spite of my enormous achievement, or perhaps because of it, I'd never felt more alone. I left the party, ignoring the waiting car, and wandered down the streets, floating through the night like a ghost, my golden statue my only company. And one thought played over and over again in my mind.

I would never give myself over to someone so completely again. I couldn't stand that kind of heartache again, not ever. It would kill me. Ava had shattered something in me that could never be fixed, and I had to accept that now—and move on.

CHAPTER 36

FRANK

My Oscar win was a lightning rod to my career.

Suddenly everyone wanted a piece of me. Movie studios, television networks, casinos in Vegas and Atlantic City, clubs . . . They threw money at me like it was on fire and soon, all my debts were paid and my bank accounts were padded and growing fast. My singles were hitting, too: "Anytime, Anywhere," "From Here to Eternity," and "The Girl Next Door." I had to hand it to Nelson Riddle, the man was a genius. He had a sound, a know-how, and something about his know-how melded beautifully with mine. He wasn't threatened by my take-charge attitude with the orchestra, or my obsession with learning all the new gadgets and technology in the world of music. He relished my curiosity and we had fun together, experimenting with rhythm and tempo.

With Ava and I officially apart, I started properly wooing women again. Gloria Vanderbilt, Marlene Dietrich, Jeanne Carmen, Jill Corey. I had them all and so many more that I lost track of their names, the times, the place. Eventually, I hired George Jacobs, my valet and right-hand man, to help me handle the ladies and all of my guests. I sent him out for roses or dinner reservations, asked him to chauffeur my friends, or anyone I wanted to show a good time. No one went without if they were in the company of Frank Sinatra, I made sure of it.

Did I have something to prove? Sure. What man didn't? If nothing else, I wanted to be *remembered.* And that was what consumed me now—creating something memorable, leaving behind the kind of legacy that was unrivaled. Who could stand the test of time the way I could? No one. That was who, and I'd prove it.

The only thing I couldn't have was Ava.

I tried to put her out of my mind. There were more important things distracting me at the moment: Bogie was diagnosed with terminal cancer. He tried not to let it get him down and we partied with exuberance. He'd always been a ringleader and the head of our group of friends that Betty called the Rat Pack. Now, he was in no shape to lead anything so I took the reins planning our excursions, encouraging him to keep things light for as long as possible. If we weren't at his house on Mapleton Drive in Holmby Hills, we were sailing on his fifty-foot schooner named the *Santana.*

One perfect morning, we took the boat out for the whole day. The sun blazed as clear and hot as oil in a frying pan, and I was glad I'd brought my wide-brim fedora. I mopped my face with a towel and thought about cracking open a beer despite the early hour.

"Hey, get me a beer, will you?" Bogie called from the deck.

"I was hoping you'd say that."

I fished around in the cooler, pulled out a couple of beers for us and poured a glass of champagne for Betty. She looked beautiful today, her sandy-blond hair swept into a braid that showed off a graceful neck and a plunging neckline. There was something intoxicating about her face, something unique. Her cheekbones were sharp enough to cut glass, but it was her arched brow and piercing blue eyes that made me want to take her to bed. And we nearly had, a few times. The chemistry between us was undeniable, but I couldn't betray my best friend that way. I loved the guy; he was a real man's man, a tough guy with an edge who didn't put up with any crap from anyone, least of all me.

"How are you feeling, pal?" I asked.

"Tired, mostly, but alright," Bogie said, taking a swig from the bottle.

He was starting to shed weight from his already-thin frame. His collarbones had begun to protrude and his cheeks were hollow, the flesh on his face appeared loose and gray.

I stared at the ocean, studying how the light played over the water, glistening in a way that made me think there really was a God, even if he was cruel. I couldn't bear to think about Bogie suffering to the end, slipping away to nothing. My anger flared at the injustice of losing someone so alive.

"Is there anything you want to do, man? You know, do you have anything you've always hoped to get around to?" I asked.

"You're looking at it." He clinked his beer bottle against mine. "Cheers. To being out on the water with my girl and my friends."

"You know I'd do anything for you," I said, trying to stanch the emotion welling in my throat. "Anything at all. You just say the word."

"I know," he said. "But enough of that. I want to keep living, got me?"

"Yeah, pal, I've got you."

We watched boats whiz by us in the harbor for some time when the sound of laughter caught our attention. I looked up, put my hand over my eyes, and squinted into the sun. "Looks like we have company."

A sailboat skidded over the top of the water toward us in the harbor, slowing as it neared. When the people onboard realized who they were looking at, they whooped and hollered, shouting for Bogie, who waved, and then for Betty and for me. Humphrey Bogart, Lauren Bacall, and Frank Sinatra—they'd hit the jackpot.

"Sing for us, Frank!"

"What do you think?" I said to Bogie.

"I'd tell them to piss off, but it's up to you," he said.

I wasn't one to let an audience down so I stood easily because of the calm waters of the harbor, and launched into one song after another, growing drunker and more sunburned by the minute. They cheered and clapped, and I had a grand old time, soaking up the unexpected praise, until finally, Bogie had had enough.

"Will you knock it off, Frank? Let these people go on about their business and give the rest of us some peace." He seemed more exhausted than irritable.

"Alright," I said. "You heard the man. That's it for the day." I waved good-naturedly as the sailboat of fans set sail.

Bogie's tolerance had waned in recent days. He coughed more, bent as some unseen pain racked his body when he thought no one was looking, and he'd snapped at me more often, too, lecturing me about my flamboyant wealth and the stupid parties I threw when I flew an entire group of friends to Vegas. I put everyone up in individual rooms and presented them with a bag of silver dollars to gamble. But that was my way; I wanted everyone to have a good time, even if I wasn't. Bogie never understood it, and I didn't try to explain it. He'd come from money and had never wanted for anything in his life, not in any real sense. I'd always wished I'd been in his shoes, until now. Despite the attempts to end my own life in the past, I was glad to be alive, to be back on top and living the dream, even when things were hard. Going out by cancer seemed about the worst way to go.

One night I sat beside Bogie's bed as he drifted to sleep. The smell of vinegar tinged the air and the shades were drawn, making the room feel more like a cave than a warm bedroom. It had been a particularly rough day for all of us. Betty seemed to be at her wits' end, racked with grief and exhaustion from the round-the-clock care. That night, I learned that sometimes death was a mercy.

We tiptoed from the room and headed to the kitchen for a drink.

Betty stopped in front of the cabinets, her back to me, clutching the counter to steady herself. Her shoulders shook slightly and I knew she was crying.

"I know," I said. "Come here." I reached for her, pulling her into my arms, wiping the tears away, and clinging to her for dear life. We were both losing someone we loved, and only we understood what that meant.

After her tears subsided, she leaned back to look at me. "I just want it to end," she said. "But I can't imagine the end either."

"I know," I said, swallowing the lump in my throat. As we gazed at each other, suddenly the distance between us disappeared. I grazed her lips with mine.

And then we did the unthinkable. We left, went back to my place, and fell into bed together, consoling each other and engaging in the kind of furious affection that I would soon—and forever—regret.

CHAPTER 37

AVA

When filming concluded in Rome in May, I flew home knowing this was it—I was finished with life in Los Angeles. I wasn't truly cut out for a life in the spotlight and the social pressures that came with it, and I learned that evermore with each passing year. I wanted to do my movies and disappear into a regular life between them, enjoying myself, seeing the world, so I next made a decision that would change my life forever. As soon as I finished filming my next picture, I'd pack up and move to Europe for good. I had Spain and its heat in my veins, the Spanish zeal for life bubbling inside me. And the best part of living there—people left me alone.

The first thing I had to do to cut ties with this godforsaken town, was to finish what I'd been putting off. I had to file divorce papers. Frank would either give me hell about it or drag things out between us, so I was left with one choice: a trip to Nevada. Filing for divorce was a nonevent, I told myself. I was dating my bullfighter still, from afar, though I knew my time with Luis would be short-lived. We'd been living out a fairy tale together—until he'd pressured me for a commitment. The last thing I wanted was being shackled to another male, and especially to one who had a flair for the dramatic. I'd had enough of that with Frank.

After dinner with Howard Hughes and some old friends in the city, I packed a few things to spend six weeks in Nevada to file for divorce. Howard was so happy I was splitting with Frank that he rented a monstrous house for me in Tahoe. Reenie and I set out in June and luxuriated in the gorgeous place that was more of a manor than a home. It was a nice gesture, but it wasn't long before I discovered that Howard was up to his old ways.

A private investigator tailed me wherever I went, which probably meant the house was wired, too. I figured staying and eating for free was worth the price of admission and what did I have to hide anyway?

The second week I was in town, Howard showed up at the door.

"I made dinner reservations," he said. "Put on your best dress."

We ate like kings at a private steakhouse and as the dessert and port were served, Howard reached into his jacket pocket. "I have something for you."

"What's that?" I sipped the tawny port with notes of butterscotch and then licked my lips.

"Open it," he said.

I reached for the small package, tearing the paper away. Inside was a box that could mean only one thing: he'd bought me jewelry. As I opened the box, I gasped. A sapphire and diamond ring, at least two carats but likely closer to four, sparkled in the lamplight. I glanced at him, stunned. Hadn't he already learned that I wasn't someone he could buy? What was he playing at?

"Will you marry me, Ava? It's my turn." He smiled awkwardly.

I tossed the ring back at him. "Haven't I answered this question, Howard? There's no such thing as turns. I'm not some pony ride at the fair!"

He sat back in his chair, defeated for the last time, or so I thought. In time, I'd be offered a diamond necklace once owned by the Romanovs attached to a few other outrageous pleas until, at last, Howard not only grasped the truth but ruined our friendship forever.

To make sure he understood, I dug the knife in a little deeper. "Besides, I'm still in love with Frank."

I wasn't sure why I said it. At the time I told myself it was to get rid of Howard, but after I'd been in Tahoe for a couple of weeks, Frank caught wind of my visit. He knew why I was there; he knew I'd given up on our marriage. I thought we were through, but when he took off after a late show at the Sands to pay me a visit, I didn't turn him away. As I opened the front door to find his famous blue eyes and charming grin, I fell upon him like a vulture on its prey.

As we made love, every nerve tingled, awakening something inside me that had been lying dormant since the last time we'd seen each other. And goddamn him, what I'd said to Howard was true—I still loved Frank.

"You missed me," he said after we'd done what we did best together beneath the sheets, more than once. "No one will ever love you like I do, Angel."

"It's too soon to tell," I said.

He laughed. "You're about to divorce me—and here I am to persuade you that I'm still the love of your life and you're mine—and it's too soon to tell?"

"You're a pain in the ass."

"Would you have it any other way?" he asked, his gaze searing right through me.

I didn't know, really. Yes, I would have liked for him to not be an egomaniac and a traditional old fool who felt threatened by every moment I left his sight. But truth be told, I would have fled the marriage a lot sooner if we didn't have sparks flying, and a deep understanding of each other that no one else could touch.

After the sun rose in the sky and another particularly tender and languorous lovemaking session, he turned over to peer at me closely, a grin on his face. "Let's go down to the dock."

"Sounds like a fine idea."

We dressed and walked down to the dock to find a sleek motorboat.

"Take it for a spin?" he asked.

I hadn't been out on the lake yet and it seemed like the perfect way to spend a romantic interlude. "Sure," I said. "I'm up for a ride. Let me grab a few things."

I returned with a basket of fruit, cold meats, some bread, and a big bottle of vodka.

"Now you're talking," he said, winking. "Hop on, first mate."

He looked handsome behind the wheel and my heart fluttered at the sight of him happy, beside me, on a day where the sky smiled down at us and everything felt right between us. My thoughts of divorce had drained away like a swirl of dirty dishwater in a sink.

As I slid into a seat on the boat, he fired up the engine and we rode out onto the lake. The wind whipped through my hair, and I reached out to take his hand in mine. He smiled and after several minutes of gliding over the water, we slowed and eased into a private cove.

I poured us each a drink and laid out the food spread, and we lazed on the boat, drinking, laughing, eating. We didn't talk about why I was here, or Luis or Frank's lovers. We drank each other in, remembering why we'd fallen in love in the first place.

Hours later, the sun began to slide down the arc of sky and I grew chilled.

He revved the engine and looked out over the water.

"Has that boat been there the whole time?" He motioned to a cigarette boat about four hundred yards away.

I squinted in the sun. "I don't know, has it?"

The man at the helm didn't bother to hide a large pair of binoculars. They were pointed directly at us. I knew who that was. It was another PI—or maybe the same one that had been following me all week.

"It's probably Howard's PI," I said, stifling a yawn after hours of loving, sun, and vodka.

"What do you mean 'Howard's PI'? Who the hell does that creep think he is? He's not the fucking president of the United States!" Frank whipped the boat around swiftly and in an instant, slammed the gear shift to crank up the speed—and immediately gunned for the other boat.

"What are you doing!" I shouted over the wind. "Just ignore him. Who gives a damn if Howard knows we're out on a boat together!"

He ignored me and, cussing, cruised in tight circles around

the other boat over and over, creating an enormous wake. I slid from my seat twice, landing in the bottom of the boat on my rear end.

"Frank! Knock it off! Let's go!" I shouted.

He ignored me, screaming at the man and nearly capsizing the other boat.

Suddenly I was reminded why I was in Tahoe in the first place: to escape the madness Frank and I made together. And it was definitely time.

CHAPTER 38

FRANK

Ava didn't show in court or sign the divorce papers she'd sworn to file after Tahoe, and neither did I. We couldn't seem to get there, and I held on to a shred of hope that we might reconcile.

If my personal life was a mess, my career rocketed to new heights. Nearly all of my singles hit the *Billboard* charts. Roles for new pictures flooded in from multiple studios. When *Time* magazine called, I lost it—I drank myself into a stupor to celebrate. I'd never forget seeing Ava on the cover, being awestruck by her fame, and now, the deadest man in Hollywood who couldn't get a single person to take a call was on the cover of *Time*. I'd even received a second Oscar nomination. I was unstoppable.

I started thinking about investing in my own record label and in shares of a casino, but those decisions were still for the future. For now, I spent money like water. Gold key chains for staff and other people who were good to me, extravagant parties with flowing champagne in my suite at the Sands. I bought my daughter her first car and I bought a car for Ava, too. She paid me back well with a quick visit and a hot weekend, leaving my head reeling and my heart wanting her all over again. We weren't together but somehow, we couldn't be apart either.

When I didn't win the Oscar for playing a one-armed man in *The Man with the Golden Arm*, Ava was the first person I called.

"What is it, Francis? You're upset." Her voice came over the line.

"I lost," I said, disappointment rippling through me again. I'd worked so hard on the role, read and researched, and met with doctors to understand what it was like to lose an arm, including the pain, the phantom limb sensation, and even the inevitable shame from people staring at you and making you feel like you've become a freak. But it wasn't enough.

"The nomination is what counts, baby," she said. "And you were brilliant, no matter who won the award. It should have been you and everyone knows it. Besides, you're on top everywhere. People aren't comfortable with winners. Not for long. And you, baby, are a winner."

Something inside me released at those words. I ached for her, wanted to be consoled in a way that only she could provide. "I need to see you. How about I come to Madrid?"

"I'll keep the bed warm," she said, her drawl pronounced.

I thought of Betty, Bogie's wife, and how we'd been quietly seeing each other the last few weeks as he declined. I wasn't comfortable sitting with that truth. Still, she wouldn't like me flying off to see Ava, but comparing my feelings for Betty to those I felt for Ava was like comparing a pastel watercolor to a Van Gogh canvas of vivid, bold strokes with layers upon layers of color and emotion. They weren't in the same universe.

"Tomorrow, Angel," I said.

When I arrived in Madrid, Ava greeted me with the biggest grin, her green eyes sparking, her curls wild in the hot wind. My heart squeezed at the sight of her, and as we walked toward each other, I knew I was done for all over again.

"It's good to see you," she said, looping her arms around my neck.

"I love you," I said, covering her mouth with mine.

When we parted, she said, breathlessly, "I love you, too. Always will."

We made our way to bed, and everything else vanished. For a time.

When I returned to the States, I felt unstable, missing her and once again slammed with guilt for sleeping with my best friend's wife. Sometimes I thought Bogie knew Betty and I were fooling around. He'd look at her with a pained expression and then at me, and contempt would flash in his eyes. I knew he loved her, but I also knew he'd been in love with his hairdresser, Verita Thompson, for years. The woman had meticulously cared for Bogie's toupees before cancer and after, and they'd had a serious and long affair. Betty knew about Verita, and I knew Bogie loved Verita more than he could ever care for Betty. Sometimes those were the breaks.

Soon after my return, I got the call I'd been dreading for months.

Bogie, dead.

It didn't matter that he'd long been suffering and I'd seen it coming a million miles off. I struggled with the fact that I'd never see him again, knock around some jokes with him, talk about things that mattered in life and things that didn't. I

locked myself in my New York apartment, smoking one cigarette after another until my hands shook and my head ached
with fatigue and nicotine. I contemplated the arbitrary nature
of life and made a vow that night to not waste a single moment.
What a fool I'd been, to attempt to take my own life. I hadn't
seen what was precious there, in those moments. Now it was
undeniable, mirrored in the life of a dear friend, lost against his
will and far too soon.

I asked Betty to marry me on a whim one night after wistful
memories and bottles of wine. A day later in the clear, bright
sunshine, it didn't feel right. I'd gotten carried away. Sometimes I couldn't stop the runaway train of my emotions.

"Let's keep our engagement quiet for now," I said the following evening. "We're not in any sort of rush anyway, are we?" We
didn't acknowledge the fact that I wasn't even divorced yet.

Though Betty agreed, within weeks, a newspaper caught
wind of our engagement—that's when I knew she'd told someone. When she called the next day to explain, I refused her phone
call. I ignored her barrage of messages and made sure I wasn't
home for weeks. With time apart came clarity: I was relieved to
have a reason to let her go. I didn't want to marry her—she was
my friend's girl—and the guilt was eating me alive. Betty and I
had shared something intense while Bogie was dying, but that
was all it was. An understanding, a companionship.

I ignored her calls and never spoke to Betty again. As for
Ava, I'd soon learn she was leaving the U.S., for good.

CHAPTER 39

AVA

When I learned of Francis's alleged engagement, I lost a few days to gin martinis, had a raucous night out with Lena Horne and her band, and followed it with a day of wallowing with my sister. In the end, the news made it easier to leave Los Angeles. Seven months after I'd vowed to pack up my life in Los Angeles for good, I finally decided to go for it. Reenie, my sister, Bappie, and my dog, Rags, were loaded into a plane and off we went.

I rented a ranch home twenty minutes from Madrid on a couple of acres of lawn with towering pines and sweeping willows, and dusty brown hills rolling in the distance. I connected quickly with the wealthy expat society I'd met a year before while dating Luis. Betty and Ricardo Sicre became my nearest and dearest friends. Not only was I amazed by their stories of being former World War II spies—and falling in love during their time at war—but they knew how to party with the best of them.

Betty and I grew so close, I passed her the scripts sent my way from Hollywood and turned down the offers if she didn't like them. I also turned them down when I didn't want to leave home. I knew I was cutting myself off more and more from life in the spotlight, but I welcomed the reprieve. The Spanish let me live my life. They didn't chase me down alleys to catch a glimpse of me or to take a photograph. They didn't behave like parasites, as Francis used to call the media, sapping me of energy and taking from me something that couldn't be easily replenished: my privacy, my happiness.

During my free time, I traveled all over the country and learned the way of the land—the mountains and cooler temperatures in the north; the seaside towns on the eastern shores; the blazing hot, dry region to the south. The customs and the endless salty, oily seafood dishes. In the end, I felt most at home among those who were considered vagrants in Spain. Bands of people who roamed from town to town, often along a river, living off wages gained from their bewitching music. I was drawn to their vivid earthiness, which reminded me of my North Carolina upbringing and reminded me just how pretentious and false everything was in the city I'd left behind. These people came alive at night like I did, beginning their evening after a ten-o'clock dinner, and carrying their music and dancing through the black hours until the sky streaked purple with dawn's first light. When the morning came and my new friends began to trickle home, sometimes I'd invite them back to my place, luring them with a currency of wine or a tidy sum I knew they needed to buy food. I felt most myself in their presence, wild with joy or deeply philosophical, and at times, celebrating my own private pain.

In the end, the wine-soaked nights began to add up and I felt the caution that had ruled my professional life in public disappearing. What did I care if I was portrayed as a wild child, participating in orgies and the like with the wicked and the banished on the fringes of society? I didn't. It didn't matter, none of it—not what others said or thought or believed. I could only be myself, even if I was changing without knowing precisely how.

As for my career, it was changing, too.

The script adaptation for another Hemingway book arrived and I called the man myself. Hemingway—whom I'd had the pleasure to meet at a bull ranch and whom I'd adored instantly—asked for a copy of the script for *The Sun Also Rises* and I sent it immediately.

When he called, I grew nervous.

"I hate to be so blunt," he began.

"Out with it, Papa," I said, using his nickname. "I need to know what I'm getting myself into."

"The script is a piece of shit."

I laughed at his directness. "Well, you really should work on telling me how you feel."

Now he was the one who laughed.

"I don't have a choice but to take the film," I said. "I keep turning down their scripts and I'm still under contract."

"Good luck, Daughter," he answered, calling me by his pet name for me. "Let me know how it all works out."

I tarried over whether to try to get out of the film, but David Hanna firmly backed me into a corner.

"I don't care if it's the worst damn thing you've ever read," David said. "You need to get on that plane to Mexico. You've turned down one script too many and you're still under contract."

I reluctantly packed my bags, knowing there was one other

thing I must do while on that side of the world. I packed the divorce papers right along with Francis's records in my suitcase.

When I arrived in Mexico City for filming, I was bused out to a horrible set and even worse lodgings—if you could call the ramshackle huts lodgings. One had already caved in on several crew members. I demanded to be given sufficient lodgings outside of the camp. I demanded my hairdresser be flown in from Hollywood. I demanded the press be barred from the set. I also charged my liquor to the studio account. I was no longer a clueless young starlet—I was a seasoned actress who wasn't in any mood to put up with the baloney that came with my ridiculous job. And if MGM didn't like it, they could cut me loose from my criminally low-paying contract. I longed to be a free agent, anyway—most of the bigwigs already were by now. I was just biding my time until it ran out.

One day on set, a member of the camera crew made a snide comment: "Tequila is the hardest on the skin, you know."

I looked a little puffy that morning, for sure, after bar time the night before, but I obsessed over the man's comment. For the first time, I stared in the mirror, noting the circles under my eyes and the little lines that had begun to form on my forehead and around my mouth. I bought up all the tabloids I could find to study the unflattering pictures of myself—and then I snapped.

"I'm not coming to set if you don't bar those photographers from the production," I said, storming out of the scene one afternoon.

"Ava! We have two more scenes left," the director called after me.

I whirled around to face him. "Then get them out of here so

I can focus and we can all go home!" I motioned to the handful of press photographers that showed up almost daily.

He did as I asked after more threats and shouting, and I stumbled blindly through the rest of the picture. The real motor behind my horrible behavior was something I thought I'd accepted—that Francis and I were through and it was time to move on. That didn't mean I had to like it.

I finally signed and sealed the divorce papers, and had them delivered.

Francis didn't even fight it. He signed and filed immediately.

I was as relieved as I was devastated on a level I didn't understand until the middle of the night, left alone, my heart racing from three gin martinis too many. I stared at the ceiling of my hotel room, my eyes drawn to a spider crawling into a crack in the corner. I didn't know what I was doing, where I was going. I didn't know what my next move would be—and God forbid my beauty was truly slipping. Hollywood would have nothing to do with me. I was only as good as my last picture, as my last photo shoot used for pinups.

I tortured myself with visions of Francis and Betty. Would he really marry her? I slipped out of bed, put on Francis's latest hit on the record player, and listened to him sing to me until I'd cried all the tears in the world. Tonight, the world was black and my chance at love was a blurred spot on the horizon.

On my first day home in Madrid after the terrible filming experience in Mexico, I received a call from Los Angeles.

"I've got another film for you," David, my publicist said. "It's in Rome."

I groaned. "How many more are there?"

"You're almost done with your contract," he said. "Hang in there. Soon, we'll start making you some real money."

The power had shifted to agents and managers and best of all, to the actors. We could call the shots about which pictures we agreed to do rather than be one of a stable of actors forced to work on a film. Now, our team negotiated the deals. I could hardly wait to be done with MGM for good.

"So back to Rome, I guess," I said, sighing.

In Rome, I was hounded every minute by the press. I was recognized everywhere, harassed, photographed, followed. It was surreal: ducking into alleyways to hide, covering my hair with scarves and my face with sunglasses, or waiting to leave the house at odd hours. Exhausted by it all, and desperate for a reprieve, I was glad to escape to Monaco for Grace Kelly's wedding.

I was happy for Gracie, but something about her getting married unsettled me deeply. I was envious, sure. What woman wouldn't want to go from Hollywood starlet—a difficult and winding career—to Her Serene Highness, Princess of Monaco? Or perhaps I felt left behind while everyone moved on with their lives and settled into a normal, fulfilling family life. One thing was certain, I was nervous as a bedbug that I'd run into Francis and his flavor of the month. I didn't think I could stomach it.

On the day of the wedding, I wore a tasteful silk dress with full skirt and pinned my hair into a smooth bun. A wedding for a princess required class and taste. Besides, the crowd would be a who's who and I wanted to look my best—especially if Francis would be there. I don't know why I cared. We were divorced, after all, and hadn't spoken to each other in months. I thought about our wedding, on a miserable day in November, the pouring rain an omen for what was to come. I should have called it quits right there. And yet, I knew I would never regret my time with Francis, even as tumultuous as it was.

Gracie, on the other hand, had a morning of cerulean skies. I marveled at the magnificent cathedral where the ceremony would be held; crowning the cliffs of Monaco and overlooking the stunning Mediterranean Sea, it was all white stone flanked by lush palms. As I was ushered inside the beautiful cathedral, I didn't have to put on a fake smile—I was truly happy for Grace.

The organ music began, and Grace walked down the aisle on her daddy's arm as MGM cameramen were poised in every corner of the church, doing their best to make the ceremony into a spectacle. MGM had agreed to free Grace from her contract early only if she allowed them to film the entire ceremony. A dirty move, but Grace had consented. I got the feeling her prince didn't want her doing pictures anyhow.

Once Gracie had been given to Prince Rainier and the Latin mass began, I found my gaze straying. I searched the crowd for a familiar face, the one that I hadn't seen in far too long. I don't know why I looked for him—seeing him with a date would have wrecked my good mood—but I couldn't seem to help myself.

But Francis hadn't come.

As the disappointment hit me, the familiar ache of missing him began. I tried not to dwell on it and put on a smile for the happy event.

Gracie was beautiful in her stunning, high-collar lace gown, glowing with happiness and assured footing, moving toward the thing she wanted most in her life. As she turned to swear her love to the prince who would become an integral part of her life, I saw myself in her, swearing my love and devotion to Francis all over again. But we weren't meant to be; our destinies had collided and now moved in opposite directions.

And yet . . .

I still wished I was holding his hand, here in front of God and everyone, in the back of this beautiful church.

CHAPTER 40

FRANK

When I received the invitation to Grace Kelly's wedding, I declined. It didn't work with my schedule, but I also had a pretty good idea that Ava would be there. We weren't talking at the moment and if I showed up, we'd argue and ruin the whole damn affair in front of half the town of Hollywood and a prince besides. I couldn't bring myself to do it.

After a year of breakups—Ava, Betty, and a young singer named Peggy Connelly—I needed a new pad; some place no one would bother me, and a home where only my kids and the closest of my friends were allowed. I bought a house in the mountains in Coldwater Canyon, a beautiful and rugged place with an incredible view of the sky. I set up a telescope and spent my few quiet nights gazing up at the stars, thinking about what was out there while classical music played in the background. I liked the house a great deal, but the reality was, I hardly spent time there. I was almost always on the road. Bright lights and even brighter women, a sea of new faces from one night to the next, cigarettes and bottomless bottles of whiskey, and hours and hours of filming or performing in every time zone—I barely knew where I was or what day it was. I topped the *Billboard* charts, had smash hit singles, and fended off the rising popularity of the rock-and-roll music that I so despised. And yet. All the success, the whirlwind of dazzling nights didn't take my mind off the one thing that meant more to me than any of it: Ava, the woman who had taught me more about passion— and about heartbreak—than any one person or one thing could ever do. My heartache kept me up most nights. My pal Jimmy Van Heusen, who crashed at my house often enough, saw the burden of that pain in nearly everything I did.

"I'm writing something special for you, Frank," he said one night, a cigarette hanging on the edge of his lip. He was curled over a notebook filled with lyrics, notes, and scratch-outs. We'd been lounging around the pool during a merciful day off, working our way through a pint of bourbon. By nightfall we were nice and lubed and far too philosophical, and Van Heusen had been channeling it to the page.

"Oh yeah?" I reached for the crystal decanter and refilled our glasses. "Hey, you want something to eat? I'm starved."

"I could eat," he said.

I asked the housekeeper to cook up a couple of burgers and then flicked a look at the pile of pages in his lap. "You ready to tell me what you're working on?"

"A suite of new songs. You've been through a lot the last few years."

I nodded. "Ain't that the truth. Can I see what you've got?"

He handed me the top page and I pored over the page of fresh ink. The song was called "Only the Lonely." "Shit, Jimmy, this is good."

He nodded. "Been tough watching you suffer, man."

I stared into my glass, avoiding his eyes. The song captured a sense of searing loneliness and despair, but also a reverence for love. My friend had me pegged. I couldn't have written the song better myself.

I cleared my throat, swallowing the emotion. It was the start of a new album, one I knew had to be dedicated to Ava, but how would I sing without making a spectacle of myself on stage? "This is amazing work, man."

"You're a pretty amazing guy," he said.

I punched him in the shoulder playfully to lighten the mood, and we both laughed.

Weeks later, I recorded that album, and though it wouldn't be the hit that my others had been, I knew it was among my best, and most of all, it was cathartic. It was my Ava album, an album about breakups and heartache—and the very first themed album out there on the market. Somehow we knew we were on to something, grouping songs by theme and we were— themed multisong albums changed music forever.

I couldn't help myself and sent a copy to Ava.

She called me to thank me for it, the first time we'd spoken in months. My heart skipped in my chest at the sound of her voice.

"Sing me the Ava song, baby," she said after we'd been on the phone for some time.

"You want me to sing now?"

"Yes. Like you mean it, baby."

"Oh, I mean it alright," I said, and I began the song that would forever spark longing every damn time I sang it.

"That's beautiful," she said, the sound of her sniffles drifting faintly over the line.

"You're beautiful."

"I miss you, Francis."

"I miss you, too, Angel."

That woman possessed my soul. I knew I held hers, too, as hard as she'd fought it, and I began to think that maybe we really were like Romeo and Juliet after all. Star-crossed lovers, forever in love but ultimately a tragedy. There was something poetic about our desperate need for each other.

Soon after the Ava album hit the radio, I headed to Indiana to film *Some Came Running*. I was to costar with Shirley Mac-Laine and Dean Martin, an Italian American comic, singer, and actor I'd heard plenty about but hadn't yet met. We got along like the Three Stooges. Dean was witty and told wild stories about running bootleg booze across the Pennsylvania border for the Mafia as a teenager and tales of the shenanigans and scrapes he'd been involved in since becoming a star. Shirley had a great sense of humor and liked to have a good time the way we did. She was young, though, and couldn't quite keep up with the long, late nights, the hundred-dollar tips to the bellboys, or the pranks Dean and I played on each other. I'd leave cracker crumbs in Dean's bed one night and he'd repay me the next with spaghetti sauce on my tuxedo.

Even though Dean was aloof and hard to know, I instantly understood I'd found a lifelong friend in him. He let me do my thing and he did his own, and together, we were dynamite. It wasn't long before Dean was invited to the Sands and shortly after, our names stretched across the marquee, side by side, on a regular basis.

One night, the house was packed and the crowd was rowdy after hours of gambling and booze, so we played to it.

"How about we sing a set, pal?" I said into the microphone, looking out at the eager, smiling faces, the dimmed lights and the cigarette cloud that hovered overhead.

"That would be swell," Dean replied. He stumbled to mimic a drunkard.

The audience laughed at the sight. I chuckled, too, and said, "The mic is this way." I pretended to lead him back across the stage.

The audience roared.

The band caught on quickly and began the song again.

Dean started to sing and then let the words trail off. He stopped and scratched his head like he'd forgotten the rest.

I looked at my watch and then at him. "I've got to catch a train soon."

The crowd howled.

This time, I began to sing—and Dean interrupted my song. As the audience hollered and clapped, I felt a heady buzz. It was a different kind of satisfaction to be considered funny, and we loved every minute of it.

We bantered more, goofing around as laughter rippled through the audience. Our energy was electric—the audience rapt—and we both knew this was the start of something. A comedy routine, a play between friends, a little music. A great new show, Vegas style.

Jack Entratter, the hotel manager, met us after the show and clapped me on the shoulder. "That was hilarious, man. Did you two plan it?"

Dean and I glanced at each other and grinned. "Nope. That was improvisation, my friend."

"I'll say," Jack said. "If you're feeling up to it tomorrow night, let's do it again."

"You've got it, boss," I said. "Now how's about a real drink and a game of craps?" We had some serious gambling to do.

"I'll roll first," Dean said, lighting a cigar and winking at me.

Our shows together were a huge hit, and next thing I knew, Dean and I had invited British singer and dancer Peter Lawford, nightclub veteran and comic Joey Bishop, and my pal, singer and comedian Sammy Davis Jr., to join us. On occasion, Shirley would join in the fun onstage, too. We'd perform for an hour, head to the gambling tables afterward, and then go upstairs to my suite for the best in booze and food and women. We were unstoppable: a group of men tearing up the town and diving headfirst into all the sin Las Vegas had to offer. The sillier we acted, the more the crowd loved it and soon a media frenzy began. People came from far and wide, paying top dollar to see us. Suddenly Las Vegas was the place to be. We'd made this town, and I was the leader of the pack.

The Summit, as we called ourselves—or the Rat Pack, according to the media—was a sensation. We drew enormous crowds who loved our slapstick, toilet humor, drunk jokes, and shots at racists as the demand for civil rights heated up. And, of course, jokes about sex. Sometimes we made the jokes for laughs and sometimes they were to make a point. In the end, we were nothing but a group of fellas having fun together onstage, and somehow, we'd become the group everyone wanted a piece of. People bought us rounds of drinks or sent us gifts, and women threw their room keys onstage.

Eventually, Peter had a bright idea that would solidify our fame.

"I bought the rights to a movie," he said one night in the cigar lounge after a show. We'd been particularly feisty that night and decided some Cubans were in order. "It's called *Ocean's 11*," he continued. "It's about a group of vets hired to hit five different casinos at the same time. And we're looking for a great cast."

"Forget the movie, let's pull the job!" I said.

Everyone laughed and raised a glass.

"Who are you thinking of for it?" I asked, giving Peter a sidelong glance.

"The script is being finished now, but William Holden would be lead, I think," he said.

"Sounds like a good one," I said. "If you change your mind, I'd be interested in a lead."

As it turned out, he did change his mind.

And that was it—the preservation on film of the legendary Summit. We'd moved from stage to movie, and the project was a blast. After shooting wrapped each day, we'd head to the clubhouse, a steam room and health club at the casino, wearing matching robes monogrammed with our nicknames: Dag for Dean, short for Dago; Sammy was Smokey because he was the worst chain smoker we'd ever seen; and Peter was Brother-in-Lawford, since he was married to a Kennedy. Women rotated in and out of the sauna, slipping their room keys into our robe pockets, arguing about who got Dean.

We were practically national icons, and, I hoped, leaving a legacy behind that wouldn't be forgotten. Admittedly, with each passing year my preoccupation with my legacy grew. I didn't want to be another Joe Schmo, erased from time like waves washing over sand. It was a depressing thought, suffering and loving and raging, only to meet the same end as every other cad before me. I wanted my life to mean something. I wanted my music and my pictures to leave a lasting impact.

And as my star rose higher and higher, and anything I wanted seemed achievable, I grew closer to that goal. At least, I hoped so. There was no telling who would share my story after I was gone, or if anyone would even want to, but that was out of my hands. All I could do now was keep on working, keep on bringing my best to the table until the lights dimmed and I couldn't go on anymore.

CHAPTER 41

AVA

Watching Francis's meteoric rise from afar and reading the wild tales in the press about him and the Rat Pack spurred me on to try to forget him. He was living his life without me and doing it well. While I was happy for him, his happiness threw a mirror up to my own. Was I happy? I didn't know and if that was the answer then the outlook wasn't good. The wild, riotous part of me began to take charge, my moods becoming more mercurial. I could see the waves washing over me as the angry, thrashing, crushingly sad person I was beneath my charming exterior emerged. I didn't try to curb my behavior. I'd spent the last fifteen years of my life trying to please everyone but myself, and now I was interested only in pleasing myself.

That was how I went looking for trouble. That was how I made another of the worst mistakes of my life.

Though my interest in matadors had waned, I still enjoyed the seductive yet deadly dance of bull and man so one idle afternoon, Bappie and I left Madrid and rode out to a bull ranch.

I'd met the owner of the ranch through Hemingway, and he'd gladly welcomed me back. Along the way, my sister and I drank *sol y sombra*, a mixture of absinthe and Spanish cognac that had us feeling mighty fine by the time we arrived—and very, extremely drunk.

At the bull ranch, a crowd of locals had gathered outside the small, dusty ring to watch the testing of the bulls. It was a yearly event, and as important to them as a Catholic feast day. There was an odd satisfaction in thinking about the way rituals were conducted in Spain: always with a practiced hand, always with layers of meaning and centuries of tradition behind them that I, as an American, couldn't quite grasp. But I wanted to, and I tried.

We arrived in time to see a bull being led into the ring. I watched, entranced, as the farmer shot him in the neck with barbed darts. It seemed so cruel, and yet, the ranch hands did it without even thinking.

Bappie gasped, tipping back the bottle of *sol y sombra* for another drink. "Why are they doing that? The poor animal. This is dreadful."

"It's supposed to make him less fierce for the riders when they enter the ring. Frankly, it would just piss me off more to be penetrated before the big event."

As we chuckled at my attempt at humor, Angelo Peralta, the owner of the ranch, headed over to shake my hand. Angelo still had that twinkle in his eye that I remembered from the first day I'd met him and the deeply wrinkled skin from years in the sun.

When he reached for my hand, the whispers began among

the onlookers, the delighted smiles, the waves. I realized they now knew they were looking at a movie star, all the way from Hollywood. Within moments, they began to chant my name.

"Ava! Ava! Ava!"

"Well, I guess they've found me out," I said, glad I was wearing my sunglasses. Secretly, I was pleased by their attention for a change. I still had it, even now, even as I creeped closer to middle age and becoming an old maid.

"They want you to ride the horse," Angelo said, nudging me.

"Well, I *am* being considered for a part as a bullfighter on horseback," I said, giggling after entirely too much alcohol. "Imagine me, a bullfighter."

Apparently the crowd had already imagined it. "Viva, Ava!" they cried, giving me a rush of adrenaline.

Maybe it wouldn't hurt to give them a little show to remember me by.

"Hold this," I said, handing Bappie my purse and the bottle of liquor. "I'm going to ride that damned horse."

"Are you sure that's a good idea?" she asked, her words slurred. She could hold her liquor, too, but not like I could—a skill I shouldn't be proud of but which had served me well. "Isn't that dangerous?"

I winked. "That's why it'll be fun."

The ranch hands lifted me onto the saddle of the largest black stallion I'd ever seen and like a shot, we galloped into the middle of the ring. I laughed, waving to the crowd, clutching the strap with one hand and the banderilla, the matador's flag, in the other. The crowd went wild and chanted my name louder.

"Ava! Ava! Ava!"

I threw my head back and laughed, drunk as a skunk, and giddy with the rush of being watched.

The powerful animal kicked up a cloud of dust, coating me with a fine film of dirt, and galloped into the center of the circle. I clung to the reins, suddenly realizing what I was doing was dangerous and that Bappie had had a point. This probably wasn't a good idea. But that was my way, wasn't it? Always stumbling into things that weren't a good idea and then paying the consequences later. No sense in changing that now.

I held my breath, gathering my courage.

The crowd frothed with excitement.

A ranch hand shouted and then let the bull loose into the ring. Without hesitating, it charged us.

I screeched as the horse, a mass of muscle and sinew beneath me, bolted, writhing and irritable and desperate to dislodge the intruder and to save itself. I screamed again and the crowd cheered, a little too delighted by the spectacle.

Suddenly the bull was upon us.

The stallion danced right, dodging the furious animal, but the bull charged again. My heart pounded in my ears and suddenly I wanted to get off this damned animal and escape the ring.

This time, the horse wasn't fast enough, and the bull grazed its side.

I clutched the reins, my vision blurring from the alcohol. My stallion didn't like being wounded and galloped away, kicking as it went. I clenched my legs around its middle to steady myself as best I could. The horse heaved and huffed, its sides contracting and expanding beneath my legs as it tried to draw in steadying breaths. The horse was as terrified as I was.

The audience roared, their voices rising into the scorched dusty air and contorting into jeers. They jeered at my choices and every wrong move I'd ever made. At the fact that I was stupid enough to climb atop a frightened animal in a danger-ous dance between life and death. Is this what it had all come to? In a desperate attempt to appease my vanity, I was risking my life? This could very well be the end, and for what? I was my own worst enemy, always had been. In that moment, noth-ing could be clearer—except wishing I hadn't gotten on that damn horse at all.

The horse bucked again and I screamed, yanking hard on the reins and squeezing its middle with my legs with all my might.

I thought of Francis then, of how he'd have not only talked me out of the stunt but taken the reins himself to keep me from making such an absurd mistake. And in that instant before the bull began to charge a third time, I missed him acutely. Missed his noisy, pushy, loving voice in my ear, his warmth at my side. Francis would have done anything to keep me out of that ring, even if it meant making a spectacle. Even if he'd had to throw me over his shoulder and carry me out of there, and right now, I wished with all my might that he had. Sometimes he knew what was better for me than I did.

I looked ahead at the steaming animal who couldn't wait to tear me and the horse to shreds. Panting, I held on for dear life.

The bull turned and charged again.

My horse reared up, his own scream echoing in my ears. And then I was flung from the saddle.

I smacked the ground—hard—landing on my cheekbone.

A collective gasp arose from the audience.

Pain shot through my skull, and my teeth rattled with it as

if I'd been hit across the face with a nine iron. I sucked in air and willed myself to get up, to get myself to safety, but for once in my life, I couldn't speak and I couldn't seem to move.

The next instant, hands lifted me from the ground and carried me swiftly over the barrier of the ring.

"Ava!" Bappie screeched. "Are you alright?"

I nodded, dazed. "I'm alright, I think. My cheek." I cradled my face with my hand.

As Bappie helped brush the dust from my clothing, someone placed a cup of *sol y sombra* in my hand, and I was pushed to my feet. My head spun and sweat stung my eyes. I wiped at them hastily and leaned on my sister.

"Are you alright?" Angelo asked, concern darkening his eyes. "Do you need to see a doctor?"

I shook my head, gulped down the strong liquor, and waved at the crowd. I had to give them the show they wanted, despite the spill. I hated myself a little for it, for that need to please an audience and that yearning for sensation—pleasures, adventure, danger—at any cost.

The crowd roared in approval.

It wasn't until later that afternoon when the booze had begun to wear off that my cheek throbbed so much I had to take painkillers. By the next day, a bruise had formed and swollen to the size of a fist. That was when the panic hit. I cursed myself as I stared in the mirror at a face I scarcely recognized. The injury continued to swell for days, and I grew distraught—terrified—that I'd permanently damaged my face after one foolish, split-second decision.

Too afraid to wait it out, I booked an appointment with a premier plastic surgeon in London and took the flight immediately. He assured me my face would heal and that for now, I needed to take care of the swelling and rest rather than take drastic action.

I returned to Spain and hid away for weeks, covering my face when I needed to buy groceries or go for a walk. Desperately worried, I cried daily, lamenting my stupidity. I'd wanted to finish out my contract at MGM—I only lacked one more film and a few months—and then make a handful of movies for some real money so I could retire. One more film to go, I thought, as I stared at the black-and-yellow knot on my cheek. Now I might not ever get the chance.

I couldn't handle the fear any longer. I needed the one person who always took care of me, even when times were difficult, the one person who understood me to my core and loved me no matter what I did.

I called Francis.

"I've hurt myself, Francis. I'm scared." I listened intently for signs of another woman in the background but there was nothing, only the strains of jazz from his record player.

"So I'm Francis again? You can't seem to make up your mind."

"You always were Francis, baby. I just get mad at you. But I'm not mad anymore. Anger is a waste of time."

He didn't say anything, just listened, one of the things I loved most about him. He was nothing if not a good listener. It was his generous side, the part of him that loved as much as he wanted to be loved.

"I need you," I continued. "I've done something stupid and now I'm hurt."

He didn't ask questions. He only said exactly what I hoped he'd say.

"I'll be there tomorrow, doll. Stay home, take care of yourself. I'll take a taxi to the house."

When he arrived on my doorstop, he folded me into his arms. The smell of his lavender cologne wafted around me and I instantly fell apart. God, I'd missed him, and I knew just how much in that moment. I'd thought our little tragedy had run its course. Time couldn't seem to align our stars. We were too distinctive, too much at odds. And yet, he was here again. Perhaps we wouldn't ever be through.

"It'll be alright," he said. "Shh. I'm here." He stroked my hair and rubbed my back. "It'll heal, baby. It'll heal."

After a good cry into his shirt, I led him inside.

"Let me get a good look at it," he said.

I turned on the lamp and watched his piercing gaze take in the damage. I knew he would tell me the truth, even if it hurt. That's what we were to each other: a mirror. Even when we didn't like what we saw there.

After a moment, he said, "Well, you ain't going to make any films looking like that, that's for sure."

I burst into tears all over again. "Thanks a lot." I pushed up from the sofa and went to find something to drink.

"I'll have whatever you've got," he called after me.

I returned with water for me and a bourbon rocks for him.

"What's this? No drink for you?"

"The doctor recommended compresses, eating well, and an

intense skin regime to help it heal. No alcohol for me for a while."

"Screw that doc, what did he do for you? Listen, I know the best plastic surgeon in New York. He's worked on a lot of celebrities. He'll give you some chemical injections. Maybe it'll break up that knot."

That's what worried me most: there was a hard knot forming, just as the doctor said might happen, and that was the worst news of all. Yet for now, I wasn't going to stray from his advice. If I needed surgery, I'd do it, but I didn't want to risk an adverse reaction to the injections. I was in my mid-thirties—the age when a love goddess usually retired in Hollywood—I had a damaged face, and no earthly idea what I was going to do next. I reached out to Francis hoping he would console me, and he had, but he'd also reminded me of something I hadn't yet wanted to admit: my beauty would fade—perhaps it was already fading—and what would I be left with? No career, no husband or family. Nothing but a broken heart and memories.

Francis stayed with me, consoling me through my doubts and after, we made love, tenderly and knowingly.

He was mine and I was his. And for now, that was the only thing that kept me going.

CHAPTER 42

AVA

Francis stayed with me a few days before he had to fly back for a show. We did our usual—argued on the way to the airport—but it was softer now, had less bite. It was as if we were going through the motions because of old habits, but we already knew we didn't mean it. Our insecurities with each other had leaked away over time and friendship colored in the empty spaces. I began to dream about what it would be like to truly reconcile. What the papers would say. Could their Romeo and Juliet reunite for good, after all this time?

Francis had scarcely left Spain when my publicist called with bad news. There were pictures of my fall in magazines all over the world and because I had been in hiding, speculation about my face was raging through Hollywood.

A Career-ender: Ava Gardner Will Never Work Again!

Beauty and the Beast: One of Hollywood's Most Beautiful Faces Ruined by a Drunken Fall

"The articles are shit," David said, his deep voice cracking. "Don't worry about them. Just get yourself ready for your last picture in Rome and then you can say goodbye to MGM for good."

I hardly heard him. How in tarnation could I do a film with this mark on my face? Everyone would see it, especially with the camera close-ups.

The swelling had receded, but I grew obsessed with the knot forming under the skin, touching it constantly, gazing into the mirror. I slept on my back, stayed out of the sunlight. I stopped wearing makeup and using creams and spent a fortune on facials from a Swiss therapist. Nothing worked—nothing could change the aftermath of my stupidity.

"I can't do it," I said, miserable. "I have this knot on my face. They'll toss me off the lot as soon as they see it."

"Look, it's the last one you have to do for them, and they know it. You're still under contract, Ava," David said.

"What if they take one look at my face and send me packing?"

"How bad is it really?"

I sighed heavily and the phone crackled with static. "It's not that bad, I suppose, but it's definitely noticeable."

"Let's look at it this way," he said. "People will flock to the movie to make sure their beloved Ava Gardner is still beautiful. And I suspect you're as gorgeous as ever. A little bump on your face can't change that. Now, make your plans. You're heading to Rome."

I packed for Rome, trying to pretend that my face didn't matter when the truth was, I was terrified. I wasn't getting any younger, after all, and the roles as a ravishing young woman were now limited. Lana had already begun to play roles as a mother and the very few other parts subscribed to middle-aged women, and she was three years older than me. So I went. I flew to France to rent a car so I could drive to Rome and avoid the press at the airport.

While not on set, I couldn't bring myself to hole up in my apartment and obsess about my face and the next phase of my career, so instead, I partied like a young thing with nothing to lose. I made my way from club to club that steamy summer with steamy men—if not for my own pleasure, for someone to keep me company. I thrived, throwing myself into the social life that Rome and the buzzing Via Veneto had to offer. The one thing that slowed me down was the cameras. As soon as the press appeared at a night spot, I ducked out, anxious to hide my aging face and the damage I'd done to it after one ridiculous decision.

Though there was a revolving door of men, the truth was, I missed Francis. I attempted to push him out of my thoughts completely so we could both move on with our lives, and yet, somehow, he stayed there, ever present in the back of my mind. I compared everyone to him, but the truth was, there was no comparison.

When I learned he was headed to London for a show—months after I'd last seen him in Madrid—I called him.

"Hi, Angel," he said, his voice turning buttery smooth.

"I heard you'll be in London. That's not terribly far from Rome."

"You miss me?"

"Something like that," I said, playing coy with him. Given the tabloids and the gossip I'd heard coming out of Las Vegas and Hollywood, he wasn't spending his nights alone.

We sat on the telephone for well over an hour. He told me a story about being up nights, thinking about us. He read me some poetry and then I read him the funny pages from the newspaper, and we laughed and missed each other all the more. We didn't only make good lovers, we made the best of friends.

"I'll stop by as soon as I'm done in London," he said. "I don't have long to stay. I have to get back to the States."

"We'll make the most of it, I promise," I purred.

The time and distance between us had done us some good, as it always had. I couldn't help but hope that maybe things would be different this time. We were older and wiser, weren't we?

The day before he was to arrive, I had a facial, bought a new dress and some negligees, and had the house cleaned to a shine the way he liked it. I went out to pick up a newspaper and to restock my liquor cabinet when my dream of a reunion with Francis came crashing down around my ears.

I reached for the tabloid on the stand and read the headline: "Frank Sinatra Courting Lady Adele Beatty?"

My stomach turned at the photo of Francis holding the door open for Adele, who was dressed to the nines in her satin gloves and mink stole. Did he plan to romance a different woman in every country? I was a fool to assume we could reconcile, or that we should spend time together at all. I drank myself into a stupor that night, ignored the ringing phone, and passed out. I hated myself for how much I still loved that man and worse, for my continued naivete.

When he arrived the following day, I made myself unavailable. And despite the voice in my head that reminded me I had seen someone behind his back more than once, I gave Frank the cold shoulder until I couldn't stand it any longer. I drove to the Hotel Hassler, where he was staying, my dog Rags at my side, my head on fire. I would give him a piece of my mind, tell him how much he'd hurt me. Tell him I wasn't the next hooker in line that he could make a quick pit stop with and leave all over again.

When Frank opened the hotel room door, Rags leapt from my arms and raced inside, barking happily.

"Hello, old boy! Glad to see your poppa?" Frank said, bending to scrub him behind the ears. He laughed as the dog licked him enthusiastically. When he sat on the couch, Rags promptly jumped into his lap.

"You traitor," I scolded my dog, the speech I'd planned evaporating completely. Instead, I removed the wedding ring that I still wore from my finger. "Here," I shoved it into Frank's hand. "Why don't you give this to your English lady."

"What the hell are you talking about?" he said, the smile sliding from his face. "And where have you been? I've been beating down your door all day."

"What do you care?" I said, gathering Rags from him. "You said the most beautiful things to me on the phone, and all along, you were planning on hooking up with that woman in London! I'm so sick of your shit, Frank."

I stormed to the door and as I slammed it behind me, his voice drifted into the hall.

"You're goddamn crazy, did you know that!"

I rushed down the stairs, the nails on Rags's little feet clicking over the wood, and when we'd reached the street outside,

I looked down at my little furry friend. He tilted his head sideways as if confused—and I burst into tears.

The next day, I learned Frank had already left Rome.

★ ★ ★

Though it stung, I went about my business without Frank, setting Roman nights on fire until filming concluded. I was relieved to be finished. At last I was ready to take my chances and have surgery on my cheek.

I called my publicist, in desperate need of a friend to accompany me to London. David flew from LA and met me there with a grim smile.

"How are you?" he said, slipping his arm around my shoulders.

I gritted my teeth. "I'm ready to get this over with."

"It'll be fine," he reassured me. "You're in good hands with this doctor. I did some research on him." He steered me inside the hospital and down the hall to check in for surgery. As they hooked me up to an IV and I began to fade into a drug-induced slumber, I considered how nervous the doctor must be to work on one of the world's most famous faces.

I closed my eyes, praying he had a steady hand.

When it was over and I came to, I opened my eyes to the doctor's smiling face. "Good news, Miss Gardner. I was able to remove the scar tissue. You'll always have a small dimple here in your cheek from the initial impact, but it's innocuous enough to look natural. I think you'll be pleased with the result."

I burst into tears.

I cried in relief. I cried for the injustice of being held to an impossible standard in my profession. I cried for the simple fact that my youth was fleeting, and that beauty did not endure. I cried for the yawning fear that gripped me when I considered the future. But I'd find what was next soon enough. For now, I just wanted to go home, to be comforted.

Only no one would be waiting for me there. And I would hate myself for missing Francis all over again.

CHAPTER 43

AVA

After the surgery, things didn't look up. Perhaps it was the blow to my confidence that the damage to my face had brought, or maybe it was my prowess with making bad choices, but suddenly, I was lonelier than ever and found myself adrift. That's when George C. Scott walked into my life. My new costar, he joined me on the set of *The Bible* and I couldn't help but be drawn to his strength. He was an ex-marine, had a muscular physique, and was playing the bad guy in the film. We talked politics, books, poetry. He was passionate about acting, though we both agreed the show business was garbage. I fell in love almost immediately. Something about him reminded me of all the men I'd loved—the sensitive, dark inside always lurking beneath the surface. He was darker than most and I'd soon learn exactly what that meant.

One night after dinner at his apartment, I mentioned Francis's name in passing. He was in Italy filming, too, and I'd wanted to see him. I thought if I was aboveboard with George about visiting Francis, he wouldn't be suspicious or jealous.

"What did you say to him?" George said, his tone curt.

I looked at George through my drunken haze and I swore I could see heat steaming from his ears. "To Francis?" I asked. "He's filming *Von Ryan's Express* so I stopped by his hotel last night. We had some dinner, talked. It was good to see him. Nothing happened. We're friends." And for once, that was true. Francis and I hadn't gone to bed as usual, and we got along like biscuits and gravy. Always had, as friends.

"What are you doing still talking to that asshole?" George fumed. "He never loved you. He hires whores and everyone knows it."

My mouth fell open. What did he know about my relationship with Francis?

"And you have a wife and a baby at home," I snapped. "How are you so different? At least he doesn't pretend to be something he isn't."

His face shifted to red and then purple, and with one decisive strike, he punched me.

I reeled backward, grasping my cheek, stunned by the reproach as much as the hit. I hadn't yet recovered from the blow when he jumped atop me, straddling me. His eyes were glazed over and a person I didn't know—hadn't seen until now—emerged in their depths. He hit me again and again, until I kneed him swiftly from the back, taking him off guard. I took advantage of his surprise and shoved him off me. Without grabbing my purse or shoes, without looking back, I bolted for the door, darting into the night, panting, terrorized, tears streaming down my cheeks.

What had just happened? I was stunned by his violence. I'd found myself a real prince among men, it seemed.

I headed back to my rented apartment, trying to hold myself

together. I swore as I locked the door behind me and promised myself I'd never see that asshole again.

The next day, the makeup artists on set did what they could to help cover the bruises George had left on my face. The crew seemed as shocked and disgusted as I was. George begged for my forgiveness, but I ignored him. I didn't care how passionate he was. All I could think about was how his wife managed to marry such a man. She must have been battered within an inch of her life on a regular basis, poor thing.

And yet, somehow, I forgave him. I found myself lured in by his profuse apologies and utter embarrassment, his promise not to ever be in that place again. He was completely sincere, and I could see it etched on his face. He wooed me and I fell for him again. In the evenings after shooting, we'd have drinks and all would be well—until it wasn't and he'd had one too many. He'd start with name-calling and progress to slapping and choke-holding me to the ground. I grew terrified of being with him—and terrified of trying to end things.

Francis called one night and we got to talking, whiling away an hour and next thing I knew, I was talking about George.

"I'm seeing an actor. War vet. He can be a little rough from time to time."

"A little rough?" Francis said. "Is he hitting you? I've heard a few things about Scott."

"No, of course not," I said quickly and then paused. "Well . . . he has a few times but it's nothing too serious."

"Angel, no man should put his hands on you. Do you want me to call in the dogs? I know a guy."

I sighed heavily. Francis and his thugs. "No, he's fine until he's had a little too much to drink is all."

"Promise me you'll tell me if you change your mind. I mean it, Ava."

"Sure, I will."

It turned out, Francis was right to be insistent. George dislocated my shoulder and ripped out my hair in chunks. At a hotel one night in London after going to the theater, he was in a temper and beat me bloody. Reenie had to call hotel security and the police showed, hauling George off for a night in jail. And that did it, I finally left him.

But he wasn't finished with me.

He followed me to California and one night he broke into my house in LA with a booze bottle, broken off at the neck, and threatened to slit my throat. I told him everything he wanted to hear then called the doctor, who arrived with haste. I slipped him a mickey, a powerful sedative. While he slept, Reenie helped me figure out what the hell to do with this man who treated me like I didn't matter, like my life didn't amount to much.

I wished violently for a different ending, for a different life. I wished for the man, who, no matter how angry we became with each other, would never dream of laying a finger on me. And after it all, I went on loving Francis Albert Sinatra.

CHAPTER 44

FRANK

These days I was on the road constantly or wedging visits with the kids into my schedule. I'd reached new heights, achieving every measure of success I'd ever dreamed of . . . and yet, for all the people around me and all the throngs of beautiful women, it was true companionship that I needed—it was Ava I craved.

From a hotel in Tulsa, I called her in the middle of the night. "Hello?"

I softened at the sound of her voice. She sounded as if she hadn't yet gone to bed—it was midmorning in Spain. I wanted her in my arms and in my bed. I wanted to talk until dawn. "Hi, Angel," I said, my voice hoarse with the emotion that rushed in every time I heard her on the line. "How was your night?"

"Exhausting, but a good time," she said. "I danced the night away in a flamenco bar."

"You sure do like it there."

"I do love Spain, but I have to admit, I'm getting tired of the blazing heat. I didn't think it was possible to have too much sun, but it turns out it is. A lot like in Palm Springs, I suppose."

"Maybe it's time to move home," I said.

"I don't know where that is right now, Francis."

That was the truth of it. Neither of us had a real home these days.

As the months passed, the gigs blended into each other. A year slipped by, and I'd have to ask one of the acquaintances who followed me on the road where we were. The only thing I set my clock by was a daily call to my kids every afternoon, and when I could, a call to Ava. Ava and I talked more often than we ever had before, supporting each other, being friends and lovers from afar, even when there were others in our lives—until a new man came into her life. Lately, she'd been seeing some actor that sounded like a real jerk.

One night after months on the road, I found myself in a Chicago theater. We'd packed the house and had a rocking night of music. As the band blasted the final notes of the final song, I waved at the audience.

"You know what time it is?" I said into the mic.

Voices shouted back at me, "Quitting time!"

I smiled, keeping the charm firmly intact. "That's right. It's quitting time. Time for a drink."

The crowd cheered.

"Thanks for coming out tonight. I hope you had a good time."

They clapped and whistled and rose to their feet in a standing ovation, looking for another number.

I couldn't deny them what they wanted so I pointed to the band and the fellas fired up my brand-new hit, "My Kind of Town."

The audience went wild but settled down quickly to listen to the song about their city.

After it was over, I headed backstage, Ava on my mind. I wondered if she'd be allowed to talk to me tonight. She was in real trouble with that boyfriend. She could have had anyone, should be treated like a princess, and she'd chosen some lousy ex-marine turned actor who also liked to beat the crap out of his women. He'd given her a shiner and bruises all over her body. I didn't understand it, the way she let him treat her. If I so much as raised a hand to her, she'd have decked me right back and probably knocked out my front teeth. She'd always been tough, a tomboy and a fighter, but this man didn't seem to have any manners. No one put their hands on a woman, especially not my woman.

When she called the night before sounding broken, I lost it. I knew that jerk would go after her again so I decided to handle things since she couldn't.

In my dressing room, I toweled off my face, threw back a swallow of Jack Daniel's, and put in a call to the Boys.

"Tony. It's Frank. Did you do the thing?"

"Yeah, we took care of it."

"He's going to leave her alone?"

"If he doesn't, at least now he has a pretty good idea of what's going to happen to him."

"Good. Thanks, man," I cradled the phone against my shoulder and lit a cigarette. "I may need you again if he doesn't get the message."

"I'm pretty sure he got the message. Never seen a guy turn green before."

I laughed darkly. "I'll send some cash." I hung up, satisfied the prick had been handled.

After that night, Ava thankfully came to her senses and left

Scott. And our nightly conversations resumed from Europe or South America or somewhere in Kansas. It didn't matter from where or for how long, just that I got to hear her voice. Somehow Ava grounded me and I needed that more than ever.

My star had risen so high, I couldn't be seen from Earth, or at least that was what it seemed like sometimes. I felt, at last, as if I'd truly made an imprint on music and in Hollywood. I was revered the world over, raised millions for charities, gave away as much as I saved. I had everything I'd ever wanted in my life except one thing. If not Ava, a someone who would be there every night, at my side, no matter what. Someone who'd look after me.

When I accepted a role in a World War II film, *Von Ryan's Express*, I thought I'd found her at last.

"Frank," John Leyton waved me over. He was playing Lieutenant Orde in the film. "I have a fan who'd like to meet you."

The fan was a slender young woman with long blond hair and wide blue eyes that made her look like the most innocent, beautiful little pixie you'd ever seen.

I headed over to say hello.

"I'm Frank Sinatra," I said, holding out my hand.

She blushed a pretty shade of pink. "I'm Mia. Mia Farrow, a friend of John's. I was just visiting the set when I realized you were in the film, and well, I love your music, Mr. Sinatra."

"Thank you. I'm playing next week. Would you like some tickets?"

Her eyes widened and her full lips curved into a smile. "I'd love that!"

What I didn't know then was how much I'd learn to love that smile, her admiration, and her attentiveness.

Mia was as different from Ava as a hurricane was to a spring breeze. Mia brought a gentle peace to my brash and raucous lifestyle. She was intelligent and well-read, and had an active imagination—she also agreed to put her career on the side and join me on the road. It wasn't long before I proposed. I took a lot of crap from friends who teased me about our age difference, but I didn't care. Maybe I did still believe in love. Maybe I could have it all, be happy. I'd found that someone, even if secretly, I knew it would be a someone for right now.

When we were hitched, I put in the phone call I'd been dreading, to get ahead of the media. I called home to tell Nancy and the kids. And there was one other call I needed to make, but I couldn't seem to do it myself. Instead, I asked my valet, George, to call Ava.

At long last, I would belong to someone else and my twisting relationship with Ava would come to an end.

Part 5

"FROM HERE TO ETERNITY"

1966–1990

CHAPTER 45

AVA

Francis had finally gone and married someone else. Even after our divorce, I'd always thought we'd never say I do to someone else, because for Francis and me, that was it. Mia Farrow had changed everything. I tortured myself with thoughts of him with that waifish child who was barely a woman—and a hippie to boot—and something inside me cracked open. I felt myself spin off like a top, twisting and wobbling, ready to crash. Why couldn't we make it work? How did that woman bring him something I couldn't?

I consoled myself with the movie roles that had kept rolling in the last few years—*55 Days at Peking*, *On the Beach*, and others—until I was exhausted and couldn't hold things together anymore. Too many late nights, too much booze, and a life untethered but for the make-believe that was my job made me feel as if I was floating through my life. As the media presence grew in Madrid, my behavior worsened. I was fired before preproduction began on the set of *The Pink Panther* for poor behavior, snubbed for the role of Mrs. Robinson in *The*

Graduate for showing up drunk at the interviews. I was tired of Hollywood and of fame, not that I was ever cut out for it in the first place. Really, what was the point? I had everything I'd ever wanted, and I wasn't sure it had brought me closer to the elusive happiness I'd been seeking since I'd first set foot in California more than twenty years ago.

On a particularly bad night when my little Rags passed away, I cried as if I'd lost Francis all over again. I attempted to pick myself up and headed out on the town, to not be alone, to find some comfort in my favorite haunts or do a little dancing. But nothing took the edge off and somewhere in the midst of the martinis and flamenco and forced laughter, I thought of my mama. How sad she would be to see me spiraling and spinning and falling. I saw the disappointment on her face and the concern in her eyes, and I couldn't take it. I paid my bill and wandered into the coal-black night until the early hours, where I didn't have to pretend anymore or be a single thing I wasn't. I was only me.

When I finally found my way home, there was a package waiting for me on the front doorstep. It was small but I recognized the handwriting instantly. I smiled so big my cheeks hurt. Francis had taken to sending me postcards and letters almost weekly, even now, and I found I looked forward to them more than just about anything else that happened the rest of my week.

I tore through the paper, my hands shaking from fatigue, too much booze, and far too many cigarettes. Inside the small box was a key and a note. Tears gathered in my eyes like rain clouds before a storm.

This is for you when you come home. I love you.
Love, Frank

His words hit me like a blow. Now someone else was home for him. I knew then I couldn't live this life anymore. I was tired—tired of traipsing through the darker corners of the world, waking up with someone I didn't know beside me. Tired of the constant scorn from my neighbors for being too loud or too scandalous and, worse, from the media even from afar. I craved a more normal life, one that moved at a slower pace and was filled with long walks and gardens and peace. Spain was through with me, and I was finished with it.

I packed up my home and moved to my other European haven—soggy London in a flat on Park Lane. I brought my precious little Cara with me, a corgi puppy I'd adopted. Reenie, bless her soul, came with me, too, at least for a little while, and when she moved back to the States, she still returned regularly to visit. I was settling down at last, easing into my new life, and I felt my soul begin to lift for the first time in ages.

I'd been in London a month when I got my first phone call from Francis.

We exchanged pleasantries. I congratulated him on his marriage and then the stiff niceties fell away and we were us again—Ava and Frank, friends and soul mates to the end.

"I'm here for you, even if I'm married," he said with that warm baritone that set my heart at ease. "You know I'll love you to the day I die."

"I love you, too, baby," I said, biting back tears. It was so good to hear his voice, to hear his reassurances.

We talked for hours. I told him all about London, what it was like to walk around town without makeup and fancy clothes and have no one recognize me. How refreshing it was to slip into bed early with a bag of Maltesers and a book and be asleep by midnight. To feel like everything was less frenetic and the alcohol less prevalent since I didn't have to worry about stage fright and photographers all the time.

"I'm getting tired, too, Angel," he said. "I'm rarely home. Being on the road this much used to be more fun. I guess that's part of why I got married. Need to slow down. Maybe having a wife will help me make that transition."

I was quiet on the line then, barely controlling my tears. I wished he wasn't making that transition with her, but I'd made my choice long ago, even if I now regretted it. We weren't good together then and now, and well, I had to get on with my life.

It wasn't long after I'd moved to London and got to know the city better that I decided to move to Ennismore Gardens in a second-floor flat of a converted Victorian house. My new flat overlooked a glorious park that was the first thing I saw in the morning when I opened the drapes. I adored its charm and soon filled the rooms with eighteenth- and nineteenth-century antiques, oil paintings, gilded mirrors, and pictures of family and friends. And, of course, pictures of Francis that I'd collected through the years. I settled in nicely and soon made friends with the neighbors, brought them flowers and books when they were sick or kept them company. I'd host an occasional dinner party and invite in anyone who crossed my path, especially the many actors and film industry people nearby.

I was slowing down, more at peace with myself, at last.

One afternoon, Gerald down at the Ennismore Arms, the local pub where I often picked up dinner, gave me a ring.

"The jukebox you ordered for us has arrived," he said.

"Oh, that's fantastic," I said. "Now you can have music! Is it fully stocked?"

"It is. Frank Sinatra records till your heart's content."

I smiled. "I'll be right over."

"There's a bloke here, too. He looks like a reporter. I just wanted to warn you. I know how you like to avoid them."

"Oh, it's alright," I said. "Maybe I'll even give him an interview." I hung up the phone, a smile on my face. Good old Gerald was looking out for me. It was nice to feel that I belonged in a neighborhood where I was liked for a change and not one in which I was notorious.

I spent the afternoon with several of the regular patrons, had a platter of chicken curry and chips, and headed home after to check in with Carmen, a lovely Ecuadorian woman who blessedly had a way with dogs. She hadn't known much about cooking when I hired her on as housekeeper, but I was a great cook so I taught her how to make my favorites: a little Chinese stir-fry, southern fried chicken, a handful of Italian dishes, and roast beef and lamb. She was a willing student, and I adored her sense of humor and her kindness. Just like Reenie, I valued her more as a companion than an employee.

"Carmen?" I called as I closed the front door behind me.

"*Si, señora*. I am in the bedroom."

She was bent over the bed, tucking the clean sheets beneath the mattress before stuffing the down comforter into the duvet cover.

"Do I have any messages?"

"Yes. A man named John Huston from New York. He wants you to call back right away. Something about a movie." She stared at me a moment, waiting for me to explain but I didn't so she added, "Why did he call to tell you about a movie, all the way from New York?"

"Why, Carmen, didn't you know I'm a lousy movie star?"

Carmen's chocolate-brown eyes widened, and she paused in her stuffing and fluffing. "You're a movie star?"

I laughed uproariously then, tickled by the fact that this woman who had worked for me for months didn't have the faintest idea who I was. "Didn't you notice all of the photographs of movie stars and the film sets around the house? And Frank Sinatra, too."

She blushed deeply. "I didn't think they were real."

"You didn't think they were real?" I laughed a second time until tears gathered in the corners of my eyes. "Well, that would make me a little crazy, wouldn't it? I guess I'm glad it's not obvious. I still do a movie now and again, and some television. John must have something in mind specifically for me."

"I'm sorry, miss, I didn't know."

I waved my hand, dismissing her embarrassment. "Not at all. You made my night. I'm glad I'm just a regular old girl."

Cara wandered in from her dog pillow in the living room then, and barked her approval, making us both laugh.

I found out the next day that sure enough, John Huston wanted me for a film called *The Life and Times of Judge Roy Bean*. Though it was a Western and I wasn't the lead, it had a star-studded cast, including Paul Newman and Anthony Perkins. It didn't take much convincing for me to agree to sign on. John was one of my favorite directors from over the years, so I packed a bag and headed to the States, stopping briefly in New York City. I wanted to see Francis, in truth, and hoped I'd run into him. I had a standing invitation at his apartment at the Waldorf Towers.

He wasn't in town, but as it turned out, his daughter Tina was.

"Oh, hello, Ava," Tina said, opening the door wide to invite me in. She tossed her long dark hair over her shoulder. "Dad said you might come by for a couple of days."

Francis hadn't told me Tina would be at the apartment, but there was plenty of room. She was quite pretty, in her early twenties, her alert brown eyes full of intelligence.

"How nice to see you. You're a grown woman! The last time I saw you, you were a child."

"I guess that's true," she said with a polite smile. "Do you want to put away your things?"

"Yes, and then I'm going to help myself to your dad's bar."

"I'll pour," Tina said, eliciting a smile from me.

We had a drink and got to talking, the two of us, and I learned all about her time in Germany, where she'd starred in a television miniseries for several years. The next thing I knew, we found ourselves on the streets of New York heading to dinner together. We got along famously; she seemed to take to my humor and I to her earnest but charming nature. I saw her dad in her that way.

"You know, your dad and me, we may fight like cats and dogs, but we love each other still, after all this time."

"That's kind of like me and Dad, too."

I covered her hand with mine. "He's a complicated man. I'm sure you have a lot of feelings about that."

She nodded. "Doesn't everyone?"

We talked right through dinner ànd as the waiter came around to check on us, he turned to me.

"Ma'am, would you or your daughter like another round?"

We looked at each other then, the irony of the comment not lost on us, and burst into laughter. Tina was a lovely person, and in that moment, I lamented that I'd never had children with Francis. Right then, I wished that Tina—and Francis—were mine.

Instead, he was with Mia, and I hoped that he was happy, in spite of it all.

CHAPTER 46

FRANK

I was hoping I'd finally found a woman that I'd settle down with, but my marriage to Mia lasted two years.

After five decades of loving women, I was no closer to understanding them. Neither was I closer to understanding how to find happiness that lasted. Mia was too young for me, just as everyone had said. We didn't have any tastes in common, didn't like the same kind of people or have the same habits. Her career was just beginning while I was looking at a nice, long break, perhaps for good.

The Summit was done—we were all tired, our jokes were tired, and our audiences had changed. What would forever be known as the Rat Pack broke its pact and we went our separate ways. My stress, however, was higher than ever. The feds had opened an investigation on me; they were after the Boys and wanted to know more about my links to Willie Moretti and Sam Giancana. They also wanted to look into my shares in the hotels in Las Vegas and Lake Tahoe where I'd performed for years. The Boys promised me we would be alright, that we were squeaky clean and untraceable, but I grew anxious as my FBI file expanded.

I was beat down, my throat needed a rest, and I craved a break from the spotlight. My well was bone dry. I needed time to recover from decades on the road and to pursue my other interests. Painting, reading, enjoying the quiet. It didn't take much of a push to make the decision—to my family's surprise— but one afternoon, I pulled the plug on the whole operation. I wrote up a statement as my daughter Tina looked on in shock. It was time to retire.

Although no one in my family could see me retiring, there was one person who could.

"You've been running yourself into the ground, baby," Ava said one night on the telephone. Our calls had become more frequent again since I'd ended things with Mia. I hadn't realized how much I'd missed Ava until I began looking forward to that nightly call again.

"You can say that again," I said. "It's over. I'm throwing in the towel. I've come to the point where I've done everything I want to do. Gone as far as I can, and it doesn't excite me anymore."

"Will you know what to do with yourself?"

"I'll find things to do. You know me."

"I do, and you have an active mind. I'm sure you'll find something," she said. "I'm working far less these days, and I'm so much happier not working all the time and running from the cameras."

When the night of my final performance arrived, I hired a limo for the big day. We drove along the winding road, through the hills covered with scrub, past movie stars' mansions and palm trees and flowering bougainvillea. We rode past the Holly-wood sign set atop the rocky hill that overlooked the teeming city below, and beyond to a wide blue strip of the Pacific Ocean. I watched it all pass in quiet contemplation. I couldn't believe this was it, my final show. It was surreal. I'd been a performer since I was a kid and couldn't fathom never rehearsing again, never warming up, never playing another winning run in Vegas or Tahoe or Atlantic City. There'd be no more lost hours on the road in buses or on planes, or talking with strangers. Though I couldn't imagine it, the idea of it sounded like exactly what I needed. Maybe now I could enjoy a different kind of living.

I arrived at the theater, shook hands with a few dozen peo-ple, and prepared to sing, one last time.

Grace Kelly stood in the wings, a smile on her face. Though she reminded me a bit of the woman I'd begun dating the last few months, Barbara Marx, I was struck by how Grace had aged. She was beautiful still, but her face and figure had rounded, the skin around her eyes and mouth showing her years. It wasn't that she looked older that jarred me, but the simple fact that her aging reflected my own. We'd all changed over the years, and once again, I was struck by what I was doing here tonight.

I was retiring, saying bon voyage and good night.

When it was time to go on, I held my head high, and greeted a reverent and somber crowd. It was a beautiful night and I had only one regret.

My Ava was still on the other side of the world.

CHAPTER 47

AVA

I couldn't be at Francis's retirement because I was on set, and given the limited number of roles these days, I couldn't turn it away. I had to keep the coffers full somehow.

Still, I regretted not being there for his big night—he'd wanted me there and I'd tried to arrange it with the director only to receive pushback. The truth was, though Francis was fifty-six years old, I couldn't imagine him retiring and I wasn't sure I wanted to see him give up the thing he loved most. It seemed tragic for him to lay to rest the talent that set him apart—no one could compare to my baby. He was a performer: for the love of music, for the love of his fans, for the release of all his big emotions. And they were big—bigger than those of anyone I'd ever known. It was what I loved most about him. To see him say a final good night made me uneasy.

I had my own big emotions. After I wrapped the film, I returned to London and moved through the rooms in my apartment like an apparition, wondering what came next. I knew Francis had been dating a woman named Barbara Marx and they were getting serious, but it didn't keep him from calling me, sending flowers and letters, or singing to me over the phone.

"Little girl, I miss him," I said, bending to scrub Cara behind the ears. She nipped at the back of my hand and then licked it just as quickly. An apology for her tendency to bite on impulse. "That's better."

She barked and wiggled her hind end.

I missed him so much, I found myself wishing we'd never divorced. So what if we fought? Didn't any couple in love have their spats? Besides, we were younger then, less seasoned, more ambitious. Now we were wrapping up those days of our lives, ready to settle in for the long haul and find meaning in other things. What could possibly have more meaning than being with my friend and lover of decades? The love of my life, as it turned out.

In the predawn hours, after a restless night, I called him.

"I need to see you, Francis. Can you meet me in New York?"

"It's always too long between visits, Angel," he said, exuberant at my admission.

"I want to wake up to you every day."

Our conversation was the only impetus I needed. Something was brewing inside of me—inside of both of us—I could feel it. We were heading in a new direction together. Something familiar yet different, something better.

The following day I arrived at JFK on an afternoon plane, all smiles though my heart fluttered with nerves. Francis picked me up in his Cadillac and we headed into the city to his apartment. Rather than our usual feverish ways with each other, we took our time putting my things away, refreshing ourselves, and dressing to go out. We enjoyed an intimate dinner in a new restaurant in Midtown, complete with candles and jazz and a back booth out of the way of the hubbub.

"I don't think I've ever been so happy to see you, baby," I said, raising my glass and clinking it against his. "To us."

"To us." He took a sip but kept his eyes on mine. He'd aged, the lines around his eyes deepened, the creases at his lips had become grooves. He was nearly bald, too, underneath his expensive toupees but not a single thing made him less attractive. His vivid eyes held more sadness and light than ever, and I felt like I was home again.

We talked long into the night, following dinner with drinks and a walk through the city streets. Back at the apartment, we snuggled on the sofa together. When I yawned, he reached for my water glass and set it on the coffee table, then took my hand in his. Wordlessly, he led me to the bedroom. We paused beside the bed. He cradled my face in his hands, kissed my eyelids, and found my lips. He rubbed my shoulders, loosening the last of the knots until I felt as liquid as warm brandy.

"That's nice," I said, groaning.

"You know what's nice?" he said, kissing my ear, trailing his lips down my neck. "The smell of your skin." His pupils were dilated with desire.

It had been too long and suddenly I wanted him more than ever, if differently. Gone was the eager burn of young love and new love and wild, insatiable love. In its place was a confident, knowing tenderness—a fulfilment we found nowhere else outside of the sphere we created together.

"Make love to me, Francis," I said. "Like you mean it."

His smile lit his face and he nodded. "With you, I always mean it, Angel."

"I hope that never changes," I said, covering his mouth with mine, wrapping my arms around his neck.

Slowly he unzipped my dress, pushing it over my shoulders until the cotton garment slid down my body to the floor. "God, you're as beautiful as ever." He buried his face in my hair.

I unbuttoned his shirt and then moved to the top button of his trousers. He was ready for me and I for him. I led him to the bed and lay back on the coverlet. His hands were tender as he caressed me, his lips upon my skin. Even after all this time, we still desired each other like it was the first time. I thought briefly of that first time. The meal we'd had, the knowing drive back to my place as the electricity crackled between us, and the all-consuming heat crowned with the sensation of falling. Falling in love forever.

"We belong together, don't we?" I whispered in his ear.

His eyes captured mine. "Marry me. Again," he said gruffly.

I smiled and wrapped myself around him. "I just might this time, baby. I just might."

CHAPTER 48

AVA

Reenie couldn't believe the news. I still could scarcely believe it myself.

"You're sure?" she asked as we wound through the streets in the West End of London, popping in and out of boutiques and department stores. "You're going to marry Mr. Sinatra?"

"Yes, I think so," I said.

We were shopping for my trousseau. I'd already bought several pieces of lingerie, two skirts, and a pair of comfortable trousers for lounging. I was still on the hunt for just the right outfit for the wedding ceremony itself. I wanted something feminine and white but not overly fancy.

"What do you mean you think so?" she said, searching through a rack of women's suit skirts. "You'd better be sure or you'll both be heartbroken all over again."

"And smeared in the media. Yes, I know." I sighed. I was completely certain I loved that man more than just about anything, but doubts had cropped up as I considered how much I enjoyed my time alone and my independence. What would

Francis and I do together? Would we be happy? He'd mentioned coming out of retirement again already, something I'd suspected would happen. I wondered if he would expect me to always come with him on tour. I also wondered if he'd really be happy selling the place in Palm Springs, far from his kids and the rest of his family, while we lived in New York.

As Reenie and I checked out at Selfridges, the smell of fish and chips wafted down the street and we followed our noses to the stand. We bought two orders of salty chips and perfectly crisped fish and found a park bench nearby.

"What do I have to lose this time?" I asked, after a deliciously greasy bite. I wiped my mouth and reached into the newspaper cone that had slowly begun to wilt as it absorbed more oil.

She smoothed her hand across the scarf she'd tied over her hair. "Well, for starters, your home here in London. You'll have to move your things, give up your apartment. I know you're lonely, Miss G, but you're also about the most fiercely independent person I've ever met."

I paused midbite. That was definitely true—I didn't like to be told what to do or to be hampered by someone else, but I also didn't like living alone anymore.

"And then there's the issue of Mr. S. Is he ready to be with one woman?"

"Am I ready to be with one man?" I countered.

We both laughed, but the certainty I'd felt the last couple of weeks teetered on the edge of a precipice as doubt did its thing, creeping into my head and planting seeds.

Suddenly no longer hungry, I dumped the remainder of my lunch in a nearby trash can.

☆ ☆ ☆

The ringing phone pierced the quiet of late evening. I rolled over in bed, turned on the bedside lamp, and glanced at the clock. It had to be Francis, at three o'clock in the morning. And yet, I hesitated as I picked up the phone.

"Hi, baby."

"Were you dreaming of me?"

"I wasn't dreaming of anything. Passed out cold after a full day of shopping and drinks with Reenie."

"You never were much of a romantic, were you?"

"You know me. I prefer a dash of realism with my romance."

"Did you find a nice dress? I want my wife looking her best."

"I did. I . . ." My words trailed off.

His wife. I'd be his wife again, and as much as I liked the sound of that, I also feared it.

He could sense something was off. I heard it in the way he cleared his throat, shifted the phone to his other ear. "We should start the official plans. I have a break in my schedule next week. I guess we should do it in Vegas. Less fuss."

I thought of Las Vegas, all red rock and dust and a sun so hot your skin felt like it was frying in the middle of the day. The noise, the crowds, the chaotic energy of too much pleasure in one place. Something I'd long since left behind.

"I thought we were going to get hitched at City Hall in New York?" I said. "We can pay a visit to your mama. I'd love to give ol' Dolly a squeeze. I've missed her."

"I can't get there in time. I have one day off and then I have to be back in Los Angeles for a shoot."

Los Angeles, land of dreams and broken people and more ghosts than I cared to confront. I never liked the city and could tolerate it even less so now. At this point, I'd almost call it a phobia.

"Francis, where will we live? In Palm Springs? I thought we'd decided on New York."

"Mostly in New York, sure, but I need to keep the Palm Springs house for now because it's closer to my management team. You can do whatever you want to the house, baby. Money isn't important. I have plenty of that now. So how about it?"

"In New York?" I said hopefully.

"In Palm Springs."

I was still for what felt like a long time, thinking, processing, working through a tide of emotions. Of dashed hopes and dreams—of grief—and finally, of acceptance. If we were really meant to be, wouldn't we have come together a long time ago? What about the hundreds of other times over the years when we met up in various cities, in various countries, had a few hot nights and then went after each other's throats again?

"Angel?"

I sighed heavily. "Baby, you should marry Barbara, not me. She'll suit you better in the end. We may love each other, but I'm not made to be a wife. I tried it three times and failed miserably. And we've tried a thousand times already, haven't we? But Barbara will look the other way when you argue or when you're gone for weeks and leave her in that city that I detest. I can't do it. If we were together, I'd want all of you the way you want all of me, and I just don't know if either of us is capable of such a thing."

This time he didn't cuss and plead. He wasn't volatile and angry.

We really were star-crossed lovers, wretched for each other

and completely incapable of being together. Tears slipped down my face as the truth I had known long ago settled into my bones. It was finally over, really over, after all these years. We were destined to live apart, and I wasn't even a wistful romantic type, but my Francis had always done that to me.

"I have to go," Francis said, his voice thick with emotion.

"I know, baby," I whispered. "I do, too."

"I love you."

"I love you, too. For always."

CHAPTER 49

FRANK

For the thousandth time, I was disappointed by the woman I loved but now, I was resigned to it. Ava and I were a perfect, terrible fit and I knew she was right. Still, in the end, I didn't want to be alone. I wanted a companion, a woman who kept me in line and looked after me. If it wasn't going to be the woman who had my heart, it would be the woman who was there, and I did love Barbara, too, in my way. We had a large wedding with plenty of star power and friends and, of course, the kids, though they didn't like Barbara much.

I gave Barbara free rein of the house and soon she had remodeled the joint, renamed all the rooms and buildings. She thought I didn't notice, but one day the portrait of Ava on the mantel was replaced, the marble statue of her in the garden was gone, and the photographs of her or the two of us together that had been scattered throughout the house were boxed up and put away. I didn't blame Barb. She was the woman of the house now and she didn't want to be reminded of the woman I'd lost my mind for, the woman who would never leave me completely.

Barbara didn't only take charge of the house. She had things to say about the company I kept, my old friends whom I'd always gotten into trouble with and eventually the Boys didn't come around anymore, nor did the friends I'd spent years with painting the town. We settled into a routine when I was home—and mostly I wasn't. Despite my attempt to retire, for the next ten years I was back on the road, being me. I'd thought I was done with show business, but show business wasn't done with me. It was the only way I could see myself, the only way I knew who I was. Without it, I was lost. So I kept on singing and holding the world on a string, until I heard the news that would change me for good.

CHAPTER 50

AVA

My life grew quiet and nostalgic and though I still did an occasional film or took a part on a TV show, I spent most of my time at home or traveling through Europe, living the kind of life I'd always wanted. One winter, though, I caught a nasty cold and spent most of the following spring in bed, coughing without reprieve. When the pounds began to melt off at an alarming rate, I had Carmen call Bappie.

"Please come home, Ava," my sister begged me. Her voice had the sort of crags that came with age, and I wondered for a moment how much time we had left together.

"This is home, Bappie. I hate LA, you know that. Always have."

"You need a hospital and to be with people who love you."

She called every day, urging me to come home—and I knew she was right. I was sick and needed the best care, and I needed my family. Finally after months of being sick, I left my corgi in Carmen's care and flew to Los Angeles. I booked appointments at St. John's hospital for a lung cancer screen, among others. As it turned out, I had pneumonia. I was told to give up smoking and drinking and to move to a warmer, dry climate.

I didn't.

I returned home when I'd regained enough of my strength to make the trip. My symptoms came and went and as my labored breathing returned, I was restricted to my beloved flat. I watched old movies, the classics featuring my former friends and foes, and the whole lot. When I watched my old films, I could hardly believe the young woman I saw there on the screen. I was so beautiful, it nearly hurt to see it—I'd changed irrevocably in so many ways. I'd never be that spitfire of a woman again, so vibrant and so full of promise. I feared the final scene of my life was upon me.

One day I received a letter from Francis. I tore it open hastily. The note contained his usual mixture of poetry and humor and he'd slipped in a photograph of us. It was creased and faded, as if a thumb had caressed it for so many years. It was the picture of our wedding that he'd kept in his wallet for thirty-five years, but now he wanted me to have it—to remember us and everything we'd meant to each other over the years.

I mourned silently then, a tired surrendered cry.

It was hard to live with Francis, but it seemed harder to live without him. And this gesture felt like he'd finally, finally given up on us. For good.

"Are you alright, Miss Gardner?" my nurse said in her East London Cockney.

"Can you bring me the letter box in my wardrobe?"

The nurse returned and lay the box gently on the bed. I opened the lid and sorted through its contents of notes, postcards, and love letters. They were from Francis through the years, and I'd kept them all. I opened each one, reading every line carefully, as if I hadn't already read them a hundred times. I laughed and cried and even cussed like the old days. For a few hours, they were a beautiful walk down memory lane. They made me feel alive again, and not a shell of the woman I'd become.

★ ★ ★

When the day came to say goodbye I could feel it instinctively, the same way I'd known how to act a part. I just knew. That day everything felt like too much: too much effort, too much pain. I was tired, and the world and the man I loved felt as distant from me as the North Star.

I rang for my housekeeper.

"Carmen, I have something I need you to do," I said, rasping through my lungs as they acted up worse than usual.

"What is it, Miss Gardner?" she said. She was bent over my corgi, taking off the dog's collar and giving my sweet pooch a good rubbing.

"Get a fire going," I said, "and bring me the package on my nightstand. I want you to burn it."

Carmen's eyes went wide. "But you love that box of letters, miss."

"It's time," I said firmly, and then dissolved into a coughing fit.

"No, Miss Gardner. It can't be time yet." The woman dabbed at her eyes.

I reached for her hand and as I cradled it in mine, I studied the contrast in her brown skin and my pale skin, nearly translucent now with a web of purple veins beneath it.

"Please, say you'll do it."

"Whatever you say, Miss Gardner." She was crying now in earnest.

I'd been good to her, but she'd been good to me, too, and right now, she was one of the few people I had left in the world. My head began to pound, my breath caught in my throat, and I made a horrible wheezing sound. Carmen looked alarmed and patted my back, helped me sit up enough to sip some water.

After I'd wiped my mouth and managed to get comfortable again against the pillow, I asked her for one final request. "Can you look after my corgi when I'm gone?"

My dog looked up and barked.

"Of course, Miss Gardner," Carmen said. "Now, why don't I let you rest a while? When you wake up, we'll try some broth and tea."

I nodded. "Sounds fine."

Carmen rose to her feet but before she got to the door, I called out, "Can you turn on the TV? I'm so tired, and I just want to watch a movie."

"Which movie, miss?"

"From Here to Eternity."

She smiled knowingly. It was a favorite of mine, she knew, and I'd watched it many times the last couple of years.

Today, I needed to see him, the Francis I knew who loved me more than anything. The young man who'd strived so hard to make something of himself, the one who would become more than a star but an icon. A legend. And the one man I would never get over, not in this lifetime or the next.

The TV flickered to life and the VHS tape whirred, and soon, the black-and-white picture filled the screen. He really was so gifted, more so than even he could contain. It had nearly destroyed him at times. But he'd made his way and he'd still enchanted people. Maybe he would forever.

When at last Francis's character, Maggio, lay dying in his friend Prewitt's arms, a faint smile curled my lips. He'd made the role transcendent. He really had, without my help or anyone else's.

Now it was my turn to transcend a role, one that had been as raucous and meaningful as it had been disappointing and, at times, utterly heartbreaking. Wasn't that the way of things? To play and to suffer and to find a way to hold your truth in your hands, and to live it the best way you could? Francis would say it was, and so would I. I wished I could hear him say so, one last time.

I blew a kiss at the screen and closed my eyes. "I love you, Francis."

It was the last time I'd ever see his face.

CHAPTER 51

FRANK

I received the news one afternoon as I lounged at the house in Palm Springs.

My daughter Tina was there, and we were enjoying a little time together when the telephone rang. I dropped the phone and slumped against the wall to the floor.

She was gone. The love of my life was gone.

"Dad?" Tina said, crouching beside me. "What is it?" She laid a hand on my forehead. "You're flushed."

"Why wasn't I there with her?" My voice cracked with anguish. "I should have gone to see her one last time in London. Why didn't I go? I never got to tell her I love her. I didn't tell her she was the one."

Understanding dawned on my youngest daughter's face. Her eyes reflected the pity she felt. "It's Ava, isn't it? What's happened to her?"

"She's gone. She died in her sleep." I choked on a strangled sob and staggered to my bedroom. "I need to be alone."

Thankfully my daughter listened to me, for once, and as I closed the door, I collapsed. I lay there alone all night and the entirety of the next day, thinking of Ava, remembering. Her talent, her beauty. That earthy charm and humor that always took a person by surprise. The gleam in her eye when she'd wake up beside me.

Had she done everything she set out to do? Did she have regrets as she inhaled her last breaths? She was so much more than she ever believed about herself. I thought of our last conversations, wishing I'd not been a coward when she'd said she was sick. I wished I'd gone to her. She'd always believed in me, allowed me to be who I was, even if that meant a life apart. Still, she went on loving me, and I would go on loving her, until it was all over and the curtains closed.

I thought back over the great accomplishments of my own life and wondered if they held any real meaning in the end. What was I leaving behind when it was my turn? One day not too far in the future, it would be. Would I leave something lasting? That was a question no man could answer.

When Tina looked in on me, I could barely raise my voice above a whisper.

"Can I bring you anything?" she asked.

"No, kid. Thanks," I said.

I had a wreath of flowers sent to Ava's funeral with a note that read, "With my love, Francis." But I couldn't—and didn't—go. I was a failure at goodbyes, especially with the ones I loved most. I was a failure at loving them enough in the way they needed, at showing them what they meant to me.

A day later, Tina knocked at the bedroom door. My dear daughter always stayed with me when it was hardest. I was rich in that way, richer than I deserved.

"Dad," Tina said, interrupting my thoughts. "You have a

phone call. It's your agent. He wants to know if you'll still do the concert. He said he can get Liza Minnelli to step in for you if you need him to."

"No," I croaked. "I'll do it."

Barbara pushed her way into the room and crossed her arms. She was furious with me again, but stood there in her passive-aggressive way, not saying the things she wanted to say. I guessed that she was glad her competition was finally gone. But the truth was, Ava would never be gone for me, not ever, and as much as I loved Barbara, she couldn't compete.

"You don't have to do the show, Dad," Tina said. "They would understand."

"I think you should do it," Barbara interjected. "Think how it will look—"

"I'm doing the show," I said. "Now everyone leave me the hell alone. I need to pack and catch a plane."

I arrived—exhausted, destroyed, unsure of what I was doing there—at the Knickerbocker Arena in Albany, New York, to a crowd of eighteen thousand. I didn't feel like myself and I certainly didn't feel like going on, but it was what I'd always done. I showed up. I made the audience happy. They looked for my music to soothe them, to heal them, to help them through the hard times. Maybe the truth was that I needed the music, too. I couldn't imagine a life without Ava in it, so I had to take that stage and wrap my pain in a song to somehow understand it, to make it more bearable.

As the night's host gave his introduction, the crowd roared.

With a deep breath, I pasted on a smile like I was a good show dog and gripped my microphone. It was time to be a professional and put the rest aside.

The curtains parted.

As the orchestra began to play and the melodious notes filled the auditorium, I looked out at a sea of faces and began to sing. One song after another, the bittersweet notes were more poignant than they'd ever been. I poured my soul into the microphone and launched my heart into the crowd. When at last the show wound down and the band began "One for My Baby," I gripped the bottle of Jack Daniel's that I always used as a prop. Tonight, it would be my lifeline.

I sang the song like I had a thousand times before, but tonight, the audience felt like something more than mere admirers. They were witnesses to my pain, a source of comfort. Emotion rushed over me until I was nearly blinded by it. I swigged from the bottle once, twice, three times and more, doing the faux stumble of a drunken man across the stage from the routine I'd perfected with my Rat Pack years before.

If I just kept moving from one note to the next, the song would soon be over. And I would no longer see her at the edge of my vision or feel her skin beneath my hands. I would no longer hear the sweetness of her sighs in my ear. My angel. I wouldn't feel the gaping hole she'd left in my chest, and I could go home.

But, as the spotlight beamed on me like a beacon from heaven, and the crowd was riveted by the spell I'd cast over them, my voice cracked. I stopped the song. I looked down at my bottle, over at my piano man, and again out at the crowd. I could see her there, in the front row with laughing eyes. She was smiling, blowing me a kiss, the diamonds at her ears sparkling in the light. She was bright and beautiful and wild as ever. She was telling me to go on, to finish the song.

I began again as I so often did, all those years. I sang the final notes, my voice reverberating with pain, and when it ended, I bowed my head.

For a beat, the crowd remained silent, stunned, and I was reminded of the power of the music. The power of our love. It had been a mess but it was also an enchantment for all those decades, and now it enchanted the audience.

Then the spell broke.

The crowd thundered with delirious applause and jumped to their feet, roaring, their voices rising to the rafters, and I imagined mine rising too, through the roof into the searing cold of a January night, the sky speckled with stars, and beyond to that infinite place. For a moment, I smiled, knowing she would feel my love again somehow, and that she'd feel it for always.

AUTHOR'S NOTE

When I was first approached about writing this novel, I must admit, I was uncertain. As a historical novelist, I'd never written a biographical novel about figures who have not only lived and died during my lifetime but whose lives were documented in very close detail. This meant an avalanche of source material and a vast array of photos, video clips, and films—a feast for a researcher—was at my disposal! It also meant relatives of these two incredibly gifted people were still living. Could I do Frank and Ava justice? I didn't know, but one thing I did know was that my childhood was touched by Frank Sinatra. After mass on Sundays, we'd head to my grandparents' house for a family meal and as we all filed in, my grandfather would pour himself a splash of something on the rocks and crank up a little Frank on the record player, waiting impatiently for my grandmother's homemade manicotti to emerge from the oven. I can still see in my mind's eye the image of my grandparents cutting a rug, all smiles, to the music when the feeling struck.

Frank's wonderful voice followed me into adulthood, too. When I was feeling blue or nostalgic, I'd switch on a big band station or fire up my CDs of Ol' Blue Eyes. Even today, I hear his melodious baritone floating down the aisles of any grocery store or creating just the right mood at dinner parties. Frank's immense legacy lingers still, almost as if he were not yet gone. So few in history have ever achieved this sort of coveted status. I think he would be proud to see how much his music is still cherished, and what he, as a prominent figure, represents: style, dark glamour, and the kind of star power that feels otherworldly sometimes. Most of the rest, and his very real flaws, have faded from view. As for Ava Gardner, I knew far less about her, only that she was a Hollywood star and about the most beautiful and bewitching woman I'd ever seen, and that was just in photographs. I could only imagine how her intelligence, and her charm and beauty, translated to real life. I couldn't wait to learn more.

It's important to emphasize that though this novel was meticulously researched, it presents only a snapshot of Frank's and Ava's lives, of them as a couple and how their fates—and their hearts—became entwined. For every scene that appears in the story, I cut two—it was difficult to let go of Frank's relationship with Presidents Kennedy and Reagan, his many friends and enemies, his son's kidnapping, the way the FBI was breathing down his neck about his ties to the Mob, and so much more. It was similarly difficult to let go of the many anecdotes about Ava, too—from being chased in Brazil on foot by an enormous crowd of crazed fans; to her interactions with Fidel Castro; and her once-upon-a-time neighbor in Spain, Juan Perón, the former dictator of Argentina with whom she argued about their dogs. I found myself wanting to include them all, and to portray every recording, every movie set, every exchange with famous names we all recognize. There is so much more to learn about both Ava and Frank as people, and about their careers, and I encourage interested readers to dig in to the many wonderful resources available.

OTHER NOTES

My favorite resources, other than the films and records them-
selves and the multitude of photographs, were Tina Sinatra's
gorgeous memoir, *My Father's Daughter* (cowritten with Jeff
Coplon), which brought a lump to my throat and a tear to
my eye more than once; Lee Server's *Ava Gardner: "Love Is
Nothing"*; James Kaplan's duology *Frank: The Voice* and
Sinatra: The Chairman; and *Sinatra: The Life* by Anthony
Summers and Robbyn Swan.

At times, the sources conflicted with each other in their details, including exactly what happened between Frank and
Ava, from their fights to their quieter moments, and even
whether Frank was involved with the Mafia. Therefore, I
weaved an emotional tale through and around these details, doing my best to preserve what has been documented but at times
making tough choices. Each resource provided its own view of
the fascinating story of Frank and Ava, and what secrets their
hearts might have held. Above all, I wanted to show how these
two individuals were paradoxical, as we all are. They were
gifted and intelligent, and volatile and passionate, sometimes
even abhorrent in their behaviors but always complex. I wish
I'd had the good fortune of knowing them in real life.

It was unclear where the initial meeting happened between
Frank and Ava; one account said they were introduced by
pianist Skitch Henderson at the Hollywood Palladium. Another said it happened one night at the Mocambo with Mickey

Rooney, and still another source said it took place at the MGM studio commissary, a cafeteria of sorts. I chose the most compelling of the three: the night Ava was with her new husband, America's number one star, Mickey Rooney.

I came across many stories stating that the Mafia pressured Harry Cohn to give Frank his breakout role in *From Here to Eternity*, while other accounts disputed it entirely. I chose to leave out this detail since there's no concrete evidence of it. Also, it's pretty darn clear the Mafia had nothing to do with his phenomenal performance and subsequent Oscar win.

When Frank is still down on his luck and he's not speaking to his mother, Dolly, I mention that he's borrowed money from her and that's what their falling out has been about, but there's no record of it. Given his financial circumstances at the time, it seemed a logical extension, so I filled in the blanks.

During the filming of *Mogambo* in Africa, rhinos did, in fact, charge and push the jeep—and one was shot—but I put Ava on the camera truck with Frank "Bunny" Allen to establish the flirtation and the short-lived relationship blossoming between them, as well as a turning point in her relationship with Frank.

Once in a great while someone comes along in this life who impacts history in a way that transcends place and time. They're not only remembered by those who knew them and the establishments they influenced, but they rise above even the stars of the day to become a legend. Frank Sinatra is one of these very few. To write even a portion of his story has been an incredible challenge and a privilege. To write the story of one of the great loves of his life, the talented Ava Gardner, has been a thrill. I hope you, too, enjoyed the ride. I'm pretty sure they did.

ACKNOWLEDGMENTS

'm always amazed when I've finished a novel and it's going to print. Writing a book is such a labor of love and a roller coaster of excitement, sweat equity, and perseverance. This novel faced more challenges than most, however, as the pandemic raged, a serious family emergency cropped up that I struggled to manage, and my life—and my deadlines—were thrown into a blender. I couldn't have finished without the unwavering support of my superstar agent, Michelle Brower, and my dear editor, Lucia Macro, as well as the great support and patience of Alli Dyer. I thank you, ladies. Having a team behind me means the world.

I'd like to send a special thank-you to my early readers and beloved friends, Kris Waldherr and Amy E. Reichert, who came to the manuscript with open minds and red pens, and also to Colleen Clark, jazz drummer and professor, and Tom Kessler, jazz musician and band teacher, for their friendship and their insights into Frank's music. As always, I'm indebted to my fellow authors, who listen, encourage, support, and are generally badass humans. You know who you are. I must also thank my favorite local hangouts that welcome me when I show up with my laptop or my research, fleeing a busy house for a little alone time. They always clear away a space for me and deliver great eats and drinks to keep the creative fires burning. Thanks to the happy gang at my local Starbucks and to Fenton River Grill, especially Steve Smith, for the support over the years.

Lastly, I would be remiss in not mentioning my readers and bloggers, and family and friends, who read and spread the word about my books. Thank you so very much. I cherish you more than you'll ever know.

About the author

About the book

Insights,
Interviews
& More . . .

Meet Heather Webb

Deasy Photographic

HEATHER WEBB is the *USA Today* bestselling and award-winning author of *Rodin's Lover*, *Becoming Josephine*, and *The Next Ship Home*, as well as *Last Christmas in Paris* and *Meet Me in Monaco* (both cowritten with Hazel Gaynor), which were award finalists and winners. Heather's works have been translated to seventeen languages. She lives in New England with her family, a mischievous kitten, and one feisty rabbit. ∾

Fun Facts and Quotable Quotes

Ava Gardner acted in sixty-seven films. She was nominated for an Oscar for her role in *Mogambo* and also for a Golden Globe for *Night of the Iguana*.

Quotes About Ava

Lena Horne, singer, actress, and civil rights activist, said about her dear friend, "[Ava] didn't feel she was born to rule. . . . She felt life was crappy and that a lot of people got mistreated for weird reasons and she liked to see people like each other."

Herb Jeffries, actor and one-time singer in the Duke Ellington Orchestra, said, "[Ava] was always very warm, very friendly, like somebody that wasn't even in the business. No big ego on her at all."

"She was sexually uninhibited, wild, all kinds of goodies, and quick," Jo Carroll Silvers, the wife of comedian Phil Silvers, said about Ava. "She was gone and off with somebody else before you knew where you were."

Skitch Henderson, Sinatra collaborator and band leader said, "Her acid tongue . . . If I ever knew a tiger, or a panther . . . I'm trying to think of an animal that would describe her. . . . To be honest—I didn't let anyone on to this—but I did what I could to stay ▶

out of [Ava's] way. I was scared to death of her."

"Ava gave the impression of being insecure, Frank of being supremely confident," David Hanna, Ava's manager said. "Actually, each had something of both qualities in their characters."

Frank Sinatra acted in sixty-two films, produced seven, and directed one, and he also acted in ten short films. He was nominated for Oscars in *From Here to Eternity, Man with the Golden Arm,* and *The House I Live In,* winning for all but the *Man with the Golden Arm.* He was also nominated for five Golden Globes, winning four, and won well over a dozen other awards for his acting or work in film.

Frank's music hits were nominated thirty times for Grammy Awards, and he won ten times. He also won *Down Beat*'s readers' poll for Male Singer of the Year sixteen times between 1941 and 1966 and the critics' poll for the same category twice, in 1955 and 1957.

Quotes About Frank

Gene DiNovi, an Italian American pianist who worked with Sinatra said, "Italians tend to break down into two kinds of people: Lucky Luciano or

Michelangelo. Frank's an exception. He's both."

When Frank's star began to rise early in his career and he wanted to be released from his contract from Tommy Dorsey's band, it's said he sent in a little help from the Boys. Dorsey confirmed this story with friend and casino entertainment director Ed Becker. "Tommy told me it was true," Becker said. "He said, 'Three guys from New York City by way of Boston and New Jersey approached me and said they would like to buy Frank's contract. I said, "Like hell you will." . . . And they pulled a gun and said, "You wanna sign the contract?" And I did.'"

"He wasn't a gabber," said Peggy Connelly, Frank's girlfriend after the colossal heartache and initial split with Ava. "He wasn't cold, but reserved, self-contained. He stored things up. He wasn't shy, but he was extremely inhibited. . . . I never saw him careless or vague, dreamy. And he never exposed his feelings, not ever."

Orson Welles saw Frank's reaction to prejudice, and knew he walked the walk. "Sinatra went into a diner for a cup of coffee with some friends of his who were musicians, one of whom happened to be [Black]. The man behind the counter insultingly refused to serve this [Black man], and Sinatra ▶

knocked him over on his back with a single blow."

Upon Mia Farrow's first meeting with Frank, she thought, "What a beautiful face he had, full of pain. . . . They don't really know him. They can't see the wounding tenderness that even he can't bear to acknowledge."

Skitch Henderson, Frank's frequent collaborator and bandleader, said about Frank, "He was absolutely obsessed with Ava. Absolutely crazy in love. It is a kind of legendary romance now, but I have to say the reality was even stronger. I don't like to say it because I loved Nancy, his first wife, and still do, but he was ready to do anything for Ava."

*All of the quotes included here were found in *Sinatra: The Life* by Anthony Summers or *Love Is Nothing* by Lee Server.

Reading Group Guide

1. Ava had one of the very few true legendary stories of being discovered by someone more or less passing her on the street and afterward she was promptly sent to Hollywood for a screen test. Given the chance, would you follow the same path as her—a person without training and perhaps even without any interest in being an actor? Why or why not? What did you think of her training?

2. During the decades that the book takes place, primarily the 1940s through 1960s, being a woman in Hollywood meant you were on display as mostly a sexual plaything. It also meant unwanted attention (to say the least) from male bosses and sometimes their fellow actors. How has this changed, or remained the same, today?

3. How did Ava's beauty—and the media attention—affect her self-image early in her career? And later?

4. Do you believe Frank could have loved more than one woman at the same time? Why or why not? What is your view of romantic love? ▶

5. Infidelity in Hollywood was very common at this time and, in fact, it still is if the tabloids are to be believed. Why do you think that is? Do you feel more, or less, inclined to like and support an actor's work when you learn of these anecdotes, or does it not affect your opinion?

6. Frank appeared to struggle with serious demons, and some would say this is why he self-medicated with various forms of debauchery. With medical advancements, do you think he would be in the same position today? Why or why not?

7. Perhaps both Frank's involvement in politics and his alleged involvement with the Mafia are what gave him a veneer of dark glamour. Discuss this idea. How does his possible involvement in an organized criminal organization add a certain appeal for his fans? Do you believe this appeal exists in real life, too?

8. Both Frank and Ava were complex individuals that couldn't seem to get out of their own way. Discuss their faults and how they led to the most tragic elements of their relationship. ᕦ

Discover great authors, exclusive offers, and more at hc.com.